My Darling Mayhem

Ashley Muñoz

Cover Design: Wild heart Graphics
Photographer: Couple Cover: Wander Aguiar

Content Editor: Memos in the Margins
Content Editor: Rebecca Patrick
Editor: Rebecca Fairest Reviews
Proofread: All Encompassing Books

❀ Created with Vellum

Content Warning

This is a motorcycle club romance, however with my other MC series, because this is primarily a smalltown romance, the MC themes are light and include talk of illegal activity relating to weapons trade, and drugs.
Other Concerns to be aware of:
Estranged family
References to foster care/legal guardian custody.
References (not shown) to parental death, and acts of violence to child's parent.
The use of guns and heavy artillery.
Suspense
Danger/Peril of two minors, abducted briefly, within the same chapter-no harm comes to the child.
Sexually Explicit scenes.
This book is intended for audiences of 18 and over.

For the ones who had to leave the nest, the trees and the entire forest. The ones who had to become a different breed of animal altogether. Never forget that you grew wings when other's said you'd never fly.

MY DARLING MAYHEM

Chapter 1

Wren

Something hit the kitchen floor with a smack.

I knew exactly which magnet had just fallen from my fridge, and which postcard was now floating aimlessly after being abandoned from said magnet. However, today, I wasn't paying attention to it as I sifted through the cupboard. I had somehow run out of instant rice, which was a travesty. My mother would have a heart attack if she knew I used it, but like mashed potatoes and canned veggies, I had found a tiny life hack in using instant meals.

"Montana fell again, Momma."

My five-year-old's voice cut through the air, forcing my eyes over to the small postcard that had fallen to the floor. I knew he was waiting for me to bend down to grab it and place it right where it had been, just like I always did, but I had hit my limit with that damn magnet.

"Maybe Montana needs to go, Bud."

"Mommm." Cruz rolled his eyes; they were whiskey-colored, like mine.

I withheld a smirk, waiting him out before gesturing at the fridge. "Colorado Springs is still up, and so is Mount Macon, that mountain town we want to go see in Oregon. Texas hasn't moved, and Disneyland is still intact. They deserve the fridge space, don't you think?"

Cruz sighed while getting up from his spot at the table. "Montana has horses."

That's right. I forgot how badly he wanted to see "Tana" when he was little after watching a few YouTube videos of some dream vacation spots. That's how we got into this whole postcard tradition. I ordered a postcard from every state that I wanted to visit with Cruz, and each day, we'd look at the fridge in hopes of fulfilling our trips.

Before I could grab the withered picture, my son bent down and curled his little fingers around it, bringing it to his face.

We didn't have religion or care much for politics or sports teams, but these postcards were our little symbol of hope. Seeing that it was becoming more of a tradition to him than to me, I sighed.

"I'll buy a stronger magnet."

My son smiled at me as if I had just hung the moon instead of an empty message with a faded image of a state I'd never been to on our fridge. My heart melted just like it always did.

"Maybe we can ask Lydia over at the office store."

An alert popped up, reminding me that my son's school was hosting an open house for kindergarteners later. While shooting a quick text to my friend, I abandoned my search for dinner ingredients because now we needed more than just magnets.

> Me: Hey, Lydia, it's Wren. Do you guys have school supplies there, or is that a weird thing to buy at an office supply store?

The dots danced at the bottom of my screen, making me nervous. Lydia wasn't exactly a close friend, but she was the closest thing I had in Atlas.

> Lydia: What do you mean by school supplies? Like calculators...or Play-Doh?

Cruz set his dishes in the sink and asked Alexa how much time he had left on his morning timer. I slid the milk back into the fridge and ensured all the dishes were put away before grabbing my cell again.

> Me: As in, do you guys have a special back-to-school line or something, like every other store does in September?

> Lydia: We're an office supply store, Wren. The only exciting month we celebrate is tax season, and occasionally, Christmas if we get in glitter pens.

I muttered a curse, quiet enough that Cruz didn't hear. I pulled up my work schedule and realized I had run out of time.

"Okay, we need to go, Peanut." I filled a travel mug with coffee and pulled open the drawer, holding my silverware, medicine measuring cups, and spatulas. I already knew I wouldn't find the lid inside, even if I did have time to sift through it. Which I didn't. Instead, I bumped the drawer closed with my hip and set my coffee by my purse.

Cruz was already pulling on his shoes, securing the Velcro strap. "Don't forget today's my last day!"

His little smile stretched, showing a row of baby teeth. He hadn't lost any yet, and I wasn't sure when he would start, but I wasn't ready for it. Just like I wasn't prepared for him to be finished with Mrs. Garza's in-home preschool.

I crouched in front of him and moved his hair aside. "Yep. Starting tomorrow, you'll be going to school like a big boy. Are you excited?"

I already knew he was, but I loved letting him tell me about it.

"Yes!" He gave a little jump, and suddenly, his arms were around my neck. I squeezed him tight and sat back to inspect him.

"Shoes, jacket and bag?"

He replied by checking off an invisible list: "Shoes, jacket, and bag."

I moved to turn off the hall light and ensure his bedroom switch had also been flipped. Our house wasn't something I would have been able to afford on my own, but my boss had a weak spot for me, and when one of their model homes didn't sell, she bought it and then rented it out to me. It was a modern two-bedroom with a generous floor plan and an office. Fresh white carpet in the living room, where I'd placed a sectional couch facing a modest flat screen.

I'd found discount deals at home décor shops and, over the years, managed to create a home that made me feel relaxed when I walked into it and calm when I locked the door behind me. It had a fenced-in backyard for my son, and it was in a safe neighborhood.

As a teenager, I wanted to be seen for what my family name meant and how important that made me. I was obsessed with the idea of being attached to my father's legacy and would go as far as hanging around members who were dangerous to me at that age, all so I could be seen. Now, I wanted seclusion, a place to raise my son in peace without a single trace of my family.

"Shoes!" Cruz called out, breaking me out of my thoughts.

I briefly glanced in my bedroom mirror, ensuring my clothes weren't out of place. I had a few notes and pictures tucked into the solid oak frame. I placed things within my eyesight, so I had to face them when I looked at my reflection. That way, I'd never forget them or what impact they had on my life. My eyes wandered to the faded image of my ex, feeling a familiar ache of regret. Not that I missed him, but I hated what his absence and abandonment did to Cruz. My brother's face stared back at me in a photo from when he was a gangly teenager, and I was in middle school. He was giving me a side hug in the photo, and we both looked like nothing on this planet could ever come between us...what a lie that ended up being.

Let go, forgive.

Move on, Wren.

I distracted myself by running my fingers over my black dress, inspecting the small red cherries printed in little rows across the cotton fabric. It cinched in at the waist and had a cute frill along the bottom, which cut off just past my knees. I wore black heels, and my caramel-colored hair was pulled low on my neck, with lighter strands framing my face. My red lip color looked striking against my tan skin, and the dark lashes framing my amber eyes made me look younger than my thirty-five years. At least, that's what people were always saying when they found out how old I was. My mother's genetics made my skin look this smooth and my hair this silky soft; even my lashes were attributed to her.

Thinking of her had me glancing at the photo I had up, showing her solemn face after I gave birth to Cruz. Even holding her grandchild, she looked upset; it nearly made me laugh at how perfectly her it seemed. Which was why I kept the photo pinned there. My smile turned down as I remembered that she was the only person I told, and I made her swear not to say a single word to anyone else in the family...or to—

"Mom!" Cruz yelled, pulling me from my thoughts.

I flipped the light off and grabbed my purse. "Lights."

He volleyed back. "Bag!"

I moved into the small hallway, past his bathroom, where I ensured the light was off, and then returned to the living room.

"Purse."

Cruz smiled up at me. "Jacket."

I pulled on a red cardigan and looked down at my son. We both smiled and said, "Ready."

The air was crisp as we walked outside. Part of the reason this model home had never sold was that the initial floor plan didn't include a garage. So, it sat vacant for months until it was finally offered to the local sales team. I didn't mind that there was no garage; I kept an umbrella by the door and wore thick coats on snowy days.

"Door?" Cruz asked, eyeing the lock.

I pulled my keys out and slid the silver into the top lock, turning it until it was secure.

This little game of ours was our way of making sure we were always paying attention and helped us to avoid forgetting things.

"Phone," I said out loud, following him down the steps. I glanced to the left, seeing the same view as I always did, with a brown fence separating my house from Mr. Plover's. I liked that my driveway was longer than several of my neighbors'; it allowed me more privacy. To my right was a similar-looking divider, but for a home that had just been built. It was strange to look up and see the two-story monstrosity whenever I left the house.

It was the last one to be completed on this street, so now our little neighborhood was whole, with a stretch of homes down each side of the street, white sidewalks, and well-manicured trees planted. At the end of the circular cul-de-sac was the new house, standing tall, like a sentry, watching over the rest of our meager one-story homes.

My focus returned to my son, who walked to the back door of my smaller sedan and placed his hand on the handle. "Lunch."

He knew I always forgot to pack one, and we didn't have time for me to run back inside, so I simply smiled.

"Lunch."

His features relaxed, and it made something in my heart ping around.

My son's love for me always made me emotional, which might have been why my eyes clouded the slightest bit with tears. My car didn't have a backup camera, so I used my mirrors to reverse while also blinking away the unbidden emotions when suddenly a motorcycle sped into the cul-de-sac. It was behind me so fast that I had to slam on my brakes, making us jerk against our seat belts. The coffee in my travel mug, which I could never find a lid for, splashed everywhere, and Cruz let out a tiny cry.

Enraged, I let the first thought fly from my mind unbidden, "What the fu—" but stopped the second my eyes flicked to the mirror, and I caught my son's worried look.

"Wait here, Peanut."

I opened my door and realized the motorcycle had pulled into the driveway next door. It was the brand-new two-story house that had just been built. I had no idea who had purchased the home, but I assumed it was someone from the city who planned to rent it out. Maybe it was, but whoever this person was had just pulled in like they were the new owner.

The man sat atop a chrome bike, pulling off his helmet—it was one of those half helmets, with just the chin strap underneath. He had on a black leather vest with a myriad of patches on the back. I didn't register what they said, but I noticed the rider had longer blond hair that looked wind-blown. His entire ensemble looked messy and wild as if he were a rogue bolt of lightning that had found a place to strike and linger.

Crossing my arms, I walked along the white sidewalk that attached our two driveways and approached the man.

"Hey!" I called toward the man, now making my way around to his side.

He twisted, still seated on his bike. He turned his engine off, which helped because I didn't want to get too close just to verbally berate him.

Narrowed eyes focused on me as if I had just done something wrong to him. "Can I help you?"

"Yeah..." I gestured behind me, where Cruz was peeking through the window with a curious expression. "You nearly hit us."

The man's eyes flicked to the car, then back to me. His jaw flexed as if he'd slammed his back molars together in frustration.

Finally, after a few stretched moments, he deadpanned, "Sorry."

His gaze swung forward as if to dismiss me.

For some reason, that just didn't feel like enough.

"Are you the new renter here?" I asked, lifting my eyes to the two-story house. This model's finishing touches were farmhouse-style. White siding sheathed the outside while black paint framed the shutters and trim, with raw wood beams for posts. It was beautifully made.

The man sighed as if this conversation was exhausting to him. His boot shot out, kicking the metal stand for his bike, and then he tossed his leg over the seat and stood while he regarded me. He was tall...like six foot two, or—

"Was there something else you needed?"

My anger snapped back in place, heating my chest like a furnace. I wanted to flip him off or get in his face and yell. I settled on delivering my best resting bitch face. "Just wanted to know if we're going to have to deal with your insufferably loud engine all the time or if maybe you were just here fixing something." I smiled as if I'd just paid him a compliment. I was being a bitch. I knew I was, but all I could think about was that little sound Cruz had made when we'd jerked forward or the way the coffee spilled all over my car.

My rudeness was warranted. His was not.

As I said, another bike roared from around the corner, speeding down the street. Then another. I stepped back, slightly concerned, wanting to be closer to Cruz.

The man glared at me.

There were more of them?! Shit, how many were going to show up here?

My breath caught right as my heel found a crack in the sidewalk, making me nearly pinwheel backward.

"Careful, princess, don't need you falling and breaking that pretty face."

He turned away from me, walking toward the house without giving me a second glance while the two other bikes stopped in his driveway, both men wearing the same leather vest he had on. One of the men scowled while I made my way to the car; the other laughed while whistling at me. My face heated, not because he'd catcalled me, but because I shouldn't have given this man the edge of knowing his presence bothered me. Now, he'd likely be here all the time with his band of misfit friends and all their loud motorcycles.

This was a good neighborhood. We didn't need a fucking motorcycle club moving in.

Sliding back into my car, I revved my pathetic four-cylinder engine and drove away, watching the men in my rearview laugh and shake their heads while I went.

Chapter 2

Wren

My face hurt from smiling.

Not in a good way, where it was genuine. No, I had been fake smiling at all the couples I had met with throughout the day. I was a sales agent for Encore Homes, a desirable builder that had sunk its teeth into the small town of Atlas, New York, where families had started flooding by the dozens.

Our little town was nestled just an hour outside New York City, and these homes have been selling left and right for the last three years. Encore had started purchasing land, creating cute neighborhoods with nearby parks built-in, tailored landscaping, and gorgeous views of the only nearby lake.

The homes sold themselves; I was just here to walk interested families through floor plans and lot choices. When they wanted to see a model home under construction, I'd drive over and walk them through the options. Then, of course, I'd take all the additional steps to help them secure the home.

It was good work. It didn't pay an exorbitant amount, but I didn't have to work two jobs; I could easily afford my bills while still shoving a few hundred bucks into savings every paycheck. Besides, I had a great boss who treated me like family and gave me a massive break on rent. I knew my little house would rent for nearly twenty-five hundred a month, being this close to the city, but she only charged me fifteen hundred. It was still a lot for my income, but it was manageable, even with my son's expenses, which no one was helping me with.

"Can we please see the Sterling floor plan again?" The woman wearing a warm gray cardigan put her hands together as she faced me. She had wavy black hair, a wedding ring with several bands added, and just a solitary diamond. Her husband wore a generic brand of jeans. While the home they wanted was close to seven hundred thousand dollars, I could tell they weren't the type that dripped with extra money. So, even though I only had an hour before I needed to leave to make it to the store in time, I pulled up the floor plan on my laptop and slid it toward them.

The woman glanced at her husband, and he turned toward their realtor with an expectant expression. Brick Hastings, the man who constantly reminded me why it was better to stay single than ever tempt fate with online dating, stared back at me.

"Wren, I think the Mathews wanted to walk the Sterling again."

The couple beamed, nodding their agreement.

The drive over to the model home wouldn't be super far, but depending on how long they took, it might mess with my timeline. It was my fault for waiting this long to get Cruz's school supplies, but things kept coming up. I'd been called in on more days off than I could even count. Whenever my boss, Denise, needed me, I'd drop every-thing and come in. Denise never cared if I had Cruz with me, so I never told her no.

I forced my face to remain open, with a smile they'd never know was fake. "Sure, let me grab my keys, and we can drive over. Brick, you know the location?"

He pulled out his phone, ignoring me while muttering a yes. It took me right back to the last date we'd been on when he'd done the same thing. I knew his job kept him tied to his phone, but he could have put

it on silent and gotten to his clients later since it was after working hours.

I walked to where my purse was and texted Mrs. Garza, letting her know I'd be there closer to four instead of three to grab Cruz, and then locked the office. Once I was departing to lead everyone over to the model home, I tried to ignore how I was the only person who had a car that was over twenty years old. It was made worse when I started the car, and the familiar squeal of the belt echoed around the lot.

My face heated as I drove forward, leading the caravan toward the opposite end of town. The small town of Atlas often felt like its own little island, separated from the world. Historic red brick buildings stood like withered sentinels along the town's main strip. Colonial homes were scattered through the older parts of the city, and during the fall, the entire town felt like we were in our own little autumn-colored snow globe.

The new suburban neighborhood appeared after we passed three red lights and a right past the old library. I passed the two freshly built homes and parked along the curb, eyeing the new three-story house. It was nearly a twin to the one built next to mine but differed slightly because it had three stories instead of just two. I smiled, exiting the car and relishing the sunshine that cut into my eyes and the warm breeze that made me rethink my cardigan.

Brick fell into step next to me as we made our way up the porch and into the house. The couple immediately passed us, gawking at the tall ceilings and the exposed beams. Once they were farther into the house, Brick hung back.

"You haven't returned any of my messages."

I kept my smile intact, making sure my voice was soft. "Well, you messaged me on Snapchat..."

"So?" He turned, so we hung back near the foyer while they moved into the kitchen.

I folded my arms, giving him a glare. "So, you're a thirty-five-year-old man...text me, call me. Teenagers use social media to talk..."

He scoffed, shaking his head, which made me think of my new neighbor and irritated me irrationally.

"Sorry, guess I got confused because of how our relationship started...you know, with you sending me nudes on social media and all."

Ohmyfuckinggod.

I turned on him, my mouth gaping as the Mathews came back into view.

"We just aren't sure about the downstairs den option; can we look at the possibilities to customize it?"

I plastered on a fake smile and pulled out the folder under my arm with the alternatives they could select. They browsed and asked more questions, all while Brick smirked behind my back.

My face warmed at the reminder of how stupid and desperate I had been. I was in a funk, missing adult conversation, and honestly just lonely. Brick and I started messaging, and things went from texting to sexting embarrassingly fast, but he's an attractive man and someone who didn't require a lot of small talk. We both already knew what the other did for work, which left us open to discussing different things and how we were essentially just looking for a hookup.

So, by the time we had eventually gone on a real date, we'd already been fucking casually for nearly three months. Mostly in the back of his car and in parking lots. Sometimes in the model houses, but never in either of our homes. He'd never met Cruz, and I ended things after we tried dating for real. We didn't have a relationship, we hooked up, and I instantly regretted the nudes after I had sent them.

I hated always having to live with regret. It was like my soul was tainted, and no matter how good I tried to be or how clean I lived, one tiny speck of dust would corrode the entire thing again.

No matter how painful it was, I never seemed to learn my lesson.

Once the Mathews were finished, Brick took off just as quickly as they did, likely too afraid that I'd call him on his shit or the fact that he was a lazy lay. He loved getting head but never went down on me. His dirty talk was weak and cringe-worthy. I didn't mind that he had a smaller dick; he knew how to use it, but he was just lazy, and his kisses were sloppy. Not worth the effort, but I still let things drag when all I wanted was someone to touch me. To literally stroke a finger down my arm or move the hair from my shoulder.

No one ever talked about how that becomes a craving. More than sex. More than sleeping next to someone. Just having touch becomes an absolute obsession. So really, even if he didn't have a dick, I likely would have continued to fuck Brick until we dated, and I realized I was falling back into the same patterns I always did before where I fell for complete assholes.

I needed a nice, sensible man—someone with a bank job or maybe a tax accountant—someone who went to bed early, had a steady job, and would be there to talk to every night. An idea sparked as I left work and headed to get Cruz from preschool.

Maybe I could start with the bookstore. I could hang around and see what sort of men popped in or change my preferences on my online dating profile.

But fuck I didn't want to do online dating again.

With a sigh, I turned into Mrs. Garza's neighborhood.

Cruz was practically vibrating with excitement as he jumped off the steps, and I checked him out of preschool, sadly, for the last time. I hugged Mrs. Garza and took pictures with her and Cruz before leaving for the store.

"We have to drive over to the bigger store in Luxy, okay?" I looked at Cruz in the rearview mirror. He was staring off into space, ignoring me. Ten minutes passed; his excitement seemed to evaporate completely the longer we drove until he finally spoke up.

"Davon's dad came to get him today. He gave me a high five."

A swelling, familiar panic started to fill my stomach like lead. Anytime Cruz brought up Davon's dad, he got really sad, and it was almost impossible to cheer him up. Part of me hoped he'd just change the subject, but then he continued talking, and my heart took an invisible punch.

"How come my dad doesn't come see me?"

I checked his expression in the mirror, hating how his little brow furrowed.

"Well...your dad, he's...well, it's complicated."

Five years, and I still had no idea how to explain that his father had gone to prison. I had no idea that he had any ties to any gangs, much less would fulfill an order and take out a rival member in broad daylight. The memory of receiving that phone call and seeing it on the news had been one of the worst in my life. The positive pregnancy test came a week after he'd been arrested. Matthew had called and asked me to bail him out and wanted me to attend his hearing and testify that he was a peaceful man.

In response, I boxed everything he owned, gave it to a charity, and moved as far away as possible. I had written to him and told him about his son and that if he wanted to see him after he got out, I'd ask him to go through supervised visitation first and that my expectations for him being involved would be high. Matt never wrote back. I sent a picture of Cruz a year later, asking again if he wanted to be involved, and he never wrote back. I only provided a post office box for him to send mail to, and that address was in Luxy, the next town over. Still, no mail had ever arrived.

"Does he love me?"

"Very much...but he's making some bad choices right now."

Cruz waited, then asked another question that was like being hit in the chest with a piece of concrete. "Like Uncle Juan?"

My eyes nearly watered at the mention of my older brother. The last time I saw him, I was only sixteen years old...he was in college, attending Rake Forge University in North Carolina. His smile was muted, his dark brows drawn in tight as he glared at me. My mother found out who I had snuck out to see, who I had been riding around with, and called Juan to come talk some sense into me.

"You're being an idiot. Do you want to die, is that it? You care so little for your life that you don't care who takes it? Stop stressing Mama out. Stop acting like a fucking idiot and grow the fuck up."

I swallowed around the lump in my throat. At how those words had wholly rearranged my soul. How my hero had made me feel so insignif-icant and stupid. Then, when I had started straightening out, I went back to school, stopped hanging out with the crowd I'd been with, and started trying...he'd gone and done exactly what I had.

But it was a thousand times worse because he stepped into a role he promised to never accept. He swore we'd be free of our father's ties to the Cartel, and my big brother picked up those reins and ran with them, all for a pair of pretty blue eyes. He was a hypocrite.

He broke my heart, and I refused to stick around another second to watch as he burned my mother's world down or his own. I couldn't watch a repeat of what had happened with my father.

"Yes...just like Uncle Juan."

The rest of the ride was silent, and I wished for just one second that I had one man...just one that I could introduce to my son that I knew was worthy of being in his life.

The small classroom was vibrant, with yellows, reds, and greens painted around the room. The back wall looked like a tree, with actual branches jutting from the wall where the teacher had nailed them. It was cute and fun. Cruz had a little laminated name tag taped to half the square table we were positioned at. Instead of desks, they had cubbies for all their things. Small red baskets containing basic supplies sat on each table.

"Thank you all for coming to our open house, I'm Bonnie Gerard, and I'll be your child's kindergarten teacher this year. I encourage all the kids to call me Mrs. G." The woman with fiery red hair and fair skin scanned the room, making eye contact with the parents. There were nearly thirty of us squeezed in, most of us sitting in the tiny chairs that our asses barely fit in. I was in one with Cruz sitting in my lap. The other half of our table was vacant, while the laminated name for another child sat, but whoever it was for hadn't arrived yet.

"The children have all been paired up in groups of two, as you can see by the small table arrangements. I did this purposefully, as we will incorporate English and Spanish into our curriculum this year. Each table has at least one student proficient in one of the languages, and the two will rely on each other as teammates when they need help."

Cruz barely knew Spanish, which was entirely my fault because when he finally started speaking at three, I was so happy that I just stuck to English. Being away from family and anyone to speak Spanish with made me not speak it as often. It shouldn't have surprised me that Mrs. G. assumed my son would be the one who spoke Spanish with our last name being Vasquez, but still...it bothered me that she hadn't reached out to ask.

"Mommy, I don't have a table friend. What if they don't show up?" Cruz whispered in my ear.

I glanced over at the empty side of the table and saw the name spelled out: Kane.

"I'm sure he'll be here soon. Maybe he just couldn't come to the open house."

Cruz relaxed into my chest as we continued to listen to the teacher. Halfway through the policies and importance of kids practicing at home, the chair beside us slid out, and a flash of white had me turning my head.

My son perked up as we both registered that it must be Kane, who just slid into the space next to him. Relief had me smiling down at the cute kid with lightning-white hair, blue eyes, and light brows. I was worried my son would be alone this year or until Mrs. G. decided to rotate kids around.

The teacher turned on a PowerPoint, and the small transition had Cruz leaning out of my lap toward his new neighbor. The two boys huddled together laughing and somehow had already exchanged pocket toys. Cruz usually carried a Hot Wheel's car with him or something similar, and apparently Kane did as well.

The new position where Cruz was huddled had me facing the side instead of the front of the room, but with the new position, I could see Kane's parent, who was crouched next to his chair.

I had to do a double take because why was my new neighbor here? Maybe I was wrong...it couldn't be him. I slid my gaze back over, and sure enough, he had the same hair as this morning, tangled and wind-blown but tucked behind his ears. Same leather vest, with patches, worn over a white T-shirt. Same asshole vibes.

Quickly returning to the PowerPoint, I tried to think through what I had said earlier this morning...and how he'd spoken to me. Irritation flared as I recalled his rude commentary and how his friends catcalled me.

Why was he here?

Mrs. G. finally got through the presentation, and she said something funny that I missed but had everyone clapping. I watched the man beside me ruffle his son's hair while pointing at his name tag. Had he noticed me yet?

Would he even remember me? I was still wearing the same clothes as I was this morning; there was no way he had that bad of a memory.

The class began dispersing. The lights kicked back on, indicating that the PowerPoint presentation was over. The teacher now stood in a huddle of parents who were all asking various questions while introducing their kids.

I would have to explain to her that Cruz didn't know enough Spanish for him to be half of the language duo she needed. I was about to stand up and join the line of parents, but she suddenly broke away from the group and walked toward our table, making apologies to the parents she left behind.

The man who had nearly run us over this morning, who was now standing, finally seemed to notice me. At least, it seemed like he did with the way his brows dipped and his cloudy blue eyes narrowed like he couldn't place where he knew me from. Seeing him in a smaller, confined space made him look taller than he had earlier. His t-shirt was boxy, as though he'd purposely bought it extra baggy. It worked for him, though, as did his threadbare jeans tucked into dark motorcycle boots.

I tried to refocus on the teacher, but when he took a step toward me, Mrs. Gerard stepped between us.

"Mr. Green?"

I looked at how his blue eyes and fair features reminded me of some Viking shows I'd seen. His dark tattoos seemed to highlight his lean muscles, which were visible even under the fabric of his shirt. His longer hair was pulled into a tidy bun at the nape of his neck. The pieces behind his ear were messy and untamed, reminiscent of something rogue and wild like I'd seen in him earlier.

"Right, but you're not technically on the approved list...so I don't want to confuse Kane on who can pick him up." I overheard Mrs. Gerald saying to him.

My eyes snapped to my neighbor's jaw, appreciating how defined it was, as it tensed and he looked down at his feet. "I realize that, but his foster parents said—"

"It doesn't matter what they say; it matters what the courts say. I appreciate that you want to be a supportive older brother, but until a judge says Kane is in your custody, it's really not appropriate for you—"

"Archer, look!" Kane turned around with a massive smile, holding up a name tag.

The nametag had a motorcycle drawing that he was proud of. When I saw how my neighbor responded to seeing it, something in my stomach flipped.

He sidestepped the teacher, who had been berating him, and bent down until he was at eye level with his little brother. "Kane, this is awesome. We're going to have to add this to your gallery."

Kane beamed. "I can't wait until I have my own bike."

Cruz was also inspecting it now with wide eyes and a huge smile. "You can ride a motorcycle?"

"My big brother takes me on rides, and one time he let me dr—"

Archer placed a hand on Kane's shoulder, pulling him closer while ruffling his hair. "Not everyone needs to hear about that, buddy."

I hid a smile, trying to ignore how cute the brothers acted together because I still didn't like this man on principle. Then I remembered what Mrs. Gerald had said about foster parents, and my smile fell. It sounded like my motorcycle club-leading neighbor was trying to get custody of his little brother, which reluctantly, I internally had to admit, was sweet. I hated that the teacher was berating him in front of an audience. It was still rude, even if it was just me close enough to hear. Archer's eyes flashed toward his little brother as a red flush began creeping into his cheeks, which made guilt churn in my chest. I didn't know him...I didn't owe him anything, and yet...

"Well, Mr. Green, I still think you shouldn't—"

"Cruz doesn't speak Spanish," I blurted, interrupting Mrs. Gerald's lecture. My neighbor's eyes darted to mine, widening slightly, showing his surprise. I looked back, unsure why I had helped him but feeling the need to do it just the same.

Mrs. Gerald pushed some of her unruly hair behind her ear; her face flushed the tiniest bit while she quickly glanced at Archer and then me. "I'm sorry, what?"

My gaze bounced around the room, seeing a few other parents looking over at us. My nerves were starting to fray as I stepped closer and tried to quiet my voice. "It's just that...you have Cruz and Kane as partners, but I'm afraid you made an assumption about Cruz being able to speak Spanish. He can't."

"Mrs. Vasquez, I ap—"

"It's Miss, and you can just call me Wren," I interjected again because I apparently couldn't control my mouth anymore.

"Wren." Mrs. Gerald gave me a flat smile while clearing her throat. "Our system isn't perfect but you did put that you were bilingual, so I figured that perhaps you could assist with a few things at home with Cruz and what he learns, he can share with Kane."

I wasn't sure how that was supposed to work, but it was kindergarten, and I appreciated that they were attempting to diversify the curriculum. I smiled and nodded my agreement. She finally turned and gave our area a break, leaving my neighbor talking to Kane while the two of them started for the exit.

"Come on, Cruz, we need to head out too."

My son grabbed his little backpack, and we started for the door, seeing that his new deskmate and older brother had stopped by the counter to drop off supplies. My neighbor's blue eyes stayed glued to us as we walked past; even as Kane talked to him about something, my neighbor watched me walk away.

I'd push the strange awareness of his gaze to the recess of my mind. Where details around my past lingered, my estranged family, and the fact that Brick had already sent me three messages since our conversation earlier, asking if we could meet up.

The place where things just didn't matter. The dead space. That's where any and all information regarding Mr. Green would go.

Chapter 3

Archer

"Prez, catch!" Thistle tossed a beer across the room with zero fucks about it shattering against the wall.

I lurched forward to grab it, glaring at my vice president. "Have you ever been inside a house that wasn't a trailer? The fuck was that?"

My VP was nearly six foot seven, bald, and stacked with muscle. His laugh was throaty as he tipped the bottle back, drinking his beer. Moving boxes littered the counter and floor. I had a singular couch in the living room and a recliner, but that was all I had set up so far.

"We always threw our beer in the club. You never seemed to mind then." Thistle burped while sifting through a box of plates and silverware.

I popped the cap off my beer and tried to calm down. My mind went to the club and how we were both absent from it at the moment. This new lifestyle change would be a lot to get used to.

Thistle tossed all the silverware into a random drawer without sorting it. "How come you only asked for me to come help unpack your shit?"

Because two days ago, I met my new neighbor, and I didn't like how she looked at me as if I were a stain on her pristine, perfect life. Usually,

I'd press in harder to piss her off, but she'd helped me out with Kane's teacher, and while I had no idea why, it left me feeling cautious about having more of my club here.

"Just wanted to ask how things are going at the club. I didn't want you to feel like you couldn't be honest with me and the other members here."

Thistle let out a sigh and started placing more shit from boxes in cupboards. No rhyme or reason to any of it, just random chaos that I'd have to sort out later. "Honestly, it's shitty, Prez. The men are testing boundaries, getting in fights, and a few scattered clubs from around the city have started wandering in...so far, nothing major, but I can tell they're scoping shit out...testing for any weakness we might have."

Several clubs made up New York City. Honestly, there were too many to fucking count, but of those, there were only about three that wore the one percent patch, which kept shit mildly manageable. Mayhem Riot didn't shit in their territories, and they never crossed over into ours. For the most part, we kept things peaceful. It wasn't broadcast that I had left because I hadn't.

I was taking time to figure this out, but I hadn't stepped down or left my post.

"I'll have to come back and make an appearance. Go for a ride next week."

Our conversation stalled as the sounds of shuffling and boxes filled the space. Thistle had thoughts but wasn't sharing them. I'd wait him out; he eventually always spoke up once he sorted out his feelings. I moved to the box on the floor that contained my new television stand and started taking out the pieces that needed to be built.

With another sigh, Thistle spoke again, "You get anywhere with the custody stuff?"

No, but I wouldn't tell him that. He was under the assumption that all of this was temporary. Me living here in the suburbs, this house I purchased, he assumed I placed in the club's name, using club funds, but I hadn't. I had told him very little about my brother, just that I needed to get him out of the shitstorm my father had created.

Kane needed stability, and I knew what it would take to provide that for him. I just had no idea how to do it.

"I'm meeting with my lawyer tomorrow; I should know more by then."

"Doesn't Kane start school soon?" Thistle moved into the living room, bending down to help me with the long wood pieces.

"He starts tomorrow...I'm going to pick him up from his foster home in the morning, bring him back for some breakfast, and see if he likes the place. Then take him in."

Thistle had a bushy beard covering his mouth, making it somewhat difficult to read his expressions. His eyes were down on the instructions and the various bolts we'd need to sort out. His mind likely whirring based on how focused he seemed to be.

"You got something on your mind; just speak it." My voice was low, encouraging. Thistle was as loyal as they came and always had my back. I had no doubt about that, but he often took his time to think through his answers before he gave them. On the rare occasion, this prevented him from saying anything at all.

"Just wish you had more support here. If any of our enemies catch on that you're here alone, it's dangerous. You should have the club out; be sure people know you're not a lone wolf or anything."

I nodded, knowing he was right.

"Not sure how my new HOA will feel about that." I smiled, but there was a sliver of truth to it. Not that I gave a fuck about the fees or whatever power those stupid organizations had, but I didn't want to attract any negative attention. I had to look like I was a good fit for my brother to live with. I had already talked with Ruth, one of our hackers, to see if we could have what was already on my record expunged, but in the eyes of the family court, I wasn't sure it would make much of a difference.

Even as the president of a motorcycle club, with all the negative connotations that come with that, I couldn't allow Kane to go to our father if he decided to pop up again. Establishing a way to balance the club's responsibilities while gaining legal custody of Kane would be a top priority, but to do that, I had to ensure I didn't draw any negative attention to myself.

"That pretty new neighbor a member of the HOA?" Thistle's question had my mind snapping back to the moment. Then picturing how her silky soft hair bounced against a narrow waist and round ass. How her amber eyes looked against her brown skin and those thick dark lashes. Even more so, how she'd spoken up to distract Kane's teacher when she didn't have to.

Wren. She'd said her name was Wren Vasquez. The name had looped around my head several times, forcing me to type it into a few social media search bars, but nothing came up.

I shook my head. "She sure acts like she is; I don't think she likes me very much."

"Just flash her that Archer Green smile, and I'm sure she'll beg you for a ride." Thistle's laugh boomed through the empty room, his innuendo clear.

We both laughed and joked before he had to leave to get back to the city to work in the morning. I grabbed our glass bottles and a few other flattened cardboard boxes and exited through the back. The recycling bins were currently set up along the side of my house because my garage was full of all my shit.

It was almost dark, but as I rounded the small alley next to the house, I could see over the fence where Wren's car was parked. She acted as though I disgusted her like my mere existence was a stain. I would almost assume she was doing it because she thought she was better than me, but her car was older, her clothes were from a discount store, and she seemed to be on her own with her kid. Maybe she just really didn't like that I nearly hit her with my bike.

Maybe I should actually apologize instead of the bullshit apology I gave her.

My hands were full as I began shifting things around to fit inside the bins, but suddenly I heard a car pull up behind Wren's.

A fucking Tesla parked, and the guy who crawled out from behind the wheel wore a suit and a tie...I glared at his slicked hair and the fact that he wore those loafers without socks.

He didn't see me watching him from my side of the fence as he pulled out his cell and slowly sauntered down the driveway toward Wren's front door.

Was this her boyfriend? He seemed too clean...too perfect for her. It would be like pairing up a wildflower with a wax plant.

I continued to watch as he knocked on her front door, and then she stepped out, wearing a pair of short pajama shorts and a thin tank top. She instantly started pushing at the man's chest until he was away from her door. She seemed surprised, almost shocked, or panicked that he was there, which only proved correct when she started yelling.

"What are you doing here?"

I couldn't see the man's face, but he raised his hands and shoulders as if to shrug.

Wren shook her head, crossing her arms tight across her chest. "No, I didn't respond to your messages. You can't show up at my house, Brick."

Brick? Oh shit, that's too easy. Such a stupid name.

He said something back to her, then shoved his phone in her face. She didn't seem to like that, and honestly, neither did I. It felt a little aggressive, especially considering she had already stated that she didn't want him there.

I took a slow walk past my bins, setting all the materials down so as not to make a sound. Then I pushed open my side gate and rounded the drive, standing at the top of Wren's. Neither of them could see me, and she was waving her hands and pointing at Brick's car, telling him to go.

But he wasn't moving.

Shoving my hands into my pockets, I made my way closer to the pair, and I heard the asshole saying something about the two of them fucking. Wren scoffed and rubbed at her forehead like she was exasperated. For no reason whatsoever, I detested the idea of the two of them together that way.

I kept walking until they both saw me and turned. Wren's lips parted while those amber eyes went wide. I decided I liked that expression on her face and that I was the one who put it there.

"Hey, sorry to bother you both. I'm the new next-door neighbor, Archer." I threw my thumb over my shoulder to indicate my house. "Just wondering if either of you had a screwdriver I could borrow?"

The man, Brick, I guess...was staring down at his cell phone while Wren glanced between us both.

"Yeah, I do. Brick, you can head out." She lifted her chin toward his car while standing guard in front of her door.

Brick finally glanced up at me, then over at Wren. "I'm not leaving until we discuss this."

I pivoted, my boots kicking up a bit of loose gravel as I moved directly in front of him.

"Yeah, you are, Dick."

Brick's eyes widened, and then his lip lifted in a sneer. "My name is Brick, and fuck you, asshole. Who the hell even are you? I'm not—"

I didn't give him a chance to finish as I pulled on the back of his shirt and started dragging him back toward his car.

I heard Wren gasp behind me, but she didn't stop me.

"Hey, wait...fuck," Brick grumbled as he tried to get his feet underneath him. His hands twisted up, trying to break my hold, but I continued to drag him until he was next to his car, and I dropped his ass on the asphalt.

"When someone says no, it fucking means no. If they say leave, then go. If they say now isn't a good time, then you leave. Period."

Brick managed to get to his feet and pull his cell out. "I'm calling the police, telling them some redneck fuck in a motorcycle gang assaulted me."

I kicked out, swiping his leg, which made him fall again, and his cell phone fell out of reach. I pressed my boot into his chest, and then I leaned down so he heard me quietly deliver my warning. "You want to find out exactly what this redneck fuck in a motorcycle club will do to you? For starters, have you ever had your leg crushed by a motorcycle's back tire? Or how about your face plastered to the side of one of our exhaust pipes after a long ride when it's nice and hot. You want to fuck around and find out, Dick? I'll make sure the police have a difficult time piecing you back together for their report."

I released my boot and reached over to hand him his phone. I dropped it on his chest; he winced but caught it. He continued to stare up at me, and finally, with a jump in his Adam's apple, he stood on shaky legs and opened his car door.

Once he drove off, Wren was behind me, her arms still crossed over her chest. Her caramel hair was twisted into a bun on top of her head, and little tendrils were left kissing her face. She was beautiful in a way that I hadn't experienced anyone yet. I'd fucked plenty of attractive women, but I had never felt like I'd just watched my first sunrise when I saw any of them.

"Did you really need a screwdriver?"

I smirked, turning back toward my side of the yard. "Nah, just taking out my trash and saw you had someone lingering on your steps who couldn't take a hint. Thought I'd offer to help."

She turned toward me until she was fully facing me, even as I tried to turn to leave.

"He's a work colleague; we hooked up a few months ago. He's trying to get things started again."

I nodded my understanding. "None of my business, but maybe—"

Her laugh cut into my thoughts. She rubbed at her temple and muttered, "Fuck, he's going to tell my boss...and when my boss finds out a motorcycle gang lives next door, she's going to—"

I cut her off mid-sentence, "The term gang is really fucking derogatory. I'm a part of a club; it's not a gang...although, based on that tattoo on your arm, you'd be the expert on them."

She tilted the back of her arm in front of her where the bleeding black heart was inked into her skin, with a bit of glare. I didn't hear what else she said because I was already walking away.

Pretty, but too much work to be worth any more of my effort.

Chapter 4

Wren

I'D NEVER BEEN ONE TO SPY ON MY NEIGHBORS...UNTIL NOW.

My life had always been too busy to care or even notice what others did with their free time. This helped me never line my life up next to someone else's and play the comparison game. The less I saw of happy families headed to soccer practice or playing in the yard, the less I envied them.

But, after last night and how I offended my new neighbor, I wanted to apologize.

Part of me wanted the divide because he was a part of a motorcycle club, and while I didn't entirely know what that meant, I knew it wasn't good. I should keep my distance, stay away...and let him think I didn't give two shits about what I called his band of misfits...but the part of me that still existed deep down in my heart that had been called names merely because of my association to a group, made me want to apologize.

I knew how it felt to be judged merely based on an affiliation to something. In my case, that affiliation was terrible, but I still remember how much it hurt.

"Are we going to give it to him?" Cruz asked, peering up at me from his place at the window, where I watched Archer's house.

I had made a pie.

It seemed so simple and so stupid. I'd told Cruz we would give it to him because he was new to the neighborhood, and that's what people did when they moved in.

I'd bought a tin foil pie pan, so I didn't have to worry about him returning a dish, and now it was covered in foil. I had no idea if he was gluten-free or allergic to anything, so I printed the ingredients out on a small piece of paper and taped it to the top foil piece so he wouldn't kill himself by eating it.

"Yes. We'll go over right now and give it to him." Archer would have to be nice to me if I had my five-year-old son with me, right?

God, I was pathetic.

Sliding into my shoes, I opened the door before I could think any more of it, slid my hand under the pie, and stepped out.

"Shut the door for me, Cruz," I said over my shoulder as we both began the walk down the drive. My nerves were shot, and even my breathing was all over the place as we got closer. His garage was shut, and no bike or any other vehicle was parked out front, so I had no way of knowing if he was home.

Cruz walked behind me, tipping his head back to take in the second-story and pitched roof of the house. "This is big."

He'd never lived in a second-story home, much less even been inside one. My mother had bragged about how my brother had become wealthy. If I had any respect left for him, perhaps I'd take my son to see how the other half lived, but I'd rather we live humbly than expose ourselves to the wolves.

Without another thought, I stepped onto Archer's stoop and pressed my finger to his doorbell.

Cruz smiled at me, and I gave him a silly look while we waited.

Nothing happened.

"Can I press it again?"

I nodded, slightly shifting so Cruz could access the button. There was no doorbell cam or any other security system set up that I could see, but I decided after Cruz pressed the bell for the second time and Archer didn't appear, it was time to go.

I turned to leave when Cruz tugged on my hand. "Let's leave it for him."

I had no idea why my five-year-old wanted this man to have a housewarming gift, but it melted my heart the tiniest bit. Enough that I crouched down and gently set the pie on his step.

"Okay, Bud. We'll leave it."

Cruz smiled and grabbed my hand, pulling me back toward our house.

"Now he'll come over and thank us for it!"

There wasn't even a note regarding who it was from, so he'd have no idea unless he had a camera set up somewhere.

But I just smiled and returned home to start dinner.

The interaction with Archer regarding my tattoo had snuck in and planted roots of suspicion and fear.

I was sorting through the various books in my son's bedroom when my thoughts finally got the best of me, and I pulled my phone out to call my mother.

"Buena?"

Her confused tone made me smile. "Hola mamá. ¿Cómo estás?

She paused as the sounds of the clanking dishes began to fade from her speaker.

"¿Mi amor?" I could practically hear her begin to grin as she connected the dots on who'd called her. It was always like this with her.

"Yes, mamá. It's me, Wren."

"Is everything okay?"

The E.B. White book fell to my son's bed as I let it go and stood. "We're okay, everything is fine. I just wanted to call and ask you a question."

Her silence had me rubbing at my temple as I tried to take a step back.

"How are you...and Leo?"

"Fina pero gorda." She sounded exasperated as she spoke, and her smile made me laugh in a way that made me remember happier times— her smile, my brother's, Leo's.

"Mom, Leo is not fat. The last time he was here, he was rail thin."

Her tongue clicked. "No, he stopped cooking in the restaurant so he's become bored and lazy. He has a panza now."

I could hear him yelling at her in the background, and the two started to argue. I sat there, listening and missing them, just like I always did...until I heard a distinct voice cut into their argument, which stiffened my spine.

"Is that Juan?"

She must have covered her phone or something because suddenly, the room went quiet, and when she spoke again, no one else was with her.

"He stopped by to check the oven. It keeps making a clicking sound."

My heart raced as I processed that I'd heard his voice through her phone. It was muffled, and I couldn't make out what he'd said, but I knew it was him.

"You called to ask me something?"

"Right..." I didn't need to know why he was there or ask how he was. She gave me updates every time we talked, whether I wanted them or not. Cruz is in a bilingual program in school, and his teacher suggested we read more books written in Spanish. I was going to see if you had any suggestions."

She was a grandmother, but I had no idea if my brother had more kids than the one he'd adopted. She had to be in her twenties now and probably didn't have her abuela reading story books to her.

"I will send you some, mi amor."

My head shook as I considered refusing because I didn't need her spending money, but I knew it was futile. She loved spoiling Cruz when she could.

"Okay, thank you, that would be great."

"Everything else okay?" she asked gently and protectively.

I wanted to bring up the tattoo and ask if she knew why a man from a motorcycle club in New York City would recognize it. I wanted to know what that meant for me and if I should be worried about it.

Instead, I asked what new TV shows she was binging, and she spent the next hour talking trash about TV couples.

The following day was Sunday, which was supposed to be my day off, but Denise had called and asked if I would come in. Packing Cruz a bag of activities for the day, I loaded him up, and we headed to my job.

The town of Atlas flew by in three blinks. There were two traffic lights, the gas station, the library, and an oil shop. Then, there was a vast park, which led into a newer development area where Encore Homes had started building. The model home was set on a block with a few houses already built and the cutest cherry blossoms. I parked along the curb, seeing the big, blue banner waving, encouraging weekend buyers to stop in to talk to us.

"Okay, Cruz, get your bag."

We walked inside, and my spine immediately stiffened.

"Hello, Wren." Brick sat in my desk chair, reclining like he'd been waiting for me. His gaze flicked down to Cruz like I'd tracked in leaves or mud with me.

"You brought your kid to work?"

Cruz frowned, glaring at Brick while hugging his bag to his chest. He always knew when he wasn't wanted somewhere, and while I tried like hell to make sure he never went anywhere that made him feel that way, occasionally, it happened.

"Yes, as it's supposed to be my day off."

I placed my hand on Cruz's shoulder and encouraged him to walk toward my desk.

"Can you please move out of my desk space?"

Brick sighed as if this was highly frustrating, then moved around so he was sitting in the client chairs we had arranged in front of my desk.

Cruz found his way to the same spot he always tucked into when he came in with me. I made a small fort between two filing cabinets with pillows and a blanket. All I had to do was pull it out and set it up for him.

"Does Denise know you bring him in?" Brick asked snidely.

Cruz's little mouth turned down again as if he hated the idea that I might get in trouble. I never wanted my son to feel like an inconvenience or a burden. I was two seconds from throat-punching Brick.

Once I set up Cruz and ensured his headphones were in place, and his show began on his tablet, I spun in my chair.

"What the fuck is wrong with you?"

Brick leaned forward. "Wrong with me? You're the one who had your new neighbor assault me."

"I didn't have—"

"Wren, hi, darling." Denise walked in, interrupting our conversation. Her white hair was styled perfectly, and her makeup was minimal.

"Hi, how are you?" I plastered a fake smile while she peered around me, looking for Cruz.

"Is my little guy here?"

Cruz looked up and saw Denise and waved. He liked her, but only so much. She occasionally gave off fake vibes that he could see right through. That's why I never asked her to babysit or accepted any invites to her house.

She waggled her fingers at Cruz, then regarded me.

"Thank you for coming in, honey. Brick emailed me this morning to tell me that his clients, the couple you two helped the other day, are considering backing out."

My brows dipped. "Haven't they already paid their lot premium?"

Brick smirked, and I knew he'd done something. I just couldn't prove it.

My laptop was out as I brought up their file.

"They were actually on the cusp of paying this weekend but decided they might go with Phurline Homes instead."

Our biggest competitor. Fuck. This was on me if it fell through, and Denise would get shit from her bosses too.

"What can I do to help?" I glanced at Brick, then Denise.

"Work with Brick. Hopefully, a good brainstorming session between you two will help." My boss turned to leave, leaving Brick smiling and tilting his head as though he'd just stolen my queen in chess.

I wanted to scream at him.

"What will it take to make this go through?" Because we didn't need a brainstorming session. He merely wanted to punish me for what happened the other night.

He leaned forward so his voice was low. "An apology for starters."

My mouth snapped shut, a million words desperate to fly at him.

Calmly and quietly, I said, "For what exactly? You arrived at my home uninvited and then refused to leave."

"For leading me on." His sharp chin lifted while his green eyes pinned me in place.

Fuck this guy.

"I'm sorry, Brick if there was anything I did that gave you the wrong impression."

"Good. Also, I want a date. One where I pick you up, you wear something nice, and you don't rush home the second it's over."

I scoffed, sitting back in my chair. "Not a chance."

Brick's nose flared while he leaned in closer. "Then you can say goodbye to this sale."

"So can you. You know for a fact our homes price out higher. Your commission will be bigger if you stick with us."

Brick smirked. "Not if I made a deal with the sales agents on what they'll tell the clients the listing price is."

I laughed. "Do it. Please. I'd love to see your face on the news for scamming someone. You know that shit's illegal, and you'll never get away with it."

Brick took a second to consider what I said, then sighed. "You used to like me."

I rolled my eyes because that was over a year ago, and that was a mistake.

He clicked his tongue. "Then let's start with something small... coffee?"

His backpedaling was insane, but I'd do it if it got him out of my face and the house sold.

"Fine."

"Tomorrow morning," Brick offered, but I shook my head.

"Tuesday. Tomorrow, I have to volunteer at Cruz's school for something."

Brick considered it, then let out a sigh. "Fine."

Leaning forward, I narrowed my gaze on him. "Let's be clear. That is all you're getting from me. The sale gets pushed through by tomorrow afternoon, or our coffee date is off."

Brick nodded his understanding and then stood up.

"One of these days, you're going to introduce me to him." He gestured down toward the filing cabinets.

He was wrong. Today was the one chance he had to make an impression on my son, and he failed. He'd never really met my son, not where Cruz shook his hand or knew his name.

Instead of saying that, I turned and started typing on my laptop.

I was running late to Cruz's school.

Our morning was more chaotic than usual. Cruz heard Archer's motorcycle drive in this morning and wanted to ask if he'd gotten our pie.

I didn't have the heart to tell him that if Archer had been gone all weekend, the pie would have been left out, meaning he'd have to throw it away. It didn't matter. I wanted the pie situation to never resurface for as long as I lived.

Once I finally got him to school, I had to rush to work and help finalize the sale of the Mathews home. Brick had come through, which meant I was getting coffee with him the following morning. I'd have to reconcile that and have him take me somewhere with good coffee, but I had to shove it to the side for now. I was drafting an email to my boss to have Brick work exclusively with Briana, the other sales associate, from now on.

Denise wouldn't like it because Atlas was small, and I was the senior agent who secured more deals than Briana did. However, I couldn't work anymore with Brick. In fact, I refused to. By the time two in the afternoon rolled by, I was running late to volunteer at Cruz's school.

I was snapping my volunteer nametag in place over my blazer when the sounds of the kindergarten class echoed around me in the hall. I slowed down and tiptoed into the back of Cruz's class, seeing a few parents helping with other kids. I smiled at another mom and then looked for Cruz.

I scanned his desk, not seeing him or Kane, his deskmate. In fact, several of the desks were empty, with a large portion of kids gathered on the reading rug near the tree wall.

"Ms. Vasquez." Mrs. G found me, giving me a broad smile.

I smiled back, "So sorry I'm late."

"Oh, no problem, but we've started storytime. I was hoping you could alternate with Mr. Green and read your story, which is in Spanish, to the kids, and then he'll read the English version."

She was walking away, and I was supposed to follow her, but I was stunned when Archer was mentioned.

He was here?

Why?

I didn't have time to ruminate on the idea as I moved halfway across the classroom and stopped on the edge of the reading carpet. At the base of the artificial tree, there was Archer, sitting on a small chair with his elbows on his knees and a book in his hand. He didn't have on his leather club vest, but he wore his worn denim jeans, boots, and a dark hoodie.

"Mr. Green, Ms. Vasquez is here now, so you two can begin your reading slot together."

My smile was as fake as it always was at work. Archer didn't smile at me so much as he stared. I carefully stepped around the kids until I could get to my seat directly next to my neighbors. I felt his body heat and could smell his spicy, citrusy cologne. There was an undertone of leather and something else that tickled my nose in a good way. The sort of way that made me want to turn my face into it.

"Nice of you to join us," Archer leaned over and whispered so only I could hear.

I snarked back as I reached for my book and started prepping it for reading. "How are you even here? Don't they do background checks?"

His eyes snapped over, and instead of humor, there was more mirth —more of what I'd caused last week when I offended him by commenting on his club. My heart felt a little jolt of regret, remembering my peace offering and how I'd wanted to mend fences.

He started reading and kept the children's attention by animating voices and changing the tone of his voice for certain characters. Listening to him read was enchanting in a way. His little brother was completely enraptured by him and clung to every word he spoke. When it was my turn to read the same story but in Spanish, all the kids turned to watch me.

I expected Archer to leave or hang out in his chair, but he shocked me by moving to the floor to sit beside his brother. Knees up, his arms around his legs, and those sharp blue eyes entirely focused on me.

Inhaling a sharp breath, I started reading through the text, doing the best I could to animate my voice like Archer had, but my nerves made my voice rattle a bit. It also didn't help that my brain kept focusing on Archer's intense gaze and how his jaw looked today. It looked the same as it did the other day, but for some reason, after a whole weekend of not seeing him, it was as though my brain wanted to examine it.

Finally, my face felt pink once I was finished, and my stomach was knotted up. Cruz ran to me and threw his arms around my neck.

"Buena mamá," Cruz said excitedly, settling some of those nerves in my gut. My son was learning Spanish, and it was beautiful. It was not perfect, but he could say "good," and Mom, that was huge.

I squeezed him to my chest, which made him giggle before I released him. "Let's go, bud. Your teacher said I could take you early."

"Okay, I'll go grab my backpack." He ran off, and I stood, putting the book back and aptly ignoring how Archer was still in the area with his brother.

Cruz ran back toward me but stalled near his deskmate, Kane.

"Did you get our pie?"

Ohmygod. My feet shifted faster than my brain, causing me to nearly trip on the carpet to stop my son from telling my neighbor about our peace pie.

Archer's eyebrows shot up, staring down at my son. "Pie?"

"My mom made it for you. We walked it over two days before yesterday." His head tilted until his eyes found mine. "That's how you say it, right, Mom?"

My face was on fire, and I avoided Archer's gaze while grabbing Cruz's hand. "Yep. We better go, say bye."

Archer moved with us. "Wait, you made pie?"

Cruz halted, turning back toward him. "As a welcome gift, it was cherry. You weren't home, so Mom left it on your porch."

Earth, please open and swallow me.

I felt my neighbor's gaze but kept mine on my phone, shoes, and walls. Anything but him.

Finally, Archer crouched down to be at eye level with my son. "Did you help make it?"

Cruz nodded. "Mom, let me stir the cherry sauce and add sugar."

Archer clicked his tongue. "Well, I'm super bummed I missed out on it. I love pie. Especially cherry pie. Thank you so much for thinking of me. It was very thoughtful."

I felt he was trying to communicate with me by saying everything to Cruz, but I couldn't be sure.

"You're welcome, but you should thank my mom. She's the one whose idea it was."

Archer stood, and my eyes finally lost the battle of avoiding him. He gave me a smile, and then his lips moved. "Thanks, Wren."

I could brush it off and tell him I gave everyone in the neighborhood one. Make him think I'm a pie whore, but instead I confessed.

"It was nothing...just a way of saying welcome to our neighborhood. I do it for everyone."

His eyes narrowed as if he knew I was lying, but before he could say anything else, Mrs. G. called the kids who weren't returning to their seats. I left with Cruz without another glance behind me or to see if my neighbor was on our heels.

Chapter 5

Wren

Cruz stood by the door, waiting for me to finish getting ready.

I could tell he was frustrated with me by how his tone hitched while we did our daily checklist.

"Backpack!"

It was my turn to say keys or purse, but I was still mid-curl with the beach waver wand. My shirt was half-buttoned, my skirt didn't feel like I'd pulled it on correctly, and there was already a mascara stain on my eyelid.

Cruz stomped over to the bathroom, clenching his little shoulder straps tight. "Mom, I'm going to be late."

For a five-year-old, he was frustratingly aware of time. If I was smart, I would have had him turn on the television so he'd completely forget about school. But he loved school, and I loved that he did.

I hadn't slept well last night, and there wasn't a decent reason. Other than this situation with Archer, it was because he felt like such a wild card, and I didn't know what to expect. While I wasn't currently speaking to him or anything...there was an attraction that I had fallen victim to.

45

It was concerning, to say the least, because every time I closed my eyes, my mind would drift to how perfectly shaped his nose was in proportion to his mouth and cheekbones. His wide jaw was deliciously defined, and a thick Adam's apple bobbed when he swallowed. I had kicked at my comforter after that one hit because who the fuck is attracted to the lump in a man's throat?

Me apparently. Fucking me.

"Okay, I'm ready." I wasn't, but I refused to make my poor guy wait any longer.

I tugged the cord from the wall, threw on my leather jacket, and slipped into my high heels. "Keys, purse, phone."

Shit, did I leave any lights on? Did I ever fix my skirt?

"Door...come on, let's go." Cruz tugged my elbow until the door was closed.

I locked it behind me, seeing that he'd already made it to the car and eagerly awaited me to make my way down the steps. I gave him a reassuring smile as I took each step faster than usual, but right as my heel landed on the bottom step, my ankle twisted to the right, making my entire body jolt to the side.

Shiiiiiiit.

I let out a little cry as I went down.

My son jerked forward, staring down at me in shock. "Are you okay?"

No. I wanted to cry and be extremely dramatic about all this. Was it too extreme to call an ambulance?

"I'm fine." My voice was breathy, my pain evident, but holy shit, what was I supposed to do? There was a really good chance I sprained my ankle.

"Mom, can you get up?"

Placing my palms behind me, I lifted my body enough so Cruz knew I hadn't died, but there was no chance I'd be able to get up without crawling back into the house. I ran through the very short list of people I could call in my head. Lydia was probably already at work, but maybe if I could get my phone.

Cruz came down and tried to help me up using his little arms. "We have to go. Can you still drive me?"

The pain was intense, but letting him down and knowing I absolutely could not drive and only had one friend I could maybe ask for was a different sort of pain. The kind that dug into my veins and tugged at my heart, mocking my attempts at this life and giving my son something better than what I had.

"Just give me a second, I can maybe—"

"Hey, you guys okay?" A male voice called from somewhere behind my car.

Cruz turned and lifted his hand in a little wave, his tense shoulders relaxing a fraction. From where I was, I could see the loud, black diesel truck parked at the edge of my driveway. My stomach did a little flip at the fact that I had already begun to recognize the cadence in Archer's voice.

I fell back on my palms and gave up as my neighbor came into view. He stood out against the backdrop of the light indigo sky, still streaked with pink clouds. His eyes were a stark, brilliant blue, too beautiful for such a stern face and an equally hard man. Although I didn't know him, all I knew of him hinted at a roughness as tough as the leather on his back.

Archer's brows dipped in worry. His gaze scanned me from head to toe, homing in on my ankle. I sat forward, trying to prove I was fine, as he knelt beside me and gently cradled my foot in his large palms.

A hiss left my clenched teeth.

"You sprained it. The swelling is already so bad your shoe won't stay on."

Fuck. Fuck. Fuck.

"Thanks for checking on it, but I can—" My croaky voice cut off as my neighbor shifted, lowering my ankle. Then, without asking, he scooped me into his arms and lifted me until I was cradled against his chest.

"What are you—"

He peered over his shoulder at my son and gestured toward his truck. "Cruz, get your backpack and your mama's purse, I'm going to take you to school."

"What? No...we don't." I panicked, my breaths too shallow, so I tried again, "I don't want to inconvenience you."

His hands weren't touching any part of me that was inappropriate, and yet being able to smell the spicy, citrusy scent that I had gravitated toward so strongly yesterday, this close, made me feel strange. I tried to lean away from his chest to create some sort of distance between us, but he shifted so I was back under his chin.

"I wouldn't have offered if I didn't want to help. You're not an inconvenience." His lips moved close to the side of my face, and the heat from his breath was like a shockwave that burned through me all the way down to my toes.

Had he forgiven me? Did the peace pie work?

"Cruz, hop in the back with Kane." Archer walked around the front of the truck as I watched my son climb up on the extended step and pull the back door open. Kane had already crawled to the back and excitedly awaited Cruz to join him.

"Can you open that for me?" Archer asked as he paused next to the passenger side door.

I extended my palm and lifted the handle, allowing the door to open. Archer gently set me in the seat, but not without shifting his hands to the front of my thighs, then slowly moving his palm down my calf. I inhaled a sharp breath, which I hoped he'd assume was because of the pain.

"You going to be okay like this until I get you to the doctor?"

No one had touched me like this in years. No one to care if I'd gotten to the doctor or was safe. His concern did something to me. It softened some titanium piece of metal that had lined my defenses. It angered me while also making me so grateful I wanted to cry. The fight I usually had reserved to keep men like this away dissolved instantly, and instead, I simply nodded.

His eyes wandered to my lips for the briefest moment before flitting away. "Give me your car keys."

His palm extended to me, and my brow furrowed. "Why?"

"Need Cruz's booster seat. Kane has to use one, and I'm assuming Cruz is still in one, too."

Oh.

That was incredibly considerate of him to think of; I hadn't even had the forethought to remember my son's booster. My face dipped, digging through my purse and handing the set of keys over to him.

Once he gently shut the door, I watched him walk back toward my car and pull out my son's car seat. An odd lump formed in my throat as I watched him. He didn't seem hurried, annoyed, or like this bothered him. Those thick motorcycle boots carried him back to the truck, the gray and black booster in his arms as he opened the back passenger door.

"Scoot over, buddy, and I'll set this up for you," Archer said softly to Cruz.

The draft from the cool air filled the cab as Archer stood there, adjusting the seat, and then he had Cruz crawl into the seat.

"I can do the buckles myself," Cruz bragged excitedly. I turned to look over my shoulder right as Archer smiled at my son.

"Yeah? Why don't you show me, and then I'll give them a good tug to see if they're good."

Cruz buckled the one over his chest and the one near his hips as if he were being timed. "See!"

Archer tugged on the two restraints, acting like he'd lost all this strength. "You did too good of a job, Cruz. How are you that strong, buddy?"

My son laughed, and it was a sound I'd want locked in my head, like a favorite song on repeat. Archer gave me a quick glance and then shut Cruz's door.

The heater continued to blast warm air as the boys chatted in the back seat, and once Archer took his spot behind the wheel, he turned it with extreme caution as if he were transporting something precious.

I bit my cheek to hold off the tears welling up. I'd been hurt plenty in my life. This was nothing new, but there was some tiny ping of pain trailing from being at the mercy of a man that I didn't even want to live in my neighborhood. Pride was a fickle, cumbersome thing to carry around.

Archer kept one hand on the wheel while shifting at the waist, reaching for the glove box. His hand brushed against my kneecap as he pulled the compartment open, which had me glaring at him.

"Relax." He grabbed the bottle of pain reliever and tossed it in my lap before gently slamming the box shut.

I held the rattling plastic, twisting the cap and pouring two pills. I could swallow them dry, although I didn't love doing that because of the taste left behind. Right as I lifted my palm to my mouth, Archer looked over.

"Here—"

A metal flask of water was handed over to me. It was on the tip of my tongue to argue with him, that I didn't need his help, or that I refused to put my lips anywhere his had been, but my fight was gone.

The pain was calling the shots, so I lifted the cap on the flask and pressed my lips against the cool metal, sipping the water into my mouth, then tipping my head back to take in the pills.

Archer glanced at me, then turned his gaze back on the window while murmuring something I couldn't make out under his breath.

I tried not to let it bother me; whatever he'd said sounded like a complaint or that he'd maybe used the word "fuck," but I couldn't prove it. So, I returned the bottle to the cup holder, watching as his jaw ticked from his side profile.

He gave me another quick glance before turning into the kids' school and making a quick comment to the boys.

"Remember to wait for the crossing guard to come and help you cross."

My gaze swung over, surprised at how considerate he was about their safety. I was so used to being the only person to look out for Cruz that Archer's consideration was like a bucket of water in the face.

The boys started pulling on their backpacks and unbuckling. Cruz lifted over the seat and hugged my neck. "I hope you feel better, Mommy."

More tears nearly threatened to fall as I hugged him back.

"Thank you. I love you. Have a good day."

Archer watched our exchange while he held the door open for the boys. I hadn't even noticed that he'd gotten out of the truck.

Once Kane and Cruz were near Archer's side of the truck, he shut the door and gently held both boys' shoulders while they made their way to where the crossing guard stood. He didn't have to do it; in fact, he was the only person who was walking their kid up. Everyone else was just dropping their kids and moving their car forward. I didn't even walk Cruz up, but the fact that Archer had made something warm and unexpected bloom in my chest.

Someone honked behind us, breaking the strange feeling, but Archer didn't even glance behind him or hurry as he slid back into the truck.

"Okay. Let's get you to urgent care."

I continued to watch him shove the gear into drive, and we started moving again. "Don't you have a job you have to get to?"

His gaze remained on the road while he smiled. "Sure do."

"Where?"

He glanced over with a blinding smile. "You're a nosy thing, aren't you?"

I clenched the seat on either side of me as he took a turn, gritting my teeth while we went.

"Tell you what. You answer one of my questions, and I will answer one of yours, sound like a deal?"

How long did it take to get to the fucking urgent care? My ankle throbbed, my jaw was starting to ache, and I really just needed a distraction. "Fine."

Archer took another turn, this time slower. I released my death grip on the leather seat and waited for his first question. He took another turn, and the silence stretched in the cab.

"Are you going to ask me something?" I turned my head, irritated that he had already seemed to sway from our deal.

Archer kept his gaze on the road, then clicked his tongue.

"Oh, I'm definitely going to ask you something. I'm making sure my first question doesn't scare you off, which would prevent you from answering other questions."

For the love of everything.

"Fine, I promise to answer whatever you ask."

He winced as if he'd been hurt. "Nah, I think I need a bit more of an assurance. How about you promise to answer five of my questions."

Why did he care?

"And you'll answer five?"

His handsome face quickly turned in my direction. "I'm thrilled that you think you'll have five to ask."

I had no idea what that meant, and I didn't have the chance to find out as we pulled into one of the parking spaces in front of the medical building. Archer didn't waste any time parking and jumping out. I opened my door and was already prepped to use my good leg to get out, but the man took the decision into his own hands by scooping me up once again.

"You know this isn't necessary, right?"

His lips were near my forehead again, and his strong hands held me tight against his chest. "Yeah, but I do have a job to get to, and waiting for you to limp into the clinic is just going to waste my time."

Asshole.

He made some agonized sound while adjusting me in his arms. "Fuck, that bratty expression will be the end of me."

I was going to tell him something derogatory and clever, but we were already walking into the clinic. The sun had me closing my eyes and almost ducking my head into his chin.

Once we walked through the sliding doors, the room came into focus. On one side, a row of maroon cushioned chairs lined the room, while a wall mural decorated the other section. In the middle, a round registration desk with two receptionists sat.

Archer lowered me to one of the chairs. "Here, let me go check you in." As he turned away from me, someone emerged from the door by the receptionist's desk.

"Wren?"

My gaze caught on brown hair, pink eye shadow, and fake lashes. "Lydia?"

She appraised me, then sank into the chair next to me.

"What the heck happened?"

"I still can't wear heels, apparently." I tried to laugh, but it came out more as a wince.

Lydia chuckled, then moved her head so she had a better look at my ankle. "Well, I can't judge you. I'm here because I slammed my finger in a drawer. Thought I'd actually broke it this time."

She sat back, relaxing in the chair as if she had all day to hang out and talk to me.

"So, you here alone? You have anyone who's gonna take you home?"

I glanced at her wrapped finger as an idea popped into my mind that wouldn't leave me at the mercy of my neighbor or answer any questions. "You aren't busy?"

"I have the whole morning open."

Lydia and I weren't close enough to talk every day or anything, but if we did see each other, we could easily converse. "Would you mind staying with me and giving me a ride home?"

Archer returned to where I was sitting with a tablet in his hand. "She says you need to fill this out." His eyes flicked over to Lydia, and based on how close she was sitting, he likely processed that we were friendly.

"Who's this?" Lydia asked, smiling up at my neighbor.

I gestured with my head while inspecting the tablet. "Archer, my neighbor who found me on the ground this morning. Archer, this is Lydia." I hesitated to define what we were because it wasn't like we were friends, but I'd sound stupid saying we were mere acquaintances. "She's a friend of mine."

Lydia held her good hand out toward Archer and lowered her lashes in an undeniable attempt at flirting.

"Nice to meet you."

Archer shook her hand like he wasn't sure why she was sitting beside me. Tentatively, with a quick glance at me, like he wanted to be sure I was okay with it. A ball of warmth hit my chest, liquid heat warming it to my stomach. I held his gaze during his entire interaction with Lydia until she reeled back with a laugh.

"Shit, Wren. This is the man who brought you here, and you're asking me to stay with you? Did you hit your head, too?"

My face burned with her insinuation that my neighbor was attractive. It was no secret that he was, but her words made me squirm in my seat.

"This way, you can get to work and not have to stay here with me," I said, looking up at Archer's stoic expression.

He gave a dreamy smile to Lydia and stuck his hands in his pockets.

"Fine by me. Have a good one, neighbor."

Before I could say anything else, he was already walking away. I felt strange, like I'd repeated my previous offense or something. I didn't like it, but I also didn't like being at the mercy of a man I didn't know.

Lydia gripped my arm in a vise-like hold, making me wish she'd hurt a finger on each hand instead of just the one. "Wren, do you know who that man is?"

I focused on the tablet in my hand, trying to push through the pain radiating in my ankle.

"He's my neighbor."

Lydia made some sort of squealing sound. "No, babes. He's much more than that...I can't believe he lives next to you. I need to call my sister."

My stare flitted to where Lydia was pulling out her phone.

"Wait, why would you need to tell your sister?"

With the phone up to her ear, she waved me off. "No reason."

The call must have connected because she suddenly dipped her head with a broad smile stretching across her lips.

"Cece, you will never guess who just walked in here."

I tried to act like I wasn't eavesdropping by selecting any known illnesses on the tablet.

Lydia laughed and then lowered her voice. "Didn't you date a guy from that dangerous motorcycle club in New York City last year, Mayhem something, right?"

Dangerous motorcycle club?

Lydia continued, "You said you wanted to marry the president. He was blonde with that great jaw...Archer, right?"

President?

My stomach churned as her voice escalated. "I finally saw him in person. You are so dumb to let that man walk out of your life. No, I know he was never in your life, but you had a rare glimmer of opportunity to try and seduce him. I just called to tell you it's my turn bitch. He's my friend's new neighbor."

Lydia continued talking, but my mind kept returning to what she'd said about it being dangerous. No matter how good-looking he was, I didn't need someone dangerous around my son. He'd been nice to me last night and today, but I wasn't risking any more encounters with him. I couldn't.

A fearful thought crept into my head, reminding me how he'd noticed my tattoo.

I blinked and shut out the reminder.

He was ten times more dangerous if he knew anything about that tattoo or who it was linked to.

I asked Lydia a few more questions while we waited for the doctor to see me. What I gathered so far was that Archer led a club that identified as a one percenter club, which meant they lived outside of the laws that made up society and lived by a set of their own. Things like trafficking drugs or weapons wouldn't be too far off the list of things for them to do, or organizing illegal street fights, races, whatever could bring the club money and help them beyond just the dues from the club members.

It set them apart from other clubs because of their notoriety.

I learned that Mayhem Riot was a big club, big enough that it made no sense that its president lived in a suburban neighborhood an hour outside of the city.

My mind pulled up the image of his younger brother, Kane, and I realized that had to do with why he'd suddenly landed in suburbia.

I needed to do more research before I knew exactly what I would do about his presence next to me. Once the doctor arrived, Lydia returned to her phone, texting and swiping away while the doctor gently examined my foot. I had a mild sprain; he wanted my ankle elevated and for me to stay off for at least twenty-four hours. An ACE bandage was provided, and an order was made to pick up crutches and painkillers.

Once Lydia swung by the pharmacy, she helped me inside and dashed off to see her sister.

I let Denise know that I'd be working from home the rest of the day. I'd called to arrange for Cruz to take the bus so I could meet him down the street at the drop-off point. It wasn't the best option, but I was limited until I could move a bit easier on my foot.

Once I managed to prop my leg up and set my computer in my lap, I started sleuthing.

I hadn't handled the purchase of Archer's home, but it was still logged in our system. So, I pulled up the address and looked at a few details: the house style, lot size, and purchase price.

"Interesting," I mused out loud, scrolling through the information while bits of sunlight strayed in through my living room window.

Archer had put in a cash offer for the house after it had been selected and built, so nothing was custom, but he overpaid by about fifteen thousand dollars. It didn't make any sense when nothing was what he'd requested, and other homes in this area stayed on the market for a few months before being scooped up for nearly ten thousand less than the initial listing price.

It also showed he chose not to have the house inspected before moving in...which was typically not allowed, but that was when dealing with lenders. He didn't have a lender or a realtor.

Odd.

What was that job he mentioned? How did he have that much money to put down on a house? I continued to dig through what he'd submitted. Typically, we had information on employment and contact info, but his information was all missing. Only his email was listed, not even a phone number.

Brianna wasn't the type to skimp on inputting data. If anything, she was over-detailed regarding our client's information. I clicked page after page, looking and inspecting, which led me nowhere. I switched to social media, typing in the club name and seeing what came up, but only a few images here and there popped up, none of them recent or of Archer. I had a social media, but it wasn't under my name, and I didn't post anything. I only watched reels and occasionally looked for people's accounts I had stopped talking to.

As if my fingers had a mind of their own, they started typing a familiar handle. Deep down, I knew nothing would populate, but a few times a week, I still tried.

@juan_hernan

A text came in, derailing my efforts.

Brick: We still on for coffee tomorrow?

Shoot. I had forgotten entirely about Brick and our agreement. He must not have heard about my accident, or he just didn't care. Biting my lip, my fingers hovered over the screen as I considered my next move. I needed a ride tomorrow; technically, I had plans with him.

With a resigned sigh and a simmering frustration in my stomach, I shot out a text.

Me: Yeah, would you mind picking me up?

His dots bounced around on the screen for a few seconds.

Brick: Yeah. I need to swing by that coffee place on Greenwood to meet a client first, so why don't I pick up our coffee to go? We can do another date at a different time.

Maybe I should just call in sick tomorrow.

The alarm on my phone went off, making my fingers freeze mid-type. It was the one I had set, indicating it was time to get Cruz from the bus stop. This was probably better anyway...I didn't need to look him up or see if I could find anything new about his life. I reluctantly put my laptop away.

I wouldn't care about Archer or what I had found, except that conversation Lydia had in front of me had stuck in my head like glue. He was part of a club, not just part of the president. I had already deduced that from his patches, but hearing someone talk about a real-life club in New York City had my mind churning.

He was dangerous, and because of him, more dangerous people would probably be arriving.

Using my crutches, I began walking toward the bus stop near the end of the street. I had barely made it out of my driveway and up to the sidewalk when I heard the familiar rumble of a diesel nearing. I kept my face down, watching the movement of my crutches so I didn't fall when the truck came to a stop next to me.

"Need some help, neighbor?" Archer's voice was playful, and it had me looking up.

His hair was tied into a bun at the nape of his neck, still messy but making him look masculine and handsome.

I lifted one of the crutches just barely. "Nope, got these bad boys, so I'm all set now."

He laughed, and the sound was so bright and complete that it nearly made my breath hitch. When was the last time I had made a man laugh? When was the last time one had stopped to actually check on me?

"Wren, it will take you forever to hobble down the street to the bus stop. Just let me take you."

Hearing him say my name was strange. It felt like I had his full attention, which also felt strangely safe like someone pulling me in from the cold on a stormy day.

"You honestly did enough today, Archer. I appreciate your help, but I'm good."

I swung my crutches again, but Archer put his truck into park and turned off the engine...in the middle of the road.

I continued down the street like I didn't notice what he was doing, but he was walking next to me, swinging something around on his key ring within seconds. He wore a regular black hoodie, but it had the name of a bar or something on the front. It matched the large sewn letters on the back of his leather vest that he usually wore.

Mayhem Riot.

Our stride was comical at best. He was walking slower just to keep pace with me while not talking to me, and I couldn't quite wrap my brain around why he was even bothering me. The sun was shining, and the air was too hot for the cardigan I had pulled on, but it was just a tank top under it. The fabric under my arms felt better than just skin to rubber.

Irritation burned under my skin, forcing me to stop.

"Why are you walking with me?"

Archer lifted his head, gesturing toward the bus stop. "Kane—."

"Doesn't live with you," I snapped, harsher than intended.

His shrewd eyes narrowed, and then his jaw started to work back and forth. I had hit a sore spot; I knew I had based on the conversation I had overheard in class that day. Not one I had been invited to hear but had been exposed to just the same. I had information on him that I had now used to wound him.

Red stained my cheeks the longer we stood there. I was ashamed of myself, but I had no idea how to even begin with an apology. Then there was a part of me that wanted a divide, to sever the bridge of neighborly kindness to protect myself and Cruz. I didn't need to know a motorcycle club president. I didn't need to be his buddy or friend and have him assume I was okay with his lifestyle.

The bus pulled up; we were just a few yards away now, and before we started toward it, I cleared my throat.

"I'm sorry, I shouldn't have said that about Kane, it wasn't—"

"You know..." Archer cut me off, forcing my gaze up to his shrewd one. "All my life, I've believed the best about people. Even if their first impression of me was always to assume the worst. I have been called worthless and told my life had no meaning, that I'd be better off dead. That I should just do people the kindness of leaving... And yet, I still smile. I still try. I still hold my hand out for a greeting. Time and time again, people just spit in my face, telling me to shove all my good intentions up my ass. I have no idea what I did to deserve your rudeness, and I know I'm not as clean-cut as that guy, Brick, but honestly, Wren, you can fuck all the way off with your judgment." His glare cut me to my bones, robbing me of breath.

I watched him turn away from me and continue walking toward the bus where Kane had stepped off. He ran to his brother and hugged him around the waist.

Tears burned at the edges of my eyes. I had no reason to be rude to him, but my guard with guys like him was rusted in place and wouldn't come down. While Brick was an asshole, I still ventured toward men like him because of how they looked on the outside. The safety they made me feel because they seemed far from dangerous, and yet under Brick's prestigious ensemble was a shitty human who treated people like they were disposable and expendable.

"Mom!" Cruz was in front of me, and the tears gathering in my eyes would give away that Archer had any impact on me at all, so I quickly swiped at them, with one hand hating that Archer was once again glaring at me while he walked Kane back toward his truck.

Kane waved at Cruz, and my son waved back. I was so mad at myself that I wanted to scream.

All I seemed to do was burrow in my little hole and kick people out. I'd removed anyone and everyone who felt dangerous or like they'd somehow disrupt what I had with my son. But what other options did I have?

I didn't have the luxury of allowing men into my life who might not stay—or really anyone who could ever hurt us.

Slowly, Brick by Brick, I closed my heart back up, hating that Archer had found a weakness inside it, and I swung my crutches so that I was moving back toward my house.

"Can I go play with Kane?" Cruz tilted his little face back, squinting at me.

My heart throbbed as I tried to verbally say the rejection sitting on my tongue.

Right as I was about to open my mouth, Archer looked over his shoulder and yelled,

"If Cruz wants to join us, we're just going to be riding in front of the house...that way, his mom can keep an eye on him, too."

So, he'd moved to not even addressing me.

Why did that even bother me? It wasn't like I knew him.

Cruz looked back up at me and smiled. "Can I go?"

Normally, I'd run my hands through his hair as a way to ground me, to keep me sane, but my hands were gripping the support bar on the crutches. With one last glance at the frustrating man in front of me, I gave a warm smile to my kid.

"Yeah, of course."

He ran ahead of me and joined his friend. Archer gave one last look over his shoulder as the three of them headed to his garage, and I veered toward my driveway, completely alone and aching in more places than just my sprained ankle.

Chapter 6

Archer

The social worker's office smelled like old carpet and burnt popcorn.

This was slightly better than the last time I'd been here when the air had an odd odor of feet.

"Mr. Green, do you have those pay stubs we discussed?" Iris, Kane's social worker, looked down her nose at me like my neighbor did. Which only had me thinking about yesterday and how I'd told her off in the street. I had no regrets about what I said, but I didn't miss the hint of red that had stung her cheeks afterward or how she'd wiped her eyes.

It seemed my little iron-hearted single mom had a weakness, after all.

"Yes, right here." I pulled an envelope out, which contained the last six months of paystubs.

Iris started unfolding each one while entering information on her keyboard.

The sound of keys clacking filled the space while people around us engaged in phone calls and murmured conversations. Iris had frizzy blonde hair that she piled on top of her head, with pieces that she very clearly sprayed down with hairspray. Her eye makeup was dark purple, her eyeliner thick black, and her lipstick blue. I had absolutely no idea how old she was, but if I was thirty-five, she had to be somewhat close to it or older.

"So, you're a freelance financial manager?" Her penciled brow lifted like she didn't believe what she saw on the paystubs.

"I'm hired through E Trust, but it's a smaller branch: Trust and Save Financial Management. They currently have three agents hired, and we handle anywhere from seven to ten clients. I oversee the other two agents, and my client list is only five clients, but they're the top five of all our clients combined."

Iris looked at me while adjusting her thin glasses. "That seems like an incredibly demanding job."

I shrugged, feeling uncomfortable in my suit and tie. "It can be at times, but I'm salary, so my timetable is flexible, and I've yet to find a reason to ever require me to stay any longer than three in the afternoon. As soon as I leave for the day, the work waits for me to return the following morning. It allows me to have hobbies and, of course, be present at home."

Iris stared, trying to find something else to say, but merely clicked her tongue.

"And you only work four days a week?"

I nodded, hoping she'd see the gap in time as a way for me to have more time with Kane if I were to have my brother full-time.

She clicked a few more keys, then glanced at me briefly before asking, "And describe what your weekends will look like if you gain custody of Kane."

Easy. "He's currently learning to ride his bike. We'll go to parks when the weather is nice; when it's not, we'll be at home playing and relaxing. Depends on what's going on. Or, if he wants to join a sport, I'll put him in that."

Iris took off her glasses and set them aside. "And what about your motorcycle club? How will you balance your club's needs with Kane in tow?"

"Well, he—"

He what? He'd come with me? I couldn't say that to a social worker. He'd stay home? Fuck.

I must have taken too long to respond because Iris sighed.

"We're not yet, but we could be going up against a parental hearing. I just got a call from family services in New Jersey. There's a petition that was just filed for Kane Green. This means another family member might be trying to contest you to become Kane's legal guardian. My guess is it's Kane's father. We will treat these sessions as though that were happening because it's a worst-case scenario. You need an iron-clad case. The court doesn't care about what you did as a teenager or even in your early twenties. You're an established adult with a home, a functioning vehicle, and a good job. Those are all wonderful things that would make a great guardian. However, you lead a motorcycle club, and if there's a chance this other family member doesn't, then you're in trouble. While I think you would make a great choice, I don't make the rules. When asked what you'll do with your ward, the only correct answer revolves around being available for them. Kane is in kinder-garten, so part of your weekend plans might revolve around practicing reading, writing, and anything that would help him progress in school."

"Right, I just—" I started, but Iris started clicking on her keyboard again, ignoring whatever defense I was about to use.

"The judge won't care for your excuses, so I won't do you the disservice of entertaining them. Solidify your free time because this question will certainly be asked of you during the custody hearing. Talk to your lawyer about pushing the date. The longer you've been in that house and away from your club, the better it looks."

My heart sank; even if I knew she was right, it felt like a knife had started carving into my back, cutting away at invisible wings. My club had always been my freedom, and no one said I couldn't return to it after a time, but I had no idea how I was supposed to balance being Kane's legal guardian and the president of Mayhem Riot.

"And Mr. Green?"

My eyes flicked up.

"It would help if you had more help in your corner. A girlfriend, boyfriend...husband, or wife that would make the judge agree to temporary guardianship faster. It would help if extra hands were in place to help you care for this child. If that's not possible, then your only option is to make the appropriate plans regarding your club. Sadly, in this situation, I don't see a way where you can keep both."

My scoff had her jolting.

"What you're talking about is community...I have that with my club. While I understand the stigma around motorcycle clubs, and while I completely agree it's no place for a child, the people within the club are decent. Did you know one of my members is a doctor, a bank manager, and another volunteer at the hospice? These men and women come together to form a community, and you're telling me I should find that. I'm telling you I have, and it somehow makes me look worse to the courts?"

Iris pursed her lips while tapping her pencil against her desk. "I don't make the rules, Mr. Green. I'm just here to explain them to you. The parenting model of taking a village rarely works with family court. They want to know you've got a stable home without a village and the chaos that would go with that."

I bit back the rest of my response because it was clear it didn't make a fucking difference. Instead, I grabbed my folder and walked out.

Thistle was working on his bike when I pulled up to his house. He lived in a single-family home a few blocks away from our club. It had been a while since I'd ridden into the city. The time on the road gave me time to process the meeting with Iris.

Several things she said were on repeat in my head, circling like a drain down to my stomach, where my nerves twisted into knots. But one in particular had me driving all the way to the city so I could share my concerns with my vice president.

"You preppin for winter?" I asked as I tossed my friend an energy drink.

Thistle gave me a solemn nod while cracking open the can. "Hate puttin' her away...I'm hoping the snow will hold off this year."

"Does it ever?" I laughed, walking closer to his bike, seeing that his exhaust had been upgraded.

Thistle sipped his drink, then continued working. "You're here... why is that?"

I never thought I'd hear the day when my own VP questioned why I was in town, but fuck my life, this was what it was now.

"Kane's social worker hinted at Saul getting involved, contesting my guardianship."

Thistle's hands stopped moving as he tipped his head back, his bushy brows crowding his forehead. "That would mean your piece of shit old man was back?"

I nodded my head, staring at the concrete.

"It's possible."

Thistle sipped from his can, still sitting on his tiny stool, glaring up at me. "What's the worst-case scenario with him returning? You think he wants to go through all that shit just for the sake of being a dad?"

"Nah, it has to do with me. He must know that I want Kane, or maybe he knew about my meeting with Brit when she asked me to take Kane two years ago. It was right after that conversation that her accident happened."

With a heavy sigh, my VP tossed a tool into his open tool bag. "Let's just do a hit, Arch. Your dad killed Kane's mom. He's dangerous...let's not give him a chance to fuck with you."

My eyes narrowed on a small crevice in the driveway with weeds growing inside as my brain worked out the possibilities. "There has to be another angle I'm not seeing. He knows Brit's death can't be proven. But there was enough speculation. I should have tried harder and pushed to get the detectives to track him down."

"It's not your fault, you know that. Shit, man...honestly, I still wonder if Kane is even his. I mean, Saul got some twenty-year-old bunk bunny who was bouncing around on various cocks knocked up? Just seems—"

I gave my VP a look, and he shook his head. "Yeah, yeah. He's your fuckin' twin."

Kane looked exactly like me. If I did get custody of him, people would assume he was my kid his entire life, most likely. Brit was a gorgeous woman, but she was a brunette with freckles and a fake tan. My father, Saul Green, looked like he'd just stepped out of some Viking show with his blond hair, white eyebrows, and beard. His stark blue eyes and pale skin. According to what my mom had told me, he was almost one hundred percent Norwegian, and those features were passed down firmly through his genes.

"If I had to make an assumption, he will try and leverage the club for Kane. We need to be ready for it. But I want all the captains out on a ride, investigating him and seeing what they can find out, but I want to tell them to be discreet. Kane's social worker mentioned New Jersey, so send the boys out; we're likely looking into the Gentry Brother's MC."

Thistle nodded, finishing off his can.

"You sticking around for the rest of the night?"

A pair of amber eyes flashed in my mind as I pictured home and remaining here. She'd been rude enough that I shouldn't continue anything there...but the image of her lying in her driveway, hurt with no one but her kid there to help her, hit me right in the chest. As if I'd been shot with a pellet gun, the wound stinging and remaining. Not lethal but agitating.

"I have work to do." I needed to see her leave tomorrow morning, knowing she'd made it into her little model home job. I'd seen her work when I first stopped in to discuss the purchase of my home, but she'd been with a customer and hadn't even noticed me.

I noticed her though.

The problem was, now that I had met her, I wanted her attention. Like a kid back in grade school, I wanted the girl next door to see me, smile at me, and talk to me. For all the women I had met in my life who wanted my time, how ironic was it that I only seemed to want a single mom with an attitude issue to have it?

"Might be good for the guys to see you for a bit at least," Thistle suggested, keeping his focus on his bike and his comments off my withdrawn attitude.

I dipped my chin in understanding. He was holding shit down, and I knew it wasn't easy for him. He was a great VP but didn't want to be president.

"Yeah, I'll hang for a bit."

I surveyed my club, trying to find the same sense of freedom I had before I decided to move to Atlas. Before I knew I'd be taking responsibility for my little brother's life and agreeing to raise him. Something humbling rooted me to the ground when I considered what the courts needed to see from me. I knew the men in my club had families and jobs; most had careers outside of this club, yet when they walked in through those doors, they seemed like the lost boys in Peter Pan.

Never having to grow up. Never having to face responsibilities.

I meant what I said to Wren about us not being a gang. Most people didn't understand that our love for our bikes drew us together. Riding was as close to flying as we'd ever get while still getting to feel the wind through our leather cuts, reminding us we weren't angels or anything holy.

Just broken men with a passion for riding and a desire to build community. Gangs built their existence around corruption, greed, and crime. We might skim a little and push the boundaries to make some extra cash, but we'd still be us if we lost that. Wild, free, and happy.

"No, I'm not running that route again. Those fuckers are crazy!"

My head snapped up at the sound of one of our prospects barging into the club, tossing his helmet across the room. Thistle's brows furrowed as he watched one of our captains, Dozer, approach the kid. I wouldn't ask until I knew more, but a tantrum like he was having in front of other members and some of the non-members was an absolute fucking no.

I couldn't hear what Dozer said to the kid, but the prospect yelled again.

"This is the third time they've intercepted our routes. We're lucky to even be alive. Those fuckers are crazy."

The kid pushed past Dozer, which was another big fuckin' nope, which is when Thistle caught my eye.

We walked to the back of my office and shut the door. This room had no windows, just gray walls, a leather couch against the back wall, and my desk on the other. Thistle stood with his arms crossed, waiting until Dozer walked in.

Dozer was Armenian with thick, black hair, tan skin, sky-blue eyes, and a sharp nose. Built like a fuckin' tank, which is where he'd gotten his nickname.

"What's this about?" I asked, leaning back in my chair. Felt weird being back in it after being away for so long.

Dozer let out a sigh and sank down onto the couch. "The routes along Manhattan. Same shit, just a new fuckin' year."

I glanced up at Thistle. He gave me a subtle nod, which made my mind go back to Wren and that tattoo I had seen on her arm.

"Is this still that gang, El Peligro?" No way I thought they had new leadership or something. For the longest time, they hadn't been an issue because the primary leader didn't give two shits about us, but something shifted recently.

Dozer nodded, staring down at the ground, lost in thought. "Their patrols are more frequent, and every time we come close to one of the checkpoints for a meetup, their men intercept us. The last few times were just warning shots, but this time, he said they tried to light their bikes on fire."

"Shit," I murmured, tracing a groove in the desk. That little black heart on her arm. Why did she have it? What connection did my neighbor have to this fucked-up gang?

"You sure it's still them?"

Dozer tossed me a card. Black heart, dripping as if it were bleeding. Their calling card.

This complicated things.

"Pull back until we can get around their patrols and figure out why they're suddenly aggressive. I might have to reach out to their new leader and figure it out."

Thistle shifted against the wall. "Leaders."

My head swung up at him, my brows dipping. He clarified a second later, giving Dozer a quick glance. "There's two."

The stars were out, and they were so much brighter here than they were in the city. I should focus on the expanse of dark sky and the bright lights twinkling above me as I sipped beer and relaxed on my patio lounger. I heard Wren's sliding door open, and then voices trailed over the fence, making me sit up so fast my drink spilled.

"Shit," I whispered, then quickly moved to wipe up the mess from my shirt while briskly walking through my yard until I was right next to her fence.

I was far too ashamed to admit that I was eavesdropping.

"It's fine," I heard Wren say, but she sounded in pain.

Another female voice joined in. "It doesn't look fine; it's swollen as fuck. Where's the meds the doc gave you?"

She sounded like the woman with Wren at the doctor's office. Liza...or Laurel was her name.

"I can't take them. I have Cruz, the beauty of single parenting. I never get to be off-duty for any reason."

There was a silence that stretched, and then the other girl started up again. "If I could stay, I would, but I promised my sister I'd meet her for a drink. Are you sure you don't remember which house he moved into?"

The woman from the office laughed, but Wren didn't. I rolled my eyes because they acted like I was a brainless animal; they could just toss a bag over and take it home. The only woman who had snagged my attention in the past year was Wren, who wanted nothing to do with me.

Still didn't mean I'd be open to fucking or doing anything else with someone right now. I had way too much going on.

"Maybe you can take it once Cruz goes to sleep?" The girl from the office asked, breaking me out of my thoughts.

"What if he needed something, or someone broke into the house. I can't just check out. I wish I could, but Tylenol and Ibuprofen will do fine."

"Okay, girl. Well, is there anything else I can do before I head out?"

I heard Wren sigh and then say, "Actually, could you take my garbage bin to the curb for me?"

I had no way of knowing what the woman said, but I decided I'd make sure she helped her friend. It was a few more minutes before she exited Wren's house, and as she walked toward her car, her phone was up to her ear.

I couldn't hear her conversation, but I caught a small tidbit before she completely ignored Wren's request and got into her car to leave.

"No, she didn't introduce me, and I looked through her phone for his number when she wasn't looking. When I asked if it was the new house he moved into, she didn't confirm it. I tried; see you in a few."

Wren hadn't said which house was mine?

Something strange tried to find room in my chest. Something like appreciation and gratitude.

Her hot and cold routine was still pissing me off, but...that didn't stop me from crossing over to her driveway and pulling the two bins that sat on the side of her house all the way to the curb.

Chapter 7

Wren

"Can't we ride to school with Archer and Kane?" Cruz whined for the second morning in a row.

My irritation flared over the Archer topic again. The man had moved in only two weeks ago, and already my life seemed upturned entirely by him. Cruz couldn't stop talking about him at dinner or how Archer had tried to teach my son how to ride his bike. I had tried working on it with him over the summer, but neither of us had gotten the hang of it. Not him with pedaling or me with how to better explain it.

After three skinned knees and a forehead cut, I called it quits. But Cruz had come home without cuts, bruises, or scrapes when he'd tried with Archer. I had watched from the front porch, my computer in my lap while I wasn't paying attention to anything on my screen, and instead couldn't stop watching my neighbor.

He was gentle and cautious with the boys. He laughed like a kid, but he was safe with them, holding the back of their seats and not letting them fall. Kane loved every second of it, bragging about his older brother so loud that I heard it from where I was. His ability to inspire young boys only infuriated me more. Then, an entire day passed, and it was as if Archer had never been here. We didn't see him, which only made my son ask a million questions and be moody over dinner.

Zipping up my son's jacket, I cleared my throat. "Not today, but if he's around after school, you're welcome to see if you can join Kane again."

Cruz stomped his foot. "But I know he'll give us a ride, and you need a ride to work. You can't drive yet, and Lydia said she couldn't help you today."

"Mommy is getting a ride to work from a coworker."

"I hate riding the bus." Cruz stomped his foot again.

I clicked my tongue. "Since when do you stomp your feet? You can't whine like this whenever you don't get your way. Now, I'd hate to take away hang-out time after school. I suggest you act like a big kid and ride the bus without throwing a fit."

My son's face fell, and his eyes found the ground. Guilt slashed at that parental pride, where I assumed I was creating character in my kid. Instead, I pulled my son forward into a tight hug.

"I'm sorry, bud. If you're mad, then be mad. I get it. Just know I'm trying my best, okay? We can't just invite ourselves to get rides from people. That's not the polite thing to do."

Cruz pulled back and gave me a small half-smile. "But what if Archer offers?"

I hated this. "If he offers, then I'll accept."

And I'd gladly cancel on Brick, which meant Archer was the lesser of two evils.

Great.

"Promise?" Cruz lit up like a cute little Christmas tree, all smiles and raised brows.

I held my pinky out. "Promise."

The bus was supposed to come in ten minutes; there was no chance that I'd likely even see Archer in that time, so our little promise meant nothing.

"Let's go outside so Archer knows we need a ride again."

I stood up and rolled my eyes so my son wouldn't see. This was ridiculous.

Even still, I grabbed my keys, purse, and phone and then opened our front door.

"But if we don't see Archer, we're just heading to the bus stop, okay?"

Cruz nodded and pushed open the door. I wore a tight wrap around my ankle and boots to accommodate the thickness. Skinny jeans stretched up my legs, where a simple floral tank flared at my hips, which I covered with a small, cropped leather jacket. It still hurt like a bitch to put any pressure on my foot, so I grabbed one of the crutches to help me as I limped down the drive away.

Cruz slowed his steps, and I assumed it was for me. Then I looked up and realized he was watching Archer's house, waiting to see if he'd drive out. I just kept hobbling down the drive, knowing that even if he did arrive, he'd never offer me a ride after how things ended between us yesterday.

We turned the corner from our drive and started down the side-walk, and my son kept peeking over his shoulder with an eager expression.

I hated this.

How was it possible that he was already attached to Archer? He had no male role models in his life, so it didn't surprise me that he wanted to be around Kane's cooler older brother, but the fear I had over his heart getting broken was terrifying. It was entirely out of my control, and I had no idea what to do to protect him.

Suddenly, the sound of someone's garage door opening and the loud growl of a diesel truck reverberated down the street, and Cruz turned excitedly.

"Here he comes!"

I glanced up, seeing the white streaks left behind by planes cut through the cornflower blue sky. Fall was drawing closer, which meant the days were colder, but summer clung to the sweet, humid air. My jacket was a tad too warm, but I looked cute, so it would stay on no matter how warm I got.

"Cruz," I lightly warned as the truck started down the street, slowly but with enough speed that he'd pass us within seconds.

My son waved, smiling brightly at Archer, and my stomach flipped around. I prayed that this idiot would stop and say hello to my son. A warm greeting would likely mean the world to him even if he didn't offer a ride.

The truck slowed, and my chest thrummed with anticipation.

Cruz stepped closer to the curb as Archer came to a complete stop and rolled his window down.

"You riding the bus today, Cruz?"

My son glanced up the road, where his stop was, and back at Archer. "Yeah, my mom can't drive yet."

The diesel truck idled loudly as Archer's gaze fell upon me. His blue eyes were shrewd and calculating.

"And how's your mom getting to work?"

Cruz tilted his head up to me as if he wanted to know if it was okay that he answered. I nodded at him with a smile.

"She's getting a ride with a coworker."

My eyes drifted over the driver's seat again, hating how nice Archer's hair looked, even if it was as wild as always; something about how rugged it seemed to suit him. I saw it in his eyes: that challenge. The words he'd delivered the day before yesterday went unchallenged, and without my response, it made me curious if he wanted one.

Archer moved his arm, and the truck was placed into park.

"Well, it seems unnecessary for you to ride the bus and your mom to get a ride from someone when I could just as easily take you both. That is if your mom is okay with it."

Our eyes locked. Maybe I could silently tell him to fuck off, and he'd get it.

"She is!" Cruz beamed while walking toward Archer's truck.

"Cruz, wait..." I started, but my son was already at the back passenger door, where Archer had met him. He pulled on the handle, helped my son inside, and then turned toward me.

"You sure you're okay with me taking you?"

I hobbled toward the passenger side of his truck, biting back a bitchy response, and instead just smiled at him.

"More than sure. Thank you so much for the offer."

Asshole. Asshole. Asshole.

Archer walked with me, slow and measured, and then opened my door for me. I slid the crutch in first, then grabbed onto the door to pull myself up, but Archer sighed from behind me.

"You already assume the worst, so I might as well prove you right." His hand went under my ass, and he pushed me up.

I let out a slight sound of surprise while glaring over my shoulder at him. He smirked, then shut the door in my face.

Once I was buckled, I realized that Cruz was in the back seat alone, buckled into the booster Kane had used the day before.

Archer slid into his truck and placed the gear into drive.

"Kane isn't with you?"

My neighbor gave me a bored look before driving down the street.

"No, remember he doesn't live with me."

It was a dig at what I'd said to him, and while I knew I had delivered that barb, it seemed to cut coming from him.

"I just mean, why offer us a ride if you weren't even going to the school?"

"Because riding the bus sucks," Archer replied as if I were a total moron.

Cruz laughed in agreement from the back seat.

I decided it was time to disengage from current company and stared out the window. The town passed by with a myriad of red brick buildings, fresh signage, and new display windows boasting of autumn. The newer and certainly more popular coffee shop was packed to the brim and even had people waiting outside, and I smirked at their ignorance.

The good coffee was served in a spot only locals knew about.

Curious how busy it would be, I shifted my head until I could see the gas station over on Larch, and sure enough, only a few cars were parked in front, and even fewer were primed to get gas. Orlo's wasn't a big enough name for any of the newer transplants to visit. Not for gas or coffee, but several people were moving about inside.

Best coffee in town.

"Do you need me to stop and get you anything?" Archer suddenly asked from beside me. "Maybe coffee?"

I turned away from the window. "No, my coworker is planning to stop and get me some."

Archer scoffed, then flexed his jaw.

I ignored him until we pulled in front of Cruz's school. Once I said my goodbyes, Archer exited the truck just like the day before and walked my son to the crossing guard to ensure he could cross safely. And just like yesterday, my heart felt like a balloon had been inserted into my chest, and something was now about to pop. Why did he insist on being so kind?

Why did he look like the typical bad boy I should avoid at all costs but act better than any man I'd ever met?

Archer slid back into his seat, steering us away from the school. I forced my face forward so it didn't seem like I had been staring.

"Where are we going?"

He glanced over. "I'm assuming this coworker is Brick?"

I didn't respond because I knew from their last interaction that he didn't care for Brick or my association with him. But I was a little surprised that he even remembered his name.

Archer pushed on, unphased by my silence, "He can keep his coffee. I'll stop for you."

Something crackled under my chest, a tiny fire lit with no purpose and no right being there.

My gaze had snapped over to the side of his face, needing to see his expression and find a way to dig underneath it. My brain screamed at me to uncover why he was so set on showing me kindness when I had done nothing to deserve it. My voice was frail as I finally found a way to reply. "It's fine. He's probably already grabbed it."

Archer kept his stare on the road as he turned the truck into one of the spaces of the gas station. My mouth parted as he slipped out of his seat belt.

"How did you know this was the place to go?"

He wasn't from around here and shouldn't know our little local secret.

A smirk lifted his lips as he focused on my mouth. "You were staring at this place, practically drooling all over my seats."

"I was no—" I jumped in to argue, but he cut me off with another smirk.

"Not that I'd mind you getting my seat wet, but I'd like you caffeinated first."

With that, he shut his door and walked into the gas station. My mouth was still hanging open...because what the fuck?

My phone vibrated in my lap, forcing my attention away from the man striding into the gas station like he owned the place.

Brick: The line at the coffee place is long. I'll be late grabbing you.

Glancing up, I watched Archer bypass the line inside to place my order. No one seemed angry with him; in fact, everyone was smiling at him as he leaned over the counter, talking to Joey, the owner and barista.

I hated how that kernel in my chest felt warmer while I watched him. Heaving a sigh, I looked down at my screen and punched out a reply.

Me: Don't worry about it. I got a ride and coffee. I'm good.

Archer returned minutes later. He'd gotten me a bagel with cream cheese and my favorite coffee.

"How did you know I liked these?"

He shrugged. "I asked Joey if he knew your order."

Clever. So stupidly clever.

I hated the way my mouth twitched in a smile and how he was

being so nice to me when I knew he was pissed at me. Or maybe he didn't care enough about me to care how I behaved...but he seemed upset yesterday.

"Well, thanks. What do I owe you for the coffee and bagel?" I asked, feeling my hands warm as I held both items. He'd started driving and hadn't asked me where I worked yet.

"Answers, Wren. Our game is still in play."

That warmth in my chest moved lower when he said my name.

"What do you want to know?"

Sipping my coffee, I ignored how he began navigating toward my job. I had no idea how he knew where I worked, but I wouldn't question it. He seemed resourceful, and maybe he was just guessing.

Archer glanced over once, then shifted his hand on the steering wheel.

"Is Wren your real name?"

My heart skipped a beat, and I could feel the color drain from my face.

"Why would you ask me that?"

He shrugged, glancing over once, and I saw a small, cruel smile curve his lips. "Because I have a hunch about you, and I'm curious if I'm right."

"What hunch?" My heart slammed into my chest.

I'd created my entire persona so that I'd blend in. I'd picked a name that presented my new life, this new role I had to play where I embraced change, but I was easily overlooked. People ignored me, forgot me, passed by me without a second glance.

Why was this man suddenly here, lifting the lid on my life and using a magnifying glass to inspect it all?

His blue eyes found mine again as we slowed.

"That tattoo on your arm..."

With a slight laugh and shrug, I sipped my coffee. "It's just a black heart; it doesn't mean anything."

Archer's eyes found me again before he turned his steering wheel.

"The point of this game is that we're honest with each other...as a way to get to know one another. Try again. You're nervous, which means I'm hitting close to home."

I could push him again, but something relaxed me when I saw all of his tattoos. There were things I wanted to know about him, too; maybe I could use this to my advantage.

With another quick sip of my coffee, I considered how much to reveal.

"I assume you know which gang this symbol is tied to?"

Archer nodded slowly with a quick flick of his blue eyes.

"El Peligro. Everyone on the East Coast knows that tattoo."

Blinking, I pushed past the way the sound of my family's legacy washed over me. It felt like someone had found an old photograph and started sharing all the sordid secrets about it instead of asking about it.

"Well, you asked why I have it. I was a teenager caught up in the wrong crowd. I wanted to be a part of something, so when I was eighteen, I got the ink. I thought this guy would stay with me, but he didn't. End of story."

"Was it Cruz's dad?" Archer's curious gaze snared me.

I shook my head. "No. Matt, that's Cruz's dad... he's in prison."

Archer was looking at the road again, but his jaw tensed as if something I said bothered him.

"Were you guys married?"

What?

"No...we weren't even together for long. It was quick, mostly physical, and then developed into something deeper from there. Then, he shot someone in broad daylight and went to prison for manslaughter. When I reached out about Cruz, he never replied. It's been five years, haven't heard from him since."

The lie about my connection to El Peligro was supposed to slip from my tongue easily enough; instead, he'd asked other questions now mixed in truth. I felt the odd need to go back and correct what I'd said so he knew what was real and what wasn't. There was another part of me that wanted to tell him the truth of why I'd gotten this tattoo. My father told me I needed to show my loyalty to the family with the ink. I had only been thirteen when he'd had me sit in that chair and have someone permanently brand my skin with an emblem that belonged to his legacy. Not mine.

"Your last name..."

"Vasquez is a common last name." I cut him off while working around the knot in my throat.

Did he know my father or worse...my brother?

We were approaching the model home where my office was located. I grabbed my laptop bag and shifted closer to the door, ready to bail, when Archer leaned over the console and covered his hand over my seat belt.

"You never answered me. Is Wren your real name?"

No.

I swallowed. "Yeah...."

He stared at me longer than he needed to.

Lowering my face to break the contact, I shifted to the edge of my seat. "Thank you for the ride, but you really don't need to help me. We don't have to be friends just because your brother and my son seem to be."

Now more than ever, I needed him out of my life. He was too close to everything I was trying to hide from.

Archer searched my face as if he was two seconds from calling me on my shit.

"More judgment...nearly forgot you don't like to be associated with people like me."

I rolled my eyes. "By people like you, do you mean hot, single men who show kindness to single moms? Because yeah, I don't need that."

His smile was slow and completely perfect. "You think I'm hot?"

I pushed open the door, reaching for my crutch as I heard Archer laughing from behind me. He had opened his door and started running in front of the truck to help me.

"So your aversion to me isn't because of my 'gang,' but because of my handsome face?"

Keeping my face down, I situated the crutch under my arm and tossed my laptop bag over my neck, holding my coffee in my free hand. Archer gently shut my door, waiting for me to reply.

"My aversion is to complications and to dangerous people being around my son. Your club is dangerous, which means you're dangerous. So, yes, I have an aversion to you. I'm not judging you. I'm just doing everything I can to keep my son safe."

I watched as his face contorted from happy and playful to hurt. I'd done it again, but I said the wrong thing.

"You don't think your son is safe around me?"

My lungs burned with the need to protect this little world I'd been hiding inside. Just tell him a lie, that he wasn't safe, even if deep down I knew he was and that I was in denial and scared. A piece of me wove together a picture of him being in our lives. He'd become a proverbial postcard pinned to my fridge with the world's strongest magnet. No matter how I buried the image every chance I got, it existed in my subconscious each time I closed my eyes.

But what if I said yes and let him in, and he ripped the rug from under me? What if he was the best thing that ever happened to us, and then he left, or he did something that got him arrested? I couldn't do that again. I refused to risk my heart or son's for someone who could break us both. It was a lie, one that was crafted as a shield to protect us. An invisible shield to keep him out, and while it hurt me to do it, I knew deep down I had to.

"No, I don't think he is. You're the president of a one percenter motorcycle club, correct?"

His jaw worked back and forth.

"I am."

"Then that's answer enough for me. Your club is dangerous, which means you're dangerous. I have to do what's best for my son."

He stared at me, his pillow-soft lips pursed tight as if he were keeping his thoughts at bay.

Then, without another word, he walked back toward his door, and with a loud slam, he reversed and drove away.

This time a few of those fucking tears slipped free as if the fears I had over losing control of my life had finally manifested into an ugly virus that kept all potential happiness at bay.

Chapter 8

Archer

THERE WAS A CERTAIN PEACE IN LEAVING THE CITY AND venturing into the country.

With the wind in my face and my club at my back, I finally felt at peace, like my mind had found a way to stop throwing the look on Wren's face when she said I wasn't safe back into focus. It had been a week since I spoke to or even saw her. She was good to drive the day after our little moment, and from then on, I hadn't interacted with her or Cruz.

Which was tough, because I liked the little guy. Unfortunately, I hadn't been able to have Kane over, so it didn't make sense to have Cruz hang out. Which was fine; this was better. Wren was right; we didn't need to act civil or hang out just because the boys wanted to.

The sound of roaring engines brought me back to the present. My VP, Thistle, twisted his hand over the throttle while watching me from behind his riding goggles. He was essentially asking if I was good. I gave him a slight nod as we increased speed and continued back toward New York City.

We'd just returned from a rival club's funeral, which wasn't my favorite way to pass the time, especially when I was in the middle of a custody situation. But for this particular president, most of the clubs along the East Coast arrived, and while everyone was pledging peace, there were glares, glances, and murderous undertones that promised violence. We had all shown up, smiled, and played pretend...but we also were taking fucking notes on who showed up and who was talking to who.

The Stone Riders were the club Simon Stone had left behind. While I wouldn't be against allying with them, we had a long way to go before any declarations were made, especially with the new crew that had been assembled from various clubs that shouldn't even be in the same room, much less the same club. It made them dangerous.

I knew it was something I needed to bring my club in on and make a plan. Perhaps even try and take advantage of the fact that the Stone Riders would be weak right now, as would Sons of Speed with the loss of their president. But I just couldn't seem to think past all the shit that was currently clouding my mind.

Now, heading home, my entire club was on high alert.

The ruthless edge I'd ridden my whole life dared me to do it. To send my men out and hit them under the guise of peace. Take their shit, build my own...but then I'd remember the way one of the Stone Riders, Wes Ryan, had glared at me, and I'd think back to when we'd nearly killed one another a few years back.

All because of the patches we'd been loyal to.

Wes Ryan was just trying to protect his girlfriend or at least someone who had once been his girlfriend, and I was just trying to fulfill a deal made with her father. It was one of the few times in my life I felt remorse...only because it was senseless and stupid. We'd nearly shot him for interfering...he'd almost shot me for following her.

Now, years later, Callie Stone's dad was dead. She'd become Wes's wife, a mother, and all because, for one second, I chose peace instead of war.

That decision was a defining moment in my life, making me reflect on my place in the club and what we stood for. That was why I continued to ride back to New York instead of turning toward Virginia, where these other clubs were currently set up.

I hated that there was a tiny voice in the back of my mind that said it wasn't just Wes Ryan or Simon Stone as to why I was choosing to get back home. I'd never admit it out loud, but it was also her that was driving me back.

Maybe I shouldn't have helped Wren after she'd been so fucking blunt...maybe I should have just accepted the fuck off vibe she was giving me, and not pushed. Either way, it seemed we'd end up right back here, where we were both avoiding each other. Maybe in the week that I'd been gone, she had started fucking that Brick guy again. Maybe her name really was Wren, and there was no mystery to that tattoo she was wearing.

She probably didn't want me in the neighborhood at all. Fuck, I knew she didn't.

Thistle's engine revved in a way that had him creeping up next to me. He gestured with his head for us to pull into a local gas station that doubled as a chicken shack. Maybe we'd been riding longer than I thought, and the men were starving.

We pulled off the road and into the dirt lot, lining our bikes in rows. Most the men took off toward the restaurant, while a few stopped in to get gas. I remained on my bike and tugged my cell phone free right as my vice president approached.

"The guys want to know if you're going to head back to Atlas or come back to the city with us."

The sky was overcast, and the trees were already yellow and orange, filling in the scene around us like a photograph. The gas station was older, with few cars, just dirt—the cracked asphalt in the parking lot and the dirt in the lot next to it. My boot found a clump of dirt to kick at while I scanned the area, my answer already on the tip of my tongue.

I wanted to get back.

Thistle's beard twitched as he watched, then beat me to the punch.

"The club needs to see you outside of a run and attending a funeral. We're all on edge."

But heading all the way back to the city and then back to Atlas would be too much of a trip, especially after the ride we'd just done.

Thistle grabbed water from inside his saddle bag and took a long swig. The leather around his shoulders revealed just as many patches as mine did, save for a few.

He swiped at his mouth and then dropped his voice. "What if we do something small at your place? Let the men see where you live and be a part of your new life. You need them to be aware of where you live anyway for those who do safety sweeps of the area."

Something small...a small gathering.

"How many?" I asked, ensuring I hadn't missed any notifications from my lawyer, case worker, or Kane. He used his foster parents' phone to contact me sometimes. Mostly just to ask what I was doing, but I wanted to be available if he needed me.

Thistle glanced at the bikes. We had about fifty with us, and the other fifty or so took a different route back.

"We can keep it low-key."

I tossed the idea back and forth. It would have to be low-key; otherwise, I'd get in trouble with the HOA. But...the idea of getting under Wren's skin wasn't such a bad thought either. I could have something safe, small and still piss her off enough that it told her I was still upset over our last interaction. Maybe give her a reason to talk to me.

Suddenly, the idea held even more merit.

"Okay, yeah...let's do it. But it stays small," I warned my VP, pointing my finger at him before heading toward the restaurant. I wanted some chicken, and then I wanted to go home and hopefully see my new neighbor get all hot and bothered over my little *gang*.

This was a terrible idea. Even with a happy buzz going, which made me feel nice and relaxed, I knew this wouldn't end well.

Thistle had managed to get his motorcycle into the backyard and had set up a ramp. Just from that information alone, I knew this would be something I had to fix. There were members in the house, drinking, probably fucking, and a few had even started fighting. Last time I walked inside, a few Bunk Bunnies and Sweetbutts had shown up, fuck if I knew from where, but I was focused on the mess outside because my neighbor's yard was so close to where all the commotion was taking place.

I may have wanted to get under her skin, but this isn't what I had in mind. I pictured the rumble of engines outside of her house agitating her. I pictured some laughter being a little too loud, but this? Fuck, this is not what I had envisioned. It was exactly what she had said: mayhem. I was doing what she'd assumed I would, creating a dangerous environment for Cruz, and while I was in charge and knew everyone here would listen to my word, I was still being reckless by ever saying yes to Thistle.

She was right about me. Why did I even think for a second that I could be a good role model for Kane? Why did I think I could do this?

The happy buzz I was feeling had started to wane, and I wondered if I needed something stronger. I didn't like how tight my chest felt or that my skin seemed stretched too thin like I needed to escape all this.

No, it was deeper than that. It was fear.

I was afraid Thistle would do something that would hit her fence or somehow hurt Cruz. I'd never forgive myself if either happened.

I started toward Thistle to tell him to take down the ramp when there was a commotion behind me. A few members started cat-calling and whistling.

I turned around and found Wren walking through the throng of members gathered near the sliding glass door. She gave one of my men a slight shove as he got too close, and then she continued toward me like none of this mayhem scared her at all. I took a moment to register that she'd come in through the house...which meant she probably saw all sorts of shit.

Shame crept into my stomach, settling like a rock. It was too dark to make out that shimmer in her amber eyes, but I saw her dark brows dipped in worry, her mouth flat, and her arms tucked across her chest, holding her sweater closed.

She wore sweats that hung low on her hips and flip-flops, showing her red toenails and cute feet. I liked her feet, her legs, and that hair. I wanted to let out a groan. Her hair was down, bouncing in loose curls against her back. It was so thick that all I wanted was to bury my hands in it.

Damn, how buzzed was I?

"Archer?" Her questioning tone finally hit me like an arrow as she stepped closer. Thistle waved from where he sat in the middle of the yard, and the rest of the men surrounding him burst into laughter.

I rubbed the back of my neck as I leaned toward her. "What are you doin' here?"

Her eyes grew, as did her mouth, as if I'd said something that shocked her.

"I'm trying to figure out what the hell you're doing here. You're gone for a week, then suddenly you're back and throwing a massive party, like you're some college kid. Do you know how loud you're being, or how many text messages have come through on the neighborhood app?"

"You miss me, Wren?" I winked at her, feeling that burning sensation return to my chest. She noticed how long I was gone. That had to mean something, right? But also, what the hell was a neighborhood app?

She leaned back with a scoff. "Doesn't matter. Why is your club here?"

"It's only half of my club." I waved my hand as if that would make anything better. I hated that my voice felt too loud and not quite loud enough at the same time. She was going to notice that I wasn't completely sober.

Wren watched the people behind us with a scowl before shaking her head.

"This is stupid, Archer. What about Kane?"

"What about him?" I snapped back.

Her mouth turned down again as if I'd silenced her with my tone. I didn't like how her silence made me feel or how she'd just seemed to curl in on herself like she'd just realized she was out of her depth.

"I just thought you were trying to get cus—" she started, but I pulled her arm until we were heading toward the side of the house where we'd be completely alone. She couldn't talk about custody or anything Kane-related in front of my club. Not when there were a few members who would leak information to my old man.

"What the hell, Archer?"

I let her go once we were halfway to the side gate, the noise a bit more muted.

"My business regarding my brother is private, and honestly, you know shit about it...why are you trying to stir up drama?"

She spun on her heel, glaring at me, but she'd let her sweater go, and my eyes immediately dropped to the way her chest heaved and her tits strained against the thin fabric of her tank top.

"Stir up drama?" Her voice cracked, her eyes roaming my face as if I'd suddenly poked a monster, and she was ready to reveal all her teeth and claws.

"At the moment, I am trying to prevent you from going to jail. I don't know why, though, it's a complete and utter mystery to me now, but I figured you'd need a little reminder of what's at stake. You're right though, I don't know shit about your situation, but it was clear to me that you were trying to do something for Kane. I don't exactly know what, but this..." She waved her hands around. "Isn't good for whatever you were doing for him."

My anger flared to life, not at her but myself because she was right. I knew that even before I agreed to host this stupid party, but there was some part of me that just fucking needed a break from being the loser older brother who couldn't seem to get ahead with the courts, and the loser neighbor who couldn't seem to get the girl he was crushing on to give a flying shit that he was even alive.

"Again, you know nothing about my situation."

She crossed her arms again but didn't drag the sweater with her, so her tits pushed up. My eyes remained on them, and I openly stared, not giving a shit. She had a fucking fantastic set of tits, almost as glorious as her ass.

"Then tell me, Archer. We were supposed to do five questions."

I started laughing and shaking my head.

"Now you want to know about me?"

"I never said I didn't want to talk," she argued, shaking her head.

"You did. You said just because the boys were friends didn't mean we needed to be, and cherry on fucking top, you said I was unsafe for Cruz...so, please do me a favor and go home."

Her face looked like I'd slapped her. Red filled in the space under her eyes and across her nose. Her lashes fluttered as if she were about to go for another argument, but she stopped and shook her head before turning toward the gate.

"For what it's worth, I know I'm messed up." She pointed at her chest as the wind picked up pieces of her hair, and her voice caught. "I'm broken and can't be fixed. There's this wall around my heart and practically every part of my life. I guard what I can for my sake and for Cruz because I can't let someone in that might hurt us. What I consider safe where you're concerned has nothing to do with physical safety. I think you're dangerous for us because of how much we both like you... or could have liked you...but—"

I stepped closer, erasing the space between us. I wanted to tell her she wasn't broken. I wanted to say I understood why she was so guarded, but I knew she wouldn't really hear it from me. Not right now. Instead, I focused on the last part of her sentence. "The idea of liking me scares you?"

She searched my face, tipping her head back.

"It terrifies me."

Ashley Muñoz

"Why?" I held her elbow lightly because I didn't want her to leave even though I'd just told her to.

Her pink lips parted as she pulled her arm free. "Because...you could just—" She blinked as if she wanted to say one thing but decided on another. "I just don't want that in my life right now."

My hand returned to her elbow, pulling her close again as I whispered, "What do you want?"

She drew her bottom lip between her teeth, searched the ground, and then shifted on her feet. "You're drunk."

I smirked, tugging her again. "I'm buzzed. Now tell me."

She scrunched her nose with a sigh, looking off to the side. "I want...a fairy tale. Something that doesn't exist."

"Why doesn't it exist?"

She shrugged, shifting again. Her eyes flicked over to the fence, and I knew she wanted out of the conversation, but my mind was churning with ideas about why this woman, hard and rough around the edges, seemed to only want a fairy tale.

"That's the point of a fairy tale, isn't it? To dream up Prince Charming coming in and sweeping you off your feet, of being called darling and other ridiculous things. To have someone obsessed with you so they say things that feel like midnight against your skin. Like all the stars exist just for you, and they were the one to put them there. That's not realistic...it doesn't exist."

I tilted my head, seeing her in an entirely new light.

"So you settle for hookups with colleagues?"

Her amber eyes held my gaze, steady and unfaltering. "I settle for human touch; I just need some sort of connection in any way I can get it."

"But the idea of settling on friendship with me was too much?" I raised my brow at her in challenge.

"Archer."

"No, tell me because you made an assumption based on my club, and it's not fair. I can be more than that, I can be—"

I stood staring at her dark lashes, her pink lips, unsure what else I

92

wanted to say...maybe that I could be charming. I could be the fairy tale she wanted, but I had to stop myself. She didn't want me, and I shouldn't want her. She was more than a fling or a one-night stand. She was the complete package, one I didn't and wouldn't have access to at any point in my life. Still, I had to say something. She was so close to me; her breaths were shallow, her lashes dark, and her hair silky. My mouth parted right as the sound of someone smashing through a fence had us both snapping our heads to the side. Thistle has driven his motorcycle through Wren's fence.

"Fuck."

Wren pulled her elbow out of my hold and glared at me. "Right, and this is supposed to be safe for my son?"

With a shake of her head, she darted toward the fence and ran back to her house.

Chapter 9

Wren

"Are you going to call the police?" Cruz whispered while staring through the back window at our broken fence.

I was so angry that my hands shook.

"No. Police won't fix this."

As we spoke, Archer was yelling at various men to leave. The man who'd run through the fence looked ashamed. His tall, burly stature seemed to nearly curl in on itself as Archer yelled at him. Thankfully, he hadn't gotten hurt; no one did—just my fence.

Cruz had been in the living room, watching cartoons when I explained that I would stop next door to ask Archer what all the noise was about. I had left my door locked and the landline next to him so he could call me if he was worried, but I was right next door and had only been gone for a few minutes.

Still, I hated myself for that split second of fear he had felt when he heard the motorcycle burst through the fence. I hated the look on his face when he'd opened the front door, crying, meeting me halfway down the driveway, unsure of what was going on.

I had picked him up and tried my best to soothe him, but my mind kept casting horrific visions of what could have happened if my son had been outside. It was unlikely because I had left, and Cruz never went outside when I walked to get the mail or even went out front to water the plants. He knew our system, but still...what if I hadn't gone over to Archer's and Cruz had gone outside?

What if he'd gotten hurt?

The spiral of what-ifs thrummed through me like a snapped guitar string. Every time I tried to stop, it would snap back front and center.

My son watched as the people next door collected pieces of fence and debris. "Archer will fix it; I know he will."

I didn't comment, knowing my temper wouldn't allow me to say anything nice. Even after the moment we had, where he seemed so affected by what I had said last week. Or how I had revealed that I noticed his absence and wanted to continue our question game.

My arms were still crossed over my chest, watching from the living room window with Cruz when there was a gentle knock at our back patio door.

Archer stood there, head lowered, jaw working. He was upset, which was good because I was too.

Cruz jumped up and ran to the door to pull it open. Regardless of what I said about safety, even at this moment, my gut still didn't give off any warning vibes about my neighbor. I knew Archer was upset about what had happened and would never intentionally put Cruz in danger.

I allowed Cruz to open the door as I stood back a few feet, still guarded and upset.

"Hi, Archer." Cruz tipped his head back and greeted our neighbor excitedly.

Archer smiled at my son, and seeing how genuine it seemed was like a hit to my chest, leaving me reeling for entirely different reasons.

"Hey bud, how are you?"

Cruz hung on the door handle. "I'm good. I was scared when the motorcycle hit the fence, though."

Archer's demeanor shifted entirely. He dipped his head while shame slipped over his face. I hated how it looked on him. The regret so potent that it made my stomach churn.

"I'm really sorry about that, Cruz." Archer lifted his face, his eyes finding mine. "I should have known better than to allow my friends to come over. Things got out of hand, and I—" His voice cracked, which had something in my chest cracking too.

I spoke up, taking over the conversation. "Why don't you come inside."

"Mom just made cookies." Cruz ran over to the counter excitedly.

Archer tucked his hands into his pockets while peeking over his shoulder outside. "I actually should probably head back. I don't want to bother you guys any more than I already have. I only came over to tell you that I'll have a crew out here tomorrow to frame that piece of fence, and it should be finished by the end of the week."

My son's little eyebrows dipped to the center of his forehead before glancing up at me. I knew he was trying to work out what Archer meant.

"Are you going to come in and try our cookies? I helped with them."

I laughed at how Cruz completely ignored everything Archer said.

"Cruz, don't pressure him."

Archer's eyes snapped up. "I don't want to impose."

We seemed to both silently communicate something as we stared at one another. I was pissed at him, at his choices, and I was viscerally angry about the fence. But underneath that, some strange part of me also wanted him to stay. I felt like our conversation from earlier wasn't finished like there was more I wanted to say, and I needed him to tell me.

"This recipe is my mother's...she cuts the larger chunks of choco-late up, and we use the fat flakes of salt."

The glass slider slowly closed as he silently accepted the invitation. Archer looked down at his feet as if he wanted to ask if he should slip out of his boots.

Cruz pulled on his wrist. "You can keep them on."

I followed both boys as they moved into the kitchen. Archer's waist met the counter as he leaned over and washed his hands. It was so weird watching him do something as mundane as hand washing. Once he was finished, he twisted to dry his hands on the homemade towel my abuela had made me when I was a teen. His expression softened as he patted his hands dry, and his unguarded eyes met mine again.

It felt like his gaze prodded and inspected for some personal thing I'd be willing to share. With a blink, I turned away.

"Here, you should have one with milk."

I handed him a cookie with a napkin, then turned to grab the milk from the fridge.

Archer accepted and brought the cookie up to his mouth while watching me. He was a few chews into his first one when his eyes closed, and he moaned. "These are the best thing I've ever tasted."

Why did I suddenly picture him between my legs, tasting me and saying that exact same thing?

"Mom makes this whenever she misses my grandma," Cruz said, looking at me sympathetically.

"You don't see her often?" Archer asked, finishing off the rest of his cookie and milk. Cruz hurriedly moved to the fridge to grab the carton again.

"No, she lives in North Carolina. She came for Cruz's birthday last year, but since then, no."

Archer took the milk from my son with a smile before pouring himself more. Cruz filled in all the remaining details I didn't necessarily want to share.

"We never go see her, though, because she lives in the same city as my uncle, and we don't see him because he's making poor choices right now."

My chest seized as I snapped. "Cruz!"

His brown eyes found mine, and his face crumpled into a wince. "But we don't talk about it with strangers."

Archer's lips quirked up as if he already knew what my son was about to work out.

"But you're not a stranger!"

"Cruz, talking about familial things with new acquaintances is still not polite."

My son came over and threw his back against the front of my body, so I had to catch him. He did that often, and it always felt like he was having random trust falls with me.

"What's a new acq—acquent." He tilted his head back, silently asking me for help.

Archer stared at the tray of cookies as if he wanted to go in for another but was holding back. Then he glanced over at us with a smile. "She just means new friends, Cruz. Sometimes, we have to give our new friends a little time to be in our lives before we share really personal things with them."

Cruz started rambling off details about the school week that Archer had missed, which somehow had him moving to the little stool under the counter's lip. The two talked about the week, and Archer shared that he'd gone to an old friend's funeral in Virginia. I moved around the counter to start washing dishes. Archer glanced up a few times as he talked with my son, but I liked that they were talking.

Cruz only lasted about twenty minutes before he was up and asking if he could show Archer his room and the toys he couldn't wait to show Kane.

Archer hesitated, glancing over at me.

"Cruz, Archer might need to return to his friends. We can't keep him captive."

Archer laughed, covering it with his hand as his eyes found my floor, then traveled up my legs, softly landing on my chest and face. "I sent them all home. When I go back, it'll be to an empty house, so if you don't mind...I don't."

Nodding, I turned back toward the counter to calm down. My face was on fire, and my heart felt like it was hammering out a warning not to be stupid about letting Archer anywhere near it.

I could hear Cruz talking from the hall, going on and on about his latest car track, which he used to launch his Hot Wheels. I knew what was about to come next.

Suddenly, there was a thumping sound, and Cruz ran into the living room, his arms overloaded with orange tracks.

"We're going to build a racecar track, Mom! Archer said he used to play with these when he was a kid."

Archer moved around Cruz, helping him take the tracks and link them together. The room filled with the sounds of cars flying down the tracks and my son laughing so hard that he nearly fell backward. An uninhibited smile stretched across my face, and I looked over and saw one on Archer's face, too. Cruz's laugh was infectious; any time he giggled, it was like a dopamine hit.

I let them play for another ten minutes while I made Cruz's lunch for tomorrow, and then I moved to the chair across from where they were playing.

"Cruz, it's time for you to brush your teeth." He'd already bathed right after dinner, so he only had one step left. I usually read him a bedtime story, but we'd done that too when I needed a distraction from Archer finally returning.

Cruz ignored me, pushing his car along the track before finally sighing and looking up at Archer. "How come Kane doesn't live with you? Is it because he's at your mom and dad's?"

Archer slowly moved, collecting little toy cars. "Kane lives with a family right now...they're helping until he can live with me permanently."

Cruz tilted his head. "Why doesn't he go live with his mom and dad?"

"Well, it's like you...how you live with your mom. Well, Kane's mom passed away shortly after he was born."

I felt like my breathing was too loud. One wrong move, and he'd stop sharing free little details about his life.

"So his dad is bad like mine?"

Archer gave my son a soft smile. "Kane and I share the same dad... and he's bad. It's important to me that Kane doesn't go live with him. I want to keep him safe and ensure no one ever hurts him."

With another sigh, Cruz dumped his cars into a little plastic tub he kept in the living room. "You're a good dad."

Archer winced as if someone had just splashed water on his face.

His lashes fluttered as he cleared his throat and scratched at the back of his neck. "Just a decent big brother."

"But you'd make a good dad too. I bet Kane thinks so, too."

I moved to help intervene and stop the flow of conversation, especially because Archer's jaw was tense, like he'd just been asked to chew on a pile of rocks. My son had struck a chord somewhere in him, and part of me wanted to let him sit with whatever it was because parenting did that to you. It was like a splash of cold water in the face all the time, and kids were blunt.

"Okay, bedtime. Say goodnight to Archer."

I expected Cruz to wave, but he walked forward and threw his arms around Archer's neck, clinging to him tightly. "Thank you for playing with me."

Archer raised his hand to Cruz's back and patted while glancing at me.

My breath had seemingly got trapped in my lungs, so I turned around and cleared my throat.

"Come on, buddy."

"I'll just head home and see you tomorrow, Wren." Archer stood behind me while Cruz darted around me and grabbed my hand.

I should have said goodbye or said I'd see him later, but instead, I peeked over my shoulder. "I actually need to talk to you about the fence if you wouldn't mind waiting."

Walking toward Cruz's bedroom, I ignored the beating in my chest as well as whatever expression Archer might have had on his face.

Chapter 10

Wren

It didn't matter that my neighbor was sitting in my living room, waiting for me to return.

At least, that's what I kept saying to myself repeatedly after kissing Cruz's forehead while putting him to bed. I had crept down the hall on my tiptoes to see if Archer was still there. He was standing in front of my fridge, inspecting all the postcards that littered the surface.

Slinking back toward my room, I quickly tugged my oversized cardigan off and threw it on the chair in the corner of my room. I wore a thin tank top with spaghetti straps, showing my tan shoulders and white bra. My gaze slid over to my closet.

I should change.

No.

I wasn't going to do that, not for him. I was fine.

But as I passed the mirror, I nearly gasped. My sweats had a suspicious brown stain near my inner thigh.

"Oh my god!" I gasped, sliding them down in a panic. How long had that been there? Did he see it?

I pulled it up to my face and inspected the stain, knowing it was probably chocolate because that's what I had been snacking on earlier.

Irritated, I tossed them in the hamper and slipped into loose pajama shorts. They were on the shorter side and gaped a bit in the legs, which meant I'd have to be careful when I sat, but they made my ass look fantastic, and since I'd just shaved my legs, it was a win-win. While I was standing there, I put on a few swipes of mascara and lip gloss before fluffing my hair and walking back out. I left my sweater behind and tried to breathe, so when I reached Archer, all I would do was talk about the logistics of the fence, keeping it casual.

"Hey." I smiled at him as I rounded the corner. He was inspecting Montana, squinting at something on the image.

"Are these all places you've traveled?"

His blue eyes flitted over my face quickly as if he was waiting for me to confirm something. Then dropped to my legs, where they narrowed.

"Nope. We haven't gone to a single one; they're goal locations."

Archer's jaw ticked as his gaze moved up. He gently returned the postcard to the fridge and placed the weaker-than-average magnet in place to secure it.

"How come you haven't gone yet?"

I shrugged, "Money...time...work...my car."

He nodded, then gestured at Montana again. "I want to take Kane to Yellowstone sometime. Go see a few national parks and let him ride a horse. I think he'd really like that. I heard of this cool ranch where they let you stay on the property and care for your chosen horse that week like a real rancher."

"He would love that, Archer."

When he approached me, I was about to ask him about his custody arrangement with Kane.

"Look, I know I said it to Cruz, but I wanted to tell you. I'm sorry. I know I messed up by allowing the club to come out. I never should have allowed any of that to happen. Cruz could have gotten hurt, and I know you probably won't ever trust me now, but I just needed to be sure you knew that I was sorry." His eyes seemed tired as if this apology took the rest of whatever reserve he had in him.

The apology tugged and pulled at my pride, melting it into empathy.

"Thank you for apologizing. I appreciate that." I had to change the subject because my neck was hot, and Archer looked at me like he wanted to kiss me. Not that I would hate it if he did kiss me, but suddenly, the idea of being kissed by him made me feel nervous.

Moving past him, I cleared my throat. "If you don't mind me asking...where are you at in the custody process?"

He brought his hand up behind his neck and tugged on his hair before blowing out a breath.

"Sorry, I shouldn't pry." I opened the fridge and pulled out two cans of sparkling water. I handed him one and walked toward the living room. Once I'd crossed my legs on a cushion, I cracked the top of the can and took a sip, letting him decide what he wanted to do.

"Can I slip out of my boots and join you...or?"

I tucked a few strands of hair behind my ear, trying not to freak out over getting to see him in his socks. "Of course."

He carefully slipped out of his motorcycle boots and set them near the patio door, then sat beside me on the couch. "You're not prying...I think we're past that. At least, I hope we are."

His eyes found mine over the top of his can as he sipped. I smiled at him and nodded. "I certainly think so...your motorcycle ran through my fence, so—"

"Not my motorcycle, let's get that straight." Archer half turned toward me, leaning closer to my side of the couch.

I shifted so my back was to the armrest, and I was facing him, which allowed me to push his thigh with my foot. "Tell me."

He gave out another sigh. "The foster parents are great and aren't making this any harder, which I appreciate, but the state seems to think Kane is better off with them or someone from the state than me. I have to prove that I've had my job for long enough and have been established long enough...the house is a great start, but they want me to have some time in it to be sure I won't move around again. They want Kane to be established in a school without having to leave. So basically, we're just waiting. Kane's case worker doesn't particularly like me, so that's not helping things."

"Can you get a new one?"

"The system is overwhelmed. They're overworked, and things that should only take days take weeks. Sometimes months. By the time I got a new one and had them caught up to speed on everything...it'd be like we were walking backward. My best hope is that I can win her over."

I considered what he'd said and felt my heart pinch with pity, which I knew he didn't want. Still, what he was doing was admirable. I pushed his leg again with my bare foot until his eyes were on me.

"Why did Kane go into the system to begin with? You mentioned that your dad isn't a good guy...but did something happen?"

"I feel like if you're going to kick me and ask me personal questions..." He gently pulled my foot in his hand. "Then I get to at least touch you while I do it."

A flush worked into my neck and face, but I didn't move my foot. His warm hands felt heavenly.

"Might as well massage it while you explain," I flexed my foot, wiggling my toes.

The smile that stretched along his handsome face warmed something deep and low in my belly. A piece of his blond hair fell over his forehead as he leaned forward and tucked my foot into his chest. He started talking before I could even process how my heel had grazed his thigh, which felt like—

"My father is a dangerous man. He was a member of Mayhem Riot...a founding member, but twenty years ago, he double-crossed the president. Nearly got him killed, and several other members too. He took off before anyone could find him. He left both me and my mom. We were too broke to move, so I grew up in the shadow of the club that hated my father and, for some reason, couldn't stay away. So when I was fifteen, I pledged."

"What does pledging mean?" I shifted so I was sliding my other foot into his lap. His smirk had heat sliding down my chest, pooling in my core. The thickness along his thigh pulsed, but I ignored it because that seemed easier than acknowledging that he was getting hard just holding my foot.

With a gentle touch, he transitioned from rubbing one foot to the other. "Pledging is similar to putting in a job application, but it's to belong to a club, and there's no money involved. If they think you're a good fit, they put you through a ton of shit and see if you stick around."

I tilted my head, smiling. "So it's like a fraternity?"

"Yes and no...a one percenter motorcycle club pledge looks much different than some hazing in a fancy private college. The club president was hesitant to accept me, but his men convinced him that I hated my old man more than any of them did, and I might be more loyal to them than to him. So he let in, made me a prospect, had me do some truly terrible shit...then he gave me a job so I could help support my mom."

"Weren't you in school?"

His thumb pressed into my arch, and I nearly rolled my eyes back. My ass slid down an inch or so, extending my leg so he had better access. I was aware that my shorts were slightly sliding up, but I was as in denial about that as I was about grazing his erection.

"I dropped out...got my GED when I was eighteen, went to a trade school for about two years until I decided I wanted to join the club. At that point, I had been a member for several years and moving up in the ranks."

His hands cradled my foot, slowly moving his thumbs over the tender places in my soles, then gently over each toe. It felt intimate and soothing...and perfect. It felt perfect. I didn't realize we'd both been quiet until Archer cleared his throat.

"Never thought I had a foot fetish before, but shit, Wren." His gaze slid over to me, his heated stare heavy and meaningful. "I think you may have converted me because all I want to do is kiss these toes." His eyes flashed, and he hesitated before adding, "Maybe even slip one into my mouth and suck on it."

My mouth felt dry, my chest all fuzzy.

"You better not because I do not have a foot fetish. I have the opposite of a foot fetish. I'm good with a foot rub, but you start kissing my feet, and I'll—"

A smirk tilted his lips up as he slowly brought my foot closer to his face.

"I ever tell you how much I love this color on you? It's not one I ever really noticed before, but red on you looks fucking orgasmic."

Pulling at my foot, I felt my face heat at his praise. "You're going to make me—"

"Come?" He smirked again, and even with my attempts at tugging my foot free, he didn't let it go. His erection pressed into my free foot, and I did something so stupid. Something only a total moron would do if they wanted heartbreak and a toxic, messy situationship on their hands, but my desire to be touched was too intense. My need for connection took over, which was the only reason I used that free foot to gently prod at the thick bulge along the right side of his leg.

His quick intake of breath only encouraged me to push harder.

"Shit, that feels good," he rasped while his eyes fluttered closed. I was almost positive this probably didn't feel nearly as good as any of those women in his house probably did. When I walked through, half-naked women were everywhere. One was even on her knees in front of someone, her head bobbing up and down over someone's cock. If that culture was what he was used to, then a little rub through the jeans likely felt very innocent to him.

The thoughts of the other women had me stopping my ministrations of rubbing him with my foot. His eyes popped open; his head turned to likely see why.

"Do you have—" How did I even phrase this without making it seem like I wanted something from him?

His deep rumbled against the sole of my foot as he brought it up to his lips and pressed a kiss there. "Protection?"

I gave him a flat look and deadpanned, "A girlfriend...or a wife?"

His beautiful head tipped back, his lips stretching over perfectly white teeth. "Do you really think I'm the type of guy who would be here, hitting on you, letting you massage my cock through my jeans while I have a girl somewhere waiting for me?"

With his eyes back on me, I couldn't fight the blush that crept into my cheeks and neck.

"Well, there were so many women in your house when I walked through it, and the typical rumors about motorcycle clubs don't exactly paint a picture of loyal, dedicated partners."

His hand moved up my ankle and slid over my calf as he shifted closer to me on the couch.

"I'll give you that. I certainly didn't grow up seeing faithful men. Most of them had wives and didn't even consider it cheating if they let some bunk bunny suck them off. But we do have some semblance of loyalty with our old ladies."

I was burning everywhere with how close he'd gotten and how he was touching my leg.

"Old ladies?"

"It sounds weird, but essentially, it means they're our women. They get a property patch, showing they belong to one person in the club, so no man will try and hit on them or fuck 'em. We treat them differently than bunk bunnies or Sweetbutts...which are women who are just around for a good time and don't really have allegiance to anyone."

"So, if you choose a woman to be just yours, then," I started, but when his eyes met mine, his free hand went to my foot and returned it to his erection, encouraging me to continue rubbing him. "So...if you had someone," I tried again, but my breathing had turned shallow.

"If I had someone that was just mine, then I'd give her a property patch that said my name on the back. I'd kiss only her. Fuck only her. Sleep with only her. Not a single person would get to touch me or be with me except her."

I pushed against him with my elevated leg, which had my legs falling open. He could see my black underwear, but I was only worried that my wetness had somehow seeped through, and he could see how much he affected me.

"But are you...is that something?" I wanted to ask if he just did

107

casual hookups or this right here, touching...fucking. If he did that with women regularly...or if he wanted something more substantial.

"Yes, but I'm okay with waiting. My last serious relationship was when I was eighteen. She broke my heart, fucked me up. I've had a ton of hookups since then, one-night stands, and whatever else, but lately, it's been less and less. Especially since this stuff with Kane started. Because of it, I haven't been with anyone in over a year."

Why did hearing that feel like relief? It shouldn't matter; he wasn't an option for me. I couldn't...

His lips pressed into my ankle, and my eyes fluttered closed.

"Wren?"

My eyes remained closed, but I nearly moaned my reply.

"Ya?"

"When I'm worked up like this, I tend to say some pretty crass things. I'm nervous that you'll freak out if I do."

I wanted to hear exactly how crass he could be and feel it against my skin.

"You can't offend me with dirty talk, Archer."

His hooded gaze remained on my face as my foot continued to massage his erection.

"But it's what I want to ask you that I'm nervous about."

In a breathy whisper, I arched my back and encouraged him. "Ask me."

"Fine. I want you to slide your shorts to the side and those lacy black panties and show me your pussy. I need to see how wet you are."

Pure fire erupted in my veins at the cadence of his voice and how raw his words were. I knew I didn't have to and, honestly, I shouldn't... but I craved his touch. He felt so good; a selfish part of me wanted to explore this.

I did as he asked and slid the fabric of my panties and shorts to the side, revealing my bare, likely glistening slit.

My neighbor hissed while lifting his hips the slightest bit. "Fuck me, that's pretty. So smooth and wet."

I smiled, feeling emboldened and slightly lightheaded by his praise.

"Can you spread those puffy lips for me? I just want to see..." he rasped while holding my foot over his hard length. It was solid rock against my soft flesh, and even if it was just my foot rubbing against it, I was extremely turned on by the fact that he was reacting to me.

I licked the pads of three of my fingers, and then with the fabric pulled to the side, I spread the lips so he had a better view of my slit.

"Oh fuck, just like that, Wren. Jesus, you're beautiful."

My chest heaved as I tipped my head back, my breathing came out shallow, and I began massaging myself in slow, measured strokes.

"How does that feel?"

I let out a breathy cry, "So good, but I need—I need..."

Archer's hand slipped to my thigh, pushing my leg to the side for a better view. "Fuck, I'm going to dream about this for the rest of my life."

He made an appreciative sound before lowering his voice and asking, "Your pussy must be aching...why don't you come over here, straddle my thigh and get some relief."

My hand paused, and with my eyes locked on his, I started to move, but his hands were under my legs seconds later, pulling me on top of his thigh. My underwear and panties stayed off to the side as I pressed my slick entrance over the bulge in his pants and began rocking my hips. The thickness underneath me was enough that I started to feel the ache in my pussy alleviate.

"That's it," he whispered, staring down at where we'd connected, "ride me, beautiful. Take what you need."

His hands were on my ass, under my sleep shorts as he pulled me against him, and then his lips were on my jaw, peppering my skin with little bites and kisses.

My hips rose the slightest bit, which pushed my chest into his, and then I readjusted so I was over his erection again. He was so hard, and the way he kept lightly moaning had me mirroring him with tiny gasps of pleasure. I continued riding his thigh, shamelessly rubbing against him, then, feeling bold, whispered against his ear.

"You ready to fuck me yet because I've been such a good girl, waiting."

His eyes fluttered shut as his mouth dropped open, a string of curses falling from his mouth as his fingers tightened against my ass. I heard him muttering, "Yes and fuck," which only encouraged me.

My tongue gently traced the shell of his ear as I gently moaned against it, then continued dry fucking him. "Think of how good it'll feel to have your hard, thick length slide into my hot, wet pussy. Do you feel how soaked I am?" My hips rocked; my knees spread farther apart. "So ready for your fat cock to fill me—"

Archer suddenly froze, forcing my hips to stop moving against him.

"Wren, I need—" His breathing sounded labored as he let out a frustrated sound. "Shit, we should stop."

My eyes shot to his, my heart thundering in my chest.

"What?"

His jaw ticked, his eyes closed as he tried to catch his breath.

"I—" He cleared his throat, keeping his eyes off me. "I think this might go too far, and we should stop."

I released my hold from around his neck and sat back, creating distance between us. A flush of embarrassment hit me as I considered how desperate I sounded and how filthy my words had been to him. I felt so humiliated.

When he didn't say anything to contradict his objection, I crawled off his lap, mortified that I hadn't been the one to stop it. I walked over to my sink and scrubbed my hands, trying to shake the way my pulse hammered in my wrists and my neck, almost like my shame was pounding through my body as heavily as bass in a song.

"It's just...you had a lot of questions, Wren...and it feels like maybe this might be too much. I just fucked up your fence...our friendship isn't even off the ground yet. This is the first civil moment between us since we met. I'd be angry if this ruined our progress or made it to where you didn't want to talk to me anymore."

"Okay," I replied brusquely, focusing on the sink and the few dishes sitting inside. I couldn't look at him.

"I'm not saying I wouldn't want this...or more than this, but you have made yourself pretty clear about where you stand on things."

He was right. I had made myself clear, and while I had considered letting that cement block around my heart down, it was a good reminder that it wouldn't do me any good. He was trying to win a custody case, and I was trying to raise my son in peace, lacking as many complications as possible.

His shoes were suddenly on, and he was standing close to the counter as if he were waiting on me for something.

"Unless—"

"No, you're right," I cut him off, finally meeting his gaze. "This is better; we shouldn't complicate things."

He stared at me. His jaw worked back and forth before he finally stepped closer.

"I don't want to stay out of your life, Wren. I might be asking too much, but I want the boys to play...I want to see you and say hi. Offer you a ride if you need it. Come talk to you about random, mundane things that don't matter."

"So you want to be friends."

I didn't phrase it as a question but rather as a summarization of what he was getting at.

He was silent while looking at the floor. "Yeah...I haven't had a real one of those in a really long time."

My stupid heart turned to goo at his confession and how his voice cracked.

I crossed my arms, then let out a resigned sigh. "I can do that."

His head lifted, a smile stretching across his face. "Really?"

"Yes, really. We can be friends, Archer. I'm good with that...but just so we're clear...I don't want to be friends with benefits or anything like that. If you ever touch me again..." I hesitated, scared of saying this next part, realizing how dangerous it was, but feeling it so strongly I couldn't stop it from coming out, "You better not stop."

His eyes were pure fire as he stared at me. His mouth parted as he was about to reply, but then his phone went off.

"You should probably head out," I suggested, turning away from him.

He stared at his cell, silencing it, then glanced back up at me. The silence stretched, and then he scratched at his jaw before closing his eyes again as if he were having some kind of internal battle.

I needed to recover from his rejection. Even though it was kind and considerate...it still stung.

His phone went off again, and with another frustrated sigh, he finally turned away from me. "Right...night, Wren." His hand went to the handle as he let himself out through the back door.

I stared at the empty glass door for another five minutes before I finally registered that he'd really left, and it was better that he did.

At least, that's what I told myself as I headed to the shower to finish what Archer had started.

Chapter 11

Archer

MY NECK ACHED FROM LOOKING OVER MY SHOULDER SO MANY times, hoping Wren would come out and check on me. I had started early, not wanting to wake her or Cruz, so I just slipped through the gaping hole in my fence, setting up all the materials. I had contacted Thistle and another member, Gunner, to come out a little later, but until noon, I wanted to be the only person in her yard.

Her back patio was a small square of cement with two loungers and a myriad of toys covering the surface. Chalk drawings covered the free space leading up the small step to her glass sliding door, but I noticed another entry point to where her bedroom door was probably. There was another small slab of cement with a plant sitting outside of it, and over the glass window of the door was a long shade closed for privacy.

Her grass looked like it had recently been cut, but tire marks had cut into it, creating patches from where Thistle had run through the gate. I'd have to find a way to fix her grass, too. She hadn't mentioned if I'd need to contact her landlord; it seemed she was dealing with everything. Honestly, I was still shocked that she hadn't called the police on us.

Glancing over my shoulder again, I checked her slider and secondary patio door to see if she'd come out and say hi.

It wasn't like I needed her out here with me while I fixed her fence, but after last night, something was sitting in my chest that needed her to come tell me we were okay. I wasn't lying when I said I wanted her as a friend. I just also really wanted to fuck her last night, and she will never know how close I was to lifting her off that couch and walking her back to her room.

It took all of my strength to stop, and it was for this reason right here. I didn't want to feel like she'd shut me out.

My muscles shifted as my mind churned over the details of last night and how I probably fucked all this up regardless of my hope for her to see me as something other than a random hookup, but by noon, she finally came out. Arms crossed over her chest, she held her sweater closed.

"Archer. Hi." Her eyes were bright, but her tone was curt.

Guilt tugged at my heart, making me want to kick my ass for making her feel embarrassed. I wanted to explain to her that this was more to me than just something physical ...that something had shifted in me while I sat there with her last night.

She'd told me she wanted a fairy tale and how impossible it would be for her to ever have it, and then I'd broken her trust by breaking the fence. Instead of pushing me out, she pulled me in. She'd asked questions about me like she genuinely wanted to understand.

She let me near her son. She sat next to me, felt comfortable enough to touch me...

It was a very odd realization, this clear and perfect moment where I looked around, saw her and Cruz, and discovered that I had a fairy tale of my own that I wanted.

Something I would be a fool to ever hope for but still wanted regardless.

"Hi."

"Just wanted to see if you needed anything before we take off." Her eyes trailed over my face and down to the grease pencil in my hand. My mind snagged on her words, which had me turning and setting the pencil down.

"Where are you guys headed?" Not that it was my business, but damn, I wanted to know.

Wren glanced back at the door and then gave me her attention again. "I'm heading into work for a bit."

"Does Cruz want to stay and help me? I can watch him play in the backyard...I mean, only if you're comfortable with it." Fuck, now I was embarrassed. There was no way she would let him do that after last night. Not just the almost having sex thing, but the fucking hole in her fence.

Her lips twisted to the side as she glanced back at the house.

My neck felt hot as I tried to shake off her impending rejection. "I'm sure he'd rather hang with you, but if it helps, Kane's foster mom offered to drop him off in an hour, so he'll be here too."

Just then, Cruz opened the sliding glass door, looking dejected. "Do I have to go with you, Mom? I hate going into your work."

Wren winced the smallest bit as she took stock of the grass before glancing up again and focusing on me.

"That's really nice of you to offer." She hesitated, then seemed to let out a silent breath. "I'd love it if he could stay with you."

My head snapped over, making sure I heard her right.

"Seriously?"

She laughed, a smile spreading across her lips. "Don't seem too surprised. I am trying, you know."

Something shifted in my chest at the sight of the sun cutting through the clouds, making her eyes brighter than usual. I dipped my head and gave her a smile in return.

"Fair enough."

She turned away to go talk to Cruz before spinning back toward me.

"Oh yeah...uh, cell phone numbers...we need to exchange them in case you need to contact me."

I felt a jolt in my chest. "Yeah, of course."

It was okay; this was fine. I stretched my fingers out so they didn't shake as I grabbed my cell, but Wren was there a second later, stepping closer to hand me her phone. She smelled so good, I didn't even know what it was. It was floral and somehow also spicy, but it was perfect on her, and every time I breathed near her, I withheld a groan. I added myself as a contact and then sent a text so she could find me easily in her text threads.

She smiled thinly before explaining to Cruz that he'd be staying with me. My heart grew inside my chest when I saw his head swing over, a huge smile taking over his cute little face. He jumped excitedly like she'd just told him he was going to Disneyland. Fuck, that made me feel a thousand feet tall, knowing he liked hanging out with me. I would do whatever it took to protect that feeling in him. Make sure I never let him down. Which meant I couldn't fuck things up with his mom.

Thistle and Gunner were helping with the fence and having a great time with the boys. The sun came out in a shock of late September heat, which honestly took me by surprise. Both Kane and Cruz kept squinting and trying to shield their eyes while their cheeks turned rosy. I knew they needed sunscreen and hats, most likely.

"Hey, Cruz." I pulled him and Kane under the covered patio where Wren's furniture was set up. "Do you know if your mom has sunscreen?"

His little cheek dimpled as he smiled. "In our beach bag, I think."

I didn't want to go sneaking around Wren's house. Maybe I should just go to the store. Although, I'd have to find one that sold hats, and most drug stores didn't.

"Where's the beach bag?"

Cruz grabbed my hand. "I'll show you."

We walked inside, leaving the slider open so Kane could come in and find me if he needed to. Cruz walked through the kitchen and crossed the hallway to a closet. Twisting the knob, he pulled it open, revealing a few shelves and a large multicolored beach bag on the floor.

Bingo.

I tugged it free, bending at the knees, and started pulling out neatly folded towels and sifting through clean beach toys. There in the side pocket was sunscreen and even a few sun hats. Right as I was about to shove the bag back into place, I noticed a clear tote to the left of it. Inside, near the bottom, was a business card with a black, dripping heart inked into the middle—the same as her tattoo.

"Thanks, buddy. I got it from here. You can head back out with Kane, and I will be out in just a second." Cruz gave me a swift nod before turning around and darting through the sliding glass door. Kane was already playing under the covered patio, out of the sun. I decided to take a few seconds while they were there to remain inside.

The clear tote sat there in the closet full of secrets. It was an invasion of her privacy...I shouldn't.

But I had to know.

I gently pulled the tote free and slipped the cover off. Inside the tote were old hoodies, tattered, torn, and smaller. As if a teenager had worn them. I pulled them out and continued to sift. Photographs were tucked inside a journal; a few sticking out showed a younger-looking Wren. Early teen, or somewhere close to that. She had a huge smile that could carry the world; it was aimed at someone who looked almost identical to her, except a few years older. Dark hair, amber eyes, same brown skin, but his smile was aimed at an older woman who looked like she could be their mother.

I knew the boy's face.

Staring down at the image, it seemed that Wren was related to him, but if that were true, then...I tucked that one back and pulled another. This time, it was of Wren and this guy, a few years older, in front of a restaurant boasting the best tacos in Rake Forge.

My hands shook.

There had to be some sort of proof that she wasn't related to him. She couldn't be.

I flipped through image after image until, finally, a name caught my attention in the journal.

Dear Juan,

I wish I'd been.

~~*Being your sister was the best thing that happened to me, but you acted like you couldn't care less. I hate that you turned your back on...*~~

DOESN'T MATTER.

Just take care of Mom and Leo. You'll never even read this, but it feels good to write. I love you. I will always love the version of you that existed before El Peligro. You promised you'd never take it over. You swore you'd never walk in our father's shoes. You lied.

You lied.

Kane and Cruz laughing from the patio broke me out of my thoughts, forcing my hands to move quickly to replace all of Wren's memories. I felt sick to my stomach for invading her privacy, for reading something so personal.

But something else was there, too...a feeling of finding a missing piece to a puzzle. Wren wasn't so different from me; she had a jaded past with an affiliation that others looked down upon. It likely shaped her outlook on being so close to danger because she wanted to escape it.

Her home was made of the same material as mine. Her memories were all ash and used up hope. She created a new life for herself while I forged mine out of the ashes my father left. She was my match.

My equal.

Mine.

Regardless of her connection to her brother's club, she belonged with me, and I'd do whatever it took to prove that to her.

After a while, Kane and Cruz both joined in and started helping carry boards, even holding the drill for me as I added in the screws. I'd pulled my truck down Wren's driveway and propped her side gate open so I could access my tools easily. I watched the boys play in the front yard while I sat on the lowered tailgate, eating a burger next to Thistle.

He took a drink of his soda before quietly talking. "Dozer texted me this morning a report of what they found when they looked into the Gentry Boys MC in Jersey."

I tried not to think of what I found in Wren's closet and how this problem had nothing to do with the gang activity in the city that was threatening my club.

Thistle continued, "Your old man has been spotted wearing their colors. Riding with them. So we're assuming he's under their protection."

"Gentry Boys grow in the past year and I not know it?"

Kane was laughing so hard at something Cruz did that his eyes started to water, and it made my own water for a different reason. I liked seeing him so happy and free. Like a kid should, in a place where he truly knew he was wanted and he belonged.

Thistle shifted next to me. "Not that we can tell unless they're pairing up with some outside club we don't know about. He won't have the numbers to make a move against you."

"Unless he's going to leverage Mayhem Riot and see if I'd give it up for Kane."

Joke was on him. I would have to do that regardless because there was no way I could win my case if I didn't prove I'd stepped away from them.

My vice president finished off his food and crumbled the wrapper. "I have a contact. They're waiting on my call to tip them off, but we can dump evidence from what your dad did in front of the detective who was initially on Brit's case after she died and Saul disappeared. They'll open it back up, and now that we have sights on Saul, he'll have to go in for questioning."

It wouldn't be enough if they couldn't pin it on him. "They'll be nervous to prosecute unless we can tie him to both my mom and Brit; otherwise, they risk double jeopardy."

"Still might be enough to make the judge give you custody."

That was true. Even if Saul was acquitted, it was enough to tie him up in questioning that the judge wouldn't say yes.

"Make the call." I jumped down from the edge of the truck bed and tossed my garbage in the burger bag. Cruz and Kane were on the ground, drawing in chalk all over Wren's driveaway. I was about to see if they were ready to return to the back and finish the fence when I heard a car approaching.

I looked up and saw a familiar Tesla.

What the fuck was Brick doing here?

When his car stopped, I saw Wren's dark head of hair in the passenger seat as she started gathering her things. Brick jumped out of his side of the car and glared at me as he ran around to her side of the car and opened her door.

There was something like electricity crackling in my chest; like any second, I was going to catch fire and burn down everything in front of me. Starting with that fucking Tesla. Brick smiled at Wren and held his hand out for her to take. I'd already cataloged how I'd break his fingers so he'd never be able to offer it to her again for any reason.

Trying to control my emotions, I made eye contact with Thistle, who knew my moods and understood what I was telling him because he called the boys to help in the backyard. They ran after him excitedly, probably hopeful it would be one of their turns to use the drill again.

Once they were in the back, my feet carried me to the Tesla.

As I rounded the car, I saw Wren still gathering her things, about to accept Brick's hand. I was there first, so I dragged Brick by the shirt, which made him stumble back. That electric feeling lit up my chest, making it difficult to breathe.

Why the fuck was she with him. Why was he here? Was she casually seeing him again?

There was no way.

Not after she'd ridden my cock through my jeans and begged me to fuck her last night. Not when I knew, deep down in my bones, that the fairy tale she talked about, she wanted with me. Maybe I was delusional, but fuck if I cared. I would be that man for her, and there was absolutely no way that Brick would enter her life again.

"Hey, what the hell is your—" Brick started, but I took his place in front of Wren, offering her my hand.

She looked up at me, kicking one of her legs out of his car. As a silent moment passed between us, she placed her hand in mine.

But Brick was there again, and I didn't see his fist coming as he sucker-punched me, which had me jolting to the side as he stood over me. "I'm really getting sick of you being here, you redneck motherfucker."

Wren was out of the car instantly, holding her laptop bag, purse, and folders while her eyes blew wide.

"Brick!"

Gunner was over at my house and heard the commotion. I saw the second he registered it was me who'd been hit because his face twisted. He dropped the box of screws, pulling something from his pocket. I knew they were brass knuckles, and his stride to Wren's house was brisk.

Shit. This was about to get out of hand.

Thistle knew what had just happened, too, but I didn't need the club's help with this prick. I held my jaw while Brick tried to go in for another punch, and before Gunner could approach, I turned, so when Brick went to hit me, his fist hit his car.

Gunner stopped, likely realizing that I was essentially fighting someone with the survival skills of a paperclip. I saw him smirk and shake his head as he headed back to my driveway.

"Brick, what the hell is your problem?" Wren yelled, but Brick was now on the ground, holding his hand.

I bent over, placing my hands on my knees. "If my brother and Cruz weren't in the backyard, and Wren wasn't standing right here, you would be headed to the hospital. You need to let that register. I have two members here with me. You attacked their president. They wouldn't have stopped until you were on life support. You and me we have a problem. You keep trying to spend time with and even touch someone who isn't yours."

Brick glared up at me and scoffed. "She sure as fuck doesn't belong to you."

"Yet," I snapped back at him, resisting the urge to stomp his ankle hard enough to snap it. "She will be, and until then, there isn't a single man on this earth that will take that pleasure from me, and that includes giving her rides."

"Her car broke down, I was helping."

I tilted my head, knowing he shouldn't have even been at her job and was probably harassing her. "Next time, call me. I'll come get her."

"Archer." Wren let out a sigh, but I wasn't going to mince words or not say exactly what I meant to this fucker.

"Do you understand me?" I asked Brick, making sure I had his full attention.

He flicked a pensive expression at Wren. "You may be used to getting your way in your club, but I have a lawyer, and I will—"

Using my knee, I pinned his bicep down while I gripped his wrist with one hand, and with the other, I pulled out my knife and held it over his forearm.

"How about I carve my cell phone number into your arm? That way, there's no confusion about what it is I'm asking. If. Wren. Needs. Help. You. Will. Call. Me." I pressed the tip of my knife to his skin and heard Wren start toward me.

"Archer."

Brick's eyes bugged out, his mouth gaping as he registered that I was serious. "Fuck, okay. Okay. I heard you. I'll call you."

A trickle of blood followed from the line I'd started on his arm to form the number two. I released him and stood up, pocketing my knife.

"Good. Now get the fuck out of here."

My hand found Wren's hip as I moved her away from his car and took her laptop bag from her shoulder. Brick's tires squealed while he peeled out of her driveway and sped down the street. Wren's shoulders were rigid while we walked inside the house alone.

I set her bag down on her little entryway table when she spun on me, her silky brown hair flying.

"You can't reject me one second and the next—" I backed her up against her door and held her chin in my hand.

Her eyes searched my face frantically, her chest rising and falling quickly, but her hands were tangled in my t-shirt.

"I didn't reject you, Wren. You said you wanted a fairy tale, then tried to fuck me out of your life. I know you probably don't see it that way, but it's what makes me different than that asshole who just dropped you off."

Her mouth parted like she was surprised, and her dark brows dipped into the center of her forehead. However, her fingers gathered more fabric, like she was worried I'd step away.

"I may have said I wouldn't fuck you, but that sure as hell doesn't mean I'll share you with anyone. I'm doing something here..." I trailed my finger down her jaw and leaned in closer.

She wet her lips, rasping, "Doing what?"

"Right now, I'm kissing you. The rest, you'll find out soon enough." I smiled before closing the space between us. Our lips met, slow and tentative. Wren tilted her jaw and opened for me. My tongue slid over her bottom lip, and then her top, and she pulled me closer with her hands while moving her tongue against mine.

My chest felt too full, there was that clashing electricity sparking and lighting every nerve ending on fire. My hands came up to cup Wren's face. She moved with me, sliding her tongue against me while her hands moved from my shirt to around my neck.

I felt like she'd pried her fingers between my rib cage and began weaving thread around my heart, stitching in words that I never imagined would be a part of my story. It fucking terrified me as I felt the weight of hope begin to fill me so much that I released her and pinned my forehead to hers.

Thistle knocked on the glass slider door right then, and I stepped away from her.

Her lips were swollen, her face a pinkish hue, and her eyes... looked like they'd finally found something she'd been searching for.

A heavy thrum behind my chest filled me, making me move toward the door. Wren was breathing hard, and so was I.

"Archer," she said softly.

I paused at the back slider and looked back over at her.

"I need a ride to work tomorrow." Her lips spread into an easy smile, and I felt my own stretch into one that matched hers.

"Done." I slid the door open, but before stepping out, I reminded her, "Oh, and Wren?"

She was holding her arms over her chest, fighting a smile. "Yes?"

"Don't think I forgot about the other thing either...I don't plan on stopping."

Her brows hit her hairline in surprise as I slid the door closed and joined Thistle outside.

Chapter 12

Archer

I'd given Wren and Cruz a ride for three days in a row, and I was starting to enjoy the normalcy of seeing her every morning. I brought her coffee and made sure when I dropped her off that I never saw that asshole's car there.

Each and every day, when she got out of my truck, she would smile at me, but I didn't move to kiss her. I had no plans on not touching her, but I also meant what I told her when I said I was trying something. I wanted to build a relationship with her, so once we did start fucking, she knew we were doing it as a couple, not two random people who didn't owe each other anything.

Now, it was early Wednesday afternoon, and I was home early because some school function had Kane's foster mom asking if I could pick him up. I was annoyed that she hadn't invited me, nor had the school notified me, even though I'd asked to be on the list for class updates. I could only find out about anything school-related if I picked him up and he had something in his backpack with information on it. This wasn't something I had seen any fliers about. Regardless, I was happy to go pick him up, just bummed that I missed what it was and equally annoyed because I didn't see Wren there.

Ashley Muñoz

"Will you ever get married?" Kane randomly asked while we were watching television.

I had my laptop in front of me while I worked on a customer's portfolio. They wouldn't hit their goals for the year if they didn't invest their money in a few places. I began pulling up options and ideas while glancing at my younger brother.

"What made you randomly think about that?"

Kane sat on the floor, his apple and peanut butter snack in front of him while he glanced back at me. "You have this big house with enough rooms for a big family. I was curious if you were going to get married or had a girlfriend."

I withheld a smirk.

"I would like to get married someday..."

Kane tilted his head while biting into his apple. "Aren't you running out of time?"

If I had been drinking anything, I would have spit it out.

"Excuse me?"

"Aren't you thirty-five? That's old."

"It most certainly is not," I laughed, trying to clear my throat. "A lot of people don't start dating or get married until well past forty."

My brother shrugged and returned his focus to the television. I also tried returning to work, but he turned around again.

"What about Cruz's mom. Do you like her? Cruz thinks you guys like each other."

I closed my laptop and set it aside. "He does?"

Kane nodded. "He thinks she likes you because she smiles a lot now whenever he mentions you, and he said it because she's letting you drive them every day."

"She might like me, I'm not sure, buddy." I tried to withhold a small victorious smile, but I didn't have to when Kane finished his sentence.

"I told Cruz you like his mom because you're always looking over at their house, and I heard you say that one night when I slept over, you were dreaming about her."

I quirked a brow. "Dreaming about her?" I hadn't dreamt about

126

Wren yet, not in any meaningful way, maybe if she passed me on the street in my dream or something.

Kane laughed, finishing off his plate of snacks. "Yeah, you kept saying her name loudly. You had to be dreaming."

Oh shit.

I was most certainly not dreaming.

I was, however, doing something else that wasn't appropriate to discuss with my five-year-old brother. I had assumed he was asleep, and I wasn't that loud; I'd just gotten a little carried away with my fantasy of Wren on her knees and my cock sliding over her tongue while those pretty lips of hers wrapped around me.

"Well, I do have a bit of a crush on her. But I don't want her to know, so you can't say anything to Cruz, okay?"

"Okay. I promise...but..." Kane tilted his head again. "Would you marry her?"

I had no fucking clue. Shit was way too complicated at the moment to figure out or sort, but had I pictured her with a ring on her finger, one I'd picked out and bought for her? Possibly. Had one of my fantasies been me taking off her wedding dress and seeing her white lingerie that was just tiny scraps of fabric?

Yes.

"Finding the right person can take time, buddy. You can't rush these sorts of things."

My brother lost interest in me and continued to watch his show after that, all while I kept thinking about what he'd said and how Cruz was on to me.

Later that evening, I got a text from Wren, which had me sitting up in bed.

Wren: Hey...so my car is ready, so no need to pick us up tomorrow.

I didn't even try to make it seem like I was busy.

Me: Did the mechanic deliver it to you or something?

Wren: Yeah, he offered to deliver it for free. Nice, huh?

No, it wasn't nice. The fucker was flirting with her, but it was hard for me to ride that line of overbearing, jealous boyfriend when I wasn't even her boyfriend yet.

Me: Yeah, what a deal.

Wren: Anyway, thank you for the rides this week.

Me: Anytime, beautiful.

I hated that fucking car. It wasn't reliable in the slightest, and I had no doubt that this mechanic didn't actually do shit to fix it. Even if he did, it wouldn't last. Winter was coming, and I knew how unreliable that car was. The idea of her stranded out on a slick highway while cars nearly slid into her suddenly crashed through my mind, making me feel like I was about to have a heart attack.

I had to fix this.

The worry over her safety took me off guard again. A new sensation for me. The last woman I had worried over or had any concern about their safety or well-being was my mom. An ache unfurled in my chest like it always did when I thought of my mom and the way she died. Car accident cut brakes.

If my mom were alive, I'd tell her about Wren. I could almost see her smile as I explained this woman who had been firmly under my skin from the moment I met her. A familiar sadness invaded my chest as I remembered her death.

I knew it was my old man, but I couldn't prove it. But he'd done the same shit with Kane's mom. The memory of Brit meeting with me privately, telling me about how abusive my dad was and how fearful she was over Kane surfaced. She'd wanted me to take him, to keep him safe. I had promised to talk about it with her more the following day after she'd calmed down and had gotten sober.

She was high as a fuckin' kite.

Kane was only three, but whatever my dad had done had freaked her out enough to come to me and seek out help. That weekend, she was in a car accident; the brakes were cut. Kane wasn't with her, and I had a shit time finding him after that. Thankfully, Brit's cousin had been watching him, but instead of calling me, she called the police to come and pick up an abandoned baby.

My brother was in the system a few days later, mainly because my dad had gotten himself on the police department's radar enough that he'd disappeared for a while, and they couldn't locate him. I was hoping he'd stay gone.

Seemed like my luck had run out.

Bringing my phone back up, I shot a quick text to Buck, one of my club members who lived not very far from here.

> Me: Need you to meet me tonight and bring your tools.

> Buck: Got it, Prez. Send me the location, and I'll be there. Is it a usual clean-out?

My stomach clenched. This could go badly, but it would mean Wren and Cruz would be safe.

> Me: Yeah, gut it. Here's the address.

I punched out my idea, hoping this didn't bite me in the ass.

The truck was already started and warmed up for my neighbors to ride with me. I was sipping coffee, watching Wren's door as she emerged in a long wool coat that went down to her calves, covering a fucking pencil skirt with cute little boots.

Cruz's hair was combed to the side, and he wore a thick coat that his backpack straps had difficulty fitting over.

I watched as she slid into her car and tried to turn the engine over, but nothing happened.

She got out, looking confused, and circled the car as if that would somehow explain it. Then she returned to her car and lifted her hood. Did she know what to look for?

I couldn't hear her saying anything. I saw her head lift, look toward me, and let the hood slam. Cruz shut his door while the two began walking to my side of the drive.

"Morning." I smiled at them while setting my coffee on the truck's hood.

Wren had stopped walking as if something had hit her or shocked her.

With her mouth parted and eyes huge, I felt a blush working up my jaw.

"You're in a suit," she said, suspiciously as if she wasn't sure if I was playing a prank.

"I have a meeting today with a pretty high-profile client. I try to dress nicer when he comes in."

Wren walked Cruz over to me, standing there with his hand on his shoulder. Her eyes hadn't stopped roaming over my face and down my chest. "Well, could we get a ride again? I guess my car isn't working after all. I'm not sure what's happening, but my car isn't even turning over."

"Of course you can." I hid my smile by raising my cup, then handed it to her. I loved that she accepted it, placed her lips right where mine had been, and began sipping.

I helped Cruz into the truck, then walked to her door, where she asked. "What exactly do you do for a living? I never did figure that out." The second she reached for the handle along the doorframe, I gripped her hips and helped her settle.

"I'm in financial management, actually. I uh…I help people manage their money and investments."

Before she could respond, I gently shut her door and jogged around the side to get in on my side.

But her gaze was locked on me the second I climbed in.

"Finance. You said you went to trade school…"

I began reversing out of the drive. "I did. I went to welding school but stumbled across these night classes focusing on finances. The professor noticed me sitting in the back of his classroom each night and decided to ask me a few questions about stocks. Then, I decided I was in the wrong class. He took me under his wing and trained me in everything he knew. Even though I was a part of a motorcycle club, I often missed classes because of it. He never gave up on me. His dying wish was to see me make a career out of it. Gave me a ton of recommendations to the firm he was a part of. Old man changed my life."

"Wow, that's incredible, Archer. Truly incredible. I never would have guessed."

I sent her a smile. "Most people don't get this far with me to learn any of this…they just write me off as some redneck with a bike."

I caught her slight wince and the way her head dipped to her lap, and maybe she had misjudged me…but really, she hadn't. I was a fuck up. She'd been right to protect herself and Cruz, and it was only a matter of time before she realized I would be more than a hookup.

We reached Cruz's school, and I couldn't help but look around for Kane. I knew he rode the bus from his foster parent's house, but my heart did a little lurch when I showed up without him. I hated that he wasn't living with me full-time and that this custody shit was still being drug out. Thistle called his contact, and I was waiting for the hearing date. My lawyer told me everything on my end looked good, and there was nothing else I needed to do.

"Hey, Cruz?" I said, hopping out of the truck with him and walking him up to the crossing guard. The rest of the drop-off lane hated when I did this, and I understood it...but they could all fuck off. I didn't care. Life was too damn short not to do what you wanted to do.

"Can you tell Kane I said I miss him and hope he has a good day?"

Cruz beamed up at me. "Yeah, I'll tell him."

"Thanks, Bud."

I patted his back, but he twisted and gave me a hug. My arms came around his little back, and I squeezed him to my chest, telling him to have a good day before he ran off with the crossing guard. I made the mistake of turning around and seeing Wren's expression through the windshield.

She watched intensely as if some puzzle piece had finally clicked into place.

I slid back into the truck, noticing that, today, no one honked.

"You okay?"

We started driving, but Wren was staring intently out the window. Her brows were dipped, and her lip was pulled under her white teeth.

"Wren?" I glanced at her, driving past the first street light beyond the school. We only had about three more until I took the turn for her job.

"Can we..." She dipped her head. "Can you pull over up here?" She turned her face, her tone urgent.

I did as she asked, pulling over into a vacant parking lot. The truck faced an empty storefront that had recently been relocated.

"Is everything okay?"

Wren wet her lips, then ducked her face. "Seeing you with him... it's..." She stared down at her lap like she was nervous. "Seeing you be so good to him does something to me. It makes me want to..."

"To?" I asked, spreading my knees apart, hoping this would lead to kissing again.

"Touch you." Her amber eyes were on me in a flash, and then she darted away. Her lips were so full and perfect. This same woman had just said the most filthy things to me with her entire chest ready to get fucked. Now she seemed timid, almost shy.

I unbuckled my seat belt, hovering over the middle console with my hands shoved in her hair, gently pulling her face to mine.

I thought up all the ways I had been fantasizing about her. How I'd wanted to lay her flat and taste every inch of her. How I had pictured exact moments like this, where we were just randomly making out in a parking lot, casually on the way to work.

My cock swelled in my slacks, which had me releasing a low groan. It must have encouraged her because Wren was suddenly shoving her coat off.

"I had something else in mind, but I'm not about to have you pump the brakes, so you need to tell me if you'll be okay with more?"

I sat back and patted my leg. "I pumped the brakes because I want you to take me seriously, but I'm at the point where I need you to touch me, Wren. I'll beg if you want."

She smiled slightly before crawling over the console and into my lap.

With her pencil skirt, she couldn't straddle me, so I just held her in my lap, tilted her chin, and continued kissing her. Her arms were tethered at my neck, and her ass was over my erection, which I knew she felt. Especially when she started rocking her hips, making her ass move back and forth.

I let out a hiss, which broke our kiss. "Thought you were going to touch me. You ready to show me, beautiful?"

"Push the seat all the way back and raise the steering wheel as high as it will go," she whispered against my mouth.

I did as she requested, providing a little more space near my legs.

Wren gave me a devilish smirk before slipping off my lap and sliding down onto the floor, where she fit between my knees. Her hands came to my thighs, and I stared down at her, unsure of what she was about to do because, surely, I was hoping for too much.

Her fingers gently tugged on my zipper, releasing the fabric button that held them up. Her red fingernails dug under the band of my boxers, and she was gripping my length, her mouth parting as she pulled it completely free.

"So thick," she whispered, staring up at me. It made me think of the other night when we'd stopped, but her filthy mouth had me nearly coming in my jeans.

"Shit," I rasped, watching as she held the base and merely stared at it in wonder. Ever so slowly, she leaned forward and licked over the tip of my erection, swirling her tongue around the precum that coated it.

"Mmmmm," she moaned, which made my balls tighten and my hand go to her hair.

"You seriously about to suck my cock right now, beautiful?"

Her gaze slid up, and with a smile, she wrapped her red lips entirely around me and slid down my length. Silky, caramel hair was a curtain around her face while she bobbed up and down on my cock. I inhaled a sharp breath, relishing how good she looked on her knees, barely fitting under my steering wheel but making it work just the same.

"That's it, Wren. You're so fucking perfect." I hissed, closing my eyes and keeping my hand on her head. Fuck this felt good.

She hollowed her cheeks, which had her going even lower, then let up, repeating the process.

"I need you to take me deeper. I want to hit the back of that throat, Wren."

She rose on her knees, and with the base of my cock in her fist, she started going deeper, but I tugged her chin, which had her letting me go. With her mouth open, her red lipstick, and a ring around the base of my dick, I smiled at her.

"I think you want me to fuck your throat the way I want to. Tap my thigh if it's too much, okay."

She smiled and nodded before readjusting herself over my slick length.

I gripped her hair and forced her down even farther. She started gagging, and I nearly came on the spot. Once she tapped my thigh once,

I let her go, and she came up for air, then immediately went back down, not caring that saliva was dripping from her chin or trailing from my cock.

She took me again, and I lifted my hips. "Shittttt."

My hold on her hair was rough as I rocked forward and began fucking her throat. She'd gag, then moan and keep me there, repeating the process until I couldn't hold on any longer.

With a deep rasp, I warned, "I'm about to come down your throat, Wren..." I was breathing harshly as I held her there. "Tap my thigh if you want me to let you go." She took me deeper, and I let out an agonized groan, pushing my cock to the back of her throat and coming so hard I nearly blacked out. I heard her gagging and moaning all at once while I filled her up.

We were making a mess, but fuck if I cared now.

My suit might even be ruined, but I'd rather go home and change before letting this girl go.

Once I'd finished, I opened my eyes and looked down. Wren was slowly releasing me, while dabbing at the corners of her mouth. She'd missed her chin and somehow even her nose. I realized I really liked seeing my seed covering her face.

"That was..." she breathed, still trying to swipe at the missed spots, "an experience...I've never uh." She flushed, and my heart nearly stilled.

"You've never swallowed?" Because I knew she'd fucking sucked cock before, she was too good not to have, but I couldn't deal with the idea of her mouth on another man at the moment.

She shook her head. "No one has ever made me feel that...excited, where all I wanted to do was—"

"Filthy, depraved things?"

Another flush worked its way into her face. "Yeah, something like that."

"I'm sure it's just the suit," I joked, but her face fell.

"It's not...it's just you."

Wren laughed and then rested her face on my thigh. I gently

stroked her hair, not hating how it felt to have her like this. She was just staring up at me like I had found a way to whisper those fairy tales against her skin.

"Also, I don't think I can get up; my left kneecap has been numb for about two minutes."

Smiling down at her, I brushed her hair to the side and laughed. "If you're gonna be stuck anywhere, darling, you may as well be..."

She pinched my calf, which had me reaching for her and helping pull her up.

Once she was up near my face, I pulled her chin and kissed her again. She moved with my kiss and fell into my lap again, sighing into my mouth.

"Thank you," I whispered, pressing my forehead to hers.

She spread her fingers over my chest and under the buttons of my shirt. "What are we doing, Archer?"

"We're taking our time. You're safe with me, Wren. Trust me." I closed my eyes and pressed a kiss to her mouth. She let out a shuddery breath as she kissed me back. Her fingers dug into my hair, lightly tugging before she released me.

"Crawl over or open the door?"

She eyed her seat and then my lap, realizing my semi-hard erection was still out.

"Uh, I'll crawl so you can zip up."

She carefully lifted her knee and pressed it into the center console, which put her ass in my face. I had to look away while gritting my teeth because I really wanted to touch her, but I also really needed to make it to my appointment.

Once she was over, I pulled my boxers back up and then my slacks, ensuring nothing showed from how much of a mess we'd made. Then once she was buckled, we started back toward her job.

When I pulled in front of the model home where she worked each day, I saw a familiar-looking car parked there.

"Is that Brick's car?" I already knew it was, but I needed a second to calm down. The idea of him being around her right after she'd just had my cock in her mouth was making something dangerous begin to claw its way out of my chest. I'd never felt this way before. The mere idea of him looking at her had me feeling murderous.

Wren's gaze slid over a spot to where I was looking.

"Yeah, he's probably here with a client." She let out a longsuffering sigh, then opened her door. "Thank you for the—"

I killed the engine and pocketed my keys. "I'll walk you in."

Her mouth pursed as she watched me, but I didn't care. I opened her door and held out my hand for her to hold.

"Looks icy."

It didn't.

I could hear her small laugh, but she wrapped her hand around mine and interlocked our fingers as we walked into her job. Laminate flooring ran under our feet with a nice-looking runner that worked to catch dirt and other things from people coming in. There was a sleek L-shaped desk that had an apple monitor on it. There were photos along the wall of all the various floor plans for different houses.

"This is pretty cool," I said, moving around to the drawers' custom carpet and fixture pieces.

I slid one out when Brick walked in.

"Wren. Finally."

I didn't appreciate his abrupt tone.

He froze when he saw me standing there, glaring at him. "What is he doing here?"

Wren started unpacking her laptop bag, mostly ignoring him.

"Archer gave me a ride today."

I snapped my gaze to hers, wanting her to say more. That we were a couple or something that made me seem like more than just her neighbor, but why would she offer more than what I had given her?

Brick moved past me. "Thought your car was fixed?"

Were they texting each other still?

Why would it bother me so much if they were? Fuck, I hated this.

"I thought so, too. I'll find out later." Wren left her spot behind the desk and walked over to where I was standing.

"Well, she's at work now. You can leave," Brick said smugly while glancing at me. I thought I had taught him his lesson without even hitting him. But apparently not.

Letting out a laugh, I ducked my face. "You won't be the one who tells me to leave, Dick. Trust me on that. I'm here as long as Wren wants me."

Wren turned toward Brick and crossed her arms. "Brick, what are you doing here?"

He bristled slightly like he wasn't prepared for her to question him. "I have a client question."

"Is it something Brianna can help with?"

He twisted his lips, almost in a sneer. "Why can't you help me?"

Wren glanced at me. "Because I'm helping Mr. Green with something related to his home. Also, I emailed Denise asking you to be assigned to Briana from now on if you have any future clients. I know Bri would love to assist you when she's back. Perhaps you could email her and make a plan."

She had already requested he deal with someone else? Shit, that made me feel good.

Brick glared at Wren, which I didn't love. I was going to be late for my own meeting, and this was one I really couldn't fuck up with all the custody shit going on, but there was no way I was leaving her here with him.

"I'll take off so you can work, Wren...but I'll see you right after work when my mechanic arrives. I already texted him to meet us after we get the boys."

Wren's lips thinned out, almost as if she wanted to say something else, when she glanced at Brick. "Okay, yeah."

I closed the distance between us, stood directly in front of her, and pulled her chin.

"Thanks for this morning," then I kissed her.

I smiled against her mouth when she kissed me back, and we remained locked like that, kissing and breathing one another in while her shitty ex watched on. Once we broke apart, Wren was breathing hard.

I gave her one last smile before I turned toward Brick.

"After you."

He glanced back at Wren angrily. He looked like he was about to throw a punch at me.

"I'm not leav—"

I stepped closer, clicking my tongue. "You're not staying here with her. So, either leave, or I will have you taken out on a stretcher. Your fuckin' choice."

"Fuck you!" Brick pushed past me, shoving his shoulder into my sternum.

I let him go, giving Wren one last look. She wagged her fingers at me, giving me a little smirk, and mockingly said, "Have a nice day, honey."

I replied in the same sugar-sweet tone, "You too, *darling.*"

Chapter 13

Wren

MY NERVES WERE RAW.

This could be because of the fifth cup of coffee I had downed or the fact that I had actually instigated a blow job this morning with my next-door neighbor. All while folding myself in half like a twenty-something-year-old to fit between his legs. My knee still had not recovered from choosing that position.

But also, I had never in my life been the person to offer to suck someone's cock, and I certainly wasn't the person who became obsessed and swallowed all that jizz down after. I had always provided a few sucks, some licking, then we'd move on to the main course of the evening. I'd never experienced getting so enraptured by making someone feel so good that they couldn't hold back or lose all sense that they came within mere minutes right down my throat. There was something sort of special that it had happened with Archer. I was glad it was with him, but it still had me jumpy all day.

Now, as I grabbed a ride home with Cruz, Kane, and Archer, I felt torn in half. Something was actively burning in my chest, like a fire had been lit, and part of me knew I needed to put it out, but some rebellious part of me wanted to keep feeding it.

"My mechanic will be here in about twenty minutes if you need to change or do anything before you tell him what's happening." Archer put the truck in park, and the boys started pulling up their backpacks and filing out of the back passenger door.

Archer gave me a warm smile before he exited as well. He looked tired, like he'd had a hard day with his suit jacket off, his sleeves rolled to his elbows and the top two buttons unclasped. He looked like he was slowly shedding this fake persona that he'd had to hide inside all day and was itching to get back into his denim and leather.

I should have let him go change so he could finally be at ease...but before I slid entirely out of the truck, I asked, "How was your day?"

Archer paused and twisted at the hips with an odd expression. "What?"

God, this was embarrassing. "Your day...did you. I mean, how was your important meeting?"

His brows arched as he held his door open. "Oh...it, uh it went fine. Thanks."

"Oh. Okay, well, good." I slid out of the truck, feeling stupid for forcing him to hang back. Cruz ran over, and we headed to the house to change and get a snack.

Once in my room, I tossed my hair up in a bun, stripped out of my pencil skirt and top, and quickly showered. I donned familiar clothes that made me feel more at home in my own skin: a pair of yoga pants and an oversized T-shirt. Cruz was munching on Pirates Booty and wiping his hands on his jeans, unaware I was watching him.

I smirked, feeling too exhausted to even reprimand him. Instead, I headed toward the fridge, hoping for something to help my nerves. I had crossed a line with Archer today, and I had no idea how to get things back where they were, where I felt like I had some semblance of control over things.

The memory of how he held my face, licked along my bottom lip, and moved his mouth over mine like I belonged to him came rushing back, making my face heat. That was the best kiss I'd ever had in my entire life. I'd never really had a romantic relationship with anyone other than Matt. Still, even then, things started so hot and heavy that we'd slid into romance after we'd already hooked up.

Cruz's cute little lilt of laughter disrupted my thoughts and brought me back to my open refrigerator. There was nothing but sparkling water and milk to settle my nerves, so I sipped on a lime-flavored water while I stared off into space, deliberating how badly I had messed things up with my neighbor. A few minutes later, a soft knock on the front door had Cruz's head snapping over, and, in his excitement, he jumped up to answer it.

"Is it Archer?"

The hope in his voice caused a small piece of my chest to shatter and fuse back together at a speed that wasn't good for my heart.

"Uh, let me see." I walked over and opened the door. Archer wore ripped jeans and a long black shirt styled under his leather cut. His wild hair was tamed at the nape of his neck, exposing his freshly-shaven jaw and blue eyes.

Beside him was a man wearing the same cut, roughly younger and shorter. He wore a brown T-shirt under his baggy jeans, and his hair was a mop of brown, tight curls. Next to him stood an excited-looking Kane whose hands were full of little Hot Wheel cars.

"Hey, Wren. This is Buck, he's a member of Mayhem Riot and a damn good mechanic."

Buck waved, and I waved back, stepping down the porch steps. Kane ran past me into the house, and Cruz waved him toward his room.

"Thanks so much for coming over and helping out."

Buck moved near my car while Archer stepped next to me; he was so close that our shoulders touched.

"Can you pop the hood for us, Wren?"

I did as he asked, sliding into the front seat of my car and popping the button that released my hood. Archer felt around for the hook, then shoved the slab of metal up, securing it in place.

Both men were suddenly behind the lifted hood, discussing something I couldn't hear. When I finally joined them, their conversation seemed to stall.

"So, any idea what the problem is?"

Buck shifted on his leg, glancing at the engine like he wasn't sure where to start.

"Well...you've got uh..." He glanced at Archer, then me. "A battery issue."

Archer snapped his head over quickly as if he was reprimanding Buck with a look. While I couldn't see his face, I felt the mood shift.

Buck hesitated. "I mean a radiator problem that can't be fixed. I hate to say this, but the car is done for."

My eyes slowly trailed to my neighbor, whose strong jaw worked back and forth while his eyes sparkled. "Bummer, beautiful. Looks like you'll need a new car."

"But I...there's no way it's just done for. You barely looked at it. Can you explain in a little more detail what's going on? I have this serviced regularly, and it just got it back from the mechanic."

Buck started moving various wires around, which all came apart as if they'd been cut. I gasped as he started going through the list of things that were wrong. "You've got your intake hose here. It's ruined. These connectors for the battery..." He held up two wires I knew had been intact last week when I checked but were now severed. "They're done for, but the worst thing is the radiator. No clue how, but there's a hole in it."

"A hole?!"

Buck nodded with a wince. "Sorry, but there's too much damage done to justify the repairs."

Archer turned his face, but I saw his shoulder slightly shaking like he was laughing.

Was this some kind of joke between the two of them?

But it couldn't be a prank because the hoses were really cut, and when I tried to start it this morning, it wouldn't even turn over.

My gut sank.

"Oh."

What was I going to do?

I needed a car to get to work. I needed a vehicle for Cruz. I was a single mom; it wasn't like I had another person with a car I could rely on to take him to school or pick him up in the middle of the day if he had an accident at school. My savings were for that trip I wanted to take with Cruz. There was only four thousand dollars in it, which I was insanely proud of, but it had taken me so long to save that. I had my medical bill coming in for my damn ankle. Cruz had strep throat two weeks before that, so that bill was still sitting on my desk, needing to be paid. I'd just bought him school clothes and new shoes, which set me back. My credit had improved, maybe I could get a loan and add the extra payment to my monthly budget.

The idea of how tight that would make things felt like someone had started squeezing a fist around my lungs. I was going to cry right here in front of these two men.

"Uh, could you excuse me? Buck, would you mind telling Archer what I owe you, and I'll get you cash? I just have to run inside real quick."

Archer said something, but I didn't hear him as I ran inside.

Heat crawled up my neck, and my throat felt tight. Tears lined my eyes as I swiftly passed Kane and Cruz, playing in the living room, and closed myself into my room. Memories of how things once were for me and how low my lows had gotten came back in a rush. I had to breathe through my nose and walk around my room to remind myself I wasn't still there. I had a home. Cruz was safe.

I wouldn't be homeless again.

I wouldn't go hungry again.

I wouldn't have to consider selling my body just to eat. I was in a good home and a good job. This was just a bump in the road.

Tears were streaming down when I heard a gentle knock on my door.

"Give me a minute," I called out, swiping at my face.

What was I going to do?

My door cracked, and Archer's face was suddenly there as his gaze swept me from head to toe. He didn't wait for me to tell him if he could enter; he just walked in and shut the door behind him.

I couldn't compose myself, so a whimper escaped my lips, and Archer crossed the space between us in three long strides. His hands cradled my face, tipping my head back. His lips pressed gently against the tears staining my face in the most tender moment I'd ever shared with anyone.

Once he'd kissed away every tear, he pulled me into his chest.

"I fucked up, Wren. I'm so sorry."

My throat still felt tight, so I let him continue talking while I clung to the leather at his back.

"I wanted to do something nice for you and Cruz. I thought I was —" He trailed off, his own voice catching with emotion. "I am so sorry. I went about this the wrong way."

Pulling back from him, I swiped at my face. "What do you mean?"

His blue eyes were dark, remorse had transformed his features into something soft and unsure. "I didn't like how fast that mechanic worked, and I did some research on the year, make and model and realized you were going to need a new car within the next year if not sooner...and I just—"

"What, sabotaged it?" My voice rose as shock splintered my chest. Who the fuck would do such a thing?

His face shuttered as his hands dropped to my waist, trying to pull me back.

"Yes, I did, but only because I have a car ready for you. It's one the club owned and was fixing up to sell."

I pulled away from him and brought my hands up to rub at my forehead, confused and frustrated.

"What do you mean, you have one ready?"

He looked helpless as he watched another trail down my face. "I figured if I impaired your car, made it seem like it was beyond hope, and then swooped in with your new car, you'd be okay. I didn't want you to feel overwhelmed by it. When you ran into the house, I was about to offer you the new car."

"Archer..." How did he think this sort of thing would be okay with me? I was so confused by his actions. "I can't afford to buy a new car from you. That's why I'm stressing out...I just need a little time to wrap my head around what you did, it's—"

He was back in my space, cradling my jaw and tipping my face up to his. "It's not being sold to you; it's being given to you."

Shaking my head, I tried to push at his chest, but he only held me firm.

"Please, Wren. Let me give this to you. It's in excellent shape, and it's going to be better in the snow for you and Cruz. I need—"

"I need to understand what made you think this was acceptable? It's crazy, Archer. I can't...this is too much."

"Taking care of you and Cruz, that's too much?" His voice pitched, and it made my heart feel frantic. It was like we were about to touch something precious, and it might break, but if it didn't, then it would be the most wonderful thing we'd ever experienced.

"It's the way you went about it, Archer."

He moved so he was closer to me again, and how his eyes flashed with concern made my stomach flip. "You have to remember who I am, Wren. I'm not one of those guys who will call a tow truck if you need it. I'd call my club my family. We operate outside of the normal laws of normal society. You of all people—"

His mouth suddenly snapped shut, and I wasn't sure what that meant, but I was too frustrated to focus on it.

"That may be how you're used to doing things, but you're trying to get custody of Kane. You have to start thinking like someone who would call a tow truck. Someone who doesn't press the tip of a knife into someone's arm simply because they keep flirting with someone who—"

"Someone who what?" He was in front of me again, his hands fastened at my hips.

My palms went to his chest as his familiar scent wrapped around me. "Someone who might mean something to you."

His forehead pressed into mine. "Might?"

"Archer." I started to pull away, but his lips caught mine in a firm kiss before pulling away once more.

"I'm sorry. You're right. I do need to start realizing I'm living here not as a motorcycle club president but as a citizen. I don't want to handle things like I'm used to and scare you off. Will you forgive me while still allowing me to protect you?"

Sunshine found a way to wind through my chest, warming my heart unfamiliarly. To have someone care for us, to need to protect us... that had never happened to us. It had been just Cruz and me against the world from the start...what would it be like to accept something like this from a man like Archer?

My gut screamed at me not to get attached to him or let him inside the safe space of my heart because if he walked out, I'd never be okay.

"Say something, please," Archer whispered against my forehead, then pressed a kiss there.

"I—" my hesitation circled my head as effectively as a drain, there and gone again. Reality hit, leaving me confused, standing there practically in his arms. I didn't hate that he wanted to take care of us. "I, well, I want to pay you something for it. Please."

I felt his smile against my skin.

"Do you want to see it first?"

I shook my head. "No. I trust you, but in the bill of sale, charge me something, please. I can afford a little bit, just not a ton."

I felt him laugh, and then I raised my hand to stroke his chest, near his throat, so I could memorize it.

"Okay, I'll charge you something, but you can't argue with what I put on the paper."

I smiled, letting him wrap me in another hug. "Fine."

Chapter 14

Archer

WREN STARED AT THE CAR WITH A STRAIGHT FACE, BUT A SMILE kept curling her pink lips. She was inspecting her new car, which I had sold for just a dollar. I'd had Buck tow away her old one once she got anything of value out of it, then drove in and parked the new one in her driveaway.

"It's so much bigger than my old one." She half crawled into the back seat. I noticed her hand lightly graze the screens built into the headrests.

Shrugging, I lightly kicked at the front tire. "Just means it'll be better for the winter and when you need to haul more stuff."

Her amber eyes skated over, pinning me in place with a look that said I was full of shit.

"Means it'll be more gas money."

I rallied, lifting my hand. "But this one is a hybrid, so it's more gas-efficient and better for the environment."

"Says the guy driving a diesel."

I smirked, tugging one of her curls. "It's biodiesel."

With a slight shake of her head, she finally let out a sigh, turning toward me.

"This is incredible, and I'm still struggling to accept that you're offering it to me."

"I sold it to you." My smirk was lopsided because she was so damn cute with her hands on her hips and her chin held high. I knew she was about to argue with me, so I aimed at her weak spot instead.

"What does Cruz think?"

Her determined expression transitioned into a soft, dreamy look. "He loves it. He's never ridden in anything this nice."

"Then let's stop arguing about it. You deserve to have something stable and good in your life, Wren. Even if I leave tomorrow, you deserve that."

Her face swung over like she was worried I would, in fact, leave tomorrow.

"I'm not, but I'm just saying."

She took a step closer to me and bumped my shoulder. "Can I make you dinner as a way of saying thank you?"

I smiled. "I'd love some dinner. I have Kane with me after school, so it'll be two of us."

"Cruz will love that. See you at five?"

My stomach dipped. It was just dinner, but the idea of sitting at a table with her, Cruz, and Kane did something to me. "We'll be there."

"Why do you have flowers?" Kane asked as we walked over to Wren's house. The sun was setting, and the sky was blue with swirls of orange and pink, creating a beautiful sunset. The red roses were mixed with baby's breath, wrapped in burlap, and in my hands, they felt as significant as walking over with an engagement ring.

"Because Wren is making us dinner, bringing the host flowers is a nice gesture."

Kane wrinkled his nose. "Sarah took a loaf of bread to someone's house when our fancy neighbors invited us over."

Sarah was his foster mom, and she was nice enough, but I hated when Kane used the term 'our' or 'my' when talking about her or Ron, his foster dad.

"Bread is a good idea, too. In fact, Wren might have liked that better." I passed by her black SUV and smiled. The windows were all tinted, and the wheels were black-walled. My mind drifted to how safe it would be and how, if she were my woman, the only other thing she'd need was a piece of leather for her back. Then, I thought of taking her on the back of my bike...in more ways than one.

Kane bumped into my leg. "Are you going to knock?"

I blinked, shaking away those thoughts, and knocked my knuckles against her door.

Cruz yelled something on the other side before Wren pulled on the knob, revealing both of them and a warm, inviting house.

Kane pushed past me and ran inside with Cruz. The two took off toward his room before we could encourage them to wash up. Wren sidestepped the two, which gave me a second to look at her without her noticing. Her hair was loosely braided down her back, but pieces had fallen free, kissing her cheek and framing her bright eyes. She wore a pair of tight jeans and a soft shirt that had a deep V cut, allowing just the smallest peek at her cleavage. Fuck, the way I wanted to trace my tongue along that cut and see what her tits looked like underneath it.

"Hi." She smiled, and it made my head feel fuzzy.

My eyes dropped to her mouth, and all I could think of was when we'd kissed in the truck. I had something else in mind...

"Archer?" Wren's brows dipped into the center of her forehead. "Are these for me?"

My hand shot out with the flowers. "Yes."

"They're beautiful, thank you." She brought the flowers to her nose, where she inhaled and closed her eyes. That fuzzy feeling returned as I stepped inside and closed the door. There was a strange sense of fulfillment as I slipped out of my shoes and followed her into the kitchen.

"Smells good in here." My stomach growled as I smelled the different spices permeating the air; it was sweet with an undercurrent of savory that made my mouth water. Wren gently set the roses down and began searching through her cupboards.

"I'm glad you think so. I decided to treat you guys to my famous root beer tacos." She pulled a large glass vase out and began filling it with water.

I settled next to her, carefully peeling back the burlap that held the flowers together. "Root beer?"

Wren gave me a smile that eclipsed her entire face, making my stomach flip. "Yes, root beer. I soak the meat in it and then slow-cook it. It makes for such a delicious kick, especially when we add the salsa. I mix in mango, purple onion, cilantro, and a few other things that create a really delicious combination. I also have chicken in case you guys don't like it."

Her face flushed pink, making me want to pull her in for a kiss.

"We'll like it."

She laughed, and it made me smile. "Don't be so sure. I can throw together something else, too, if you want."

"If you made it, we'd be honored to eat it, Wren." Since the boys were in Cruz's bedroom, I stepped behind her and placed my lips at her ear. "In fact, I can't wait to taste them. They're making my mouth water." I traced my tongue over the shell of her ear, which caused a trail of goosebumps to erupt down the side of her neck and along her arms.

She sighed deeply as her hands sorted the flowers into a vase. Her mouth parted just as the boys ran in, and I stepped away from her.

Wren's voice cracked as her fingers gripped the counter. "Boys, ready to eat?"

"Yeah, I'm hungry as an elephant." Kane laughed, and then Cruz slid into the chair next to him. "I'm so hungry, I could eat an elephant."

The two laughed while Wren shook her head, smiling while serving our plates. Smaller tortillas were pulled from a circular container, steam rising as Wren used tongs to pull out a pile. She prepped each plate with double-layered tortillas, then lifted the lid off the meat. My stomach groaned again, as I had never smelled anything so good.

"Here, let me help." I took Kane's plate, dished his meat, and added the mango blend.

"You can add lime. I like adding it," Cruz said excitedly, reaching for a half-cut lime from one of the bowls. He used both hands and squeezed a generous portion onto his tacos, which caused Kane to do the same. I caught Wren's gaze as she laughed, and a smile stretched along her beautiful face.

My chest ached. That fuzzy feeling was replaced with the one where I felt like a pellet gun had shot me. Like my chest burned and ached and needed to be soothed.

"This is so good," Kane murmured while he took a generous bite.

Cruz nodded while sipping his milk. "Mom made my favorite, I told her you'd like it, Kane."

Wren blushed, then gave Kane a soft smile. "I'm glad you like it." She'd also texted and asked me if he had any food allergies, which was incredibly considerate. But she didn't ask about me, which I gave her a hard time about. She replied with, "You're a big boy."

To which I replied, "Want a reminder of just how big?"

"So, boys, how is school going?" Wren asked before taking a modest bite. She'd also prepared pinto beans, homemade chips, and guacamole. Everything tasted so good that I was practically inhaling my food.

Kane shifted in his seat while chewing, so Cruz answered, "Good, we're learning the word for food in Spanish and English right now."

Wren lit up. "Oh yeah?"

Kane nodded, jumping in, "Leche means milk, and strawberry is fr..." He swung his gaze over to Cruz, who tilted his head as if trying to remember.

"Fruz or fez..."

Wren replied, with a smile, "Fresa?"

"That's it!" Kane said excitedly. "We learned that cow is, vaca."

"Wow, you guys are learning a lot." Wren beamed while dabbing at her lips. She glanced at me as if silently telling me to keep the conversation going.

"How did you learn to cook like this?" I managed to ask around another massive bite of food. I was being rude, but fuck if I cared. This was the best meal I'd ever had.

Wren flushed, but her smile was infectious.

"My parents actually own a restaurant in North Carolina. My stepdad would let me sit on the counter when preparing meals, but even before my mom married him, she would have me next to her when she'd cook. It—" Emotion suddenly swept over her features, transforming them from happy and proud to sad as if this was a painful subject for her.

Her throat cleared, but her eyes smarted as if she was about to cry.

Shit. What had I done? I quickly recovered by changing the subject so she didn't feel obligated to continue to talk about her family.

Unfortunately, my new topic had Wren leaving the table ten minutes later.

"You guys are so gross." She shook her head, taking her plate with her.

I tipped my head back, still laughing. "They're just noises."

Kane blew a raspberry into his arm as if on cue, then laughed. "Fart noises!"

The boys giggled, and to apologize for my part in the fart conversation, we agreed to clean up dinner while Wren went and took a bubble bath. She argued, saying she was hosting, but we insisted on making more noises, which had her leaving. I watched as her ass swayed, and then she was tugging the elastic from her braid and digging her hands into her hair, letting it cascade down her back in waves.

My mouth went dry, and I had to resist the urge to follow her.

Thirty minutes later, the boys were sitting on the living room floor playing cars while I continued to check my phone to see if Wren had texted for me to come join her. Not that I would have, or even could have, but my stupid brain couldn't quite get the message to my dick.

Finally, Wren exited the hallway wearing sleep shorts and a baggy T-shirt, but her damp hair hung against her shoulders as she brushed it out.

"What are you guys up to?"

I froze.

Cruz smiled up at her. "Just playing."

My younger brother made engine noises while he made his car fly through the air. That fuzzy feeling was back in full force, twisting into something that warmed my chest. I hadn't felt this way since middle school and had the world's largest crush on that brown-eyed girl who rode my bus. She never seemed to notice me, not even when I had given her a piece of gum, until one day. One glorious day, she sat next to me, and I thought I might die of happiness.

That's how this felt, seeing Wren freshly bathed, her hair wet, in her living room, curling up on the couch next to me while the boys played.

Wren suddenly appeared beside me, leaning close so no one could hear her. "What time do you have to get Kane back?"

Shaking away the strange feeling, I let my lips graze her ear as I replied. "I get him for the night. He'll have to go back tomorrow mid-morning."

I saw the wheels turning in her head and had already considered it, so I gave her a slight nod.

"Kane, would you like to do a sleepover with Cruz tonight?"

His little head whipped up as Cruz let out a gasp. "Can he?"

"Can I?"

They both asked simultaneously. She nodded graciously.

"If it's okay with Archer."

I nodded, then laughed when Kane asked, "Can Archer stay, too?"

Wren's face flushed pink. "No, he'll have to go home soon, but you can stay."

The boys returned to their game of cars until it was time for me to go get Kane's sleep clothes from the house. When I returned, Wren had transformed the living room into a huge fort with stools, cushions, and blankets.

Once we both said goodnight to the boys and turned on their little string of lights that Wren had hung inside the blankets, Wren walked me to the door and stepped outside while she pulled the door shut.

"So, this was nice." Her arms crossed over her chest.

I matched her stance, stepping down from her steps. "It was."

The silence stretched while the stars winked above us, reminding me of what she said about what she wanted someday. To have someone obsessed with you so they say things that feel like midnight against your skin. Like all the stars exist just for you, and they were the one to put them there.

"You headed to bed after this?" Her hair was still wet, and it was cold outside.

"I was actually thinking about how when I put up the fence, I couldn't help but notice that private, patio door you had that led to your bedroom."

Her eyes widened as a smile spread across her lips.

"You happened to notice that, did you?"

I stepped on the lower porch step, which aligned our chests.

"Maybe you could invite me in, using that door, of course...and I could braid your hair for you."

In the darkness, I couldn't make out every line of her face or how her throat bobbed, but I heard it.

"You want to braid my hair?"

My hands went up to her wet locks. "Meet me at your patio door, and watch a movie with me while I braid your hair."

I thought she'd fight me, but she pulled back and turned away, giving me one last smile while saying, "I assume you know the way to my door?"

It was like muscle memory, even in the dark, as I made my way along her house and opened her side gate, securing it behind me. Then, in the cover of darkness, I sauntered along the perimeter of her home until I was in her backyard, facing her closed patio door.

Seconds later, the lock was unlatched. Wren's eyes twinkled while she pulled the door open. "Hi."

I decided to surprise her by placing my hands under her breasts, picking her up while I pushed inside.

She let out a little yelp while her arms came around my neck, and my boot kicked her door shut.

"Shhhh." I laughed as we landed on the bed, her on her back and me hovering over her.

She pulled me close and wrapped her legs around my back like a koala bear.

"Don't play games, Wren. I'll win."

Her lips were at my ear as she giggled. "You promise?"

Leaning down, I pressed my mouth to hers and gave her a slow kiss while her hands came up around my neck. She released me a few moments later, trying to catch her breath.

"So, you really know how to braid?"

Wren sat up and pulled her hair in front of her so it rested against her shoulders.

I kicked off my boots and crawled onto her bed until my back was up against her headboard. I'd been in her room that one time, but I didn't really get a chance to take any of it in. She had a queen-sized bed, bringing us closer together as we huddled against the headboard. Her feather duvet was white with purple flowers, and she had a tan, woven throw blanket draped across the edge of her wooden sleigh frame.

A lamp illuminated the room from one of the matching bedside tables. In the corner of her room was an oversized chair with another little table right next to it. I pictured Wren sitting there, watching Cruz play in the backyard while she read a book with a peaceful smile on her face.

"I do."

"Okay, fine, but fair warning, I might cry." She handed me a comb and hair elastic and pointed her remote at the modest flat screen that rested on her long dresser across the room. She chose an older TV show and let it play on a low volume. My eyes flicked to the tall standing mirror near her closet, which had several pictures, including only one postcard tucked into it. I wanted to ask about them but didn't want to miss this story.

"Why are you going to cry?" I spread my legs and waited for her to crawl between them.

Once her ass was nestled against my cock, I set my jaw and focused on her hair. It was silky and smooth as I gently combed through it, separating it piece by piece.

Wren let out a sigh as she tipped her head back. "Because when I was little, my brother used to braid my hair. My mom always made him, and it felt like the only time we'd go without arguing, laughing, or doing anything. We'd both just be quiet and still like I was this piece of art he was too scared to mess up on. I remember feeling so safe when he'd start my braid like he'd never hurt me, but only in that setting. It was like touching a base in a game of tag."

My mind went back to what I'd found in the box. Discovering exactly who she was connected to and how I still hadn't told her that I knew. The truth was, I wasn't sure I ever would. At least not until I figured out if her brother was even in her life anymore, which it seemed like he wasn't. "How far apart in age are you and your brother?" I gathered her middle part and separated it into three parts while she closed her eyes.

"Five years."

"That's not much...you must have grown up really close. How long has it been since you've seen him?"

I saw Wren's throat bob and her lashes flutter while I slowly braided down the length of her scalp. "Uh..." She swallowed, and her voice cracked. "It's been a long time."

The silence stretched as I gathered strand after strand, ensuring the braid would hold. A tiny ache in my chest started at how her voice cracked and how painful this subject seemed for her. All I wanted to do was find her brother and punch him in the face for making Wren feel like this. I wasn't sure what happened, but I knew Wren. She was fierce, loyal, and protective. If she had a reason for being away from her family, then I knew it had to be a good one. But she didn't need to talk about it now, not when her voice sounded so small and frail. Instead, I changed the subject.

"I lied about that one meeting going well."

Her eyes flashed open, staring up at me from where her head was tilted back. She only saw a glimpse of my face, but she still tried regardless. "What do you mean, what happened?"

I got there late, and he decided to treat me like shit because of it.

"He wasn't happy with the numbers and decided to take it out on me."

"Oh no, Archer, I'm sorry."

Fucker was going to experience a little Mayhem, so it was fine, but only because he'd called me trailer trash. I'd made him a million dollars in investment trading this last quarter, and I was only fifteen minutes late. I offered to reschedule when I called and let him know, but he insisted on me just getting there as soon as possible. The second I walked through the door, he began berating me on how I had wasted his time and how different he was from me because he had real money.

The blow job was worth every second of his miserable sneer and the chance to see his true colors.

"Don't be. I much prefer knowing someone's true nature when working with them. He did me a favor. I cut him as a client, and now I'll never make him another dollar."

Wren rubbed just above my knee. "Good."

Shit, her hand felt so good. She was going to know I was hard any second, with her ass nestled up so close to me.

"But, actually..." I started, unable to get the images of her in my truck, her mouth taking the tip of my cock between her pretty red lips, out of my head. "I couldn't help wondering how you did after our little time in the truck."

I tied off her braid, and she half-turned between my legs. "What do you mean? I went to work and had to deal with Brick. You were there for all of that."

"Yes." I dropped my gaze to her lips. "But you were moaning while you slid that wet tongue over me, sucking my cock and then swallowing my cum like a..." I trailed off, unsure how free I could be with my words.

She wet her lips, staring at my mouth and holding onto my leg with her hand.

"Like a what?"

I felt a flush working its way up my neck. I'd never hesitated to speak however I wanted to with a woman, not ever. But Wren had me wanting to talk about flowers and how she smelled like lavender while also making me feel like she had started weaving her own fairy tale in my chest. She was folklore, and I was just a boy falling in love with a story.

Wren twisted until she was on her knees in front of me, her hands running up my chest, her lips a breath away from mine.

Her mouth trailed over my jaw lightly, and then her teeth latched onto my ear. "Like a what, Archer?"

My cock twitched in my jeans, hardening to a painful point.

Gripping her hips, I rasped in the air between us. "Like a dirty little slut."

Wren drew her bottom lip between her teeth and bit down.

Then, leaning forward, her lips trailed my ear. "So you want to know if I had to touch myself after I sucked your cock? If I went to work with slick thighs because of how badly I wanted you?"

My fingers dug into her hips as I guided her to straddle me.

"Well, if you must know, I locked myself in the bathroom of my job, Archer. I had to take off my thong because it was soaked." Her tongue traced the shell of my ear as she continued to whisper, "Then I slid down my skirt and started circling my clit with my fingers, desperate for relief."

Fuck, I was going to come in my jeans. "Did you get it?"

She shook her head while slowly rocking her hips against me.

"So that's two orgasms I owe you now, is that right?"

Biting down on her lip to suppress a smile, she nodded.

"Well, we better do something about that."

Wren looped her hands around my neck loosely. "I mean, if you say so."

Ashley Muñoz

"You're going to have to do exactly as I tell you. No arguments, no questions." I slowly shifted her off my lap. "I will not fuck you tonight."

Wren's mouth parted the tiniest bit, but she searched my face and nodded.

"Also, if I do or say anything you're uncomfortable with, you need to tell me."

I shifted, leaving the headboard and moving toward the bottom part of her bed.

"Say yes, Wren," I rasped near her ear as I stroked down her ass.

Her eyes were wide, her neck flushed, and I saw her chest rising and falling fast. "Yes."

"Good." I slipped my shirt up over my head. "Strip out of your clothes and put this on."

Her brows dipped, and I knew she was likely confused, but I didn't care; I was finally about to see her completely naked. I sat back, watching as she slid her shirt over her head, revealing silky, smooth, tan skin. She had a beauty mark above her left breast that I wanted to kiss. She slid her sports bra up and over her head, letting her tits fall free, which had my mouth parting.

I refrained from touching her as she moved to her shorts.

"Underwear, too. All of it," I demanded.

She hesitated momentarily, her nails lightly scraping over the thin band of her white panties. They arched up over her hips and looked fucking sinful against her tan skin. She was a goddamn vision in just that underwear and the long white socks on her feet with her dark hair braided behind her, those tiny tendrils of hair kissing her neck.

Fuck. Me.

"Wait...just." I tried to breathe through the sight of her naked, save for those two items, but she was so stunningly gorgeous that my brain felt like it was short-circuiting. I'd never experienced this before. The mere sight of someone stopping me in the moment because they robbed me of breath. I didn't have words, but I had thoughts stitching together and forming things that would make me sound like an idiot.

160

Things that seemed to come naturally as I stared at her because her idea of a fairy tale suddenly didn't sound so far-fetched. No, it felt like she'd found a way into my chest and embedded herself into the lining of my heart. Now, it was as if I had no clue if that organ had even functioned before her.

Nothing had ever felt this real or terrifying.

This felt better than riding. Whatever this feeling was.

Sparks seemed to jolt under my skin as I stared, and that fuzzy feeling returned. I wanted to tell her that she was beautiful, the most gorgeous thing I'd ever seen in my entire life, and I was positive that she'd continue to hold that title for as long as I lived.

I wanted to tell her that she made me believe in impossible stories, that I wanted to learn whatever language spoke of midnight caressing her skin and using dialogue like darling because all I'd ever known was mayhem. I was desperate to exchange it for peace.

"Archer?" Her hands traced along my knuckles, over the tattoos inked on them. My face flushed as all the emotions began invading me, seemingly shaping something new and unfamiliar.

Was this love?

Was I in love with her? I caught her gaze, and the flush of pink on her neck made it difficult to swallow.

"Are you okay?"

No.

I'd never be okay again after this. She'd be there for all of time. Beyond stardust and the vast expanse of all the dark layers of this universe, beyond all the precious things that ever existed within this lifetime. She would remain.

My throat was thick as I finally found words. "Keep going. Remove it, then slide my shirt on."

She hesitated again, then slowly slid the panties down her tone legs and tossed the garment on the floor so all she was in were those tall socks. I continued to stare as she slid my shirt over her bare breasts, her nipples peaking beneath the soft fabric. Once it fell against her thighs, I took my position.

First, I unzipped my jeans and slid out of them so I was in just my boxers.

"That's dangerous of you, Mr. Green," Wren chided with a smirk.

I knew it was, but my cock ached.

"Do not touch unless you're positive you can keep from sliding it inside your cunt."

Wren raised her hands like she was being held at gunpoint, a playful smirk on her mouth.

Once I laid on my back in the center of her bed, my head nearly touching the end of her frame, I waved Wren over.

"Place your hands on the frame and face your television, so you can watch your show."

Wren began crawling on her hands and knees. "Where should I sit?"

"On my face."

She paused while my hand went to my erection, slowly stroking through my boxers. Finally, she moved into place next to my chest.

"Just..." she asked, staring down at my mouth and then at the television.

I stroked down her calf. "Straddle my face."

She lifted the hem of my shirt and turned to face the edge completely. Finally, she did as I said.

Her hands were up on the wood frame of the bed, her knee moved over my face, and then her hot, wet cunt lowered right over my mouth.

My hands came up to her thighs, holding her in place, while my tongue slid up through her center and circled her clit, tasting her.

A hiss left her mouth as she froze in place, and then she was pushing down against my mouth while she rocked her hips.

I hummed encouragingly, and she seemed to grow bolder with how I held her thighs and moved her over my face. Her breathing was coming in tiny little bursts while I roughly adjusted her to my sucking and licking. I was devouring her, and fuck, she tasted good. She was sweet and tart, but it was more than that; her sounds and the way she desperately fucked my face told me she loved this. She'd never swallowed another man's cum while sucking his cock, until me. Now, she'd had another first, which had me hard for entirely different reasons.

Over and over, her hips rolled, sliding her pussy over my tongue while I pushed it farther inside her. I began squeezing her ass and sliding my fingers along her crack, poking and pushing while sucking on her clit.

Her thighs clenched when a rasp left her, then her fingers were in my hair, and I knew she was about to come.

"I'm...I'm, Archer," she whispered in a cracked plea while she moved against my chin.

Pulling firmly down against her thighs, I slowly lapped at her clit, focusing all my attention on the little nub until she shattered, and I felt that warm, creamy arousal coat my tongue.

I didn't release her until I'd licked it all up, every fucking drop. Then, and only then, did I let her move.

She lifted her knee and then crawled until she collapsed flat on her back, trying to catch her breath. I slowly slid my cock out of my boxers and stroked along my shaft.

"That's never happened to me before. That was...I can't even." Wren started but kept stopping when she tried to articulate what she wanted to say.

"That was one, beautiful." I rolled over, caging her in with my arms.

"It feels sensitive," she whispered into my neck as if unsure if she could take any more.

"Okay." I kissed her stomach and helped her sit up. "Just sit in my lap while I have a little fun."

She followed me back to the headboard, where I placed my back and pulled her into my lap. Her naked pussy notched right up against my cock, which had her letting out a sharp exhale. Using my thumbs, I slowly pushed the material of the t-shirt up, revealing her perky, full breasts. I saw the moment when she realized what I likely meant by fun.

"You don't have to do anything," I assured her while I lifted both her tits and began slowly licking her nipples.

Her hips rocked immediately with a jolt of pleasure.

"Mmm, you like this, don't you?" I caught her gaze while I bent down again to lap at the two nipples.

She arched her back, rasping curses low enough that I couldn't hear them. But her pussy began sliding against my erection.

I moved faster with my mouth and my tongue, even grazing my teeth over them, all while she matched my rhythm with the cadence of her hips.

"You want me to slide inside your slick pussy, don't you?" I kissed her neck, pulling her against me. Her wet nipples slid warmly into my chest while I pulled her hips against me, and her clit continued rubbing against my shaft, making me pant painfully as I tried to restrain from pulling her on top of my erection.

"Fuck, baby. Fuckkkk," I rasped, pulling her harder against me and sliding through her lips while the tip of my dick wept, nearly about to explode.

She nodded while lifting her hips and pushing down over my restrained girth. "You're so wet for me, and I'm about to cum all over your stomach, let it drip down along this pretty pussy. Want to see you covered."

A low moan left Wren's chest while she rotated her hips against me. My cock was so thick, and my balls ached with the need to be released; I had practically notched inside her. She continued to bear against me, rubbing herself shamelessly against me.

"If you grip me this well, just sliding through your pussy lips, I can only imagine how well you'll take me. You're going to clench around me so good, aren't you?"

I slid my hand to her ass and gripped her cheek, pulling her closer. She let out a louder moan while her breathing increased. She shoved her face into my shoulder while her thighs clenched around my waist. I was about to cum.

"Archer," she breathed into my ear, kissing me sweetly before trying to withhold a cry. Fuckkkkk."

Wren shuddered against me. I glanced down and made sure the tip of my cock wasn't somehow buried inside her because it felt so good, then gripped my shaft. I started pumping my hips, my dick still sliding along the outside of her cunt. It was so wet, and my breaths were so short as a tingle started in the base of my spine, and then groaning into her shoulder, my release shot out in hot spurts against her stomach.

Wren's breathing was ragged as she sagged in my arms. Leaning back the slightest bit, I saw how the mess dripped down her lower stomach to the top of her smooth mound. It was so perfect, and all I wanted to do was paint different pieces of her body with it. See all that beautiful skin smeared with what she did to me.

"I think you should stay, just to sleep."

My skin prickled with nervousness. Something had happened between us tonight, and while she might not be aware of it, I was in a monumental way. Part of me wanted to get on my bike and run away, let the night air carry me somewhere. But another part of me, a stronger part, wanted to hold her all night and wake up with her in my arms.

"Okay, but I'll need to leave early because I don't think Kane should see me here when he wakes up."

Wren shook her head. "Definitely not, Cruz either. I think it would confuse them."

"Okay, I'll stay." I kissed her forehead while she adjusted, so my shirt fell back around her thighs. I slid out of bed and walked into her attached bathroom, not flipping on the light. Grabbing a hand towel from one of her shelves, I returned to Wren, swiping up the mess from her stomach. Her sleepy smile and a gentle squeeze of my wrist tightened my chest. That feeling returned tenfold.

I was in love with her.

"Do you want this back?" she asked, her lashes fluttering, her big amber eyes dreamy and tired.

I gave her the most genuine smile I'd ever felt as I said, "Never."

Chapter 15

Wren

My face was against something warm and firm, while something equally strong seemed to wrap around my back, securing me. I opened one eye and saw my bedroom was still gray and mostly dark, but I could make out Archer's peaceful face as he slept.

His chest rose and fell under my cheek, and I had to resist the urge to trace the bridge of his nose and down along his jaw...over his lips. The same lips that tasted me last night.

The memory returned in a rush, like liquid heat activating in my veins, burning all throughout my body. I chose not to focus on the way his hands held my thighs against his face or how he expertly licked and sucked my nipples while I rode him into orgasmic oblivion.

No, I was focused on the gentle way he'd braided my hair and seemed to pick up on the fact that talking about my brother affected me. Archer was more considerate and far more careful with me than I'd ever been handled by a man. Yet, when his hands cradled my thighs or his mouth tasted me, he wasn't gentle at all, and the contrast between the two actions was something new that I never knew I'd crave at some point.

My thoughts faded and tangled, and I came to a rushing halt when I heard the little giggles of two five-year-old boys near my bedroom door.

Oh shit.

I tried to sit up, but Archer's arms were like steel around me.

"Archer!" I whispered, and I instantly felt his hips press forward, his morning erection pushing against my stomach. I had to bite down on my lip and ignore it because I wanted nothing more than a repeat of last night...and, honestly, more. I really wanted to have sex with him, but I wouldn't push it since he had made such a stark stance against it.

"Mmmm." He buried his face into my hair while sliding his hand down to my ass and gripping my left cheek hard. It felt so good that I let out a breathy gasp while trying to detangle our bodies. Archer's hips continued to press into me while he held me, and suddenly his lips were tracing my collarbone and up my neck.

"Archer, wake up. The boys are up." I slammed my eyes closed, trying again, desperate now because if he started touching me, I would begin to shamelessly ride him. But having the boys not see him here was important to him. Doing this, whatever we were doing, and establishing it the right way, seemed paramount, and I didn't want to do anything to ruin that.

The man under me seemed to freeze when another, much louder lilt of laughter echoed outside the room.

"Is your door locked?" Archer's husky voice was close to my ear, and I loved how gritty it sounded. I'd love to feel that skate against my thighs on another morning just like this, but with an actual plan in place to ensure no one was able to sneak in and see us.

"No. I always unlock it before I sleep because I worry about Cruz. Last night, I nearly forgot, but sometime in the night, I slipped out of bed and flipped the lock when I remembered."

"Well, shit. Will he come in here?"

"I doubt it because Kane is here, but if he's hungry..."

Archer started to move, sliding out of the bed and dropping to the floor on silent hands and feet. I withheld a laugh while I watched him tiptoe over to my door and quickly flip the lock. Then he dipped to grab his jeans but seemed to pause near my standing mirror.

With gentle hands, he plucked my postcard out and inspected it.

"Why do you keep this here instead of on your fridge?"

My heart seemed to leap into my throat as I watched him hold one of my silly, meaningless dreams in his hands, so easy and carefree, as if he were curious why it was bound to the mirror instead of tethered to my heart.

"My father was a horrible man, and I have very little love or care for the fact that he passed...but back when I was a kid, when I used to look up to him and miss him, I had always wished he'd think of me on his trips. Yet, each time he returned, he'd merely pat my head or give me a quick kiss, but there was never any indication that he'd cared or even missed me. Until this one time, this one, long trip."

"He'd been gone for weeks, and when he'd returned, he handed me this postcard, while telling me a story. He talked about how he visited this place, and while he walked along the sand and looked up at billowing white curtains in one of the villas, it was like he saw me there. He told me how he'd pictured this beautiful life for me, full of sunshine, warmth and fairy tales. He spoke of regret, how he'd wished he'd been a better father to me, how I was everything he'd ever hoped for when he was young and imagined being a dad. He said I was special to him, not just a jewel in his crown, but I was the crown. For whatever reason, he said that town, that place he went, made him reflect on all that. He told me to always remember I deserved the unrealistic, outrageous sort of life, where I'm loved and cherished."

My throat felt thick, remembering the one and only kindness my father ever showed me.

"That was the only gift he'd ever given me."

Archer glanced at me, then the image on the postcard. "Cabo San Lucas?"

It seemed silly when he said it out loud. My dad probably just found me an easy tourist gift and made up some elaborate story while he was vacationing in some resort, likely cheating on my mother. But, to the little girl inside me, it was the fact that he'd thought of me, and the picture he'd painted for me was a beautiful life. One I had hoped to one day have, no matter how outrageous it seemed.

"Have you been then?" Archer walked closer after tucking the image back into the frame. He buttoned his jeans and pulled his hair back into another little bun at the nape of his neck.

I shook my head. "I can't even get to Montana. I definitely haven't gone to Cabo."

His lips twitched while his knee pressed into my mattress. His hand slid along my jaw and into my hair.

"You'd look good in Cabo, beautiful. I think I need to see that at some point in my life, you, on that beach, wearing a bikini, looking back at me while you walked along the sand, knowing that moment had been etched into your chest as a dream."

My heart skipped a thousand beats as his blue eyes locked on me and his lips brushed against mine. Heat and skin slid against each other as I lost myself in his steady eyes and allowed the rhythm of my heart to mirror his, wishing I could somehow tuck it away in his chest and ask if he'd carry it for the duration of my life. I'd never had anyone tell me they wanted my heart or were in love with me. Matthew and I had been together as a couple, but it had only been a few months before he went to prison.

A lonely, painful reminder seemed to balloon in my chest that I had gone through my life without being told that I was loved. My mother had said it to me growing up...Leo had even said it a few times after they married. Juan had said it; surely, he had. Why couldn't I remember if my brother said he'd loved me?

Archer's mouth moved to my ear as his hands traveled down to my hip, which broke me out of my thoughts. He was here, he was real and he'd continued to show up...he brought me flowers. He asked to come in last night, and he wasn't just here for sex. This meant something to him. I meant something to him.

As if he could hear my racing thoughts, he whispered, "Come with me this weekend."

"What?" My hands went to his wrists, trying to hold him in place so he wouldn't leave me. The boys laughed in the living room, but I could hear a cartoon playing, too.

Archer's gaze searched mine as he swallowed.

"There's a family barbeque for club members. We're riding out to a big state park. There's stuff for the kids and a great view…" His forehead pinned mine as he seemed to struggle for words. "It's a good way for you to meet my club."

Didn't that seem like we were serious then? Maybe we were. I felt serious about him and how he treated me; it felt like this was real for him. Something told me his no-sex thing came from a very serious place, and I just needed to trust him and let him show me.

"I thought you had to take Kane back."

His fingers found mine, intertwining ours together. "I'll ask if I can have him longer."

I liked the idea of riding with him into the city, taking the boys, and seeing this piece of his life, but then I remembered one of them running through my fence.

Turning him down was on the tip of my tongue, but instead I asked him. "Will they be how they were at your house?"

I felt him smile, even if I couldn't see his features due to our position. "No. They're never like that when families are around. Old Ladies, kids, even Moms and extended family come out. No bunk bunnies or Sweetbutts."

He pulled back so I could see his face and how his lips tugged up.

"Those are the ones who aren't patched to members, right, with property something?" I tried to remember what he'd said about that.

His smile was sweet and perfect. "Exactly."

That meant he was making a statement by taking me. And he was making it to his club, not just a few friends.

Still, I couldn't find enough reason to turn him down. The weather was nice, the kids would love it, and I wanted to be seen on his arm. I wanted women like Lydia and her sister to see me and know that Archer wasn't available.

My gut sank. Fuck that meant I'd already placed him in my head as my boyfriend. Someone who would be loyal to me and monogamous.

"You're overthinking it, beautiful." Archer kissed my lips as the boys got louder, coming down the hallway. He glanced at the door, then rose above me, about to leave.

I inhaled a cleansing breath. "Yes. We'll go."

Archer moved to the door and smirked at me from over his shoulder. "I know."

He was about to leave without a shirt, which jolted me up. "Do you want the shirt? You have nothing to walk back home in."

His gaze narrowed. "No. It's yours. I'll be back in a few after I go shower."

I watched his muscles shift as he slipped out my back door. One of my neighbors was definitely going to see him and speculate that he was doing the walk of shame, but I couldn't find it in me to care. Let them see him. Let them know he's mine.

My stomach flipped at the idea of truly belonging to him and, likewise, him to me.

Perfect.

Two seconds later, someone tried to turn my doorknob. I slid out of bed and pulled on a pair of sleep shorts before flipping the lock. Right as I swung the door open, I yelled, "Boo."

Cruz and Kane both brought their hands up to their mouths in a giggle fest. I walked past both boys toward the kitchen, trying to shake the feeling that I'd slept with a man last night but truly just slept. There was something infinitely more intimate about just being held by someone all night than just fucking.

"How did you boys sleep?" My hands moved independently, grabbing a flat pan and a large mixing bowl.

Cruz slid onto the stool first. "Good."

Kane followed his lead to the second stool. "I had a dream about a magical toilet."

Cruz laughed, and the two started a whole conversation about what a real magical toilet could do while I mixed ingredients for pancakes.

I cracked an egg into the bowl when Kane tilted his head at me. "Hey, my big brother has that same shirt."

Oh shit. Archer had been wearing this shirt at dinner last night.

"Oh really?" I moved away and grabbed the melted butter, adding it in.

Kane's keen eyes continued to inspect me.

"Yeah...it even says his name, just like his shirt."

My face was on fire because how on earth had I missed that his T-shirt had his name on it. I was too nervous to look down, but after a second, I just gave in and pulled the shirt away from my chest, inspecting it.

It was black with white lettering and carried the club insignia for Mayhem Riot. A few other symbols and words made no sense to me, but along the rib cage, in white ink, was printed "Archer."

There was no way of getting out of this, but I would try.

"I think I got this as a gift from the club when they broke the fence...maybe they made several with his name on it?"

Kane merely shrugged and spun on his stool to watch the cartoon Cruz had picked out.

My heart felt like it was in my throat from the lie, which only brought back the reality that this thing between my neighbor was getting out of hand. Twenty minutes later, Archer came to the door, lightly knocking. Kane asked if he could open it, and when I gave him the okay, he excitedly greeted his brother.

Archer's gaze was down, listening to Kane until he walked in, and those blue eyes landed on me. The pancakes were done, and we were about to eat, but he looked at me, standing in his shirt as if I were the meal.

"Hi." His smile stretched along his handsome face as he drew closer. He had showered, and seeing his wet hair was doing things to me.

"Hi."

He slid out of one of the stools and sat while nodding toward my chest. "Crazy, I have that same shirt."

Kane smacked his forehead like his brother had misspoke. "I already told her that."

"Is that right?"

I brought the dish towel up to hide my laugh while Archer watched me, shaking his head with a full smile.

Chapter 16

Wren

A PAIR OF SUNGLASSES PERCHED ON MY FACE WHILE I WATCHED the city fly by and trees begin to appear. Archer had driven us an hour south, narrowly missing the main artery of New York City, until we started veering West toward a national park.

Kane and Cruz talked in the back seat while a few toys sat scattered between their little booster seats. Archer's bike was tied down in the back of the truck, and the way he kept looking over at me and smiling had something in my belly swooping and catching fire.

I smiled back and realized I needed to tell Cruz about my feelings for Archer. It was only a matter of time before he caught us holding hands or kissing. Our touches were becoming more insistent as if we couldn't keep our hands off each other.

But was it smart to do that before—I shook my head, hoping to displace those thoughts. It didn't matter what Archer did or didn't do. My son deserved to know how I felt about our neighbor because Cruz was the center of my life, and I knew he loved me. I needed to share this part of my life with him. Because even if Archer wasn't sure how he felt, I knew that I was.

I watched the countryside pass us while trees with orange and yellow leaves came in and out of focus along the windy road down the canyon. Archer was talking to the boys about this lake and how he used to play in it when he was a kid, but suddenly, the sound of thunder had me sitting up and looking around. It was so loud.

Archer caught my confusion and started laughing. "Look behind us, Wren."

I turned and tried to catch what I could from the glass in the window. A few yards back from us, traveling down the canyon, were dozens of motorcycles. Men, some with women on the back, others alone. They all rode in unison, taking up both lanes of traffic, and they all wore those leather vests that Archer did.

"How many are there?" I mused, unsure if I meant for Archer to answer me, but he did anyway.

"We're expecting around a hundred or so today."

One hundred? My eyes likely matched my shock as I tried to register how many riders were behind us.

"They're not passing you."

Kane was the one to answer my question this time. "That's because Archer is the president. They're showing him respect by riding behind him."

Something like pride flickered through me. All these men loyal to Archer, to the club.

This didn't feel the same as El Peligro. His club...he was right, they weren't a gang...I wasn't sure what made them different, but I wanted to discover and figure out what it was and honor it. Nerves rattled around in my stomach as the rumble of their engines eclipsed our music and seemed to increase in sound as we neared the bottom of the canyon.

Once we finally pulled into a parking space, my fingers felt like they were trembling. What if they laughed at me or thought I was stupid for being here? What if they thought one of their own women would be better suited for him, or if Lydia's sister showed up and tried to—

Suddenly, Archer's fingers gripped my chin, forcing me to look at him.

"Hey."

I relaxed into his hold, loving how his eyes seemed to peel back layers of my fears and step inside them as if he was physically taking them from me.

"It's just a barbecue. Don't overthink it."

Cruz sat up, watching us with his head tilted. He was going to ask about Archer holding my face. He was going to ask what we were, and I wouldn't know what to tell him.

"Will there be hot dogs here?"

Archer laughed, and I found that I did, too. Then, I lowered my face and began a few breathing exercises. This was ridiculous. They were just people like me, like Archer.

We exited the truck, and I helped Cruz out of his door. He jumped in my arms and clung to my neck, then whispered a question that made me freeze.

"I think he wants to be your boyfriend, Mama."

Playing along, I whispered back, "Who?"

He giggled, and I shut the truck door, still holding my son to my chest. "Archer."

"Ohhhh, I see." I smiled while walking around the hood, keeping my eyes on the people starting to park around us. The engines rumbled and echoed, thrumming through me like thunder.

"What would you think of that if he was?"

The sun was bright and warm, even with the autumn leaves covering the ground. The air had a slight chill, but it was cool against my overly warm-skin. We had on light jackets and snug boots with jeans. Kane was walking ahead of us with Archer, holding his hand while peeking back at us every few seconds.

Cruz got closer to my ear and spoke louder. "Well, I'm the one who wished for it, silly."

My nose burned as tears lined my eyes. He'd wished for Archer to like me, for us to be here with him. A peace settled over me that I had never experienced. Something so foreign as I watched Archer walk like I was being pulled by him or like we were connected. For once in my life, I wasn't all alone.

The other members began pulling into rows, lining up their bikes without fitting into any set parking spaces. It was as though they'd just created their own. My steps picked up, hurrying a bit to get closer to Archer. Not that I was afraid...I just, I was nervous. I had arrived with their president, and I still wasn't entirely sure what that meant or how serious that was.

But something told me I was about to find out.

I had occasionally imagined what it might mean for Archer to be the president of a motorcycle club when thinking of him in those moments I swore I wouldn't. Or when I was trying to justify why it would be such a bad idea to place my trust in a man who held the allegiance and attention of such a group, but nothing could have prepared me for actually witnessing it.

I was very good at determining how a man watched other men in power and Archer's men...they watched his every move as if he were the most important person in the world. These men didn't want Archer's position or think someone else should have it; they looked at him like they'd do anything to protect him. It was the closest, I thought, that I'd ever come to seeing men look at a man they considered their king.

"So, Wren, right?" A woman named Rosy had sidled up to me, handing me a can of beer. "How did you tame the untamable?" Her brown eyes were bright, and her smile seemed friendly as she spoke with me. I cracked the top of the beer and sipped it carefully, knowing there was no way I'd ever drink enough to lose my faculties while my son was here, surrounded by strangers. I hoped that Archer understood how much trust I was putting in him to even be here with Cruz, to begin with.

My eyes trailed over to Archer, seeing him sit in a circle with a few other men, but Cruz and Kane took up both sides of where he sat while he helped them arrange their marshmallows for roasting and prepping smores.

"I'm not sure what you mean." My attention slid back to Rosy.

She was tall with frosted white hair, dark roots, and bold makeup. She wore a leather cut; I was learning they weren't called vests but cuts, over her long-sleeved shirt. Her patch said she was the property of someone named Nolan.

Rosy sipped her drink and then lifted it toward Archer. "Never seen him with anyone like this. These outings are for families. In the past, he'd arrive late, eat a burger, drink a beer, and then just take off again. It was like being around all of us was difficult for him. He always seemed to fit in the role of president, but none of us ever imagined he might settle down."

My heart rioted, feeling swollen as I considered her words. Archer smiled at Cruz as he helped pull his marshmallow stick out of the fire. He looked happy, smiling and laughing while the men around him helped their kids.

He looked like a dad.

Rosy took pity on my lack of conversational skills as I watched the man I was slowly but positively falling in love with. "Looks like maybe he isn't the only one this is new for. You seem like the type to not let random men around your kid, which makes this much more interesting."

I was still watching him as I muttered in reply, "How can you tell?"

"You're a single mom, and I can tell you're a good one. Which means you've fought like hell for your kid. People mean well, but no one really understands until they've lived it. Being the only person your kid has in the whole world. It's a scary and daunting feeling to wield that alone, to protect your kid's heart and make sure they're safe from anyone who might hurt them. You pay for everything on your own; you're the only one on duty when they're sick or scared. All the bills are yours to worry about. The damn grass has to get mowed, that's on you. The garbage, holidays. Even if you have helpful family, it's not the same. It builds up this thickness around you and gives off a vibe. I can feel it from you."

My focus was on her now, her kind eyes and meaningful gesture as she spoke about things no one had ever seemed to understand about me. My throat felt thick as I battled a rogue emotion that wanted an escape. No one had ever quite surmised me in that way before.

"I was a bitch to him in the beginning." I laughed, sipping my drink and feeling my voice crack slightly.

Rosy laughed, shaking her head. "Guess you'd have to be."

"He was so nice and helpful. Scared the living shit out of me, to be honest."

"Didn't hurt he looked like that on top of it, right?"

My face broke into a smile as laughter spilled out of me. "Right."

"Well, for what it's worth. All of us Old Ladies really like you, and we're excited to see him so happy." Her hand came to my arm and gently squeezed before walking off. I watched as she bent down and pulled a little toddler from a man who wore a cut that said, Nolan. He kissed her, and she fell into his arms while holding the toddler. Something shifted in my chest.

Was that envy?

Did I want that with Archer, a toddler with his hair and a piece of leather on my back that said I belonged to him?

Yes.

Archer's eyes found mine from across the distance, and I held his gaze while I made my way over. It felt electric, as if that piece of lightning really was trapped inside him, and now it wanted a way inside me, too.

Kane and Cruz relaxed in the little camping chairs that someone had brought. Once I was in front of Archer's knees, he tugged on my hand and pulled me into his lap. I went easily, feeling protected and safe, as he pulled me under his chin and began talking to his men. They spoke of rides they'd been on, crazy things they'd done, and old memories of times past. Laughter erupted nearly every five seconds, but it was refreshing and freeing. My son had a smile that hadn't waned since we arrived, and that was a feeling I'd never thought I'd have.

Of being whole and a part of something.

It was well past dinner when Kane and Cruz played with other kids, happily yelling and running, when Archer tugged me close.

"How would you feel about Thistle watching the boys for a second while I take you on a ride?"

I'd met his best friend and vice president the day they worked on my fence. After Archer had dealt with Brick and kissed me, I calmed down and took them all snacks. He'd seemed so remorseful about the fence that I had no choice but to forgive him. He was also extremely protective of Archer and Kane, which was something I had picked up on immediately. It didn't go unnoticed by me that Archer had asked him to take the boys in the back when Brick had arrived that day so they didn't witness any violence.

Thistle had done it without question and kept the boys safe. I had a good feeling in my gut about him, so I nodded.

"I'd be okay with that."

Archer's brows raised like he was shocked. "Really?"

I slapped his stomach, feeling his muscles underneath. "I'm trying. I keep telling you this."

He kissed my jaw, smiling against my skin. "My darling, mayhem. There's anarchy under those beautiful lashes and that fucking sinfully smooth skin. You're a wildfire, and I love it."

He let me go and walked ahead to get Thistle's attention, but my pulse had skyrocketed at his words. They felt like midnight against my skin. Like he'd found me in a forest and started singing, just like in the cartoons. Like he was a rugged, misunderstood prince trying to sweep me off my feet from the moment he met me.

Fuck, I was done for.

I was in love with him. My steps slowed as the realization washed over me. He laughed with Thistle, then bent low to talk to Kane and Cruz, making a circle with his finger and pointing to where they could go, then up at Thistle. I knew what he was saying, and still, my mind went to how my heart had officially caved, opening up for him and letting him have space in a place I'd never allowed anyone.

Most of all, I couldn't stop thinking about how incredibly dangerous it was to let him completely in and have something he'd never even asked for.

The ride up the canyon on Archer's bike was beautiful and peaceful. I had never been on the back of a motorcycle, and it felt like a hidden secret or something; it felt like flying. My hair whipped behind me while my fingers held firm to his waist, and we crested the top of a ravine, looking down.

Archer parked his bike, pushing the kickstand down, and I untangled my arms from him.

His hand came out and held my thigh in place. "Stay put."

I sat back on the leather seat and watched as he swung his leg over and stood. The wind blew pieces of his hair lightly askew while he walked to the saddle bag on the side of his bike. The gravel crunched under his boots, and rushing water echoed from the canyon. The sun was setting lower in the sky but still bright enough to offer warmth.

"Close your eyes." His playful smirk had butterflies shooting off in my stomach.

My eyes fluttered closed, and I felt the breeze caress my face. Archer's hands returned to my thighs, and he held me in place while the bike slightly shifted. I felt his knees cradling mine, which must have meant he was back on the bike but facing me.

"Before you open your eyes, I need you to know something." Archer's voice was soft and gentle but prodded at that place he'd taken up in my heart, making it throb. "This, what I'm about to say and do... it's not a light thing. This...in our lifestyle, this means something. It's important, and while it won't hold the same weight for you, I need you to understand that for me, it's almost as serious as a..." His voice trailed off, and I could feel hesitation or fear in his lungs. I wanted to open my eyes and see his face, see that flush of red hit the hollow part of his jaw, and see how he grabbed at his neck.

"This is serious for me, Wren. I just need you to know that."

He gently took my hand and whispered, "Open your eyes."

I did, seeing his smiling face in front of me, his body close to mine, cradling mine between his wide legs. A folded piece of leather sat between us, and my breath hitched.

"This is yours. It's probably too fast, but...I just..." He trailed off and cleared his throat. "I know that it's still new, and I told you I wanted you to take me seriously, and I mean that, but I also want others to know you belong to me. I want you to know that you belong to me."

I grabbed the black leather and held it up, gently tracing the words and letting the finality of this moment soak into my soul.

White stitching printed out the words "Property of" along the upper part of the material. The insignia of Mayhem Riot was sewn into the middle, and along the bottom was the word "Archer." But then my fingers moved to the shoulders where two patches were sewn. The left shoulder patch said, "President's, and the right shoulder said, "Wife."

My eyes flew up to his.

His Adam's apple bobbed, and his voice came out rushed and almost panicked. "It's just a term we use. I know it seems intense, but it just means you're mine, and no one can mess with you or try to touch you...it's just a—"

I cut him off by throwing my arms around him.

He pulled me into his lap, my legs going over his as he kissed me, and I kissed him back.

My heart felt free, my soul on fire, and I was happy. The happiest I'd ever been in my entire life. I was in love. The kind that made my belly swoop, my nerves rattle, and unbidden smiles stretch along my face. I grew up seeing the kind on television and reading about it in books. He made me feel like reality was better, richer than fiction.

Like my dreams were his mission to see fulfilled.

Pulling away, I pressed my forehead to his, staring at the leather in my lap.

"I'm so honored, Archer. I love it...and I." Hesitation caught my words as fear lassoed around them, pulling me back to reality. What if he didn't mean it this way? What if he was just possessive, and he didn't really mean—

His whisper danced along my mouth. "I'm falling in love with you, Wren."

My eyes flew up, finding his, my breathing shallow.

"You are?"

His hand was on my neck, his forehead still pinned to mine. "I... fuck, no, I'm sorry. I lied."

Fear ricocheted like a bullet hitting a piece of metal. My mouth parted, but he merely laughed and kissed my jaw and then my ear.

"I'm past that. I fuckin' fell, hard. I'm in love with you, and I'm scared shitless."

Tears pressed against my eyes, and I let them fall while I smiled.

"Really? Because me too...it's terrifying."

He had tears gathering in his eyes, too, while he laughed relieved. "I have so much shit going on with the custody stuff, it's the absolute worst time to bring you into my life, but I can't imagine it without you at the same time."

"Then don't. I'm here. I want to be inside it."

"Yeah?"

I kissed him again and let him taste my tears of happiness. "Yeah."

Archer helped me into my new leather cut, my property patch, as they called it, and it felt like I'd just knit a piece of my future into place. It felt right. It felt different than belonging anywhere else ever had. This felt like I was part of something bigger and better; strangely, it felt like home.

We rode back down the glen, returning to the kids and his club.

The smile on my face couldn't be rivaled as we flew down the road. The second we parked and people saw what I was wearing, there were shouts and excited yells. Women came up to me, pulling me into hugs, while men made all sorts of shouts of approval. A few lifted Archer and congratulated him.

I laughed while I went over to where Thistle was with the boys. There were people everywhere, but at one point, the group had separated Archer and me halfway to where I was headed. It wasn't a big deal as I passed people who wished me well and were happy for me, but then suddenly, there was a man in my way, and I realized we were slightly off to the side.

"Property of the president? What an interesting plot twist. I bet your father would have loved this." The man smiled, showing all-white teeth. He was tall, broad, and stacked with muscles. His hair was nearly as white as Kane's, and sharp blue eyes reminded me of Archer. Something like oil began to slither in through my chest.

Where was Archer?

I took a step back, and he stepped closer. "Wonder what the new leaders of El Peligro will think of your latest relationship. If Archer knew about your connection to his biggest enemy, do you really think he'd place that piece of leather on your back?" He took a step forward, but I refused to back away or cower to him in any way. Mostly because I was shell-shocked that he'd just talked about my past and Archer...and somehow made a connection to both.

Something told me not to look away from this man, even for a second.

But his eyes drifted to the side, and he sighed like his time was up. "Enjoy it while it lasts. El Peligro isn't your brother's anymore, but he'll be sent to deal with you just the same. He'll have to before the new leaders find out. Your blood ties to that gang are a complication for Mayhem Riot. You're a problem now whether you realize it or not."

What was he talking about?

The man suddenly shifted on his boot and turned around, disappearing into the crowd. Archer was next to me a minute later.

"Who was that talking to you?" His voice was panicked.

I shook my head, my mind too muddled to even have an answer for him. I needed to get to Cruz. Archer helped me push through the crowd until we were finally in front of both boys, seeing they were safe and sound. I tugged Archer close and whispered in his ear.

"He looked like...you, and he looked like Kane."

Chapter 17

Wren

I SAT WITH MY HANDS FOLDED IN MY LAP AND MY HEART hammering against my chest. Thistle looked over at me and winced.

"I know you're probably freaked out, but Archer can handle this."

My smile was pathetically weak, as were our voices as we ensured the boys didn't wake. "This is just new for me."

It was dark outside the truck windows, but my gaze drifted to the side mirror where I watched the singular headlight following us. Two men rode ahead of us, and several more were behind Archer, taking up the rear. The second I had mentioned that man's looks, Archer's brows dipped then raised as if all at once it dawned on him who had been there, and then he stared at me as if he expected me to move my new property patch and reveal a bullet wound.

His panic shot through me as he pulled Kane into his arms, then told Thistle to take Cruz. I was so confused at the way his tone had turned militant and how everyone around him seemed to mobilize without question. Archer's truck was up on the grass within minutes. Only the driver's door and back passenger were open. His members had guns drawn, keeping them low to the ground while Thistle and

Archer continued to usher us to safety. My head spun, still trying to piece together what had just happened.

The threat I'd felt from the man had settled in my chest like a poisonous fume, clouding and deteriorating tissue with each second that passed, but there was too much going on for me to even have a moment to wrap my head around it. The man who'd spoken to me was obviously dangerous, and as I tried to collect the pieces, I had to assume that perhaps this was Archer's father. He'd told me he was dangerous, wanted to potentially take Kane, and looked so much like them both.

I climbed over the console to the passenger side while Kane and Cruz were buckled into the back. Thistle took the driver's seat, and Archer approached the side of the truck moments later. He pulled the door open, and within seconds, his hands cradled my jaw and pushed into my hair.

"I need to watch from the road in case something happens..." His voice caught, and as he started to pull away, I gripped his wrists to keep him with me.

His eyes searched mine, and I found fear in his gaze, making my stomach flip. I knew Archer wanted to hear what the man said to me, but it seemed he needed to ensure we were safe first. I wanted him in the truck with us, but I also knew this was his role with this club. He needed to be the president, and I needed to trust him.

"Be safe." I pressed my mouth to his in a quick kiss.

Archer held my face as he kissed me back, then pulled away. "Thistle will drive you home. I'll be right behind him, but in case something happens, I will ask him to stay outside to protect you. A few members will be down the street, scouting as well. Don't be alarmed by them, okay."

I nodded, and then, with his eyes on mine, he moved out of my space and shut the door.

Thistle glanced over at me, bringing me back to the moment. We'd been driving for a while, but I had no idea how long. It wasn't like I could text Archer, so I hadn't looked at my phone. Instead, my only connection to him was watching his headlight as he followed us.

"Are you able to tell me who that man was?" I asked, letting my voice echo softly in the cab, knowing the boys wouldn't hear us.

Thistle shifted his hand on the steering wheel before checking the rearview mirror.

"I didn't see him, but based on what you said...I assume it was Saul Green. Archer's old man."

Just as I thought.

"How would he have gotten the chance to be around your club without anyone noticing?"

I stared ahead. The taillights of a few motorcycles showed, and then the brake lights as we took a turn.

Thistle seemed to think this over before giving me a simple answer.

"He was wearing a cut with our colors. Blended right in."

I perused the side of Thistle's head, seeing his hair was shaved, leaving him bald with the smallest bit of growth. His bushy beard covered his mouth, making it difficult to read his expressions, but his eyes were kind, and those were much easier to understand.

"What does it mean that he was wearing your colors?"

Thistle's long, tatted finger came up, pointing to his patches. "We call these our colors. It's a way to identify which club you're affiliated with. Can be dangerous if you're in the wrong part of town."

His comment only reminded me of what the man, Saul, had said about my connection to El Peligro and how it seemed that Archer would have known who I was or should have known. It made me think back to when Archer had recognized my tattoo...and asked about my name.

"Thistle?"

His head turned quickly, then returned forward. "Yeah?"

"Did you know who I was...when you met me and knew my last name?"

I observed his features, but they didn't change at all.

"As in, knew that you were Archer's neighbor or that you worked at the same place he bought his house from?"

That answered how Archer knew where I worked before I had told him. How did I bring up what Saul had mentioned without bringing up my family? What if Thistle kidnapped me and my son, thinking he was being loyal to Archer...I trusted Archer, but did I trust the man he considered his second?

Something in my stomach flipped with nerves, making me look out the window. Archer would be asking what his father had said to me, and he'd tell Thistle if not all of his men. There was also a chance more of his men knew, especially if Saul did, which might put Archer in danger. I had no idea what Saul's affiliations were, but if he knew who I was, I might be in danger not telling Archer's men.

There was no running from this.

With a deep sigh, I turned to face Archer's second.

"The man who talked to me...Saul. He knew about my family."

Thistle flipped his blinker as we turned onto the main freeway, which would take us back to Atlas.

"Your family?"

Did he really not know, or was he just pretending? I hated not knowing.

"I'm the daughter of Manny Vasquez."

I waited, watching his reaction to my confession, knowing I didn't need to say anything else. His eyes remained forward, and then I saw his chest move with a deep inhale.

"Fuck. That complicates things tremendously."

"Why?" I searched what I could of his face, desperate for more information. How did my family and Mayhem Riot interact? How did they know each other?

Thistle glanced over; his brows crumpled.

"Because we've been at war with your family for nearly twenty years."

Archer still hadn't arrived home by the time Thistle pulled into my driveway. Thistle turned off the engine, and we sat in silence, with the awkward tension that I was the daughter and sister of their enemy.

"What will happen now?"

Thistle peeked over the seat, seeing the sleeping boys.

"I'm sure Archer will talk to Kane's foster parents and get an extension to have him overnight. But we should head inside, get you somewhere safe."

"So you won't..." I started, nervous about what I was going to ask. "You won't hurt me or hold me as leverage or something?"

I had no idea how they operated, but from what I could remember from how my father ran El Peligro, that was something they would have done.

Thistle narrowed his gaze like he was confused.

"What do you mean?"

"Because I'm your enemy."

His chest shifted in what I thought might be a laugh. "Wren, you're family. That patch on your back means Mayhem Riot will be there for you forever. You're not just a patched Old Lady. You're our president's woman. You have our loyalty; we only ask that you remain faithful to us."

The knots in my stomach eased as I let out a relieved breath. "I haven't spoken to my brother in nearly twenty years. We had a falling out...so, I don't know what or how he runs El Peligro."

Thistle tilted his head like he was confused. "Don't you mean brothers?"

My mouth parted in question when someone knocked on Thistle's window. He turned, opened his door, and began talking to one of the members who wanted to help us get inside. I allowed them to open my door and usher me to my house. There were three men aside from Thistle helping us.

Thistle checked the house while I waited on my couch with both boys curled up under blankets. My heart beat erratically as he moved from room to room, a gun drawn but pointed down at the floor while his eyes were alert. A member was at my back door, and another two were standing near the front.

This was crazy.

But it was also familiar. My father's men were always around as I grew up, even after I moved in with my aunt Maria. Her husband worked for my father, so the men were always around.

Once it was clear, Thistle came back into the living room. "I'll be outside with the rest of the men. Archer will want you to get ready for bed, get some sleep, and don't worry about anything. You're safe."

I gave him a solemn nod, wishing we could talk a bit more about the conversation we'd started but understanding that he needed to leave. I watched as he exited through the front door, and I decided I would sleep on the opposite couch so the boys weren't alone while we waited for Archer to return.

Hoping that once he did, he'd still want me.

The next morning, I woke up to a note under my face.

Plucking it up, I read it and felt my stomach tilt.

Wren,

I didn't want to wake you or Cruz, but I had to return Kane to his foster parents. I know we need to talk, and we will, but for now, you and Cruz are safe. We were able to track down Saul, my men are watching him. I'm going to see if I can push Kane's court date up. If you leave, a few of my men might trail you; otherwise, they're staying out of the way. – I love you, Archer.

... I'm on my cell if you need me.

That was great news, and while I knew I should be grateful, I couldn't help but feel completely thrown off balance. I wanted to sit down with him and ask how last night went. He was gone, but I had no idea for how long, or if he encountered any trouble. I hadn't heard if Thistle had told him about my father or the fact that we were essentially enemies.

This almost felt silly. I'd been removed from that world for so long that it was about as believable as hearing I was once related to a monarch centuries ago. It had no bearing on my current life situation whatsoever, but still...I couldn't understand that someone had brought it up, pinned me to it, and then acted as though my life was about to be upturned because of it.

Now that I knew Saul was under surveillance, my biggest concern was how to tell Archer.

Deep down, I felt like he'd understand...but the smallest piece of doubt lingered on the fringes of my mind. Stretching, I watched the white blanket drop from around my chest. Archer must have brought it out from my bedroom for me. Cruz was still asleep on the other end of the couch, curled up with his own blanket. I smiled, feeling my heart thump happily in my chest, remembering what we'd said to each other on top of that canyon. With only the sunset as our witness, we moved to a new level. I had a piece of leather that felt nearly as important as a ring on my finger.

He'd told me he loved me.

How could he really feel that way for me, though, if he didn't know my family was his enemy? Saul's words came back, whipping against my conscience. If Archer knew about your connection to his biggest enemy, do you really think he'd place that piece of leather on your back?"

What if I lost him?

I'd pushed him away so effectively in the beginning, yet he kept coming back, trying, and never giving up. What if he realized all that was a waste...

I was spiraling, and the fact that Archer and his men seemed to have left made me feel even more off-balance. I wanted time to slow down and just give me a second to acclimate.

Coffee.

I needed to caffeinate first, then I could figure out how to break the news to Archer.

Right as I slid my mug under the Keurig, my doorbell rang.

Cruz lifted his little head from the couch, being woken by the sound, then covered his ears when it was pressed again.

My feet moved, and I wasn't even thinking about who might be watching us or if Archer deemed it safe to go about my life now, when I swung the door open.

My mouth dropped.

"Mom?"

Amber eyes that I'd inherited narrowed on me as she pushed me aside.

"¿Entonces soy un extraño ahora?"

Chapter 18

Wren

I moved aside, my mouth still open. "No, you're not a stranger... I'm sorry. I didn't—"

Then I stopped because how was she making me feel guilty when she hadn't even called ahead to see if she could visit? Granted, I would never make my mother ask, nor would I get angry if she just showed up —which she had just now.

Securing the door and ignoring how my son had already ran from the couch and thrown himself at his grandmother, I tried to piece together how she was here...and why.

She usually planned her trips months in advance with me, so she knew I would be free to visit extended family with her. She also wanted to be sure I had a clean place for her to stay, which, at the moment, I did not.

"Mom, I'm so glad to see you."

Her intelligent gaze slid back my way as she fought a smile. "You are not."

"I am," I tried to add a little extra enthusiasm, but she knew me better than that.

My house was a disaster. She was right. I wasn't excited that she was here. I would be if she left and gave me two days to prepare for her.

I decided to change the subject. "Can I get you coffee?"

"¿Dejaste de hablar español?"

The urge to roll my eyes was strong. "No, mama. I haven't stopped speaking Spanish."

Yes, I had.

"I'm merely more comfortable with speaking English. Besides, you raised me on both."

She scoffed. "Your father did."

She meant Leo, not Manny. She never spoke of Manny or acted like he was a part of our lives. Which was why my brother took Leo's last name. I had considered it, but my cousins all remained Vasquezs, and while my father was terrible, he was also my dad. That damn postcard lingered in my mind, a little golden symbol of parenthood that shouldn't belong to him but did.

I knew she'd never turn down a cup of coffee, so I started brewing her a cup.

"Do you have bags?"

"Grandma, you can stay in my room if you want," Cruz offered excitedly.

My mother smiled at him warmly. "Gracias, nieto."

Cruz tilted his head. "What's nieto?"

"I thought he was learning Spanish." My mother accused me with a click of her tongue.

"He is, but he hasn't learned everything."

I moved so I didn't see her face reflect what I already knew she was thinking.

"It means grandson."

Cruz smiled, then darted back to the living room, already bored with the conversation. I prepared her coffee how I knew she liked it and hoped she'd remove her sweater and shoes. Every time she did, she seemed to relax a bit more.

She was seated on my couch, pulling a framed photo of just Cruz and me into her hand.

She smiled warmly, tracing a finger down my face. It took me back to when I'd first had that photo taken. It was black and white, and I was crouched in front of Cruz, smiling up at him while he pinned his forehead to mine.

I watched as her hair shifted in front of her, and I saw that her hair was completely white now. When had that happened? I took in the rest of her, ensuring nothing else had changed. Her dark brown skin, while still impeccable, was starting to show her age. She was getting close to seventy now, and it made my chest ache. My mother was beautiful, but seeing her age felt strange. She still had arched, dark brows that never seemed to need to tweeze or wax, at least for as long as I had ever known her. Her lashes were thick and full, framing her amber eyes that were still just as bright as ever.

She was taller than me, probably closer to five feet seven inches, and she still dressed like she was about to head out on a cruise with her wide-legged cotton pants, simple button-downs that she kept rolled at her elbows, and a silk scarf tied around her slender neck. She was well-toned from her hobby of playing tennis every Tuesday and Thursday with my aunts. I smiled, seeing how she matured with grace and remarkable beauty.

"You're staring, Henrietta."

A shudder nearly had me dropping her coffee. "¡Mamá!"

Her dark brows narrowed as if she knew exactly what she'd just done. "Am I supposed to visit my only daughter's home and call her Renny?" The derision was evident in her tone as she reared back.

"Everyone else has called me that, Mom. My entire life."

She sipped her coffee, glaring at me from over the rim. "Not your whole life. You've picked a new name."

I needed to change the subject. "So, what brings you to town?"

"Perhaps I missed my daughter and wanted to see her." Her thin shoulders lifted as she returned the photo to its place on the side table.

I'd believe her if I didn't know her so well. It was the end of October, and her church was planning some sort of harvest festival. Besides, she had other grandkids besides Cruz; surely, they kept her busy.

"Okay, Mama. I'll let it go for now and get you set up in the office." I stood and walked toward the back of the house, trying not to get annoyed that she'd arrived just when it seemed of all the times, she shouldn't.

> Brick: Did you get my email about the couple interested in Lot 42 in the Hemlock neighborhood?

The text came through while I was grocery shopping for my mother. She'd thankfully agreed to stay home with Cruz. I felt like I needed a moment to clear my head and process the silence from Archer. My gut was in knots over the idea that Thistle had told him about my connection to El Peligro.

I'd texted him several times, but he hadn't replied yet, so I was so annoyed when Brick's text popped in.

Once I was in my car with the groceries loaded, I responded.

> Me: Please direct all emails to Brianna.

My fingers drifted back to Archer's text thread, seeing I'd already messaged him twice. Dammit. I couldn't keep harassing him, but something felt off with my mother's sudden appearance.

> Brick: Wren, I'm not going through Brianna.
> Now, calm down, and let's try again.

My fingers flew.

Me: FUCK OFF.

As I was staring at my phone, a call came through, which had me jumping.

It wasn't Brick, and the area code wasn't even local...I would never typically answer it, but I was too paranoid over what had happened with Saul and my mom showing up.

"Hello?"

There was a pause, and then, "Wren?"

The voice was familiar yet not. I had only heard it periodically from talking with my mom over the years or if she wanted to show me a video and he was in the background speaking. Yet, I knew it was him.

"Juan?"

My heart pounded chaotically in my chest, like a trapped bird in a cage.

"Yeah...it's me. I wanted to—"

I pulled my phone away from my ear and pressed my thumb to end the call.

I was going to throw up.

There were zero chances that I would start speaking to my brother again after almost twenty years, the day after what happened with Saul and now my mom. Something was wrong.

Was Archer in danger?

The number called again, but I ignored it and started toward home.

It was dinner time, and I still hadn't heard back from Archer. My nerves were shot. I refused to ask my mother about my brother's calls. Her loyalties were more than clear. However, I was determined to wear my mom down and figure out why she was here.

She was stirring my son's favorite soup while humming a song to herself when she suddenly stopped.

"You're too thin and pale..."

I folded the clothes before me, resisting the eye roll I wanted to send her. "I'm not pale. It's just almost winter...and I've actually gained weight since you saw me last."

She laughed while tossing a tomato and then a few peppers into the blender. "En las nalgas."

I snapped my head around right as she hit the blend button, drowning out any response I might have.

Cruz came out a second later and hugged my mother's side. Once the blender had finished, he tipped his head back.

"Why do we need salsa, Grandma?"

My mom clicked her tongue. "Salsa goes on everything, Mijo."

"But aren't we having soup?" His little nose scrunched, and I smiled, remembering when I stood in my stepdad's kitchen, asking him question after question until he finally set me on the counter and let me watch him cook.

"We can put salsa in the soup, too, if we want. But I'm going to have your mom make us some chips. How does that sound?"

"I love it when she makes chips."

I knew better than to argue.

"So, Henrietta, mi amor. When are you going to tell me about this boyfriend?"

"Why do you assume I have a boyfriend?" I pulled a handful of corn tortillas from the package, then grabbed a knife and cutting board.

My mom stirred and prepped the salsa while keeping her head down. "The leather property patch on the back of the couch that says you belong to a man named Archer Green."

My hands froze, my pulse hammered, and my eyes scanned the living room. I had left it out.

Shit. Shit. Shittttttttt.

Wait. How did she know it was a property patch? My mother clicked her tongue and reached for the pan she'd gotten out for me. "Warm your oil. You act like you've never done this before."

I grabbed the oil, poured a generous amount into the pan, and then flicked the burner. My mouth was dry, and my voice cracked as I tried to explain. "It's new, but we've been friends for a long time."

"You never said." She moved around me, putting things away. I hadn't talked to her since Archer arrived and we started our friendship.

It wasn't that I didn't want to, but my mind was so preoccupied, and the deep loneliness I usually felt wasn't there.

"He just moved in last month, but we've been around each other almost every day."

I didn't see her face, but I heard her scoff. "He's dangerous, Renny."

Cringing at her nickname for me, I started quartering the pile of tortillas.

"Can you try calling me, Wren? I picked it out; it keeps me safe…"

Her eyes rounded as she gaped at me. "That's literally what I just called you. Renny is Wren, and you're lucky I called you that instead of your given name, Henrietta. You were named after my grandmother, who would roll over twice in her grave at how you've spit on her."

Shaking my head, I continued to slice. "I mean no disrespect, but Renny is a part of Henrietta. Wren is a beautiful bird that can endure and last in tough environments…they're resilient."

My mom's hand was on her hip as she glared at me. "And this name keeps you safe?"

"Yes, it does." However, that wasn't true after Saul had recognized me. My new name didn't do shit for me.

"If safety is so important, why are you willingly driving around with ¿el diablo?"

I leaned in, whisper-yelling back at her in shock, "Really, the devil? Archer is the devil, now?"

My mother's face didn't change; she merely shrugged slightly. I shook my head while slowly adding the chopped tortillas to the pan.

"Do you know what he's a part of? You have no idea why it's so dangerous to be near him."

My stomach flipped around, trying to find purchase, but it was like a fish on land. "What do you know about it, Mama?"

"I know he's been a problem for far too long."

I stirred the frying tortillas so they didn't burn. "What is that supposed to mean?"

With a lowered voice, she murmured, "He uses territory in the city to run guns and pharmaceutical drugs...it's been going on long enough and has been growing that someone needed to intervene."

I had a lump forming in my throat. "Who?"

My mother's lips pursed while turning away from me.

No.

I followed her as she turned away and lowered my voice to a harsh whisper, confirming the fears that had been stirred up last night. "Are you saying my neighbor is running illegal activities through territory that belongs to my...brother?"

My heart felt like it had galloped straight through my chest. This was why she'd come. Somehow, she knew I was in close proximity to Archer...I had no idea how she knew unless I was being followed or he was, and I fell into the report. But why was she even still working with Juan? She'd left my biological father because of this life, but my father had yanked her and my stepdad back into it without a choice. It wasn't until he died that she finally started living freely...but as soon as Juan resumed the role, it was like she happily stepped right back into it.

"It's more complicated than that, Henrietta."

My fingers were shaking from how angry I was. How dare she only come here to keep tabs on me. How dare she use our relationship as a way to communicate something from Juan.

"Did he send you?"

Her silence was deafening, which meant he had.

"He's worried about you now that he's aware of your connection to the problem."

"How come he won't just come himself?" I still refused to think through what it meant that he'd called me or considered it an attempt to reach out. Why now when there'd been nothing for long?

My mother shook her head, flipping her burner and spinning to grab bowls. "Because it's not his decision regarding what happens to you. We both came here to protect you and Cruz."

Fear pierced me like a bullet, shallow and dull.

"What do you mean, whose decision is it?" My mind tugged at her other words that implied my brother had also traveled here.

My mouth was so fucking dry. Anger surged and swirled inside my chest like a hurricane. It slammed against my reasons, my past, and all the hurt I'd filed away where Juan was concerned.

"Cruz, come eat." My mother moved away from me and joined my son at the table. I hadn't even realized she'd finished the chips and ensured everything had been cleaned and put away.

My phone buzzed in my back pocket with a text, so I moved to the laundry room to check it.

> Archer: I'm so sorry. I'm back, at home. Can I come see you?

My fingers moved briskly as my heart continued to pound.

> Me: No. I'll come to you. My mom is over and staying with Cruz.

> Archer: Okay, I'm hopping in the shower, but my door is open. FYI, my men are parked up and down the block, but none of them will bug you.

Tucking my phone back into my pocket, I returned to the kitchen, seeing my mom and Cruz already about to eat. "I uh...I've been waiting for Archer to get in all day, and he just texted me that he's back. I need to ask him about a school email I got regarding Cruz's class."

"You can't just call him?" My mother quizzed, watching me as she scooped soup into a bowl.

"No. I need to see him in person. I might be out for a bit. Do you mind putting Cruz to bed?" I walked up, pressing a kiss to the top of my son's head. My mother's gaze was cold as she watched me.

"I suppose, but we need to talk at some point, Henrietta, and it needs to be tonight."

My answer came in the form of a slight nod. I knew she was right, and deep down, I knew there was a chance I'd even encounter my brother over the next few days if my mother's arrival was anything to go on. I just needed a second to withdraw from the situation and check in with Archer.

He'd been gone all day, and all I wanted to do was ask him if he knew and whether he still loved me. My stomach had been in knots all day. I needed this.

My mother and whatever the hell else was going on there could wait.

Chapter 19

Wren

THE STARS STRETCHED ABOVE ME AS THE CHILLY AIR KISSED MY cheeks. I tucked my sweater tighter over my chest as I walked down my driveway. I thought back to when I'd first arrived in Atlas, and all the years leading up to this moment when my past came to collect.

I conjured up the image of the bird I'd renamed myself after and dug deep for courage. I could do this.

Just because my past had returned, didn't mean I had no future.

If Archer didn't want me, then...I'd survive.

Before I even noticed, I was on Archer's doorstep. Remembering what he'd said, I wrapped my hand around the knob and entered.

The house was dark, save for the track lighting built under the kitchen cabinets that lit up the counters. His living room was shadowed and empty, so I made my way to the stairs, where Archer appeared, holding a towel to his hair. He was shirtless, with a pair of sweats resting low on his narrow hips. I soaked up the way his stacked muscles moved and shifted. The tattoos all along his torso looked like wisps of shadow in the dim lighting.

His smile was what had me practically running up the steps.

Once I was at the top, I threw myself at him. He was ready for me, pulling me into his chest while his mouth found mine. We moved back a few steps while our mouths moved in heated desperation. We were a song ready to be released after weeks of writing and harmonizing. We were ready.

"Where were you?" I finally pulled away, trailing my nails down his chest while his fingers dug into my hair.

"Tracking." Archer's mouth moved down my jaw and neck while his hands cradled my face. I noticed we were moving toward a bedroom.

"Did you sleep somewhere last night?" My voice was practically a whisper as I asked it, slamming my eyes closed as his hands skimmed up my rib cage and under my shirt.

He smirked against my lips. "Where do you think I slept?"

Archer pulled me down the hall, pulling my shirt up as we went.

After a few steps, we were in a large, spacious room with oversized windows and a massive king-size bed. No lamp was on, but he had the shades wide open, so the streetlight bounced inside, providing enough light to see by. He continued to pull me until we were both crawling onto his soft bed.

"I don't know, my mind played a lot of things out. I didn't think you came home because I didn't hear your bike."

His hands were on my chin, digging into my hair as he brought me back for another kiss. I let his tongue sweep inside my mouth, and I allowed him to deepen the kiss until our entire bodies were moving with it; my fingers tangled in his hair, his in mine.

"You didn't text me." I breathed harshly against his lips.

Lowering the straps of my bra, his mouth returned, marking me with open mouth kisses and dragging his teeth along my cleavage. "By the time I stopped riding, I was walking into your house. Because where you are feels like home. I saw you sleeping on the couch and decided to just sleep on the floor below you."

Firm hands held my breasts together while he lowered his mouth, sucking and licking along the expanse of my nipples. My bra was gone, somewhere on the floor, after his hand slipped around my back. My breathing was shallow as I tried to collect my thoughts.

"There's something—" I started, but he pulled me onto his lap, and his erection underneath me felt so good that I nearly moaned, "I need to tell you—"

He was sucking and leaving marks all along my chest, and I was rocking against his cock through his sweats. I had to tell him.

He had to know.

"Archer. I'm—"

His tongue delicately slid along the shell of my ear where he whispered, "Mine."

"Yes."

He pushed me back until I was staring up at him. My hands went to the band of his sweats, where I pushed them down. He helped, so his cock sprung free. The velvet smooth head pushed into my palm as the tip leaked. Archer's hungry glare cut through me as he retreated, pulling my sweats and underwear entirely down my legs. Then he drew his cock into his palm and stroked up and down the massive length before using his other hand to spread my pussy lips apart.

I watched with rapt attention as he harshly spit right along my slit, then used his fingers to rub it into my clit. It was so hot it had my legs clenching together, which he stopped by spreading my thighs apart.

After he spread his blunt fingers down my slick center, his hand landed near my ear. His chest hovered above mine, and ever so slowly, he began inserting the tip of his cock inside me.

"Can I wet it for you first?" I asked, remembering how hot sucking his cock had made me. I ached for that fullness back in my mouth even days later.

"No, you're going to lick it clean once I come inside your pretty cunt, Wren."

Oh god. Archer's hips nestled between mine while my legs came up, caging him. He locked his hand against my hip, adjusting more of his length inside me. My chest rose in anticipation as he placed his other hand under my back and began pulling me up while his knees came underneath him. His biceps flexed as he held my weight as though I weighed nothing at all until I was sliding down along his shaft and straddling his hips. My chest smashed against his, my gaze focused on his hunger as I stared down at him and shifted the smallest bit. His length was long and thick, so the adjusting took a second or two of acute pain.

Once he'd fully sheathed himself, he began kissing me again. My hips slid forward over his cock, and my eyes rolled into the back of my head.

"Fuck."

His hands came to my hips as he pinned me in place. "No, baby, but we're about to."

My eyes flashed open as he pushed into me with a groan, deeper than he'd been. My mouth parted as he adjusted his grip and lifted me so his slick, veiny cock was revealed, and then he slammed me back down onto his shaft.

"Oh my god," I cried out, clinging to his shoulders.

He leaned forward and sucked on my neck, harsh and brutal. "Do I need to remind you that you're mine, Wren? I'm yours. It's not God you'll scream to. It's me. Call my name." A vicious kiss rendered me speechless, and he repeated the process of slowly pulling me up and off his thickness, only to slam me back down.

I cried out each and every time, feeling impossibly full while also unprepared for the way he hit that perfect place inside me each and every time. I'd try to fuck him on my own by rolling my hips, but he'd only click his tongue, chiding me.

"My little slut, so eager for my cock. Didn't I just tell you to call my name?" His mouth was back on me, sucking my nipple into his mouth. He shifted us so I was on my back, and he pulled out of me completely.

"Archer!"

"That's it, beautiful. Now, open your mouth."

He moved us until I was on my back again. He swiftly pulled out of me with a groan. Gripping his cock, he moved on his knees.

"You're going to taste what you do to me."

He held my chin and slid his slick cock into my mouth while kneeling next to me. I took him in, opening and not caring when he hit the back of my throat. He groaned deeply while he pulled my hair with one hand and held my chin with the other.

"So fucking deep for me. You take me so well." He pushed farther into my throat until my eyes watered, and I was gagging around his length. Pulling out, he'd gently push back in and repeat the process, making spit leak out of the sides of my mouth and down my chin.

"That's it. Take all of me, Wren. You look so beautiful when your lips are wrapped around my cock." His length slid out, and he held the base while he traced the tip over my lips.

"Get on your hands and knees, push your face into the mattress, ass up."

I did as he instructed, moving slowly and keeping my gaze on his cock. Before I moved, I took one last suck of his length, moaning around him before he pulled my hair back.

"Do what I said, Wren. I don't want to put any marks on that perfect skin, but I will. We don't have the proper time."

I moved, pushing my face into the soft duvet but to the side so I could breathe while leaving my ass up in the air.

He didn't play with me or spit or do anything but hold my hip with one hand and shove inside me so hard that I cried out. His hand came down in a punishing slap to my ass as he pulled out, then slammed back inside. Suddenly something wet landed against my tight hole while he continued to fuck me ruthlessly. Then, before I could process that he'd spit again, his thumb was pressing into my ass.

"You need both filled, don't you? Such..." He slapped my ass hard on one cheek, then the other. "Filthy, little..." He spit on my asshole again, rubbing harder with his thumb. "Slut."

I screamed as my orgasm ripped through me in a way that had never hit before. Darkness danced behind my eyes, my breathing was shallow, and I didn't notice how hard Archer was slamming into me until he froze, cursing above me.

"Shit, look at that. You're so fucking beautiful."

I could hear his harsh breathing and even more mutterings of appreciation and happiness, but I felt like I was drifting in and out of a fog. Somewhere, I knew I belonged forever, yet I had never once visited.

Archer left to grab a warm rag, but I was still so out of it that I hadn't even realized his arms were around me, and he was holding me in his bed until a few minutes later. His lips gently pressed into my shoulder as he whispered something I couldn't hear.

"I need to tell you something."

Archer stroked my hair, his lips close to my ear.

"Is it about your brother?"

I froze, even as he pulled me closer. His mouth was still close to my ear as he tried again.

"I already know."

I pulled away from him and sat up. "What do you mean you already know?"

Archer's eyes frantically searched my face as he slowly sat beside me.

"This was before our talk about how I couldn't handle things like an MC president..., but something happened recently on one of our routes. The member who came back mentioned El Peligro and what the new leaders were doing... in addition to our conversation in the truck, it made me suspicious. That day I worked on the fence, it was really sunny out...I had to go find sunscreen for the boys. Cruz mentioned you had a beach bag in your closet."

Oh my god.

"You didn't."

He had the decency to look disappointed, even ashamed, but the same feeling slithered through my chest as I pictured him sifting through a box that was so deeply personal to me.

I moved off the bed and started searching for my clothes.

Archer jumped up and moved to stop me. "Wait, I'm sorry, Wren. I know I messed up and should have told you, but I never assumed it would even come up again. I assumed it would just be something I could use to protect you if the time ever came."

The floor was too dark for me to see where my underwear had landed. My shirt was out on the stairs or near it.

"Wren." Archer's tattooed fingers were on my jaw.

I tried to pull away, but he held me.

"Even if I wanted to overlook you invading my privacy, Archer. My issue right now is the fact that you never told me. Did Thistle mention what Saul said to me?" Tears edged into my vision as Archer held me, his own eyes silently begging me to stay with him.

I didn't wait for him to finish because it didn't matter. I'd been waiting all day for this conversation with Archer, and now...it felt like I'd been sucker-punched.

"Saul knew who I was too."

Headlights flashing from the street below lit up the wall, revealing the dread on Archer's face.

"I'm sorry he talked to you. I'm sorry I took you somewhere that he could get to you. I've been beating myself up all day because I can't accept that I was right there, and still, you could have been hurt." His voice cracked.

More headlights beamed through the window.

"I've been worrying all this time that..." I paused as the memory of when he braided my hair came back. "You let me tell you about my brother and never said—"

We shifted, and Archer had me back on the bed, cautious and careful as he settled beside me.

"You never said, Wren. I was the one who had initially asked you about all this, and you lied to me. You lied about your name and your connection. Even when we talked about your brother, you chose not to tell me. So, as much as you're hurt about me finding out, I'm equally hurt that you didn't tell me on your own."

I shook my head, my eyes finding my lap. "See, this is why I don't let people in. You're right, and I can't even argue because I never planned to tell you until Saul mentioned the connection and that you wouldn't want me—"

He tipped my chin so my eyes were on him. "I love you, Wren. I want you. With this, without it, with another lie, or anything else that comes our way. I want you. But for the record, I am sorry. I want you to know you can trust me and that you're safe with me."

"I know I'm safe." That was true. I had never felt safer with anyone than I did with Archer.

"You keep expecting people to give up on you, that if you push them hard enough, they'll stay away for good, and you can just rebuild something new out of all that rubble. I'm not leaving, Wren. You can't push me away. You can't scare me or do anything that would make this too much."

As he talked, I was hiccupping and swiping at my face with the bottom of my shirt. Because it was all I'd ever wanted. Someone to just accept me, defective, mean, bitchy, all of it. Just me. Juan never had. My parents had given up on me until I finally tracked them down and showed them I had changed.

But no one had ever just wanted me exactly how I was.

"How are we supposed to get past the fact that my brother is your enemy?"

Archer's eyes narrowed like he had no idea what I was talking about.

"Why would we need to get past it?"

"Because I'm—"

He slid closer to me until his arms were around me. "Mine. I don't care about your past, Wren. I care that I'm the only one in your future."

A lump formed in my throat.

His hand came up, pulling my hand over his heart and placing his hand over mine. "I belong in there, you in here. Anywhere else we go, whatever we do...it won't matter because of that."

Tears fell from my lashes as hope filled me. I let him pull me into his arms until we lay down and slid under the covers.

Archer had gotten me water, a washcloth, and then pop-tarts.

We sat in his room with the side lamp on and his shades shut while the television played something in the background.

"Did you get anywhere with Kane's custody hearing?" I asked, taking a bite.

The silver wrapper crinkled as Archer swallowed his bite and cleared his throat.

"Really good. I spoke with the judge. We're transitioning into a conditional living situation where I have to check in a ton with them, and allow them to come check on Kane, but it's the next step for us and a good one."

"That's amazing!" I beamed up at him, swiping a crumb from my cheek.

"Thank you. I'm happy about it. Especially after last night, I needed to know he'd be coming home with me."

"When?"

"Next week, but his foster parents are being really cool. Said I could get him as much as I wanted leading up until then. Even the case manager signed off without needing to be the go-between, saying we can transfer when ready."

Archer balled up the remaining wrapper and reached to grab mine before walking to a trash can and tossing it all in.

"It will be nice to return to how things were," I mused softly, leaning back into his pillows. Although I wasn't even sure that would be possible with the strange visit from my mom looming over my head.

Archer came back to bed and gently gripped my thighs, pulling me toward him. "Wren, I need you to understand that because of my role in Mayhem Riot, there might be moments like this that don't feel normal. I don't want that to scare you."

"But what about Kane...and Cruz? This isn't safe for them to be exposed to this sort of danger."

I knew I had said the wrong thing because his face shuddered. Like I'd just slapped him. It took me back to when we just met, and I continued to hurt him by saying the wrong thing.

"I just mean—"

"I know what you mean, and I—" He trailed off, sounding sad and worried. "I haven't worked that out yet. I guess maybe dropping Mayhem Riot or leaving them. I just haven't figured it out yet. I just know I can't give up Kane. I won't give up you or Cruz either."

I stroked his jaw, leaned closer, and pulled his mouth to mine. Archer kissed me back and hauled me down next to him, cradling me in his arms.

"Tell me what happened between you and your brother."

I stared at our joined hands, tracing over Archer's tattoos, trying to go back in time while I kept my emotions at bay. I had done enough crying for one night.

"When Juan was twenty-one, I was sixteen, and I was being especially careless with my life. Which included not going to school, getting caught at street races, and other idiotic things that kept my parents worried at night. Juan would check in and tell me how senseless I was being. At the time, his opinion really mattered to me, so hearing him say he was ashamed of me, was devasting. So, I started to change...I went into a credit recovery program at my school, I stopped smoking and drinking...and I pulled away from El Peligro entirely. I was home every night, missing parties and skipping out on anything my friends did. I was lonely, but I thought my big brother...my hero, would notice and be proud of me. Whenever I tried to tell Juan I was doing better, he was busy or didn't care. I felt like I'd lost his respect, and there was no way to get it back."

My throat suddenly felt too tight to continue. My eyes burned as I tugged at the duvet underneath me. It was soft, gray, and masculine.

"Then months went by, and I was so hurt that I started to feel depressed. I'll never forget the night I overheard my mother crying on the phone to my tía. Juan had taken over the very gang my father started. The one he judged me for being attached to at sixteen. The hypocrisy was more than I could bear."

Archer took my hand and gently held it. "What did you do next?"

I used him as an anchor as I drifted back to the bad memories of a life of fear. "I left. At first, I was just being dramatic. I thought my mom would call or one of my cousins would push Juan to find me. I had been away from El Peligro so long that no one even welcomed me back to their old haunts. But I was too prideful to go back home."

Archer processed it all, then brought my hand to his lips and pressed a kiss to it.

"Your mom...did she come after you or your stepdad?"

Another tiny slice of hurt radiated through my chest as I recalled how easy it was for them to let me go. "They assumed I had just fallen back in with El Peligro and was back on the streets. I hadn't exactly been the model child before that, so I think once I left for good, everyone was just sort of relieved."

Archer squeezed me into him. "I'm sorry, beautiful. That sounds like an extremely lonely journey."

It was. He had no idea. I slept under bridges, in shelters, and worked shitty jobs, saving every penny I got. I made friends and rented rooms from them occasionally, only to always have it blow up in my face. It was always some argument, drugs, or a creepy boyfriend who snuck into my room at night. I was even desperate enough one extremely depressed night to consider prostitution, but I'd walked into a diner instead and asked if they were hiring.

I finally found a rhythm, living in the city, working multiple jobs, and living in the basement of my elderly boss. It wasn't until I heard one of my regulars talk about some tourist town that was like a movie set just outside of New York City. I was dating Cruz's dad at the time, but I was too nervous to tell him my big dream of having a small house in a cute suburban neighborhood. It was only two weeks after that when he was arrested.

"It was," was all I managed to say. I hated going back through my memories. Most of mine were terrible.

Archer tugged his hands through my hair while propping his head up with his fist.

"So your mom is visiting?"

I gave a slight nod, toying with a thread. "She just showed up...it's strange." I glanced up, catching his gaze as he reached for his phone. "My brother called me today, too."

Archer seemed to freeze behind me. "Is that normal?"

Shaking my head, I started to explain, but my phone dinged with a text.

Leaning over, I pulled it off the side table. "It's my mom. She says I need to come back so we can talk."

"I'm coming with you." Archer slid out of bed and started pulling on clothes. I followed suit, tugging my bra on, then my shirt. "It's late... shit, nearly eleven. I'm not sure it's—"

His side drawer opened, and he pulled out a handgun. Pointing it down, he checked the clip and slid it into the back of his jeans. I knew he was in a club that didn't obey the laws of the land, a one percenter club. His patch meant that, but seeing him with a gun was different.

"Archer..."

"Wren, if your brother called you and your mom just showed up, something is wrong. My men are mostly here, in Atlas. The ones who aren't are watching Saul's movements. He's back in Gentry territory, so we can't attack him. All that means is we're not watching our regular routes. I have no idea if we angered the leaders or not."

"Why does everyone keep referencing that? What new leaders?"

Archer stopped gathering supplies while he slid into his leather cut and faced me. "Your brother doesn't lead El Peligro anymore. Two brothers do, as far as I know, and they're ruthless as fuck. If they're after me for some reason, they have targeted you. I'm coming with you to your house."

He held his hand out for me, and I took it. He was right; there was too much going on for what he was saying not to make sense.

Chapter 20

Wren

THE SKY WAS DARKER, AND THE MOON WAS HIDDEN BEHIND DARK clouds. The stars were visible but not nearly bright enough. I'd kept my porch light off, but Archer's hand anchored me as we walked down my driveway and scaled my porch steps.

A chill ran down my spine at how quiet the neighborhood was. "Your men are out here?"

Archer's hand found my lower back. "They are."

I pushed inside the door, holding Archer's hand, and tried to brush the feeling off. The soft lighting in my living room filtered into the foyer, where I slid my shoes off, but Archer didn't. In fact, he was completely frozen as his gaze went over my shoulder.

I turned to see what he was staring at and tried to calm my breathing.

My mother sat on one of my couches, her hands folded across her chest and an angry scowl on her face. On the other couch, twisting at the waist to see me, was my brother.

A gasp of surprise cut into my voice as I greeted him. "Juan?"

His eyes grew as he looked me over, and then a smile. A genuine one. "Henrietta."

Archer's gaze never left Juan's. Even as my real name was spoken out loud, and I'd never even told him. Regardless that he insinuated he knew, I still had never shared it.

"It's Wren now."

Juan merely dipped his face, nodding. "Heard that, actually, but figured the first time we spoke in almost twenty years, I'd use your real name."

My gaze flitted over his form, trying to pick at who he was and compare it to who he seemed to be now. He appeared older yet looked almost the same as I remembered him. He had the same defined jaw, a narrow nose, and the same dark brows that arched nicely over his amber-brown eyes. A few lines appeared near his eyes and near his mouth. Smile lines. Which led me to believe my brother led a happy life. He had the same black hair but with a few streaks of gray styled so it fell back from his face, just a tiny piece touching his brow. He was as tall as Archer but not as broad. Juan had a narrow frame, and everything about him seemed as it was nearly twenty years ago when I last saw him, all except the gold wedding band around his left ring finger.

He stood slowly as if he didn't want to scare me off. Archer took up residence behind me, like a guard on duty. I was grateful that my mother had been here for my son to put him to bed, especially with how late I had come in; guilt still tugged at my belly, making me feel like I'd done something wrong by leaving.

"What are you—" I started, but he dipped his head, shoving his hands into his pockets. He wore tan cigar pants with a thin, long-sleeved knit shirt. The gray hue made his dark hair pop against his brown skin in the low lighting of my living room.

"Been a long time." He cut me off.

As I stared at him, my eyes watered, and I processed how much time had passed. How he'd been a part of so much of my childhood, and then when my mother took him with her, he wasn't. They'd left me behind, and I'd never even explained how much that hurt.

Examining his face, I tried again and skipped over whatever pleasantries he wanted to share. "What are you doing here?"

His eyes flicked to Archer, then me. "Right to it then. Okay."

My mother muttered something in Spanish, and at that moment, I wanted to stop everything and introduce Archer. I wanted to tell them that I had a boyfriend and was happy and in love, but I knew my family wouldn't be excited for me—not if our families had been at war for twenty years.

Archer shifted so he stood next to me, then wrapped his hand around mine.

Juan caught the movement and glared over my shoulder. "I'm here to deliver a warning. One I hope you both heed because as much as I have tried to fix things, it's officially out of my hands."

I glanced up at Archer, but his jaw was tense, and his gaze was locked on Juan.

My brother continued, "Over the past month or so, there has been a change in leadership within El Peligro. The new leaders are not only young but ruthless. Archer, I'm sure you've noticed a few warnings being issued to your men."

I saw Archer nod out of the corner of my eye, but he was tense, too, like he was ready to run at Juan at any second.

My brother toyed with a string on his slacks before continuing. "I was made aware of a plan they have to take you out. Since you're seeing my sister, I came here to remove her from the situation. You need to stop seeing each other."

My mother scoffed, adding, "Should have never started to begin with."

Take him out. What did that mean? My heart raced at my brother's words; he was already talking again before I could respond.

"Renny, you either come home and allow Archer to remain here, or Archer, you need to go back to where your club is. Leave my sister and nephew alone."

"Neither of those options are happening." Archer's voice was calm but deadly.

My mother muttered something about me being irresponsible, and I shot her a scowl.

Juan watched Archer, steady and solemn. Both of them looked like they were two seconds from pulling weapons on each other.

Archer gave in first, asking, "Want to clue me in on why this is happening with the new leadership? I don't understand what changed."

Juan's jaw tensed before his eyes found the floor. It was a move he kept making, and it seemed so strange compared to the person he used to be. My brother used to stare people in the eye until they backed down. He'd never lower his head in shame like this. It made me want to press pause on all this and pull him away, asking what the hell was going on with him.

"We've been at war with each other since my father ran things. He always wanted the territory west of Manhattan. Ten years ago, it came into our possession through a game of cards, but your club never recognized the change of ownership. At the time, I was running things, and because I was pushing to improve the route, and what you were pushing wasn't damaging the neighborhoods, I didn't care that you kept it."

Archer shifted next to me. "Pardon my language, but what the fuck are you talking about? Ten years ago, I was president. I would have known about such a game and something as big as territory shifting."

Juan's head tilted. "I didn't play for it. Looks like you didn't either."

"No one in my club would have been authorized to make a decision that big, although it sounds like someone on your end was given that freedom on behalf of El Peligro."

My brother's mouth curled into a smile. "Several years back, a player came onto the scene. Most mob bosses on the Upper East Side dealt with him, but you might have heard of him. They called him The Joker. He reset the scene, took territories, and essentially wiped the board clean of players. He participated for me."

Archer squeezed my hand. "And what proof do you have that my club was involved?"

"Just the word of that man," Juan lazily drawled, stroking his jaw.

I watched his body language, seeing the differences in all the years we'd been apart. I knew how his fingers drummed against his thigh that he was itching to grab a throwing knife. I knew he likely had at least two on him right now. In turn, he might be watching my movements, and while I hadn't thrown a knife in years, muscle memory had my fingers flexing.

My father taught him, but he also instructed me. While Juan was with my mother in Mexico, I was with my aunt and my uncle, training, learning, and listening.

"Regardless. The territory has been ours, but we didn't enforce it. New leaders feel differently."

"What changed?" I asked, trying to piece together what was going on. But I wanted a bigger picture. I wanted a detailed list of what he'd done over the past nineteen years. I needed more than these tiny crumbs he was giving me.

The smallest wince crept into Juan's expression. I probably would have missed it if I hadn't been studying him so intensely. "While I ran it, I wasn't focused on making money. I merely wanted to help people."

"How very Robin Hood of you," Archer joked with a scoff.

My brother flipped him off. "Think what you want, but it was helping. We were changing things."

"But then why—"

Juan shook his head. "I can't tell you everything you want to know right now, Renny. I wish I could. I'd tell you why I let go of our father's legacy, but it would take too much time. Right now, I need you to leave and I need you to understand that for the foreseeable future, you can't be with him."

"How will us breaking up stop a war?" Archer's fingers stroked the inside of my hand.

"It won't," Juan said, adding, "I just don't want my sister or nephew here when the war starts. I know you're about to get custody of your kid brother. It might make more sense for you to stay and have Wren leave. But let me be clear." His gaze was deadly as he stared Archer down. "You are not staying together. It's no longer safe for my sister to be near you or your club."

Juan glanced over his shoulder at our mother, giving her a soft smile before addressing Archer again. "I'd invite you to meet my mother, but she's far less pleasant than me."

My mother stood up and walked over to us.

"Let me meet him." Her shrewd eyes took him in, drank him up, and I saw the flicker of something like admiration there.

I had expected her to spew horrible things at Archer, but suddenly, he let my hand go and stuck it out for her.

"It's nice to meet you. I'm Archer Green, and I'm in love with your daughter and care for your grandson like he's mine. I sincerely hope you understand when I tell you I won't be going anywhere, and if Wren leaves, I will follow."

My mother's lips pursed. "You love her?"

"I love them both," Archer clarified, and my heart felt like it had swooped into my belly. Her eyes seemed to stay on Archer's, and then she swung her head over to look at Juan.

"Fui terrible con Taylor al principio".

Juan's eyes flickered as if he was going back to what my mother had said about how she'd been terrible to his wife at the beginning of their relationship. A wife I had never met, a daughter he'd adopted that I had never seen. He smiled and nodded.

"You were pretty terrible to her in the beginning."

My mom gently took Archer's hand in hers. "I misunderstood and don't wish to do that again."

Archer's eyes watered the slightest bit as my mother's face lifted, and a smile curved her lips.

"I am Anna. It's lovely to meet you." Then she hugged him.

My mother hugged my boyfriend, the man I loved and had just been told to break up with. Archer hugged her back, and my brother sighed like this frustrated him.

"Mama, you can't hug him. We just threatened him."

"Then unthreaten him," my mother said, untangling herself from Archer's hold.

I decided to be bold, and I stepped closer to my brother. One step. Another.

I was directly in front of him, and I could see more wrinkles. He was forty now, and seeing the change up close broke my heart.

"We've been apart for almost twenty years, Juan." Tears gathered in my eyes, and I saw them also start to cloud my brother's.

His voice was thick with emotion when he said, "You didn't stick around long enough to hear that I was changing everything. We turned El Peligro into something good. It helps the community. People get excited when they see us in the streets. We protect people...we—" His voice trailed off as emotion clogged his throat.

"We did...at least. I made it something I could be proud of."

I wrapped my arms around my brother's waist and hugged him as tightly as possible. His scent hit me, taking me back to being sixteen and getting my last hug from him. To when I would sneak into his room, looking for cigarettes. Even further back when I wanted to see if he'd stolen my Barbie or had a spare GI Joe that I could use as one of my Ken dolls. I didn't dare go back to when he'd braid my hair and play with me like I was his favorite person.

He hugged me back, and I heard my mother sniff, and then Juan pulled away.

"You need to listen to me, Henrietta. I have tried to stop them. I have done all that I can do, but a war is on its way. You need to be as far away from him as possible. If he really loves you, he knows I'm right. You and Cruz need to leave with us and go back to North Carolina, so you remain safe."

Archer cleared his throat, and I felt his hand find mine, lightly tugging me back. But I had to ask because I was so confused.

"Juan, who's leading El Peligro now, and wh—"

A clicking sound started near the front door, making me stop mid-sentence. All of us turned toward the sound, and I watched in horror as my deadbolt slid back and the knob turned.

Archer shifted in front of me, pulling me behind him right as my mother ran around me into Cruz's bedroom. My heart was in my throat as I tried to process what was happening, but it was all too fast.

"Fuck." My brother spat, running his hand through his hair while he took a position to stand in front of Archer, and a mere two seconds later, I realized why.

My front door opened, and a younger version of my brother stepped inside.

No.

Two near-identical versions of my brother stepped inside my house, smiling as if they'd found something extremely amusing.

"Hola Daddio." One of them gave Juan a nod while swinging his focus to Archer. He was taller than my brother but years younger. He looked young, maybe eighteen or in his early twenties. His dark hair was thick and swept back, similar to my brother's. His skin was lighter, though, and his eyes were blue, which he must have gotten from his mother, or so I assumed. He wore a black hoodie over black jeans and thick boots.

The second twin stepped in, somber and seemingly more serious. His attire was identical to his twin's, but his hair was shaved closer on the sides and left longer on top. His eyes were amber like his father's, and like mine, and his skin was more tan than brown. But what set him apart other than his hair and eyes was the scar that ran through his left eyebrow. The way he watched us and surveyed the room gave off a sinister feeling.

Fear slithered into my stomach, deep down grabbing hold of old memories and tossing them around in my chest like shrapnel. These boys had the same look in their eyes that my father used to get. These boys were the leaders. While they hadn't said it, I knew it in my bones. My brother couldn't control them...and they were his sons.

This was bad.

Juan's jaw flexed as ten men filtered into my house behind my nephews. Finally, there was silence once the door was shut until Juan spoke up.

"I told you to give me tonight."

The one with blue eyes clicked his tongue. "Father, you should know that we don't bend to demands, even when they come from you. We know you have a soft spot for our aunt." His eyes flicked over to me quickly, then back to his father. "Whereas we do not, seeing as we've never met her."

Archer started laughing, making my head snap over to him. "These are the new leaders of El Peligro? Your sons. These are the ones you can't control?"

The twin with blue eyes seemed amused and took a step forward. "Tía, you may want to slide to the side if you don't want to get blood on your face. By the way, I'm Giovanni. You can call me Gio. It's nice to finally meet you. My mother will be happy to hear that you're well. She's requested we keep you that way."

Archer produced a gun, and in the blink of an eye, it was pointed at my nephew's head.

"My men will be here in thirty seconds if I don't check in with them. I suggest you leave before this turns into a blood bath."

Gio smiled while the other twin looked like he'd found a complication with a furrow to his dark brows.

Juan stepped forward. "Kingston, Gio. This is your family; you're crossing a line. Let me get her and her son to safety before you start this."

Kingston was his other son, the serious one.

They didn't look at their father; they continued to watch Archer, waiting to see what he would do.

"Your men are dead," Gio finally confessed, letting out a tired sigh.

Archer froze, and I knew his breathing had stopped.

Kingston slid his hands into his pockets, and I watched as Juan's gaze slid down, his jaw tensing.

"Don't," he warned Kingston.

The serious twin finally spoke, tilting his head. "He is not a part of our family."

It was as if, on cue, one of his men walked out of my bedroom, holding my property patch.

Gio moved to the left and clapped his hands together softly. "Well, well. Looks like maybe Archer is a part of our family."

"Brother, should we give him a chance to explain why he's still using our territory and recently stole from us?"

"I have never stolen from you," Archer spat, his breathing ragged, "and as I told your father, I was unaware of any territory shift."

Kingston's gaze slid to my brother, and I saw Juan nod. "It's true."

"Who brokered it?" Gio asked, holding my property patch and inspecting all the patches.

"Kyle," Juan answered.

Kingston froze, his eyes swinging back to his father too quickly for me not to notice that whoever this Kyle person was, mattered in some significant way.

"You know damn well I have more men than who was patrolling here. This is going to be a blood bath. Get her and Cruz the fuck out of here!" Archer yelled, raising his gun, surrendering.

My heart dropped. It was like watching a powerful storm bow down to a tiny current of wind.

"Please, just get them out."

I tugged on his arm. "Archer, I'm not leaving without you." But my mind raced to Cruz. Would they do this, really do this, knowing he was here?

The sound of a lighter clicking had my head swinging over. Gio held my property patch in one hand, and under it, he held a silver zippo lighter.

"No!" Archer's voice cracked, and then something inside me snapped. I wasn't going to lose him. I couldn't.

Gio smiled. "Not family anymore." The leather caught fire, and I screamed while lunging toward my nephew. Juan caught me at the waist right as the back sliding door burst open. Glass flew everywhere as I ducked down, and Juan's hands came over my head, protecting me. Gunshots rang out, making the couch and chair explode with fabric and cotton. My kitchen table was suddenly flipped over by someone and used as a shield. I crawled to my son's room, glass and debris under my palms and knees as I went. Then, it all stopped in an instant as Archer started screaming.

"Stop. Stop."

Juan was yelling, too. My brother and Archer stood in the middle of the room with arms stretched out, their panic-stricken gazes landing on all the chaos in the room.

Tears streaked my cheeks as I looked up and saw men in Mayhem Riot cuts with guns raised, pointed at my nephews and the men with them. Kingston and Gio had guns extended toward them.

It was silent for two seconds without anyone shooting when all of a sudden, I heard the smallest crack of a door, and out walked my mother, holding Cruz to her chest.

He was crying, and so was she. My chest pinched with something tight, a coil of fear wrapping around my lungs and squeezing as I watched my son helplessly. Everything I had tried to protect him from just exploded in one night all over our living room floor. My mother soothed his back, and a sob escaped my mouth.

Archer had tears in his eyes as he lowered to the ground, sitting on his knees with me.

"Please, let them leave." He cried, and it shattered something deeper in me.

"Kingston. Giovanni," My mother snapped, and I saw both of my nephews pale, lowering their guns immediately.

"Abuela," Gio whispered.

My leather cut was on the floor somewhere. I had no idea if it was still burning.

"Why is she here?" Kingston snapped.

"Trajiste la muerte aquí."

"Grandma, we—"

My mother's body was shaking. "You disgrace your mother, your sister, and your entire family."

Their heads bowed.

"You will leave this instant. You will not return here. Whatever debt you have with this man will be settled outside this neighborhood. Away from families."

I screamed at my brother, at my nephews, "What the fuck kind of monsters did you breed?"

I ambled to my feet, stepping on glass, moving to my mother, taking Cruz from her, and then I took several steps behind Archer's men, knowing I was safest with them. They moved forward, I knew they were trying to get their president behind their line of fire, but if they did, it would cause another gunfight.

"We're leaving," Juan said, placing his hands on his son's shoulders and pulling them aside.

Kingston's eyes shuttered as he looked at my son who'd raised his head, staring right at them.

"Who are they?"

I pat his back, glaring directly at my nephews. "They're no one."

Juan's head snapped back, staring at me, and something like a knife slid through my sternum. This hurt. All of it. I wanted to go back and find out what had happened. My brother was always a good man, until he'd taken over my father's gang. But why had his sons chosen this if he was telling the truth about turning El Peligro around? What happened to them to cause such darkness?

Both of my brother's sons walked with him, their men exiting as if they'd never been here to begin with.

Archer's club remained in place, their guns up. My mother turned toward me, tears in her eyes.

"I'm so sorry."

Archer was there, pulling her into a hug. His eyes were red as he stared at me with my mother tucked under his chin.

It wasn't her fault, and it wasn't Juan's, either. I didn't know who to blame; I just felt angry and scared.

"We need to go." Archer finally released my mother, then slid his gun into the back waist of his jeans. "You need to pack bags for both of you."

I moved on frozen feet.

"I will help pack Cruz's," my mother offered, moving to his bedroom.

I handed my son back to her so he could tell her what to pack. He was particular about what toys and blankets he took. Thistle was in the room with us, which I hadn't really processed, and moved with my mother, so they had someone with them in the room while they packed.

He gave my arm a gentle squeeze before striding after them.

Tucking some of my hair back, I turned toward the hall where Gio had held my property patch and found Archer crouched down, gently cradling it.

That pain came back, slicing through me. My feet moved over the carpet, and a few pieces of glass were in my way, so I tiptoed as best I could until I was next to Archer.

The bottom of my leather cut was singed and melted, but it hadn't gotten so far that the entire thing was ruined. There was a burn mark on the back where Archer's name was, interrupting the c and h in his name.

I stroked over his neck and bent down next to him, pulling it from his hands. "Still mine."

His red eyes shuttered as his head lifted.

I gripped his hand and pulled him until he followed me to my room. I knew his men would be directly outside the door and likely outside our window, but I just needed to have him alone for a few stray seconds.

The door closed behind us, and I carefully set my property patch on the bed.

"Talk to me, Archer." I went to my closet and pulled down a duffel bag.

He sat down on my bed and placed his head in his hands.

"I can't—" he started, but then he coughed, and I realized it was a sob, and he was falling apart. Shifting away from the closet, I went to him, bending on my knees until I was directly in front of him. I stroked his hair and kissed along his jaw.

"We're okay." I kissed the shell of his ear and pushed the stray strands of hair back before moving to the next ear. "We're going to make it. All of us."

His hands moved to my face, pulling me in for a kiss. His mouth moved over mine, hungry and desperate. His tongue slid into my mouth, and then he pulled me up and carried me into my bathroom.

He shut the door and turned on the shower. We stripped hastily, our mouths returning to one another in a rapid desperation. My fingers were at his neck, tugging on his hair. His hands were in mine, stroking and pulling while we ambled into the shower.

We stood under the hot spray while he continued to kiss me. Then, once he finally broke away, he rasped low and guttural against my ear.

"Turn around and place your hands against the tile."

Chapter 21

Archer

I needed her.

This was pain and agony all wrapped around the danger that made up my life. It beat like a drum in my chest and ached in my pulse as a reminder that happiness was always a thread ready to snap.

I didn't get happy endings. Joy wasn't going to be a part of my life.

Memories of when my mother died thrummed in my chest, a reminder that injustice happened every day. Seeing Kane being taken by strangers ricocheted like a bullet slamming into me. Seeing him through a piece of glass when he'd been in the state's custody. Witnessing the death report for Brit, his mother, knowing he'd grow up never knowing the love of either parent.

Fuck, I was so tired of the bad...then Wren happened, and she was sunlight.

She was good.

The only thing I'd ever hoped to have, that actually became mine, and now they were going to take her from me. My heart wouldn't withstand it. I couldn't exist in a world that she wasn't in. Would Saul cut her brakes next? Would he do something to Cruz?

"Turn around. Place your hands on the tiles." Had I already told her that? I blinked, seeing the water drip down her back, her long thick hair soaked and dipping into a v right above her perky, round ass. Fuck, she was perfect.

My cock twitched, which had me wrapping my fist around it, stroking while Wren peeked over her shoulder at me. Her lip was pressed between her teeth, her thick lashes lowered as her eyes trailed down to where my wrist slowly moved.

I stepped forward, wrapped my arm around her, and placed my hand against her stomach. Lifting her the slightest bit, I lined up my erection while I rasped against her ear.

"Breathe, beautiful. I'm not going to be gentle."

I felt her back arch into my chest, and I slid the tip of my cock into her tight cunt. I lightly kicked at her leg to make her stance wider while sliding further into her heat. She moaned while her hand came back, holding my wrist.

I pulled out and, with a sharp inhale, pushed back in, in a heavy thrust. She was so tight that I had to stand there for a second to calm down and not come on the spot. After adjusting, I grumbled closer to her ear while pushing her chest against the tile, "You're mine. No one is taking you from me."

Her tits were smashed while I fucked her. My hand was flat against her lower belly while I slid in and out of her, creating a chaotic rhythm. On her tiptoes, she used one of her hands to dig her nails into the tile while the other squeezed my wrist.

"Archer," she said in a rush, her mouth agape as I continued to pump in and out of her.

I lifted the hand from her stomach up to her neck and added the slightest amount of pressure while my hips pushed forward at a rapid pace, making her ass bounce. The sight only spurred me on as I held her body against mine.

One of her hands came to mine, and she guided my fingers over her clit.

I rubbed her, sliding my fingers through her heat; my cock swelled inside her as a tingling in my lower back started, and my balls began aching. She was gasping, breathing hard as a moan erupted from her, echoing around the shower. The water slid over our bodies, making us slick as we slid against each other, and then I burst, groaning into her shoulder while I came hard, spilling inside her.

There were so many words tangled in my head. There were so many fears and worries, but the only thing I could manage to get out was something she already knew.

"I love you."

I released her neck and pulled her into my chest. I slid out of her and let the water rush over us. Her arms came up, cradling mine as she repeated her own vow of love for me. I had to figure out a way to get out of this mess. I needed to go back to my club, talk to Thistle, and tell him we needed to dig into what happened ten years ago.

I needed to ask Juan about this guy, Kyle, who had been in that game.

The image of the guns, the glass..., and all of the fear in my chest when Anna walked out holding Cruz came back in a painful flash. They had to remain safe. I needed them to be okay. Kane too.

"Talk to me, baby." Wren's lips pressed into my chest over a few of my tattoos.

She didn't understand how I felt for her. Not really. I'd said I loved her, but she didn't understand how deep she'd dug inside me. If I lost her, I'd lose myself.

"Need you to be okay," I managed to rasp while stroking along her sides and up her back. We stood naked under the spray, wasting time we didn't have. I knew we needed to go. The back door was shattered; the house was getting cold. Cruz was scared.

I shut the water off and let out a silent breath.

Wren's amber eyes pinned me in place as I ran a hand through my hair, letting the drops of water flick against the shower door.

Her arms came up, crossing and shoving her tits up. "I'm not leaving you."

She knew deep down what was about to happen. Even if I didn't tell her, she knew.

My fingers tangled in her hair as my forehead rested against hers. "I can't breathe knowing you might be in danger. I can't think. I can't focus. I—"

How did I explain this to her? I'd never felt this way about anyone. This fear consumed me, and if there was even a chance that she was in danger, I couldn't do what needed to be done.

"Please, Wren. My love, I beg you." I pressed a gentle kiss to her jaw and then her lips. "I need you to go with your brother and your mom...I need you to get away from here."

Tears lined her eyes as her lip trembled.

"I'm going tonight to get Kane; I know Sarah will let me take him. I need you to take him with you. My gut says my father is linked to all of this somehow. I think he plans to try and take or leverage him somehow. I don't know, but I need to figure it out, and I need you three safe while I do it."

"But you—"

I leaned back and kissed her forehead. "I will meet you there and the rest of your family."

Her voice shuddered, "Archer, I can't lose you."

"You won't." That felt like a lie. She nearly lost me tonight. There was no way I should be saying this to her, but I had to do whatever it took to get her out of here.

Her voice was thick as if she were on the verge of tears. "Promise me. We just started our story, we can't--" Her voice cracked before she cleared it. "Say something that lets me know that this isn't our ending."

She was a vision, standing wet and naked in front of me. I smiled, tracing a drop of water that trailed down her breast and over her nipple.

These were thoughts I'd had but never spoke. Things I'd thought I'd keep in a journal or locked up in my head where my dreams remained.

Smiling against her cheek, I whispered in her ear.

"The first time I saw you, I thought you were more beautiful than any sunrise I'd ever witnessed. Then you walked up to me like you owned the dirt under our feet, and something happened in my chest as I realized I wouldn't mind if you did and that perhaps one day you'd own everything in me, too. Your eyes are the color of the sun trapped in honey, and every time you look at me, my breath stalls. Your skin is the softest thing I've ever felt, and after our first touch, I knew I would be ruined forever. Your heart slid into mine, shoving my organs aside and making room where I was sure there wasn't any, and now, all I can think of is making sure you stay there for good."

My lips stopped moving right as her hands wrapped around my neck urgently. Fevered.

"Please come back to me."

I traced the shell of her ear, feeling that same urgency in my own movements.

"Darling, it'll be as though I never left, and you should know by now that not even death will separate us."

I ignored the tears rolling down her face and turned to grab us towels.

Wren's mother went with her; Juan hadn't shown up. They got into her car, the two of them, with Cruz in the back, and drove over to the city's east side. I followed them on my bike and ensured Thistle and my men watched over the side roads so we weren't followed.

Sarah, Kane's foster mom, had agreed that I could take him, even at this late hour. I told her I had some urgent business that would take me out of town and that I didn't want to miss my date to get him. She packed his things for me and had him ready to go. Sleepy but happy, I grabbed my little brother and pulled him into my arms, holding him tight.

Then, under the cover of darkness, I walked him to Wren's car and buckled him in.

"Kane, I need you to be brave for me, okay?"

His blue eyes searched mine as if he understood how serious this was. I knew he would, and I knew he'd adapt to this change, just like he had to being in foster care, and now removed from it. My chest ached with all the change he'd been forced to go through and how unfair it was that he just kept being expected to deal with the hand he was dealt.

"Wren and Cruz are going to visit some of their family, and I wanted you to go because—" The words caught in my throat because I was still so scared about the possibility of losing him.

Cruz took over, reaching over to grab Kane's hand. "We're going to be a family. You get to live with Archer, and he loves my mom. We're going to be brothers."

Kane's eyes slid back over to me. "But Archer is my brother. Unless can you be my dad instead?"

I caught Wren's smile in the mirror, which had mine stretching while a few tears tugged at my eyes. I pulled him into a hug. "I'll be whatever you need, buddy, as long as you're mine. Okay?"

His little hands wrapped around my neck, and I inhaled deeply, knowing I needed to let them go. But it was so painful.

I buckled him, closed his door, and moved to Wren's door.

Her smile was encouraging. I dipped to kiss her, and then she hugged me.

"If something happens, he'll be with me, Archer. I'll have Juan forge the papers. Whatever it takes, I'll raise him. Okay. Don't worry about us. We'll be safe."

I nodded, but words wouldn't come. "I love you."

Thistle was next to me, and I knew he was silently telling me we needed to move. I let her go and stepped back.

"We'll have six of our best follow them and stay out of sight until we know she's safe in their territory."

Dipping my head in thanks, I turned away, shutting my eyes. I heard the gravel crunch under her tires as she drove away from me.

The reality that my club was at war still hadn't settled in, not entirely, until I arrived in the city and found that our club had been completely destroyed. I walked through the shattered glass and found all the pictures on our walls smashed, our pool tables tore up, our liquor bottles emptied.

My men were somber and angry. They were really fucking angry.

"How are we supposed to respond to this?" Dozer kicked at an upturned chair.

Buck was there, pulling up a table, and replied, "We fight."

Yeah, but their operation was much bigger and far more lethal than ours. They had been planning this and preparing. They surely would have the numbers on their side. I could get a few allies in my back pocket to be on the safe side, but our club was far from any other clubs that might be an option. The only ones on my mind were those I had considered double-crossing just last month after Simon Stone's funeral.

I didn't doubt that Killian Quinn wouldn't want to solidify a stronger alliance by backing me up, but their club was too fragile and had gone through too much recently.

"We need to be smart about it. El Peligro's previous leader said something happened where our territory became theirs, and we've been essentially stealing from them ever since. I need to know what happened and with who."

Thistle glanced over. "We can get, Ruth."

She helped us with hacking skills when we needed them. She was an unofficial member of Mayhem Riot, but only when it suited her.

"Do it."

Thistle pulled his phone to his ear while I looked at my captains.

"Call a disaster repair crew, have them come and get this place fixed up, and send a crew to Wren's place, too."

Their cells were out, huddling together while a few other members started brushing glass and picking up pictures.

I had to find out what the hell happened before we were at war because something told me we wouldn't survive it.

"It was offsite; there were no cameras." Ruth spun in her chair, facing us, while she fixed the blue-light glasses on her face.

"You're sure?"

Thistle shifted nervously. Ruth had always made him act like a kid in middle school, and I didn't think it was because she didn't seem to have a single thing on this earth that scared her. No, I had a feeling it had something to do with the fact that she looked like a model, and when she set her sights on him, she acted like he was the only one in the room.

"There are cameras showing who walked into the building. That's as close as I can get, but there's none set up anywhere in the room at all."

I was still impressed that she was able to dig all the way back into digital files from ten years ago; I would punch a gift horse in the mouth by complaining that we didn't have enough information.

"Can you pull that up?"

Ruth spun back around and started typing. I took the opportunity to pull up my phone and check in with Buck.

Any movement?

Buck texted back immediately.

Buck: We're watching, but not so much as a drive-by.

They'd rigged the club to look like we were all inside. We paid extra for the disaster crew to come out, same day and board up what they didn't have on hand glass wise. There were lights on inside, and we'd even set the television back up so that it played and could be seen through one of the boarded windows. Their bikes were parked in front, but my men were scattered along rooftops and streets, watching for El Peligro. They were ordered to shoot on sight, and until I figured out what the hell had happened, I planned to keep that order, even if it meant Wren lost her brother and nephews.

"Okay, we'll have to play it at two times the speed; otherwise, it will take forever. The players all arrived at staggered times. It doesn't seem like there was any set period for them all to arrive."

Shit, it was going to be difficult to narrow them down.

Thistle slid into a chair farthest away from Ruth while glancing at her from the side of his eye. She wore blue light glasses that were cherry red, which seemed to complement her beautiful Black skin. She kept making an exaggerated show of pulling her sucker in and out of her mouth while glancing over at my VP. I covered my mouth, hiding a laugh as Thistle shifted in his chair, but I saw his eyes trailing over her tight braids that went down to her waist. It was the same way he watched her every other time we'd been here.

"I won't bite, Thistle. Not with an audience at least." She winked over my head at my friend. I shook my head, ignoring them while I leaned forward to view the screen.

It was black-and-white footage, a little grainy, but I could make out the one-story brick building that boasted Gusto's Bar. Based on the clientele entering, it seemed to be a front for street fights.

"Was there a fight booked on this night?" I asked, and Ruth started clicking away on her keyboard, looking at a different monitor.

"No."

So, why so many people? Dozens started at six in the evening and continued until ten. I had no idea what this Kyle person looked like, but I'd know if one of my men showed up, and that was all I was looking for at the moment.

Thistle cleared his throat as if he were gearing up for the courage to ask Ruth something. "Could we do a search on The Joker and cross-reference it with the name Kyle?"

Ruth paused, peering over her shoulder. With a smile and pursing her lips like she was blowing him a kiss, she said, "Anything for you."

I couldn't smother my laugh this time because Thistle turned bright red.

She clicked away on her computer as I watched the people enter the establishment on the video feed. There was no one wearing our patches, no one at all. Who the fuck had he talked to?

Ruth didn't look over at us as she read from her screen. "The Joker popped up a few times in different redacted reports. There was one person...looks like he used to be with the FBI, he got messy. Seemed obsessed with this guy and had a few notes in there that have the first name, Kyle, but the last is redacted as well. I can't seem to find a clear shot anywhere, but give me a few more minutes."

I had a feeling it wasn't going to make a difference.

"I need to talk with Juan," I told my second in command, but I knew Ruth heard it. I had no idea if she knew who I was talking about, but she'd earned my trust years ago when she started working with us. I didn't have secrets because she'd just dig them up anyway.

"I can get you his number," Ruth said, clicking away on her keyboard, which lit up with a variety of colors every time she tapped.

My eyebrow rose. "Really? The last name is Hernandez based on a few reports we gathered over the years, but at birth, it may have been Vasquez."

She clicked around, and I just kept adding to her information pile.

"Mother is Anna. Father would have been Manual Vasquez. Sister Henrietta."

What else was there?

"Location, North Carolina...wife, no idea. Kids...Kingston and—"

"Got it." Ruth interrupted me and then spun around with a piece of paper in her hand with a number written on it.

Thistle let out what sounded like a dreamy sigh.

Fuck, the guy was gone for her, and he was too chicken shit to admit it. I stood up, gently squeezed Ruth's shoulder, and walked off, leaving my second-in-command to deal with his crush and pay her.

Dialing this number could go one of two ways...but either really couldn't be worse than what had already happened.

I punched in the number and let it ring.

On the third ring, he answered.

"Bueno?"

I paused, curious at his cheery tone.

"Juan, it's Archer Green." I waited a second to see if he'd hang up, and when he didn't, I continued, "I need to talk to you."

There was some shuffling on his end. "Where are you?"

A dark city greeted me as I walked to one of Ruth's windows in her apartment. "I'm in the city."

"Good. She left?"

I knew he meant Wren, but admitting I'd let her go still hurt. "Yes, with your mother and Cruz."

Juan paused again. "And your brother."

He must have eyes on them right now. My stomach flipped. "Are they safe?"

"Of course," he replied easily, but I wasn't buying it.

"Even my brother?"

Juan let out a sigh. "I would never hurt an innocent kid, Archer."

"No, but your kids would."

That made him go quiet for so long that I thought he might hang up.

"My sons aren't perfect...there was an incident that sort of transformed them both...they weren't always like this."

Didn't give a flying fuck how they used to be.

"Don't care. I need to meet with this Kyle person; you called him The Joker. How would I go about talking to him?"

There was more shuffling in the background.

"How do you know it's not a trap, you agreeing to come meet us... what makes you assume I just won't let my boys kill you?"

I had no assurances whatsoever, but it wouldn't make a difference at this point. I had to try for the sake of Wren.

"I plan to ask your sister to marry me. I plan to have a child with her. I plan to buy your mother earrings for Christmas next year. I plan to meet whoever else is over in North Carolina. I think that means something to you, and because Wren means something to you, you'll make sure I stay alive."

Juan was quiet, and then he let out a small laugh.

"Get my mother pearls."

"Why?"

His voice sounded light as if he were amused. "Because she hates them, but she'll feel obligated to wear them. I would pay money to see her put on an act for an entire evening just because she wouldn't want to offend you."

I was curious if perhaps his wife had made that mistake once, remembering what his mother had said about treating her poorly.

"What else?" I asked, hoping this was a negotiation.

Juan waited, then added, "I want to attend your wedding. It's non-negotiable. I want to see my baby sister walk down the aisle."

"Deal, but I'm on the fence regarding your spawn."

"Fair," Juan chuckled, "I'll text you a meeting location."

Urgency raced through me, along with panic and a little bit of fear. "It needs to be this Kyle person."

"He headed this way the second I told him King and Gio had gone off book."

My brows caved in as I processed that, and while I knew he probably wouldn't answer, I asked anyway.

"Why would he do that?"

Juan was stoic as he replied, "Because they fear him."

A text message from Buck came through on my phone, but my mind must have run away with me because while I pulled the phone away from my ear to check the text, I asked.

"Why fear him and not you?"

Juan was quiet for so long that I assumed he had hung up. Then he finally said, "We'll just say they gave Kyle a good enough reason to be feared."

Something about his tone told me it was a painful story, which I'd imagine would be hard for any parent to tell. I hadn't known Juan for more than two seconds, so I understood that.

"I'll text you the address; we'll meet you there in twenty minutes."

Chapter 22

Wren

THE SMALL TOWN OF RAKE FORGE THAT MY BROTHER AND HIS family lived near was roughly an eight-hour drive. We had to stop and switch drivers by hour four because I was falling asleep. By morning, the boys were hungry and ready to stretch their legs. We ate, we walked, and then we got back into the car. All while we drove, not once did my mother speak of the twins.

She didn't speak negatively of their behavior or try to justify it. She kept a stern hold on the wheel while she remained focused on the road, but she didn't bring up what had happened or how much she'd seen or heard.

My nervous system needed the quiet and the peaceful drive to process what had happened. My heart throbbed with pain from that look in my brother's eyes when I mentioned that his sons were nothing to me.

Why did I feel torn regarding those boys?

They'd come into my home, where my son lived, and threatened the man I loved. They even said they didn't exactly care for me...

But they looked so much like Juan.

I wondered what mischief they must have gotten into when they

243

were kids. Were they terrors, or were they peaceful children? Juan was calm for my mother from what I remembered, but he was five years older, so I missed his toddler years and had no idea what he was like before then.

A phone call came in for my mother, distracting my thoughts. I saw that it was Juan and reached for her device.

"Can I answer it?"

She nodded and refocused on the road. We were getting closer, based on the signs we had passed, and my nerves were starting to fray. What if Juan's wife hated me? What if there were more members of his family that would be hostile toward my boys?

My boys? When did that thought slip in, and why did it feel so right?

"Hello?" I answered, desperately trying not to think about all the things clouding my head.

Juan's voice was crisp as he answered. "I just wanted to thank you for leaving. Mamá was worried about you."

I glanced over at my mom, seeing her tired eyes, and felt my heart soften. "Just mom?"

My brother paused, then chuckled. "Not just mom. I was worried, too. I've been worried about you for half my life, Sis. I hate myself for being so cruel to you and not trying to fix it. Back then…"

I didn't want this apology over a phone call, but I didn't want him to stop talking.

"It was a stressful time, which caused my priorities not to align perfectly. I wasn't thinking what my silence would do to you. By the time things settled, you were gone."

How did I articulate why I had to go and how deep his rejection had gone? There wasn't a way to explain it, so I remained silent.

"Anyway, I just…I wanted you to know that I will do everything possible to keep Archer safe and get him back to you. He told me he plans to marry you and knock you up, so—" he laughed, but suddenly I sat up straight, my eyes wide and my heart in my throat.

Oh my god.

"Wren?" I heard him, but my mind was pulling out dates and plugging in numbers.

Shit, what day was it? When was the last time I took my birth control?

Fuck. Fuck. Fuck.

I had a plan. I wanted to get an IUD for when Archer and I started having sex, but I ran out of my pills, and since my appointment was set up for next week, I figured it would be okay if I held off. Mostly because Archer kept pushing sex off the table every single time we did anything. I assumed he'd continue doing that for at least a week longer.

How could I be this careless? Archer had finished in me last night, twice.

Shit.

I put the phone back to my ear. "Sorry, dropped the phone."

"No shit. Look...when you get to my house, you should know a few things."

"You have even more kids who wield knives and want to murder me?"

Juan didn't laugh, and my mother sighed in disapproval, making me feel guilty for joking about it. I had no idea how hard it must be for him to have his sons act like that.

"Sorry—"

"Actually, yes...it's not your typical family scene. We did our best to raise them, but with Taylor's family ties and Kyle's...our kids were raised differently. Taylor and my daughter Alex will make sure you and the kids are okay. You can trust them; just don't be alarmed by what you see."

I had no idea what that meant and how he knew I had two kids with me. Peeking over my shoulder, I saw that both boys were munching on snacks while watching a movie from the headrest, a pair of headphones over each little head—one dark, one light. I returned forward, feeling a strange fire burn in my lungs as I gripped the phone.

"I heard you adopted Taylor's daughter when you married her. Surely you can appreciate that I will fight as hard for Kane as I would for Cruz. They're mine, with or without Archer, they're mine. If anything happens—"

"Nothing will happen, Renny. I promise you. I'll guard them with my life as I would guard you."

"Even if—" I couldn't say it. What if his sons murdered Kane's brother? What if they wanted to come back and finish off Kane so he wouldn't grow up wanting revenge?

Juan was quiet as he replied, "I'm getting him back to you safe and sound, even if it means my own sons shoot me."

I rolled my eyes because that sounded absurd, but it also seemed to give me the slightest bit of hope that Archer would be okay. My mind flashed briefly with an image of me in a wedding dress, standing outside under a pergola covered in ivy and white flowers. Our family surrounding us while Archer stood in a suit, smiling at me. Our sons standing next to us.

The rightness of the feeling settled into my heart like one of my postcards pinned to a fridge. Cruz was mine, and so was Kane.

"Thank you, Juan." My voice was thick, and my brother went silent.

Until he added, "I'd like to have another chance to be your brother, Renny. I'm sorry I haven't tried before this. I'm sorry I waited. I'm so—" His voice cut off with a choke.

"It's okay if you need time, but I love you. I want to be in your life and see your son and have you meet mine the right way. I wish I was going to be there when you meet my wife and my daughter. They're the best, and you're going to love them."

That made me smile. I wanted to meet them and try again with him. I wanted Cruz and Kane to have cousins and an uncle.

With a shuddery breath, I replied, "I'd like that too."

Mom had wound her way up a glen with overhanging trees and a narrow road. I wasn't sure how long we'd travel on this secluded lane, but it felt like forever. Just as I spoke up, she suddenly turned onto a private drive.

White gravel ran along the path, with fruit trees lining the road for nearly half a mile until it stopped at a large gate. Beyond the entrance was a massive house that resembled a mansion.

I leaned forward, my mouth dropping open. "Juan is rich—rich."

My mother's face remained impassive. "This is their safe house...or it was once upon a time. It was supposed to be temporary, but they kept returning, so they made it their home."

The gate opened as I looked over at my mother. "They?"

"Yes, Henrietta. Your brother created a family of his own, and it's made up of people who do not share his blood. While others live here, you will find more than enough space for you and the boys. Don't worry."

I was worried, though. I didn't want to expose the kids to strangers. We drove forward; the gravel had transitioned to black asphalt that was smooth under the tires. Another half mile took us up the driveway that spilled into a massive courtyard. A myriad of vehicles were parked, each one looking durable and extremely expensive. Past the courtyard were acres and acres of green grass, and along the edge of the property was a dense forest.

My mom pulled up to a free spot near a small entry gate that led to the front door.

"Where are we?" Cruz asked, taking his headphones off. I wasn't even sure what to say. I had no clue where we were or what we were about to encounter, which was visible in how my hands shook.

"We're on an adventure. Doesn't this look fun?" I said, all smiles, as both boys smiled back at me.

My mother exited the car and grabbed Cruz while I pulled Kane up and carried him against my hip. Tipping my head back to take in the mansion, I noticed a man appear in one of the upper windows. He had a solemn expression on his face like he was pissed that I had arrived. It seemed to sour the air as I followed my mother up the steps to the massive home.

An oak door with a wreath made of baby's breath awaited us, with an oversized brass handle in the middle of the door.

"That's funny, like in The Hobbit," Kane said, giggling.

How did he know about The Hobbit at five? I held him closer as my mother pushed through the door.

A woman appeared, her hair flying behind her as she stopped before us. Her eyes were blue, which matched Gio's, and her pink lips spread wide in a smile I could feel all the way to my toes. This was my brother's wife.

"Wren?" she asked, as if she knew my fake name all this time and had been in my life, seeing my personal details, and was all caught up. Unlike me, who had no idea about her other than I resented her...or I used to.

She walked over and hugged both me and Kane, then Cruz and my mother.

Another woman appeared behind her. She looked just like Taylor but much younger—probably in her early twenties. She wore black leggings and a tight yoga top. Her feet were bare, and her hair was braided back.

"This is Alex, my daughter." Taylor pulled the woman to her side. Alex.

Alexandra. I had heard that was what Juan had named her from one of my mother's lectures years and years ago. She never mentioned the boys, though. Not once.

"It's so nice to meet you." I smiled, feeling a little less nervous at how friendly they were.

Alex stepped closer and hugged me. "You look just like my dad."

Taylor had tears in her eyes. "Right? I know there's an age difference, but you could be twins."

The mention of twins had my stomach souring. I wanted to comment on them. I wanted to share what horrors they'd done, but then I pictured her doing the same thing to me, talking about Cruz, and I couldn't stomach speaking poorly of her kids to her.

"Well, come inside, Juan called and told me you'd be staying for a bit. I have two rooms for you, ready to go. The boys are in one together, but you'll be right next to them." Taylor led the way down a long hallway.

Off to the side were two sets of staircases that led to a separate part of the house. Through the middle was a large area strewn with chairs, couches, and a relatively long table. We just kept walking until we went down a set of steps. The floors were some kind of marble, waxed so nicely I could see my reflection on them. The drop from the stairs led to a platform that transitioned into a living space.

Thick rugs were laid out. A large sectional sofa faced a rather large entertainment system. Matching armchairs were off to the side, facing a circular coffee table with glass candle holders and melted white tapers inside. Pictures were scattered all along the walls.

I tried to catch what I could as we walked. Alex was in several of them; she was next to a dark-haired girl with reddish brown hair, bright green eyes, and a happy smile. She seemed a few years younger than Alex, but the two seemed like sisters in every picture.

Them playing piano.

The two of them were eating ice cream and making silly faces at the camera. Then the pictures shifted to Alex with two younger brothers. She held each one in her arms and smiled down at them. Taylor and Juan held the boys while Alex sat between them, smiling like she was the luckiest girl on the planet. The boys were in diapers.

My eyes watered. I had missed so much of his life, of their lives.

Now, it seemed I had been wrong about Juan. The sorrow cut deep into my heart, making guilt flare as painful as a rogue flame.

I kept walking, taking in all I could of these lives I had missed, only to pause in front of a particular image. The picture was recent; Alex was the age she is now, and Gio and Kingston looked the same. Next to Gio was that girl with reddish brown hair, but Gio's eyes and Kingston's were on another girl. One with dark hair braided into a crown on top of her head. She had bruises on her face and on her hands like a fighter would. Her smile was infectious as she leaned into the girl with reddish hair, but the boys... were transfixed by her. I was curious why they'd hang this photo when it clearly would have been one of the outtakes, one that would cause you to take another, so everyone would be looking at the camera.

Assuming Taylor was nearby, I asked, "Who is this?"

There was something about the photo that was hauntingly painful. An ache seemed trapped in the photo, begging to be released.

I startled when I heard a male voice speak up behind me. "That's Presley."

The man I had seen in the window stood behind me, and I realized I'd lost Taylor, Alex, and my mother. Cruz and Kane had followed along with them as I hung back by the pictures.

My finger traced over my nephews' faces, their eyes glued to this girl.

Then I whispered the only thing that kept circling my mind. "They both love her."

The man moved closer. "Took you two seconds to realize something that took them nineteen years to figure out."

Nineteen years.

That's how old my nephews were.

I suddenly felt like I was stepping into pain that was none of my business. Something had obviously happened to Gio and Kingston. Something that transformed them from the happy teenage boys in these photos to the monsters that appeared in my living room.

"Is she..." I didn't know how to ask because what if something had happened?

The man seemed to know what I was asking. "Is she alive?"

My feet shifted until I was facing him. It seemed too painful to keep watching something that looked so intimate.

His features were sharp and angular. He had green eyes, similar to the girl I'd seen in the photo, with reddish brown hair. Thin brown hair was almost messily styled on top of an almost bald head. His clothes were dark, nondescript, and plain. There was nothing notable about this man other than something that felt like a thrum of danger that seemed to radiate from him. His intense gaze remained on the photo as he replied.

"The twins' mother chose that photo. She wanted it hung where they'd always be able to see what they did to this family. Taylor speaks in ways that require no words. The boys spoke back by leaving the house shortly after she hung it."

I noticed he wasn't answering me about if the girl was alive or not.

"Something happened to them?"

The man glanced at me; his scrutiny felt like someone had placed me in the sights of a sniper. "You met them."

I nodded. "They're why I had to leave."

"You left alive?"

The fact that my nephews left me intact shocked him, making fear flicker in my gut.

This close I could see this man was older than me by several years. Closer to his fifties or so, but it also spoke of a life lived in the shadows. He felt dangerous, and perhaps I should walk away instead of standing here talking about a photo and two nephews I didn't know. Instead, I answered him.

"My mother is the only reason they stopped, and the fact that she was holding my son."

His stare remained on the photo. "Nice to see they do have some hard limits. I was beginning to wonder."

"Do they—"

"Scotty, I wasn't aware you were done training," Taylor said firmly, coming into view, her lips pursed like she wasn't happy the man was speaking to me.

The man, Scotty, turned toward my sister-in-law. "I wasn't aware you were breaking protocol by bringing in a stranger."

Taylor's arm came around my shoulder protectively. "Wren is no stranger. She's Juan's sister, Anna's daughter. She's family."

Scotty glared at her almost like he wanted to say something else, but instead he walked back toward the steps that led to this part of the house.

"Come on, Wren. I'll show you your room." She pulled me toward the stairs I had watched her use before getting distracted by the images.

"Who was that?" I asked.

Taylor's hold on my shoulders went slack as she let out a sigh.

"Come on, there's a few people you need to be introduced to. Scotty is...he won't hurt you. That's all you can really know about him until you meet the others."

I followed after Taylor, feeling like there was so much more I would have discovered if I'd been allowed to stay and talk with the man who stared at that photo as if he was looking at a ghost.

Chapter 23

Archer

THISTLE WAS WITH ME AS WE WAITED IN THE DESIGNATED SPOT TO meet Juan and this Kyle person.

My men surrounded the location because as much as I wanted to trust Juan, I didn't. They were given a timeline of events and what to watch for if I didn't respond by certain times using a flashlight. Dozer would be watching from the building across the street. Thistle had a few things he'd do just to let them know we were alive.

I hoped things would go well because Wren texted me that she'd arrived safely at Juan's compound. I wasn't sure what to make of that, but she sent me a photo of the boys playing in a rather large pool, and I had to just accept that it would be okay.

Thistle murmured quietly, "Ruth said if it wasn't possible to find anything on this guy, then it meant he was essentially a ghost. That or someone dangerous enough to erase ghosts from ever existing. Might not be worth messing with someone of that caliber."

I watched the street below us, the glass window from the empty warehouse providing a clear view of everything below.

"He's our only lead."

Thistle turned toward me. "It's more than likely a trap. Juan tossed

253

a story at us that we're being forced to swallow. What are the chances he's even telling us the truth?"

I didn't know how to explain it to him, but I felt it in my gut. Juan wanted to do right by Wren, which meant he would do right by me.

"I—"

The street lit up with the arrival of one car. Just one.

Thistle joined me at the window, staring down.

"He didn't bring back up."

I kept staring at the two men exiting the sleek, black car. "That we can see."

Thistle waited for Juan and Kyle to step into the stairway before flicking his flashlight to the building across from us. Indicating that we were about to start the meeting.

Thumps from the stairs echoed around the empty room until Juan finally pushed through the doorway. He wore what he had earlier, and the man behind him was my age with lighter hair, cut short and styled. He had pale skin, covered in tattoos, and wearing black eyeliner. He had an eyebrow ring and a loop in his lip. His hands were shoved deep into the pockets of his suit slacks.

"Gentlemen," the man I assumed was Kyle smiled, which reminded me of the jovial demeanor of the kid Gio, who had burned Wren's property patch.

Juan sauntered closer, lifting his hand toward the other man. "Kyle James, this is Archer Green," he paused when looking at Thistle.

"Theodore Barns. Call me Thistle." My vice president answered with a gruff voice. I hadn't heard his real name in years.

Juan continued, "Now that we're all acquainted, let's get this going."

Kyle messed with his cuffs. "Nice to meet you both. Glad the boys didn't kill you, Archer."

Irritation flickered in my chest at his cavalier attitude.

"Where are the boys right now?" I raised my eyebrow toward Juan.

Buck hadn't said there was any movement or chatter near our club.

Juan glanced at Kyle, who looked down at his phone. "Occupied."

Thistle shifted, silently communicating that he still assumed this was a trap and that the longer we were there, the more likely we would die.

I stepped forward and asked, "Kyle, Juan says that you were present for a meeting of cards where my territory was placed on the board. Something you won?"

The man who had been referred to as The Joker continued to lean against the counter, staring at me like he was happy to be there. "Yes. I remember that card game. I felt wildly successful securing so much territory for my buddy."

Juan laughed and then shook his head. This made me curious about their story and where things started for them.

"I wasn't there, as you can see from just meeting me. My second wasn't there." I gestured toward Thistle. "So, do you recall who agreed to hand over my territory?"

Kyle seemed to think about it, tilting his head back and closing his eyes. His arms were linked over his chest, and his ankles were crossed.

"Your patches." He pointed at Thistle, then me. "His says the nickname he goes by; yours is just your last name."

"Just depends on what we go by; it was something I saw my dad do." I stopped mid-sentence because it had just connected with who had sat in that game and bet my club as if he had the right to.

Kyle seemed to realize I'd figured it out. "This man, who bet, he was a big guy. His patch had your last name on it."

My adrenaline surged. "So, some guy randomly says he has the right to sell off some of my territory, and you just take him at his word?"

Kyle's brows furrowed. "No. Not at all. He had papers proving what routes you had and where you'd gotten them, and I knew the President of Mayhem Riot had the last name of Green. I took that at face value and went with it."

Shit.

"Well, that man wasn't even a part of my club at the time, so this is fucked."

Juan glanced at Kyle, and the two seemed to speak without saying anything.

"He had your patches, your colors...how—" Kyle's brows dipped in confusion.

I shook my head. "It was never retrieved after he'd been banned from the club."

Kyle searched the ground before he lifted his head. "Unfortunately, the man had papers...we considered it legitimate. You'd have to go back and figure out how you lost such important documents. So, the ownership stays with us. However, I will ensure Juan's spawn has been pulled off you and told to heel."

"Fuck off, Kyle," Juan muttered, pulling out a vape pen.

It still confused me why they might listen to him over their own father. But Juan had said they had good reason to, so I didn't care.

I just wanted to get back to Wren.

"Okay, make the call."

Kyle laughed, tipping his head back. "Oh no. One doesn't call the Phantom Twins and simply tell them to stop murdering. You need to go in person to get them to stop."

Juan took a long hit of his vape. "Kyle, you're pushing."

"No. I'm not. If I pushed, Juan, then your boys would be at the bottom of a fucking ravine. You'll know when I'm pushing."

Kyle shoved off the wall. "Let's go then. You'll need to come with us."

Thistle's jaw tensed, and I knew what he was thinking. Too dangerous.

"Why do we need to be present?"

Kyle turned back to us, his eyes searching our faces as his hands disappeared into his pockets again. "Because that man I made a deal with ten years ago was just spotted driving toward my home. He's a few hours out, but the direction is too coincidental. He wouldn't be sniffing around for anything I own; he's on his way because someone he's looking for just arrived. That would be your woman and your two boys if I'm correct."

No.

How had my father found out about them? Did he follow them?

Thistle already had his phone out. He stepped away, yelling at whoever the fuck he'd put on watching my father. How the fuck had he slipped past our detail?

Kyle continued, "That fire in your eyes, that's what it will take to get the twins' attention. They're monsters, and they only respond to other beasts. You need to show them that you're going to tear into their throats with a jaw of steel. Anything less, and they'll ignore you like one would a housefly."

"Are they working together?" My voice was rough as I walked behind Kyle, and I felt urgency in each of my steps as we trailed down the stairs to the street.

Juan was the one to respond. "That man and the boys? I doubt it, but we won't know until we talk to them."

Fuck.

Chapter 24

Wren

I spent the night staying in Juan and Taylor's wing of the house. That's what these people had, wings. Alex, Taylor and my mother kept us company while the boys played in their indoor pool, then over dinner. The conversations always revolved around me or the boys. Taylor would share stories of Alex, Juan and even a few of my mother or Leo, my stepdad. She never spoke of her sons. They were all smiles and sunshine, and I was too engrossed in the warmth to destroy it by bringing up other, more complicated topics.

I had about a thousand questions, but I respected my brother's life enough to not barge in and demand answers on anything. I had sauntered back to the living room with all the photos and inspected each and every one, twice, before taking a glass of wine up to my room. Sleep didn't come as I worried for Archer, and now with a new day dawning, I was tired and scared.

The sun came up with no news from Archer. I had another text from Brick come through, which confused me

Brick: I just want to go on record saying, we can start over. I'm going to give you the chance to apologize and we can try again.

I stared at the text and reread it three times before just blocking Brick's number. He was delusional, creepy and starting to freak me out. There was too much on my mind to think through it or focus on him.

A gorgeous view greeted us as we pushed through the patio doors outside. I decided to venture through the double glass doors, holding Kane and Cruz's hands while I went. The breeze hit me first, chilled with hints of autumn clinging to it.

The boys were bundled in thick sweaters, running through the freshly cut grass, laughing while they rolled down one of the steeper hills. I tucked my arms in close and watched them with a smile on my face.

"Good morning, Wren." Taylor came up next to me, holding a thin blanket around her shoulders.

I turned to greet her, seeing her differently out in the sun. Pieces of blonde hair flew around, trying to escape her low chignon her hair was tucked into. Her makeup was light, highlighting her lips, cheeks and eyes. With her light blue dress, her features were a little washed out, but there was something haunting in her gaze, something that spoke of a heartbreak that only a mother would know. It made me feel strange, like perhaps I should walk over and hug her.

"I met your sons." I decided to say instead.

Taylor's blue eyes flashed, her nose flared and then she found the grass by our feet.

"I'm sorry."

Her response threw me. "Why?"

She looked down. "You know why."

The breeze blew between us while the sun warmed our faces. I watched the boys while I tucked my arms in close and stepped closer to her, hoping to encourage her to continue. She watched the tree line near the back of the property and let out a small sigh. "Once upon a time, I had these beautiful baby boys that worshiped their father and looked at me as if I hung the stars. They adored their big sister and this life we gave to them, with their friends who became chosen family. Once upon a time, our lives were beautiful and full of wonder. Not perfect, but full of color and laughter."

Her face dipped, which only made me feel something in my gut twist, as if that haunted look was more pronounced. I had to look away, so I found the boys and trailed them as they ran toward us, giggling and playing tag.

"What happened?" I asked softly, hoping I wasn't overstepping.

Taylor's posture shifted, just the slightest bit. Her fingers gripped the edge of her blanket tighter, and her hair swayed in the breeze. The house stood like a tall monument behind her with glass windows that faced grassy acreage and was bordered by a thick forest. The cream color of the stone made the home feel like a castle sitting on the edge of a coastal cliff.

"Did you know that when I met Juan, I was pregnant with another man's baby?"

I kept my expression impassive while I shook my head.

Taylor dipped her face. "Not only that, but I was also engaged to a man that was neither the father of that baby nor Juan."

"Sounds messy," I mused, wishing we had coffee to go with this chat.

I had stopped into the massive kitchen this morning and made the boys two bowls of oatmeal, but the coffee machine was more complicated than my Keurig back home, so I didn't touch it.

Taylor tucked her blanket tighter while she continued, "I was in danger and completely alone. Juan saved me, saved Alex. Stepped up in a very big way, and because of us...because of me, it forced his hand and had him taking the reins of El Peligro again. Your mother hated me for it."

I couldn't tell her that I also hated her, but perhaps I shouldn't anymore. It seemed there was more to her story than I understood.

Taylor gave me a look as though she heard me. "I'm sure you did too."

I replied with a half-smile to which she laughed.

"Sometimes we do things for the love we know we can't live without. The thing we know will change our life forever. We go the furthest, act the most irrational, and make the boldest claims...and sometimes, even that isn't enough. You asked what happened...My sons found themselves at the mercy of demonstrating their love for someone."

I turned the smallest bit, tucking hair behind my ear. "And it changed them?"

Taylor's lip wobbled while a harsh whisper left her.

"It destroyed them."

A tiny ping stung my chest with empathy for them. For Taylor and my brother. "So they became monsters?"

"They became whatever they had to become. Same as Juan...same as me. The difference was the love Juan and I shared, we shouldered together...when you don't have the person with you to share it...it goes deep inside you, and it rots. It turns all the good you clung to, to something unrecognizable. It makes you stop believing. You trade sunshine for darkness. My boys shared a womb. They shared the same birthday every year for nineteen years. They even shared the same first love, and the force of that love ruined them both."

"Is she..." I still wasn't sure how to ask this question.

Where was this girl that these boys seemed to love. Fear had me thinking the worst but right as I was about to open my mouth, the back patio door creaked and someone stepped outside. A strong wind that seemed to roll up through the hills along their property forced a sheet of dark hair to fly as the girl exited. Her angular face was familiar, even without the bruises she had in the photo I'd seen. This was her.

Presley.

Her body was toned and lithe, like she'd been honing each and every tendon to be used as a weapon. Her lashes were dark and thick, framing beautiful blue eyes. She wore light blue jeans, ripped at the knee, a tight black, turtleneck and Doc Martens.

"Scotty wants everyone to come inside, he said there was something off about the sensors around the property."

Taylor gave her a warm smile. "Okay, we will. Presley, come here, meet Juan's sister."

Presley stepped forward with a warm smile. I eyed her hand, seeing her knuckles were puffy, red, and shredded. Did she train without gloves or any protection?

"Hi." I held out my hand, but Presley leaned in and took a hug instead.

"Hi."

Presley was warm, and her hug felt genuine, even as she pulled back and faced Taylor.

"When is Juan and my dad coming back?"

Taylor replied, "I'm not sure...."

Presley's brows furrowed as she seemed confused. "Where are they anyway?"

Taylor seemed to hesitate the smallest bit before she replied, "King and Gio...they—"

I missed what Presley said because I was searching for two little boys who had stopped giggling...I wasn't seeing their little heads pop up around the grassy field. There were a few hills that might block my view, and a foot deep cliff that dropped into a garden bed. I jogged over, calling out for them.

"Cruz. Kane!"

There was no response. My heart began pounding so hard that I felt like it would push through bone and skin at any second. My gaze cut to the left, searching, and then the right, as my voice rang out again screaming their names as loudly as possible.

Taylor and Presley stopped talking and turned to see what I was doing.

The moment it seemed to register that my boys weren't here, Taylor joined me in yelling, while Presley turned back toward the house and threw the patio doors open.

"Uncle Scotty!"

The man from last night burst from below where the courtyard was, and four large dogs trailed after him. He spoke in German to them as their noses slid to the ground. Scotty had a large gun in his arms, running toward the back of the property. I was about to yell at him to lower it, that having a gun out was unnecessary when suddenly the world tilted, and I saw him.

White hair.

Broad shoulders and a leather cut that he shouldn't be wearing because it said he was a part of a club he was no longer in. The same man who'd approached me at the barbeque. Saul materialized just outside the tree line with at least ten men. His arm wrapped around Kane's middle, while another man held Cruz.

My feet froze, my heart twisted in my chest as the air left my lungs.

I could tell even from where I was that Cruz was crying, Kane was kicking against the man's hold, but I couldn't make out his reaction other than that. He had to be terrified though.

Scotty aimed his gun at them while running, the dogs' legs picked up as they burst into a run.

No one else was here. We needed more people, more backup. My legs lifted as I started running. I didn't even have shoes on, and I knew my white socks would be stained green and covered in mud, but I just kept running toward my boys. Taylor was behind me; she'd dropped the blanket, and her dress was unbuttoned enough from the bottom so her knees could rise while she ran. At least she wore boots. In her hand, she had a gun just like Scotty did, but hers was much smaller and must have been pulled from a holster somewhere.

My hair flew behind me as tears streamed down my face. I drew close enough that I could make out Saul's expression. He gave me a sly smile as he turned away and began to walk away with Kane. The man holding Cruz used him as a shield, stepping behind him knowing we couldn't shoot with him in front of them.

My heart was going to stop. I felt it. This terror was ripping through me at a rate that I couldn't breathe. I couldn't—

A shot rang out, loud and powerful, from behind me.

I saw a burst of red coming from the man cowering behind my son. He went down, dropping Cruz. My son began crawling away right as another shot echoed through the air and the man directly behind him had a cloud of red burst from his head as well.

Then another perfect shot.

I paused for a second to check that I wasn't about to get shot and found Presley lying on the tallest hill with a long-range rifle set up. She was sniping them one by one. Her hair blew in the wind while she leaned forward and pressed her eye to the scope, and then I heard another shot, and when I turned to look, another man went down.

The dogs were still running past the dead men into the trees where Saul had taken Kane.

Cruz was crying, holding his little arms over his chest while tears streamed down his face. My feet felt nearly frozen as I skid to a stop in front of my son, pulling him into my arms, against my pounding heart.

"Are you hurt?" I asked, breathlessly.

Cruz shoved his face into my shoulder. "No."

My gaze searched the tree line frantically. Taylor, Scotty and the dogs were all gone, chasing Saul. Presley was running toward us, the gun strapped to her back. I opened my mouth to say something when all the sudden a rugged off-roading vehicle came racing toward us. The tires were massive and slotted for terrain. Alex was in the passenger side, and the girl with reddish brown hair I'd seen in the photo was driving.

Within seconds the vehicle slid to a stop, kicking up grass as the girl with dark red hair from the photos jumped out.

"Pres!"

"Carter?" Presley asked, narrowing her focus as if she was confused.

Alex opened the passenger side door, exiting while sliding a large clip into what looked like an automatic machine gun.

"What are you doing here?" Presley asked, sounding shocked.

Alex glared over the top of the Jeep at Presley. "Don't start, Pres."

"Whatever, we need to drive along the edge and trail him. He has a kid." Presley was about to get inside the Jeep but then she paused, glancing back at me. "He might have more men; I think Scotty would want us to hang back and protect Wren and the little guy."

All three women glanced over at me. They were barely over eighteen, maybe early twenties, how on earth did I feel like the inexperienced one?

"She can come with us," Carter suggested.

I liked that idea, but Cruz was still crying into my shoulder.

Alex's lips twisted. "No, Pres is right. Scotty would never risk them if—"

Presley's head suddenly snapped back toward the house. "My dad needs to know that our perimeter was breached. My mom is in town; she'll need to be warned too."

My head was spinning as they spoke, all holding weapons like it was nothing. They'd all obviously been trained in some capacity to do this...like the twins.

They were all monsters.

Whatever happened twenty years ago with my brother and his friends, their legacy was this. Girls who looked like they should be out shopping with their girlfriends, holding sniper rifles and automatic weapons.

"I'll stay with them, take them to a safe room. You two go out, back them up. Juan won't be happy when he realizes Taylor went out without him."

Alex's face shuddered the smallest bit, her gaze moving to the trees. "No. Dad is going to lose his shit when he hears this."

"Carter, you think you can remember how to hold a gun?" Presley asked, while securing her sniper rifle against her back once more.

Carter flipped Presley off and then crawled back into the driver's side of the Jeep. Within seconds, they took off, shooting grass behind them as they headed toward the perimeter.

I picked up Cruz and moved toward Presley who waited for me while watching the perimeter. How did she just walk away from the fact that she shot so many people? Was this her first time, or had she done this before? She didn't seem phased in the slightest by it.

We started back toward the house all the while my gut sank because I'd promised Archer that his brother would be safe with me. I failed him.

The only thing he'd tried to do since I met him was keep Kane safe, and one night with me, and all that was undone. Shame slipped in through the tiny cracks of my heart, along with fear over this life. How could I do this to my son? How could I do this to Kane, placing another young person in danger.

I lived a safe life with Cruz when it was just the two of us. I had nearly gotten him kidnapped by dating Archer and stepping outside of the safety circle that I'd drawn around my life. The one where I had kicked everyone out and refused to ever it open it up...at the risk of being lonely, it would have been worth it if it meant everyone remained safe exactly where they were.

Archer's easy smile flashed in my mind while I walked back inside, leaving his brother in the woods. I'd do whatever it took to undo this and get us back somewhere we'd be untouchable again.

Chapter 25

Archer

THE NIGHT CAME BACK IN FLASHES AS THE UNDERBRUSH CRUSHED under my boots.

Kingston's amber eyes as he sipped from a glass. Its contents mirrored that color that reminded me so much of Wren. He stared at us, glaring while we talked.

The memory of when Kyle walked through their door, Juan on his heels. Thistle and I had walked in after, but Juan's two sons didn't even pay any attention to us. Their only focus was Kyle James, and the man seemed to know it as he gave them a sardonic smile.

"Boys, seems like you fucked up."

Gio leaned forward like he couldn't believe he was being blamed. "Us?"

I was already annoyed that this was the jumping-off point. The two boys sitting on the couch smoking weed while they watched a UFC fight.

Fuck them.

My kids and my woman were in danger, and fuck if they were going to sit here and wage war with me while my dad moved in close to them.

I walked over and kicked the coffee table in front of them so all the shit on it flipped over.

Kyle smiled, leaning against the edge of the couch.

"Yeah, you fucked up by going after him. But it seems we had ourselves an imposter at that game where the territory was being gambled. Mr. Green, the true president, had no knowledge of the trade."

Their gazes hadn't left me, their hands were on their guns, but Thistle was behind me with one trained on them. Juan seemed withdrawn like he didn't want to watch if his kids were about to get shot. Couldn't say I blamed him.

The one with blue eyes, Gio, had leaned forward to sip his drink. "Not our problem."

Kingston remained stoic, staring into his liquor that he held off to the side, on the back of the couch. There was enough space between it and where Gio sat.

I pulled my gun out and shot through his glass. The shards hit his face and splattered against the wall.

Gio jumped up and screamed, "Are you fucking crazy?"

Kingston scowled at me as he tossed the remainder of the glass in my direction.

"Get the fuck up and answer these questions," I ordered. They wouldn't respect anyone who wasn't a fucking monster to them. Fine by me.

Kyle surveyed them both. "It just became your problem. Archer intends to join the family, which means we owe him a second chance. A new deal."

Kingston flicked his amber eyes up, inspecting me as though I'd produce something of value at any moment.

"What kind of deal?"

"How about one where you apologize by leaving my territory the fuck alone."

Kyle smirked and let out a small laugh. "That won't work."

He stood and began pacing in front of the overturned coffee table. "We keep the territory. We go back to pushing what we did when Juan led. No more bullshit. In exchange, we let him and everyone in his club live. We also help him kill whoever the fuck the man was who impersonated him all those years ago."

Gio produced a vape pen from his pocket while shaking his head before sinking back into the couch. He must have forgotten there was glass because he lifted his hand with a wince and cursed.

"This isn't our problem. We don't need this motorcycle club bullshit in our way. It's easier with them gone, and while I love your angel wings, Daddio, we're not doing that shit again. We made triple what you did on these routes."

Juan's jaw was tense, his eyes deadly as he glared at his son. King seemed to return the sentiment with the way he stared at his brother.

I expected Kyle to speak up, but it was Juan who quickly stepped in front of the boys.

He flexed his fingers and then he smacked Gio's face, so the vape pen flew from his mouth. Kyle's phone was out, and he tossed it over to Juan, who caught it without even looking. I couldn't see what was on the screen, but as Juan pushed it in front of his sons' faces, it had both boys going ghostly pale.

"Not your problem?" He shoved the phone closer. "He's circling our property as we speak. How long before he goes traipsing through the woods, until he gets closer to our home? Do you know who else is home right now?"

Gio looked away, but Kyle lunged forward and grabbed his jaw until his eyes were back on the screen.

"Presley is home. Your mother is home. Your sister. Your grandmother. And we are here. So, tell me if you think it's a problem or not."

Kingston muttered a curse while pulling out his phone. Gio glared at the screen before shaking his head.

"We'll agree to the terms. His club is safe," Kingston said, glancing at his device and then at me.

Kyle stayed where he was. "Get it all in writing. Call off your men. No one goes after him or his men. We're allies from here on out. He'll respect the route, but no harm will come to them."

"Fine," Gio sourly agreed while pushing away from the couch he was on and pulling on his jacket.

We'd left shortly after that, Thistle and I following their car at a speed that had us arriving in half the time.

The sound of a snapping branch brought me back to the moment.

Thistle was next to me, but he froze when the branch snapped. It was early morning after we rode through the night from New York to North Carolina. We had no idea if we'd make it on time, but I hoped Juan alerted whoever needed to be notified so that everyone remained safe.

But my stomach churned. Something was off. Thistle felt it too. I could tell from how he gripped his gun and kept his eyes on the dense tree line.

Then we heard it. A loud crack from a gun.

It was far enough away that I knew it wasn't anywhere in our immediate vicinity. Still, I slowed my steps, searching around. The trees were thin enough that I could easily see several yards away. Kingston, Gio, Juan, and Kyle were in the forest with us, all approaching from a different angle because based on their intel my father, fucker that he was, had entered through some forest that connected to their property.

Another shot rang out, echoing from the north. We started toward it, only to hear another shot ring out, then another. All from what sounded like a rifle of some kind.

"Do you hear dogs barking?" Thistle glanced over, looking nervous.

Shit. Dogs wouldn't know if we were friend or foe; they'd just know our scent wasn't familiar and likely tear the fuck into us. I was about to panic when Kingston suddenly ran toward us as a large black dog approached.

It immediately started growling and barking.

"Rex," Kingston snapped, followed by a quick whistle. The dog's ears and snout lifted, as though he responded to the command. Rex seemed to heel, trotting next to Kingston's side, right as another dog darted for us.

"Fuck. You might have to shoot him, which will mean that Scotty might shoot you in return. I'll do what I can, but if the dog seems like he'll attack then you need to shoot."

I didn't want to shoot a dog. My eyes bugged the fuck out as the second dog barreled toward us, only to pull left with his ears lifted. The dog named Rex followed him, while I heard several people running.

Adrenaline hit my chest as the scenario finally played out for me. These dogs were chasing someone; the shots were aimed at an enemy.

My dad was here. He'd made contact somehow, and now they were after him. Was it merely because he'd trespassed or had something happened?

"Kingston!" a man yelled, running toward us while his arm was raised, a black assault rifle pointed directly at us.

Kingston reared back until he was watching a man break through the trees.

The man with the gun wasn't even breathing heavily; he was merely focused intently on us.

"Are you with him?" he asked, directing the barrel of his gun at my patches.

Thistle lifted his hands as if surrendering. "With who?"

Kingston spoke up on our behalf. "Scotty, they're with us. What's going on?"

The man gave us one last once-over before searching the surrounding woods with a frantic gaze. "Male, late fifties. Stocky, white hair, tattoos, patches, leather cut like theirs." He gestured at us. "He took a kid. The kid that came with your aunt."

No.

I stepped forward, my heart tangled in my chest as it tried to push out of my skin.

"Which kid?" Not that it made a difference, but I needed to know how panicked Wren was. If he had Cruz then I'd imagine she would be behind this man any second, tearing into the tree line, looking for him. Unless something happened...

The man regarded me and then did a double take. "He your son?"

Kane.

A lump was in my throat as I replied, "My brother."

"Will this man hurt him?" Scotty asked as two of the dogs circled back to us, their tongues wagging from their mouths as they tried to cool down.

I pictured Brit and when I'd been the one to identify her body because her family couldn't do it. I thought of my mom and how I was too young, but I'd also been in the morgue with her as well. "Yes, he'll hurt him."

Scotty lifted his gun and spit something to the side. "He has exactly four minutes on us. We need to spread out and find him."

Kingston fell into step next to him as we turned and started moving, my mind feeling like it was outside my body.

"Who else is out here with us?"

Scotty fell into a light jog, answering the twin. "Your mother. Your sister and Carter are in the jeep, trailing up the far side of the tree line."

Where was Wren and Cruz?

Kingston must have someone else he was concerned with too because he fell into a run next to Scotty. I hadn't even realized I was jogging to keep up with them.

"Where is—"

Scotty turned, snapping at him. "She's guarding the woman and her son in the house."

Relief found a tiny place in my sternum. She was safe, which meant all I had to do was focus on Kane.

We ran in a singular direction as the dogs led us until we came to a clearing in the trees, and there was nothing but a blonde-haired woman wearing a faded blue dress, the hem muddied and torn. She clung to Juan as he hugged her, and then Kyle was on his phone, pacing around, while a gun dangled from his hand.

"What happened?" I pushed forward. Thistle was right behind me, but the longer I was around these people the more I felt like they were less of a threat and more of a terrified family. I'd brought the devil to their door, but perhaps this wasn't their first time dealing with one.

The woman was breathing hard but faced me with a grim expression.

"We lost his trail."

Juan pulled the woman back into his chest.

"What do you mean, wasn't he headed straight through the tree line?" I glanced at Kyle who was talking to someone. Scotty's jaw flexed while he scanned the surrounding area.

"Directly through. His men were taken out; it's just him and the kid. He couldn't have gone far."

Yet the dogs whined as though they couldn't pick up his trail. My stomach spasmed with fear as the thought of losing my brother hit me in full force. What if I found his body in the woods? What if Saul wanted to send a message to me, sick fuck that he was, and decided to use a five-year-old little boy to do it.

I had to think.

Pulling up my phone, I slid through my contacts, discerning our timeline. He had men with him they said had been taken out. I could ask Thistle to call Ruth and see if she could pull up satellite images, but we were on Juan's property...and Kyle's. However, the fuck that worked. It didn't seem like they'd ever allow themselves to be put in a position to be hacked into.

Kyle was yelling at someone through his phone. I heard bits and pieces before he lowered his arm, glancing over at me.

But it was Scotty who spoke up after checking his cell.

"She left the boy with his grandmother in a panic room."

Kyle and Scotty locked eyes.

Kingston searched both their faces and all it did was remind me his twin still hadn't resurfaced. "I thought Presley was watching them."

Scotty spoke up again. "Presley took the woman—"

"Wren. Her name is Wren," I cut in because calling her something as generic as a woman was making me insane.

"Presley took Wren, they left five minutes ago."

Fuck.

"Which direction did they go in?" That came from Kingston, even though I was thinking it.

Scotty slid his gun onto his back with a thick strap showing over his chest. "They went through the tunnels."

Chapter 26

Wren

"You look like you left your heart out there."

Presley's words were still echoing around my head after we'd walked to the panic room. We'd found my mom and told her she needed to come in with us, but at Presley's words, I had searched her face and found a small smile tugging at the side of her mouth.

As if she understood me.

"Taylor is out there, so I'm going back because there is no lifetime in which I'd ever let something happen to her." Presley lifted her shoulder.

She seemed so young, as if she should dart around the corner and grab her book bag to head off to college. Yet she seemed infinitely more mature than me in how she held herself and how confident she was with her abilities.

I knew what she was offering me, and my heart leapt at the chance. I'd die to keep Cruz safe, but I had already pulled Kane into my heart in a way that made it to where I couldn't leave him out there. I knew people were out helping, but I had to help as well.

I promised Archer that I would take care of Kane. He worked so hard to protect him; there was no way I could just sit in a panic room while I worried about his fate. So, I walked into the room with my mother and Cruz and saw they had snacks, carpeted flooring, a couch, and a large-screen television. They'd be perfectly fine.

"Stay here with grandma, I'm going to find Kane." I pressed a kiss to his forehead, then felt his little arms come around me.

"I love you, Mommy."

My eyes burned as I hugged him back and made eye contact with my mother. She pulled something out of a large bag. It looked like the one she'd packed from my house.

"Mi amor, take this, show this man who you are."

She held out a piece of leather to me, and my heart leapt at the sight of the singed material.

My property patch.

Fresh tears gathered as I stroked over Archer's name and the term President's Wife along the shoulders. Then I slipped the buttery fabric on over my sweater.

Presley appeared again, this time holding out a pair of boots, flat on the bottom and sturdy.

"These might do you a bit better than just your socks."

I laughed, swiping at my eyes, and followed her out.

Water dripping down the concrete wall near my left side brought me back to the present.

Perhaps this was a crazy idea. I wasn't trained like she was. I had some muscle memory with the use of a knife, way back when Manny used to have me practice, but I hadn't done that in almost twenty years.

I hadn't even asked why we slipped through a hatch that opened, or why we scaled down a ladder and began walking down this concrete tunnel that seemed to run under their property. For whatever reason, I trusted Presley. Perhaps because she didn't hesitate to start shooting the men near my son, or the fact that she hugged me when we met. I didn't know, but I felt safe with her.

"He had to assume we'd have dogs. Any property like ours would. There are too many security checkpoints he made his way through. He had to have had an insider help him get past the exterior walls. They're supposed to light anyone up like a Christmas tree if they so much as pass through the first layer of trees. Obviously, that didn't happen, which means he had help. If they helped with the barrier, then they told him to bring something that would throw off the scent of the dogs or go as far as to tell him about the tunnels."

Presley talked quietly, and smoothly.

I had so many questions, but I was trying to keep pace with her, and we were moving fast, so I kept my thoughts to myself.

We turned a corner, but not until Presley had scanned it, lifting her gun, like I'd seen on the cop shows. She had perfect posture, as if she'd trained for this a thousand times.

She must have seen me watching because she gave me a quick smile.

"I didn't have the typical upbringing that other girls had. Not even like Alex or Carter...I was different, always have been. Just took me a while to embrace it."

We stepped around another corner, a long corridor greeted us, and nothing but silence.

I whispered in return, "Why was your upbringing different?"

Weren't they all raised together?

Presley walked a few steps and then replied, "My dad...it's hard to explain but he and Mom never had a boy, they just had me. I liked the training though...my uncle Scotty did most of it. He used to work for some of the most gruesome Mob bosses alive. Took my dad with him when he was little, was essentially a second father to my dad. When my dad was old enough, the two of them turned against a pretty big player, and then just kept taking from everyone else on the board. He changed things in a significant way...so much so that we've never really walked away from it. The entire operation...it's not really El Peligro anymore. Juan handed that over to my dad years ago and came under the umbrella of his family. He allowed Juan to operate El Peligro as a charity for those who needed it, but my dad is the one who runs it."

Her information swirled in my head, confusing me but also helped connect a few dots.

"But I thought Kingston and Gio were the new leaders."

Presley let out a small scoff. "They're trying to protect me."

"From what?"

We rounded another corner and suddenly a loud gunshot rang out, echoing all around us. Presley pulled me back just in time for the bullet to land in the wall across from us. We waited for more shots, but none came. Presley crept around the corner to be sure no one was there and once it was clear, she waved me over.

She smiled at me from over her shoulder. "No one else sees it as their attempt at protection, but no one else knows them like I do."

Another shout rang out down the corridor, which had Presley freezing then picking up the pace again.

"Come on, I think we're close."

The tunnels poured into a large garage that held several tactical vehicles and a wall full of weapons. An additional room with tactical gear was next to a platform. Presley ran for the platform, aiming for the door at the top. I followed her, trying to process who we might find on the other side.

Fear gripped me hard as we raced toward the solid, door that looked rusted or as if someone had manufactured a shipping container as a door. Was Saul on the other side? Was I really going to do this and possibly get myself killed?

Where was Archer, had my nephews killed him? Had my brother helped? I hoped beyond hope that he was safe and on his way to me. That he'd show up and take us home, that we could put all this behind us like a bad dream. That I could forget this insanely dangerous life that my brother led with these friends of his.

This was madness.

I pushed my eyes closed and kept moving, knowing deep down I had to do this for him. I had to get Kane to safety and trust that Juan would be sure he and Cruz were kept safe. However, if they were left in his charge, I had to wonder how the two of them would end up if his sons, King and Gio, were anything to go by.

Presley was at the door but paused momentarily and looked back at me.

"Get your gun out. Keep it aimed at the ground, keep your eyes open. I don't want you to get shot. In fact, maybe you should stay here."

I pushed closer. "No, I'm going."

It wasn't a gun that I pulled; it was two knives that I had found amidst the myriad of weapons that Presley had offered me.

She glanced down and smiled. "Just like Juan, he trained me to use them too, but I'm better with a gun. How many of those do you have on you?"

My fingers shook as I gripped the blade, ignoring how long it had been since I'd thrown one. The memory of a black handle sinking directly into a target flashed back. Once upon a time, I was a really good aim.

"I have four."

Presley gave me a brisk nod. "Good. Remember to aim for the neck, or the hand if they're shooting. But the neck would be better. I took out ten of his men. I don't think he has many more."

"He'll use Kane against us. Try to use him as a shield," I explained, still trying to remember how I used to grasp the handle and what my father used to say when he'd correct me.

Hold it like this, Henrietta. Looser here, then flick your wrist.

"Then let's make it so he can't. The little guy is how old?"

Presley began adjusting her rifle scope. It was a newer model of what, I had no clue, but it was sleek in design with slate black knobs and grooves.

"He's five." My mouth was dry as I tried to swallow.

Every part of me was screaming for me to run. To turn around and leave, just like I had when I was sixteen. This wasn't the life I wanted. But Archer had said danger would be a part of his life...

"He'll be short enough," Presley commented before she pulled on the door and graying skies greeted us as we exited the tunnel. Dense trees were all around us, along with dirt mixed with gravel under our feet. Below us there was a deep boot imprint of someone much larger than either of us.

Presley started moving, gun raised, following the prints in the mud.

Rounding an outcrop of trees, my eyes widened as I saw Saul standing in place, facing an all-terrain vehicle. The back passenger door was open, but Kane was still in his arms, one of his meaty hands over Kane's little mouth.

Kane looked so brave, staring at me with relief. Not tears, as if he knew all along that I'd come. "You two bitches come any closer and I'll kill him."

Saul jerked away from the vehicle, adjusting his hold on Kane.

I locked eyes with Kane, and his little blue gaze remained on me. He still didn't cry. It was like he knew he'd be okay.

Saul's gaze flicked over me, looking over my property patch.

"Gotta say, I didn't expect you to show up. Figured you'd be cowering under the bed somewhere. That's what you do, right? I heard all about how you ran away from your family, how you hid and ended up falling for a pussy-whipped president." His chuckle slid down my back, making my grip on the knife tighten.

"Put my son down," I ordered, deadly and firm as I stepped forward, allowing the second knife to slide into my palm.

The driver-side door pushed open, and another man ambled out. Familiarity had my eyes bulging and my mouth gaping.

"Brick?!"

His smarmy smile made me feel like a thousand bees were under my skin. "Your son, Wren? Really? This kid isn't yours, he's the kid brother to that fucking redneck neighbor. He belongs back in the city in foster care, and that's exactly where I'm taking him."

Presley shifted next to me. I knew she was trying to decipher which one to target.

I stepped closer. "How did you get mixed up in this, Brick?"

He was an idiot; hopefully, he'd leave an opening for us to use it to our advantage.

Brick toyed with the keys while he watched me. "Saul called your office looking for you. I was at your desk when the call came in because, once again, you were missing work. We started talking, and it seemed some of our interests aligned. He wanted to know where you were, and had knowledge of an employee tracking app that Encore Homes uses for its agents. It's so if there's ever a safety concern with a client, the data can be given to the police."

Oh my god.

My mind went back five years to a long-winded safety instruction meeting that would outline Encore Homes' new policies for all agents who interacted with clients. I was pregnant and exhausted and skipped half the class. Shame flushed through my chest, turning it bright pink. How had I not realized my phone could be tracked?

"You forgot about that, didn't you?" Brick beamed, then paced a few steps, still toying with the keys. "Saul didn't even offer me money, Wren. He simply offered me the chance to intervene in your life and ruin your new budding romance with the redneck. He needed a driver, and I was told to take the kid back to the foster care system in Atlas. Simple as that. I might not have a motorcycle club at my disposal, but I can deliver an effective 'fuck you,' when I want to."

He chuckled, and I had a moment where all I wanted was to murder Brick. I wanted him dead, to not be in my life anymore, but I wasn't that person. If he managed to get Kane away from Saul then I'd fight for Kane in court...assuming Saul let me live.

Presley pushed the smallest bit closer, aiming her gun at Saul.

"Lower your gun, or I will kill him. This is my son to do with how I see fit. *Mine.* That bitch of a mother took him from me. Tried to give him to Archer to raise, and now you think you can step in and do it."

His eyes were wild, making fear slither around my heart and squeeze.

My voice was even and strong. "He's mine now. Put him down." My gaze was on Kane as I tried to convey this new truth that I felt down to my bones.

He was mine now, and he always would be.

Brick glanced up at him, his face wary, as if he just processed that threatening the life of a five-year-old kid was actually pretty fucking serious.

"Hey Saul, I—"

Saul produced a handgun from his side and swung it over so fast, Brick never saw it coming.

He pulled the trigger twice, and two holes appeared in Brick's head. My mouth dropped as I stared at Brick, lying dead in the mud. His eyes stared up at the endless sky. I didn't feel anything but shock. He was gone...he'd just been talking, breathing, texting me earlier in the—

I heard a loud crack from behind me, making me flinch. Saul's kneecap exploded. I waited for Saul to fall, but he didn't. He merely shifted his weight, and before he could recover how to protect his other knee, Presley let another shot fly.

His scream echoed around us as blood burst from his leg. He dropped Kane, and I didn't hesitate. My knives flew, landing directly in the jugular of his neck.

I wanted to run over, pull them out and sink them into his heart. Then do it again and dig them into his gut. But Kane was running toward me and right as my knees hit the mud below me, Archer burst from the tree line, ambling toward us with a heaving chest, trying to catch his breath. Archer's gaze darted down then slid over to us right as Kane's little body slammed into mine.

"I knew you'd come." His little voice echoed in my ear, and it made my heart lurch.

Not Archer. He knew I'd come for him.

Tears begged to be freed as I sat back and pulled him into my chest. "I'm sorry it took me so long. I'm so sorry he took you, and you thought you were going to have to go with him."

His arms were iron around my neck as he clung to me.

"I didn't cry because I saw how you looked at me when he took me."

Pulling him away so I could check his face, my smile wobbled. "How did I look at you?"

His white hair was muddied as I ran my hands through it, checking him to be sure he was okay.

"You looked at me the same way you look at Cruz. I know I'm yours now. Yours and Archer's. You're going to be my mom. I've never had one before that I remember. I'm glad it's you."

I tried to laugh as a sob came out, and I pulled him close. Presley was behind me, placing her hand on my shoulder. Then one of the twins burst through the tree line just as frantic as Archer had.

Gio.

His eyes were wild as he searched the area, and then frenzied as they landed on Presley. He stumbled over, dropping his gun.

"Gio," Presley started. She put her hands out, almost as if to hold him off. His hands were on her face seconds later, pushing into her hair as he pulled her closer.

Her fists clung to his waist, holding onto his hoodie. Then more people came through the trees. Kingston found Gio and Presley, and his jaw worked back and forth like he was processing a rather big emotion. Presley looked up, and as soon as she saw Kingston, she pushed Gio away. Pain radiated on her face, as if she'd just been reminded of something she lost.

I moved my gaze away from them, so I didn't keep watching something that looked so intimate and personal.

Juan and Taylor held hands as they came closer and then Archer finally stopped examining Saul and Brick's bodies. His hands were bloody as he pulled my daggers free and wiped them on Saul's chest.

Kane remained in my lap as they all closed in, and it hit me then.

My brother led a life of danger, but he'd made it so nothing could hurt his family. He'd raised soldiers because he was always at war.

Archer knelt down in front of us. His eyes were red, like he'd been fighting emotions too.

"Brick?"

I shook my head, still in shock that my colleague was lying dead just a yard away. Archer moved closer. I stared at how the red blended in with his dark tattoos for a moment before I reached for him. He seemed to hesitate, but I wasn't having that. I pulled his hand into mine, unphased by the blood.

"Help me get him home."

He took Kane from me and held him to his chest and then pulled me up. My nose found his neck and I inhaled deeply, closing my eyes. Home. Archer was home, Kane and Cruz...they were the home I'd been searching for all this time and while I had my brother back, nothing felt as right as this.

Kane knew I would come for him.

Courage filled a hole in my chest, one large and vast that had been a canyon in my chest since I was sixteen. It replaced a broken piece of my heart and reforged it out of steel.

My brother watched me carefully as we turned back toward the tunnels, and I knew what he was seeing.

For the first time in nearly twenty years, he was seeing his little sister again. The one who used to ride the edge of a knife, flirting with danger every chance she got. The one who loved this life and craved its edges and all the serrated pieces around it. The one who used to smile and laugh and create joy. She was still inside me, and now I knew I could let her be a part of my life instead of shutting her out like I'd done since I left.

I could be the president of Mayhem Riots' wife, and I could lead next to him with strength and courage.

I could be brave, and my world wouldn't end.

Chapter 27

Archer

WREN'S FINGERS WERE IN MY HAIR AS I WOKE UP.

She stroked gently along the nape of my neck and over my ears. My back was to her, which meant sometime during the night, I'd shifted away from her, or she left the bed. I had a feeling she'd left the bed to go check on the boys. The room was dimly lit with just a small piece of sunlight cutting through the split curtains, which meant it was still early.

We'd come back to the property yesterday and the entire day was a blur. Kyle and Juan disappeared, along with Kingston and Gio. I was so exhausted that all I focused on was Wren guiding me to a room where I showered and promptly fell asleep.

I tried to focus on how Wren's fingers gently scraped against my scalp and how good it felt, watching the wall on the other side of the room. My mind tossed up the image of her throwing those daggers, and how she'd claimed my brother. I swear my heart grew in size after seeing how protective she was over him.

I had no idea why she did it, but on my way through the trees, I could hear them talking. I hadn't reached them, but their voices carried, especially hers.

285

Put my son down.

Those were the words she'd used. She'd called Kane hers, and then when he was free, it wasn't me he'd run to...it was her.

"You're awake." Her soft voice carried over from her side of the bed. I smiled, then turned over on my back.

"How did you know?"

Her hair was up in a chaotic pile on her head, but it somehow made her look sexy and like she'd been fucked all night. She hadn't been, but it was still making me hard, thinking about it.

"Your breathing changed." She smiled at me and then leaned down to press a kiss to my forehead. We still hadn't talked about the fact that Brick had essentially worked with my father and was now dead. Thistle was going to help frame his death to look like a car accident, so there weren't any ties that would come back to our club, Saul, or Wren's family.

I pulled Wren until she was lying down next to me.

"I'd like to hear your breathing change." My lips found her neck then I trailed lower, kissing along her collarbone while I slid my hand over her stomach and down between her thighs.

"Archer." She sounded as if she was about to protest, so I covered her mouth with mine while using my thumb to swipe over her clit through her little pajama shorts.

"Oh." Her breathing did change then, and I smiled against her mouth, applying more pressure with my thumb.

Our kiss turned messy as our tongues slid against each other and I couldn't help myself. I gently tugged at the lace camisole that was barely covering her heaving breasts. Once she was uncovered, traced my tongue over her taut nipples, swiping over one rosy bud and then the other. Her tits were pushed together from her tank top, so I took my time sucking and licking each one while she began writhing under me.

From how she kept trying to rub against me, I knew she was aching so I slid farther, kissing down her stomach and swiping over her belly button until I got to her shorts, where I pulled them down her legs and then began licking along her slit.

Her fingers came to my hair and pulled as she let out a sharp breath, her legs lifting on either side of my head. I pushed them farther apart as I fucked her with my tongue. It wasn't enough.

I wanted to consume her.

With that in mind, I gripped her by the hips and flipped her over. The sight of her bare ass had my cock weeping. She let out a tiny yelp from being tossed over, followed by a throaty laugh. I'd never had a woman laugh while I was in the process of fucking her. It made my own smile appear as I shook my head.

"I love you," I whispered against her spine as I dropped a kiss there.

Moving lower to the top of her ass, my tongue traced a path over her left ass cheek, and with a hiss, I let my teeth graze along her flesh.

Her hips lifted as if she needed pressure or friction against her pussy. I repeated the process of licking and sucking her right ass cheek before grazing my teeth and sinking into her flesh with a soft bite, which had her moaning.

"You like that?" I whispered, repeating what I'd done, but this time, I spread her cheeks apart and stared at her crack. My mouth watered as the bare skin led to a dark, tight circle, and farther to her bare, glistening slit. Her hips reared again as her hand came back to hold one of her cheeks for me.

"Hmm, I like when you help me, Wren. I like when you get so desperate to be fucked that you'd even silently beg me to lick you in your tight little hole." My hand gripped her cheek while holding it apart from her other, and then I dove in swirling my tongue over her in a deep, lick.

Her words were muffled as she shoved her face into the pillow.

I liked that. Way too fucking much.

My strokes were vicious as I pushed into her tightness and used three of my fingers to sink into her core. I heard a low, guttural moan, muffled by the bed as a shudder ran through her. Her hips lifted, her pussy rising from my fingers, only to sink down on them in an attempt to get pressure. My tongue remained buried in her hole while my fingers worked her pussy, and she fucked my hand.

She dripped all over my fingers as she moved. I didn't dare pull them out as she used me, moaning into the bed as her arousal soaked the sheets. I knew she was about to come based on how another shudder moved up her back, but I wanted her to come on my cock. So, I pulled away from her, only to rise up, and press my knee to the bed as I angled closer to her ass. Then holding her hips up, I gripped my shaft in one hand and sank into her in one harsh thrust.

Her fingers clenched the sheets on either side of her head while her face remained shoved into the mattress. Her tight heat wrapped around my cock, gripping me so well that I had to breathe for a second before pulling out and pushing back inside.

"Wren." My voice was a plea as I began thrusting.

My hands returned to her ass, gripping her skin harshly while I lifted her hips the smallest bit and continued to bury my cock deep inside her. Over and over, I pulled out and thrust in, making the headboard slam against the wall, but I was too far gone to care. My chest heaved as I kept pushing my hips forward, sliding my cock in and out, until I felt her walls closing around mine, a muffled scream erupting from her as she froze and came hard on my cock.

"That's it, beautiful. Let go, cover my cock with the proof of what I do to you."

Her muffled moans and garbled curses continued as I pulled out of her. I could see her creamy release create a ring around the base of my cock and it had me so fucking hard that with one last push inside her, I filled her with a groan, coming so hard I saw spots.

"So fucking tight, beautiful. You grip my cock like you're begging me to keep fucking you. Like you can't live without it."

My release began spilling out of her as I pulled out and the sight was so fucking good that I pushed it all back in with another groan.

"I like the way you look when you're dripping with my cum."

Suddenly she froze and her head lifted, frizzy, wild hair falling against her tan back, as she twisted to see me still sliding my half hard cock in and out of her cunt, playing with our joint release.

"Shit." She stared where we were connected and then bit her lip.

"I need to tell you something that might make you upset."

Her tone had my cock finally softening, so I pulled out of her completely and stood up. She'd need a warm rag anyway. So I walked into the bathroom and returned with one so she could drop whatever bad news she needed on me.

Her gaze went to my still glistening cock that I hadn't cleaned yet.

"Wanna lick it clean?" I smirked, knowing we needed to get going and didn't have time for another round, but I wanted to get that panicked fearful look off her face.

She didn't respond, which had anxiety churning in my chest.

"What's wrong, Wren?"

Her knees curled under her while she let out a sigh. "I'm not—" Her eyes found mine while she tried to get it out. "I had a plan to go get certain kind of birth control...because we hadn't been having sex. I thought I had time and then it just happened, and then all this transpired."

She tugged on the edge of a blanket.

I didn't see the problem.

"So, you might be pregnant?"

Her eyes snapped up to mine.

Why did that sound so fucking good to me?

She nodded sheepishly while her face flushed pink.

"Does that make you scared or upset?" What was the problem?

Her beautiful eyes found a way to arrest me.

"Neither...I just, well in case you weren't looking forward to that because of our new situation, and now with custody stuff. I didn't want to be a burden."

I pulled her hand until she was closer. I was still naked, and my cock wasn't hard anymore, but she crawled into my lap anyway.

"You aren't a burden, and if you become pregnant, that wouldn't be a burden. That patch you were wearing, means you're mine. I'm yours. It's as close to a wedding vow as we get without actually saying any. You essentially agreed to marry me." I smiled at her, lopsided and happy.

She smiled back. "You never asked."

"And I never will because it's a done deal. The sky is blue. Your eyes are the kind of gold that makes me wonder if you're even real, and you'll marry me someday. Facts are facts, Wren. No need to mix up words."

She rocked into me the smallest bit. "So if I'm pregnant right now?"

Shit, the idea of her round belly had me fighting another erection. Her pussy rubbed against me as I squeezed her ass.

"If you're pregnant right now, then in nine months we're gonna have a beautiful kid."

I pictured one with her hair, her eyes, her smile. A little baby girl.

"Fuck, now I sort of want to get you pregnant on purpose," I joked, laughing into her shoulder.

Her cunt was wet again as it slid against my shaft. "Yeah?"

I gripped her ribs while I rubbed my now hard length against her slit. She hadn't used the warm rag yet so her pussy still had my release coating her slit. Her mouth parted as I lifted her and adjusted her over my shaft.

She went slowly as her breathing regulated and she adjusted to me filling her up.

Then with a moan, she rocked forward. "Fuck me again Archer." With her lips right at my ear, she whispered, "Then fill me so full you leak out of me all day."

Her hands were around my neck, and I placed my hand over her mouth as I began moving my hips.

Wren and I emerged from our room forty-five minutes later, showered and dressed. The boys' room was empty, so I assumed Anna had come to get them. Wren practically glowed as we made our way down to the kitchen and while I knew she wasn't pregnant based on the first time

ve fucked without protection, she still seemed like there was a bright-
ness to her that hadn't been there before.

"Good morning," Wren said happily to her mother who was
sipping coffee at the table while Kane and Cruz watched a tablet.

"Morning." Anna gave us both a knowing smile.

I wasn't embarrassed. Let everyone know I fucked my woman this
morning. Speaking of everyone...where were all the other people who
seemed to be here yesterday?

Wren asked for me as she looked around.

"Where is Juan, and everyone else?"

Anna set her mug down gently. "Presley is in her family wing with
Kyle and his wife, Rylie. The twins are training in the gym with Scotty.
Juan and Taylor are walking together in the garden."

I was about to mention needing to leave when Anna stood up from
the table.

"Would you be willing to stay a few more days? Just a few so we
can spend time with you all? So everyone can meet the boys, and get to
know Archer." Anna's gaze gently landed on Wren. "So we can know
you."

Wren's eyes watered as she looked over to me. I needed to get back,
but I'd sent Thistle on his way this morning after he slept in one of the
guest rooms. He could handle what I couldn't for a few days.

So I smiled and replied, "We'd love to."

Chapter 28

Wren

My face hurt from smiling but in the realest, best way possible. I hadn't laughed this much in my whole life. It was our third evening visiting with my brother and his family when his sons finally joined us.

It took a few days for them to come around, not just because of how they had acted with us, but the leak they'd discovered that allowed Saul to know about the tunnels, the perimeter, and the dogs were linked back to them. Now Kyle was out hunting this person down, and the boys acted like two pups who'd had their noses rubbed in their mess.

Once they finally did come around, things were tense at first. Archer watched them warily as if he were watching a thief move near his home. Juan's gaze was hard as he watched his son's walk in, and even Taylor was somber. It wasn't until Cruz walked up to Kingston with a remote controller and asked if he knew how to work the game that the tense atmosphere began dissipating. They moved into their large living room, wearing sweats and t-shirts like they were little kids coming in for a family gathering on some holiday. Kingston had messy bedhead, and Gio's was covered by a backward-facing hat.

They sank into two large chairs and faced Kane and Cruz.

"You want to learn how to race?"

Cruz agreed excitedly, and Kane joined in, sitting right next to him. The large, flat screen lit up with a game, where players were being chosen.

The antics of seeing the twin boys become kids by helping my sons learn how to play a video game was what had me laughing so much. It was like getting to hit rewind on their lives and peek into so many moments and memories that I had missed. Juan and Taylor came in and settled in the living room with us, laughing while they watched, and I wondered when the last time was for them to be able to experience their boys like this.

I still wanted to know what had happened to them, but I knew it wasn't my business, and perhaps one day I would get the chance to find out. Maybe by staying in their lives, I would be privy to hearing from them once in a while.

It was later that afternoon that both boys cleared their throats and asked if they could talk to Archer and me while we walked in the garden that Juan and Taylor were so fond of.

The sun was beginning to set, which would thrust us into our fourth night in North Carolina and would mark the fourth night that Archer and I had been fucking like rabbits, actively trying to get pregnant. I didn't know why I wanted it, and I had no clue why he did either, but every time we were alone, it was as though some frenzy would come over us, and suddenly we were ripping each other's clothes off, and we weren't even bothering with foreplay and we both loved foreplay. I just knew I needed him inside me as fast and as hard as he could. Then once he'd finish, we'd wait ten minutes and go again. It was madness and stupid.

We were being so senseless, and yet as I looked over at him, I smiled, hoping I was carrying some piece of him inside me.

Kingston cleared his throat then tucked his hands deep into his pockets.

"We wanted to apologize for our behavior."

Gio rubbed the back of his neck and kept his gaze downcast.

"We know we've been taking things too far lately and we feel guilty about how we handled things with you. We hope you can forgive us and let us show you what family means. We honor a code, and it's never been a blurred line for us, so...we're ashamed that you felt afraid of us, or even like you had to protect your kid because of us."

Kingston added softly, "Our dad used to tell us stories about you. When you were young and what it was like to have a sibling to care for and protect. He always got sad when he talked about you, and how he lost you for so long because he didn't protect you in the ways that mattered. He would tell us that how we spoke to each other mattered as much as how we acted with one another."

That made a swarm of warmth hit my chest as I pictured Juan talking to much younger versions of these two boys while he remembered me.

"It might not mean much, but we wanted to be sure you understood how sorry we were," Gio said sweetly then the two shuffled their feet adorably as if they were waiting for me to forgive them.

It was Archer who placed his hand on their shoulders. "I know better than anyone how difficult it can be to lead and have to be ruthless while also being wise. On my end, I forgive you for what you thought needed to be done. I'm not perfect and have had my moments of being harsh when needed, of following law and rules even at the expense of my own humanity."

I didn't want to think of that. Of the way he'd said the mayhem would be part of our lives no matter what because that was a part of him.

"It means a lot that you apologized," Archer finished then removed his hands.

I stepped forward and pulled them both into a hug.

"I have my own reasons to be sorry and most of that revolves around being gone. So if you can forgive me for missing your entire lives, then I will forgive you for burning my patch and scaring my son."

They both chuckled against my neck and squeezed me.

"We want to see you more, tía," Gio said, giving me a boyish smile.

I nodded, smiling at them both while we made our way back to the house. Juan and Taylor had planned a big feast because they wanted us to meet the rest of their chosen family. The friends who shared other wings of the house, even if it was seasonally.

Centered in the middle of the house, where a connecting hall with marble floors and tall ceilings sat, there were dozens of chairs spread out on either side of the long table. I was introduced to a man named Decker, his wife Mallory, and their daughter Carter, who I had sort of met when she pulled up in the Jeep. Then came Scotty by himself in the middle, but two of the four dogs were lying near his feet. Next to him was Kyle, Presley, and then a woman who looked almost identical to Presley, her mother Rylie. On the other side was my mother, Juan, Taylor, Alex, the boys, and the four extra spots for my family.

There was more laughter, and I noticed both Alex and Carter glanced at each other quite a bit as if they were keeping a lot of thoughts and opinions to themselves. King and Gio kept their gazes on their plates unless Presley spoke up. In which case they both looked up like lost puppies, clinging to every word she said.

It was such an interesting dynamic to watch and experience.

Archer's hand found mine as everyone talked and brought us into something that seemed so delicate and intimate. They had all been together for so long, it seemed as though they were blood-related, but then King and Gio would look at Presley and I'd realize how untrue that was. Alex and Carter would glance at Presley then each other and sip from their wine glasses. There was so much not being said that I felt like I was on a gameshow trying to piece together expressions and body language.

Juan finally stood, making a toast, and it made me feel warm and healed inside.

"I wanted my family to meet my baby sister. The one I let fall through my fingers all those years ago then was too prideful to help bring back. I wanted to take a second to thank you all for showing her and Archer kindness as you know we don't allow any outsiders in here. You were all gracious enough to allow Wren, her two boys and Archer.

Something tells me they're going to be around much more as time goes on, and if that does happen, I want you all to know who they are and understand how Taylor and I consider them a part of this circle."

Everyone raised a glass in our direction, and I looked over in time to see my mother's eyes water as she sipped.

I knew right then my days of being alone, with or without Archer, were over.

I'd returned to my family, and they returned to me.

Chapter 29

Wren

WE RETURNED HOME EXACTLY ONE WEEK AND TWO DAYS AFTER traveling to North Carolina. The boys had quite a bit of homework to catch up on, but during our time away, Archer and I had come to a conclusion regarding our lives.

We wanted to start it. Together.

With what happened to Brick, things felt too strange to return to work. Word of his car accident came out, which caused a rumble amongst the team. A funeral was prepared for him, and while Archer was supportive of me attending, I truly had no desire to go. From what I'd known of Brick, he wasn't someone I wanted to remember. He'd gotten himself into a horrible situation with Saul and had betrayed my safety and trust by using my location against me. He also threatened to take Kane from us.

As far as I was concerned, he'd received his due, and perhaps that made me harsh, but I could never get the way Kane's face looked being held captive by Saul while Brick just stood there watching. Once the funeral had passed, I had put in my two weeks' notice. Denise had been a wonderful boss, but my heart wasn't in the job. I'd been hiding for five years in that job and in that city. I was ready to focus on something else.

I hadn't had time to discover what I wanted to do for myself. I'd never considered any hobbies or jobs that I could pursue that felt like me, that would bring me joy. I moved out of my house and packed all of my and Cruz's things into Archer's home.

We lived with him while he finalized the last step of becoming Kane's guardian.

Archer and I had been looking for a new place to live now that he wasn't required to stay in Atlas. We were taking our time, finding a place that had property, where we could homeschool the boys while having the freedom to go see my family and allow them to visit us. I was heading out of the gas station with my coffee and bagel when I saw Lydia pull up.

I hadn't returned any of her texts or talked to her since that night she'd been at my house after my sprained ankle.

Her blonde hair was dyed blue, matching her long sweater dress. Her steps slowed as she drew closer, holding her clutch in one hand and keys in another.

"Wren?"

Her eyes trailed over my leather cut, the size getting larger the more she took in. Throughout the months, I'd gone to visit Mayhem Rio with Archer. I'd gotten to know his men, and in turn, their women. I had new patches on the front of my cut that Thistle had given me. I had one from a woman named Ruth I'd met that was more like an honorary member but was by far my favorite of all the women I'd met.

My leather cut had become like a second skin, but Lydia's expression only truly manifested into shock when she realized my stomach was much bigger than the last time she saw me. It was nearly Christmas, and my shirt had a reindeer flying over a house, which incidentally took up the entirety of my abdomen.

Lydia's mouth dropped open. "I was wondering what happened to you."

She hadn't tried texting more than the one time, but it was fine. We weren't really friends. I knew she had looked through my phone for

Archer's number when she was over that night, which was probably the only reason she even helped me.

The sliding door from the gas station opened up behind me, and suddenly Archer was putting his arm across my shoulders, pulling me into his side.

"I knocked her up. Excuse us, Lindsay, we're gonna be late for a party. Can't keep Wren's mom waiting."

Archer kissed the side of my head as I took a bite of my bagel, smiling as Lydia gaped at us. "You know her name isn't Lindsay."

Archer opened the door for me, holding my hand as I slid inside the car. His smile was bright as he looked down at me. "You know I don't give a flying fuck, beautiful."

He shut the door, and another smile stretched along my face. I'd been doing that a lot lately.

"Your mother is going to love my gift," Archer said happily as we pulled out of the lot. My mom was home with the boys, decorating for our last Christmas in Atlas. We were scheduled to move into a farm-house, closer to the city, in January.

Mom came here to see us, but Juan, Taylor, and his kids would be coming as well.

I was nervous, but excited.

"What did you get her?"

Archer smiled over at me, a smug expression on his face.

"Pearl earrings."

Chapter 30

Archer

I WAS NERVOUS AS THE GIFTS BEGAN DWINDLING DOWN.

Juan kept laughing as he watched his mother touch the pearl earrings I'd gifted her. She'd wince every few minutes or so, then loudly declare how much she loved the earrings. I noticed Juan's wife hiding her face in her husband's shoulder, her body shaking with laughter each time Anna would make one of her loud declarations.

I tried to let the comedy of it calm me down, but Kane and Cruz were out of gifts. Which meant it was time for Wren and me to give them their last presents.

"Excuse me, everyone, there's something we need to do that we'd like to have your attention," I declared shakily.

Kane and Cruz were both playing with toys, not paying attention. Wren came up, stroked one hand over her small bump, and squeezed my hand with the other.

"Boys, there's something we need to give you."

They both looked up, and Wren walked toward Kane, handing him a small paper.

He gently unfolded it, but he couldn't read yet, so he just looked up at her with a big smile on his face.

"Is it a ticket?"

Wren knelt in front of him, taking the paper. "It's a promise, baby. says that I adopted you, and so did Archer. It says that you belong to s now, forever and ever no matter what. I'm your mom now."

Kane's blue eyes watered as he swung his gaze over to Archer. You'll be my dad?"

"Yeah, buddy." My voice cracked as I knelt in front of Cruz and anded him an identical paper.

His eyes lit up as he took it from me. "I got one too?"

We'd had to reach out to Wren's ex, Matt to get his signature which e took nearly two months to get back to us about. I wanted to talk to im, man to man. I even had a contact on the inside try and set some- ing up, but before I could, he'd sent the papers back. His signature, aiving all his rights was included with a small note for Cruz that Matt ad asked Wren to deliver to Cruz on his sixteenth birthday.

"Yea, Bud. You're mine too. Forever."

He didn't even open his paper from me; he just threw his arms round my neck and hugged me.

"We're a family now?" Kane asked, joining our hug.

Wren replied, pushing Kane's hair back, "We've been a family this vhole time, but these papers just make it official. A judge signed off, aying no one can ever take you away from us."

Kane's face fell the slightest bit as he looked down. "But what if omething happens to you, like it did to my first mom?"

Wren's lip wobbled at his phrase of "first mom."

Kingston stepped up, gently interjecting with his hand on Kane's houlder. "If something happens to either of your parents, you'll have s, little man. You inherited all of us. We're your family now."

Kane smiled up at Kingston, then Gio as he walked over and nessed with his hair. Wren rubbed a hand down her belly again and leared her throat.

"You two will be the best big brothers to your little sister. Just wait." ihe pulled Kane and Cruz into one more hug before Anna walked)ack into the room.

"I REALLY do love these earrings. If they get misplaced, I'd be heartbroken. Please, everyone, make sure you keep your eyes open in case they slip out."

Wren laughed into Cruz's hair as Juan slapped my shoulder.

"Best Christmas ever."

Epilogue

Wren

Two Years Later

Montana was beautiful, but it was also full of mosquitos.

"Mommy, it's ewwww," Hannah, our two-year-old, whined while rubbing off the lotion I'd put on her arm.

Archer chuckled and gently took her arm in his.

"It's eww?"

Her chubby cheeks were wet from something and glistened in the firelight as she tipped her head back. "It's sticky eww."

Maybe that wasn't lotion after all...maybe it was marshmallow remains from the smores we'd made.

Kane and Cruz both had a better handle on their graham crackers and marshmallows.

I smiled as Kane leaned back and handed me one he'd made for me. "Aquí tienes, mamá."

I took the treat and thanked Kane. Archer's pride could be seen through his smile as the boys became more comfortable with speaking

Spanish. I had even started saying it more, as their homeschool lesson picked up, and both Archer and I shared teaching our sons. We moved to a farmhouse, much closer to the city, but still on the outskirts enough that we had privacy. It allowed us to be closer to the club and gave us more room for when my family came to visit.

We'd started traveling more, once Hannah turned one. We incorporated each trip into the kids' lessons while getting to fulfill our postcard challenge.

"What's after Montana?" Archer asked our little family, knowing it would be Cruz and Kane who decided. Hannah didn't even know we were traveling via postcards on the refrigerator yet.

"What about San Francisco?" Cruz asked while taking a big bite of his marshmallow sandwich. The sunset was beyond gorgeous as it lit up the shaded areas of the tall grass and shadowed parts of the nearby mountain.

Kane seemed contemplative when suddenly a different voice joined our little group, which had Archer reaching for the gun he kept in his saddle bag.

"How about North Carolina?"

Juan walked out of nowhere, hands in his cigar pants. He seemed out of place in the outdoor terrain of the Montana mountainside.

My mouth was open in shock as I stared at my brother. We'd just visited him for Easter, it was June now, but it hadn't been that long since we'd talked.

"Juan?" I asked, but the way he was looking over at my husband told me there was something I didn't know.

It had me pulling Hannah out of the chair she was in and into my arms.

"Why North Carolina?"

My brother stared at the flames and then let out a sigh.

"We need all the families to come in...it's just for a time until things get smoothed over."

Archer held my gaze while I slipped mine back over to my brother, feeling a jagged warning prick my chest.

"What things?"

Juan's clear gaze caught on ours before he replied.

"The twins reacted poorly to a situation that involved Presley."

Still had no idea what their history or beef was, so I resisted the urge to ask and instead waited for the rest.

"And?"

Juan's jaw flexed. "Their reaction wasn't received well by someone with a lot of power. They sent one of our close friends to us in a body bag. We're not taking any chances with our friends, certainly less with our family."

I peeked over at Kane and Cruz who were watching each other. I hugged Hannah close to my chest and took it all in. Archer brought his phone up to his ear, and I already knew who he'd be on the phone with.

"Thistle. I need a favor."

Looked like we were heading back to North Carolina and this time we'd be staying for a while.

Want to read Juan & Kyle's stories? Read the Rake Forge University Series Here

King, Gio and Presley are up next in the second gen installment of the Rake Forge series coming later this year. Click this link for bonus content, including a scene from Presley, Gio and King when they're in highschool.

Also by Ashley Muñoz

Stone Riders

Where We Started

Where We Belong

Where We Promise

Where We Ended

A Rose Ridge Christmas

Rake Forge University Series

Wild Card

King of Hearts

The Joker

Mount Macon Series

Resisting the Grump

Tempting the Neighbor

Saving the Single Dad

Standalone

Only Once

The Rest of Me

Tennessee Truths

-

Finding Home Series

Glimmer

Fade

Anthology & Co Writes

What Are the Chances

Vicious Vet

Acknowledgments

Now, this book...I honestly don't even know where to start.

I guess with Amanda Anderson, because back when we discussed what would be coming next for me, never in a million years did I think you would sign off on this combo between worlds that happened here.

But you did, in fact, you were such a huge supporter that it boosted my confidence enough to step completely out of the box and wield this story into something incredible.

Thank you for helping me shift my branding so that I could complete next gen for my Rake Forge series and thank you for always being in my corner when I think about doing wild, ridiculous things.

A huge thanks to Melissa McGovern who also stood firmly in my corner and not only helped me shape this book into something that was concrete but also ensured it was going to be something I would be proud of. I am always so grateful to have you with me. Rebecca Patrick, my sister, my friend. I love you and you know that your support has always been something I hold firmly to, but this year, you really stepped up in a huge way. I can't thank you enough for stepping in and helping me with PA responsibilities along with content editing and ensuring my stories are nothing short of something you wouldn't DNF, which we all know is a miracle.

Thanks to Amy and Kelly my other ride or die beta readers who always step up when I need them and always make sure they catch the outlier things in my stories that need to be fixed.

Savannah, you're the best agent I could ever ask for and I am eternally grateful that you believe in me and always ensure I reach fo whatever dream I want, and make sure to help me attain it.

The whole Dreamscape team, thank you for your patience with this story, and ensuring the best narrators are cast and the delivery is streamless.

Rebecca Barney, thank you so much for your editing assistance, a well as thoughtful content suggestions, I always feel so prepared when know that last draft reaches you.

Cat Byrd, thank you so much for all your help with managing Book Beauties, you are such a gift to me. Gel Mariano, thank you so much fo all your help with graphics, and help with my branding.

Echo, as always, your expertise with these covers was incredible and more than I ever imagined.

To my Book Beauties, thank you for always loving my books, and being excited with me. You will never know how much that means to me. You make me want to keep writing.

To my family, and especially my husband, thank you. After so many years, we make it work but it always takes teamwork and it always takes all of us to make that happen but Jose, you are my anchor You are the steady beat, I set my world to and because you do not falter you never shift, or change cadence, I know I can trust you with all of this. My dreams are vast and sometimes feel too big to carry. I merely whisper them to you and you tell me you'll carry them too. I never dreamed I'd have a partner in this way. Someone who not only loved me as a husband should but a business partner who does whatever h can to ensure we're doing the very best we can.

I love you.

To everyone who has loved me since Rake Forge, get ready- second gen is coming next!

About the Author

Ashley is an Amazon Top 50 bestselling romance author who is best known for her small-town, second-chance romances. She resides in the Pacific Northwest, where she lives with her four children and her husband. She loves coffee, reading fantasy, and writing about people who kiss and cuss.

Follow her at www.ashleymunozbooks.com

Printed in Great Britain
by Amazon

59145371R00179